LOSING NELSON

LOSING NELSON

Barry Unsworth

HAMISH HAMILTON · LONDON

HAMISH HAMILTON LTD

Published by the Penguin Group
Penguin Books Ltd, 27 Wrights Lane, London w8 5tz, England
Penguin Putnam Inc., 375 Hudson Street, New York, New York 10014, USA
Penguin Books Australia Ltd, Ringwood, Victoria, Australia
Penguin Books Canada Ltd, 10 Alcorn Avenue, Toronto, Ontario, Canada m4v 3b2
Penguin Books (NZ) Ltd, Private Bag 102902, NSMC, Auckland, New Zealand

Penguin Books Ltd, Registered Offices: Harmondsworth, Middlesex, England

First published 1999
1 3 5 7 9 10 8 6 4 2

Grateful acknowledgement is made to Faber and Faber
for permission to reprint an extract from *The Waste Land*,
from *Collected Poems 1909–1962* by T. S. Eliot

Set in 12/14pt Monotype Bembo
Printed in Great Britain by Clays Ltd, St Ives plc

A CIP catalogue record for this book is available from the British Library

ISBN 0–241–13700–4

For Aira with my love

I

I had a bad fright that morning. I wouldn't have left the house at all on such a special day if the man at Seldon's hadn't phoned to say they had a piece I might be interested in. It was an oval plate, bone china, frilled at the edges, slightly curved at the sides, pale cream in colour, with a central medallion enclosing his profile in dark blue. There was an inscription of the same colour in slightly worn cursive, running round the upper half of the medallion: *Hero of the Nile*. They had used the De Vaere profile made for Wedgwood in the summer of 1798. Nothing very remarkable about it. But of course I agreed to buy it. It bore his image. It was seldom indeed I could resist that.

I was on my way back home with it, back to Belsize Park. It was a raw day and the sky was darkly overcast. Nevertheless, I decided to walk as far as Knightsbridge for the sake of the exercise. I had time to spare – or so I thought. As I was crossing Pont Street it started to rain, not very heavily. The platform in the Underground was crowded and became steadily more so while I waited. There was a silence among the people there, silence of waiting – they were resigned. I began to feel the first twinges of panic. Then an Asian voice on the loudspeaker: a delay on the line due to security checks at Gloucester Road Station.

It was thirteen minutes to twelve. Imagine my feelings. This was the 14th of February, it was the two hundredth anniversary of the Battle of Cape St Vincent, Horatio's first great disobedience, the day he became an angel. On this day, at 12.50 p.m. – just over an hour's time – his ship, the *Captain*, went into close action. And here was I, among this mute herd, sweating despite the cold, a good two miles from my table and my models – the ships were not even set out. It mattered so much to get the time right, therein lay the whole meaning, how else could I keep my life parallel with his? Before my father died – he died last April – I fought out this battle wherever I could: on my bed, on the floor, one freezing day in the shed behind the house. We never missed, year after year we broke the line at ten minutes to one. Now I had the basement all to myself. The thought that I might fail the appointment now was unendurable, it made me feel sick.

There was no time to be lost. I struggled back to the surface along with numbers of others who had made the same decision. I was feeling distinctly unwell by now, my breath came with difficulty and there was the usual suffusion of blood at the temples, obscuring my vision, making me feel hemmed-in. It was still raining and there were no free taxis anywhere near the tube, nor outside Harrods. I had to walk some way towards Hyde Park Corner before I found one, and even then I was lucky, the previous fare was alighting as I came up.

I gave the address and sat back and concentrated on keeping my face composed and my breathing inaudible. Closing the eyes has always helped me to cope with anxiety, but now I waited two minutes by my watch before allowing myself the luxury. Timing is the key to control and control is the key to concealment. The driver, if he glanced in his mirror, would think it strange if his passenger were dozing too soon. My father was a master of concealment, he kept it up so well that nobody knew just when he died, nobody registered the precise moment.

We made it with twelve minutes to spare. I was still gasping a little as I went down to the basement. I did not allow myself to be sidetracked by considerations of where among the shelves and cabinets to put my new acquisition; such a decision would involve extensive rearrangement, it could easily have taken the whole afternoon, in these last months I had got steadily slower. I simply left the plate, still in its damp wrapping, on the floor and went straight through to my operations-room and began setting out the ships, the Spanish first in their two loose groups, 9 in the van,

18 in the rear, these last headed by de Córdoba in his great flagship, the *Santissima Trinidad*, four decks, 136 guns, the most powerful wooden warship ever built. One of the first models I made, I was fourteen, home from school for the summer holidays. Odourless now, the ship in my hands, but still seeming to bear the spirituous, heady scents of its making, glue, paint, freshly cut shavings. The shed had a smell too, dust and hot creosote and the rank weeds that grew against the boards outside. Smells are intenser for solitude and remembered more intensely, as every lonely person knows. Sounds too. But I wasn't lonely, I had him.

Now for the English fleet, under Admiral Sir John Jervis in the *Victory*, Horatio's death-ship at Trafalgar eight years later – eight years, eight months and one week. In contrast to the disorderly Spanish, our ships are sailing in impeccable close order, 15 warships in perfect line-ahead formation, approaching from the south at right angles, making for the fatal gap in the enemy fleet, two feet wide on my table, roughly seven miles in actual fact.

The sight of them now, disposed for battle, gun ports open and cannon run out, quite restored my calm. In full press of sail, with their flags and pennants and painted hulls, their figureheads picked out in gold and vermilion, they made a fine show. How much care and devotion I lavished on those models, those sloops and frigates and ships-of-the-line, what pride I took in them. Before my father died I had to keep them in cardboard boxes in my bedroom, together with all the other Nelson memorabilia I had collected over the years. My room was full of boxes, you couldn't get the door more than half open, you had to edge your way in. Now my ships had for their manoeuvres the whole surface of the billiard table that had always been a feature of the basement. My brother Monty and I used to play on it sometimes, before he left. I had covered it with dark blue baize and had a sheet of glass fitted exactly over it. In the light of the lamp overhead – no daylight ever entered that room – the surface glinted like dark water and reflected the colours of the ships.

Eight minutes to go. Since first light these stately, deadly vessels have been slowly drawing closer together, approaching in a fashion apparently leisurely the thunder and carnage of a close encounter. Incongruous, and to me entirely fascinating, this dreamlike slowness. Consider the ferocious firepower of those ships, their capacity for destruction, more devastating than anything known before, on sea or land. Jervis is taking well over a thousand cannon into action with him. Now they are twenty-five miles west of the Portuguese headland of St Vincent, one hundred and fifty miles north-west of Cadiz, for which port the Spanish are running with a fair wind.

They would avoid the engagement if they could but they cannot be allowed to, they must be intercepted. A heavy weight of responsibility lies on Jervis's shoulders today. The French revolutionary war has reached a crucial phase. The Dutch fleet has joined with the French at Brest. One attempt to invade Ireland has already been made. Admiral Lord Bridport's Channel Fleet has been driven back to England by bad weather and forced to abandon the blockade of Brest. Only this same bad weather has so far prevented an enemy break-out and an unopposed Irish landing. If the Spanish are allowed to join them, the odds will become impossible. Not only have the English been forced to quit the Mediterranean − a vital sphere of influence − but the whole of Continental Europe is now dominated by the armies of France. Drained by the subsidies she has been obliged to pay to keep her allies in the field, her trade routes curtailed, her merchantmen harassed by privateers, England is on the verge of bankruptcy. Ireland is simmering with rebellion. There are rumours of mutiny in the ships of the Royal Navy. It is indeed true, what Admiral Jervis is heard to remark as the weather brightens: 'A victory is very essential to England at this moment.'

Words that are remembered, recorded, famous words. But this brightening weather has revealed an awesome discrepancy in the strength of the opposing fleets. Jervis has 15 sail-of-the-line. Six of them are three-deckers, but only the *Victory* and the *Britannia* have as many as 100 guns. All the rest, including Horatio's, are two-deck ships with 74 guns, the standard warship of the Royal Navy at that time. In addition Jervis has 4 frigates, faster than the line-ships, essential for scouting and intelligence, a sloop and a cutter – I set them out now, on a diagonal, to windward of the English line. This is the force with which Jervis is proposing to engage the Spanish Grand Fleet, 27 ships-of-the-line, 10 frigates and a brig. Six of the Spanish three-deckers are carrying 112 guns and there is the mighty *Santissima Trinidad* with 136. Altogether they have twice the firepower of the English. But there are compensating factors. The Spanish have put to sea in haste, they are undermanned, their officers are inexperienced.

Everything is in place. It is fourteen minutes to one. One hour and four minutes previously, while I was panicking at Knightsbridge, Jervis had given a bold and unconventional signal. On this occasion he cannot follow the rigid procedures laid down by the Admiralty in London for the conduct of sea-battles, procedures that have not changed in a hundred years: you lay alongside, preserve strict in-line formation and pound away in a duel of broadsides until the enemy is crippled or surrenders or runs. Jervis cannot do this because his force is too inferior, he would be overwhelmed. So he has given the order to put on press of sail and break through the gap in the enemy formation. It is the only tactic possible. Once through, the English fleet can attack to windward, concentrating its fire on the 18 ships of the rear, disabling them before the van can make the turn into the wind and come to their aid.

A perfect day for sea-fighting, calm, with a light breeze, no rolling to disturb the calculation of the gunners. I check that the English ships are in correct order of sail as they pass through the enemy, Troubridge leading the van in the *Culloden*, Collingwood bringing up the rear in the *Excellent*. Third from the rear is Horatio in the *Captain*, flying the Broad Pennant; he is a commodore now – since the previous March.

So they pass through. The Spanish spine is severed. But now

Jervis blunders. He cannot altogether break from his conditioning, free himself from the rigid code of line-ahead formation. He hoists his signal: once through to the westward of the Spanish, the fleet is to tack in succession and bear down on them. *In succession.* No sir, wrong. It should have been simultaneously. For 15 ships to make the turn, one after the other, each waiting till the one ahead has completed the manoeuvre, and then to reform in line, this will take too long, the advantage will be lost.

But of course they obey, they are bred to obedience. Here they are now, in a wide inverted V on the ocean as they begin to execute the manoeuvre, in perfect formation still, the *Culloden* still leading. But the Spanish have the wind, de Córdoba has understood, he alters course northwards, he means to bear over the wind and unite his fleet. Then he can fight or run as he chooses and he will have time to do it, only the first 6 English ships have so far completed the turn and they have not yet come up with the Spanish, they are still out of range.

One man sees this and that man is Horatio Nelson. It is now 12.50 p.m. Without a second's hesitation, disregarding his commander's signal, he veers the *Captain* away from the wind, *he breaks the line.* The audacity of it, the impetuous logic! To recognize absolute necessity and act on that instant of recognition. Now again, in this silent room, as I send the *Captain* into the attack and her colours glint on the dark surface, I feel a constriction in the throat, and my heart beats faster at the dash and defiance of it. The move has brought us, at a stroke, across the bows of at least 7 Spanish ships, among them the huge *Santissima Trinidad*, the *San Josef*, the *Salvador del Mundo* and the *San Nicolas*, these 4 alone possessing 440 guns against Horatio's 74.

At the moment that he swung away from the wind and broke the line, risking the outcome of the battle and his whole career on this one throw, at that moment, in his thirty-ninth year, Horatio became an angel. He entered a different sphere. I will say what I think angels are. They can be dark or bright, but they all have the gift of spontaneity, of creating themselves anew. This is a pure form of energy, and Horatio was winged with it. All the same, angels are not complete, they need their counterparts, the dark needs the bright, the hidden needs the open, and vice versa. Sometimes they meet and recognize each other. Sometimes, as with Horatio and me, the pairing occurs over spaces of time or distance. He became a bright angel on the 14th of February 1797 during the battle of Cape St Vincent. I became his dark twin on the 9th of September 1997, when I too broke the line.

I had no presentiment of this on that February afternoon, as I moved my model ships about on their glass ocean. Since my father's death I had been experiencing bouts of gloom – not sorrow – and at times a sort of excited restlessness that made it difficult for me to keep still. And I had run into a difficult patch in the book I was writing, *The Making of a Hero*. I had got bogged down in the events of June 1799 in Naples and Horatio's part in them. This book had been going on for more than five years, ever since December 1991. I started it on Boxing Day – the anniversary of his mother's death. The Naples business was worrying me; I could not leap over it. Progress was slow; lately in fact there hadn't been any. I kept retreating, rewriting pieces of his earlier life. It was for this reason that I began to feel slightly uneasy now, as I went on with the battle. Because at this point I had to bring Troubridge into the action and at the time I did not much care to dwell on Troubridge, Horatio's brother officer and friend, closely associated with him in this battle but also in the treatment, two years later, of the Jacobin rebels in Naples – the business that was holding me up with my book.

Certainly there is no doubt of his fighting spirit. Horatio is not left long to fight alone. He is joined by Troubridge in the *Culloden*, the leading English ship, which has now completed the turn ordered by Jervis and come within range. For nearly an hour these two exchange broadsides with the Dons, superior discipline and gunnery making up for inferiority of armament.

Now here is the gallant *Blenheim* coming up to give them a respite, passing between them and the enemy, pouring fire as she goes. The *Culloden* is crippled, she falls astern. Collingwood ranges up in the *Excellent*, last ship of the line. He passes within ten feet of the *San Nicolas*, 80 guns, and blasts her in masterly fashion with two broadsides in succession.

Ten feet. The length of this table. That would be about it. Almost jumping distance. These towering ships, fighting so close, hardly more than the length of a man between them, launching their thunderous fire, shuddering from stem to stern with the repeated recoil of the guns – the English gun-crews could deliver a broadside every seventy-five seconds. Dismemberment and maiming inflicted almost within range of an embrace. Hard even for a landsman of the time, the notion of such closeness, such promiscuous intimacy of destruction. How much more so for us now, with our concept of war as distant erasure, a button touched, a figure or a thousand figures obliterated on a screen.

The close-quarter fighting gives Horatio his second great triumph of the day. The *San Nicolas*, reeling from Collingwood's fire, falls foul of her compatriot, the huge *San Josef*, three decks, 112 guns. The two Spanish ships, both badly damaged, are inextricably locked together. I set them together here, side by side, to the windward of Horatio. His own ship, by now, is completely disabled. She has lost her fore topmast; her wheel has been shot away; neither sail nor rigging is left. She is incapable of fighting in line, incapable of giving chase.

Again Horatio demonstrates the promptness of genius. The genius of a hero lies in his extreme readiness to action – which is not the same as rashness. He lays his ship aboard the starboard quarter of the *San Nicolas*. His sprit-sail passes over the Spaniard's poop and locks in her mizzen shrouds. Three ships tangled together now, here they are, side by side. Horatio calls for a boarding party. Short of stature – he is only five feet six inches – slight of frame, with one eye more or less useless to him after the wound he suffered in the Corsican campaign two-and-a-half years before, newly fledged angel with bright sword in hand, he leads the way, passing from the fore-chains of his own ship into the quarter gallery of the *San Nicolas*. In the exchange of fire that follows the Spanish commander is mortally wounded. They surrender, but while Horatio is receiving the officers' swords his party is fired upon. Seven English seamen are killed in this fusillade. Where is it coming from? From above and beyond, from the stern gallery of the *San Josef*, still helplessly tangled aloft. Without a flicker of hesitation Horatio orders his mariners to return the enemy fire, stations sentinels at the hatchway to keep the enemy below decks and charges on. He will board an enemy ship from the deck of another already boarded and taken!

His friend Berry is at hand, helping him into the main-chains, keeping beside him during the headlong scramble from ship to ship. But on board the *San Josef* there is no resistance. A Spanish officer hails from the quarter-deck to say that she surrenders. The flag-captain, on bended knee, presents his sword. The admiral is dying of wounds below. With his own ship disabled, Horatio has captured two enemy ships, both more heavily armed, using one as a stepping-stone to the other. An action without parallel in the annals of naval history.

Luck, some might say – the right man in the right place at the right time. But angels make their own luck. Otherwise how can it be explained that it was always he who broke the mould? Collingwood was equally well placed to veer out of line and throw himself across the bows of the Spanish. Not a question of courage or skill, Collingwood had plenty of both. But he stayed in line.

Late afternoon, the light is failing. Jervis has only 12 ships now that are capable of fighting. The Spanish have been defeated, 4 of their ships have been taken. It is time to disengage. Gradually the fire ceases, the fleets separate, the English stand for Lagos, the Spanish for Cadiz. After this terrible local storm, these hours of thunder and slaughter, peace settles down, the ocean comes to herself again and swallows the corpses and the drifting spars.

I sat on there, after the battle. I have never been at sea, except twice on the cross-Channel ferry. That was a long time ago, before my illness. No, I am his land shadow. I have been abroad only once since then, just once in twenty years. That was when I went with my father to Tenerife to see the place where Horatio lost his right arm.

2

I sat for quite a while without moving, sensing the winter dusk that was falling beyond my shuttered room, muffling the streets outside as it had the blank sea after that ferocious encounter. The short duration of these battles has always stirred my imagination. Fifty or sixty miles those ships could make in a day, not more. They had only recently invented instruments that could tell them where they were. For weeks or months they tracked each other across vast spaces of ocean. Then, one day, the sail on the horizon, the gradual closing of the distance, the routine activity of preparation. Finally the moment that gave this murderous patience its meaning: the twitch on the lanyard, the crash of the guns.

My models sat there, unmarked, immaculate. No decks slippery with blood. The glass showed nothing but the reflection of the hulls. No pools of tar, no wreckage, no swirl of sharks. Silence in the room had been unbroken. No storm of grapeshot, no shrieking tangles of chains and nails and razor-edged splinters of metal and wood, no groans and screams of wounded and dying men, no cheers as the gun-crews saw their shots strike home. Cheers and screams, the two conflicting sounds of eighteenth-century sea-battle.

I was visited by a sense of desolation, something like bereavement. Could one who had never known it in his own person grieve for the din of battle and the confusion and the blood? The question, coming to my mind in such a form, made me feel restless and somehow awed, a sensation difficult to describe, like a brush of wings, quite unaccustomed at the time though it became more frequent afterwards. Usually when we fought these battles I had a feeling of fulfilment, they brought me closer to him, I shared in his triumphs. I know now that this first taste of mourning was a sign to me. At the time I thought it was no more than delayed reaction to my panic of earlier, my fear of failing him.

The feeling of unrest set me walking back and forth from one end of the room to the other, passing between the table and the wall, from the zone of light and the reflections of the ships into the shadowy area at the far corner of the room. I found in my raincoat pocket – I had forgotten to take the raincoat off, so great had been my haste – a cheese and cress sandwich, still wrapped in its clingfilm, which I had bought the day before at a Safeway's, and then forgotten about. Living alone as I did, and preoccupied with my book, I quite often forgot to eat and was only reminded of the need to do so by onsets of faintness. But I never forgot times and dates. Mrs Watson still came, as she had done in my father's time, only twice a week now, in the mornings. I didn't want her shopping or cooking for me. I used to leave the week's money in an envelope on the kitchen table. Usually I stayed down in the basement, out of her way. She had no key to the basement, naturally; I had changed the lock.

I ate the sandwich as I walked about the room. I was thinking still about the battle and its aftermath. It had not been an over-whelming victory. The Spanish, though severely mauled, had not been put out of the war. But there had been a great boost to national morale and – of crucial importance – the Mediterranean was opened to our sea-power once again. From that moment, and for the rest of the war with revolutionary France, we would never allow these waters to be closed to us, our ships would patrol them freely, enabling us to frustrate French invasion plans and defeat Napoleon's purposes in Egypt.

For Horatio, of course, an important stage in his career, bringing the first taste of the fame he longed for. He was no humble hero, a contradiction in terms in any case, no, he wanted to have his being in glory and he wanted the world to see it, see the beautiful shine of it. That is the nature of heroes, they are nourished by fame.

He was cheered throughout the fleet after the battle, wherever they saw his pennant flying. Crowned with victory, moving through a rain of cheers, how wonderful to be Horatio at that moment. I felt my heart dilate with the pleasure of it. Nightfall, the lamps on the ships, lamplight over the water, cheers raining on him as he passes through in his launch on his way to the *Victory*, to present his respects to the admiral.

We have Horatio's account of the meeting, as given some months later in conversation with his brother-in-law Bolton. He had come straight from the fighting. His shirt and coat were badly torn, he had lost his hat, his face was streaked with gunpowder, he was bleeding from a wound in the back made by a shell-splinter. Jervis, who greeted him with outstretched hands, was immaculate in silver and blue. This was because he had been obliged to change his uniform. During the battle a marine standing close beside him on the poop had had his head blown off and the admiral's face and chest had been splashed with blood and brains and bits of bone and tissue. An officer, believing him to be badly wounded, rushed to his side. No, he was not hurt, he said calmly, and he turned aside and asked a midshipman to fetch him an orange. This in the heat of the action. When the fighting was over and the day was won he went below and washed away the evidence of mortality and changed. *The Admiral received me on the quarter-deck and, having embraced me, said he could not sufficiently thank me.*

This was to be an important friendship for Horatio. He had a gift for friendship. All through his career he won respect from superiors and subordinates alike; not only respect, affection too, he was always loved. On the 20th of February, in the normal course of seniority, Commodore Nelson became Rear-Admiral Nelson. Later, when news of the victory reached England, the Order of the Bath was conferred upon him by a grateful sovereign. Rear-Admiral Sir Horatio Nelson, KB.

It would have been a baronetcy, almost certainly, but he had hinted in a letter to Sir Gilbert Elliot, viceroy of Corsica, who was returning to England with despatches of the battle, that he would be reluctant to accept a hereditary title as he had not the means to support one. Of course there were some, sneaks and subversives being always with us, who attributed other motives to him. Chief sneak was Sir Gilbert's aide, Colonel Drinkwater, who had a conversation with Horatio on the morning after the battle and afterwards published an account. He suggests that Horatio was really attracted by the very conspicuous nature of the knighthood, which carried with it the right to wear a prominent and glittering star, and that he pleaded poverty in order to obtain this.

According to the colonel, it was he who suggested to Horatio the possibility of a baronetcy, but he was stopped by a hand on his arm: 'No, it must not be in that manner.' 'Oh,' Drinkwater reports himself as saying, 'you wish to be a Knight of the Bath, then?' And Horatio's immediate answer: 'Yes; if my services have been of any value, let them be noticed in a way that the public may know me or them.' Drinkwater is not sure about that final pronoun, but he professes himself to be sure about the rest and pronounces his judgement with confidence: *I could have no doubt of his meaning, that he wished to bear about his person some honorary distinction to attract the public eye . . .*

I could not take this seriously. It seemed to me, unmistakably, the voice of the cynic. The two men were alone, Horatio never spoke of this conversation, there is no independent support of it, he was dead when the account was published. Would Drinkwater, whom he hardly knew, have questioned him with such impertinent directness about his wishes and ambitions? Surely not. A radiant light would have been upon Horatio that morning, the morrow of one of the greatest days of his life. Drinkwater was trying to sully that light, as there will always be people ready to do.

It was not the imputation of vanity that I found offensive. I always knew that he prized the trappings and insignia of fame. His decorations killed him in the end, the stars on his breast made him a sniper's target at Trafalgar. The attainment of public honours is a hero's vocation, he bears them for all those who cannot, just as he bears the nation's dignity. No, it is the hinting at ambivalence, even duplicity, in Horatio's attitude, the suggestion that he lied about his means for the sake of the glittering star.

To hold this smear in mind long enough to repudiate it, let alone defend him from it, made me feel I had betrayed him, stirred a feeling of nausea in me, similar to that I sometimes felt in those days when I tried to understand the events of June 1799 in Naples. I had devoted myself to a study of his life, I had followed him through the succession of his days and the succession of my own, though sometimes the course had run below ground. I was nine when this started. That was in 1964, the year my mother left us. Chess led me to Horatio – chess and my father and my absent mother and the fact that on that day I broke the rule about not showing what you feel.

I thought my mother had gone because she did not love me and Monty enough to stay. I suppose I already knew, in the way that children know such things, that she did not love my father. He, no doubt intent on setting a good example of not showing what you feel, did not succeed then or later in explaining the matter to us. He did not say she loved us or had been sorry to go. Our mother had gone to India, he said, because she had become besotted with Oriental religions. *Besotted.* I did not know what the word meant, but I knew that my father was expressing his loss through contempt.

My form-master of that year at the private day-school I went to was a chess enthusiast. He explained the rules to us, he encouraged us to play. He was kind to me and I admired him, more than admired: I wanted to be where he was. I suppose I was more than usually responsive to kindness just at that time. To please him I tried hard to be good at chess and I discovered that I was good. I had a natural talent, the master said. Mr Lyle was his name. I don't remember much about him now. He had glasses. I seem to remember that he wore his hair brushed straight back. Blurred remains of a focus once so intense. I joined the school chess club. I took part in tournaments and distinguished myself. Shining at few things, for a brief season I shone at chess. I see it now, the stark arena of the board, the ruthless game that hung so paradoxically on feelings of love.

I studied the game, I read the accounts of historic encounters, the ploys of long-dead masters, and I played them out alone. I would set out the pieces at random, then sweep them off and try to replace them from memory. At night, crying for my mother, I would picture the chess board, go through the moves of some legendary end-game and find consolation.

A colleague of my father was there one Sunday afternoon – my father was a senior official at the Treasury. 'Your father tells me you are quite a chess-player.' On his reddish face an indulgent look. 'At least by his own report,' my father said. He seemed to suggest I had boasted. Perhaps I had. 'Not up to your level, Henry, not yet.' Henry, Harry, Humphrey. A chess-player of note. 'Fancy a game, young man?'

We played and I won. He still had half his pieces on the board when I checkmated him. Pleasure in victory, expectation of praise – face and voice were not yet practised enough, I suppose I showed my feelings too clearly. My father looked at me but uttered no word. He went out, came back with a book from his study, brought it over for me to see. 'Look here,' he said, the colleague meanwhile looking on. 'Look at these people here.'

He had opened the book roughly in the middle. There were two faces, one on either side: William Pitt the Younger and Horatio Nelson. Neither name meant anything to me at the time. Later, of course, I knew them for close contemporaries – Horatio was a year older and died three months earlier.

'Take a good look,' my father said. 'These two men saved our country, they had reason to be pleased with themselves.'

He meant it for my benefit or so I like to think. He did not want me to be jubilant in victory, to overrate small achievements. He wanted to inspire me with worthy ambitions. But in his manner and tone I sensed displeasure; he was not pleased at my success, it had disturbed his sense of the natural order.

Two faces side by side, two lives in parallel. I think I was fascinated by parallel tracks even then. Both plates were in colour, but for some reason the two men were depicted at quite different times in their lives: Pitt, dark-suited, close to his end, ravaged by alcohol and the strain of government, Horatio the twenty-year-old captain, in the dark blue and gilt of his full-dress uniform, his youthful face severe, intrepid. There was no comparison, none at all; I scarcely looked at the statesman, the architect of victory; my eyes were all for the splendid young fighter, so slender and small-boned, so different from me in physical form, even then. I am on the heavy side, with thick wrists and big hands. Not clumsy, though; I am good with my hands, good at making things.

My interest in chess did not long survive that day, the lesson in humility proved the death-blow to it. I continued to play during what was left of the term, but my heart was not in it, I lost the appetite for victory, my game fell off. In the autumn Monty and I were sent away to boarding school. I never saw Mr Lyle again and I never played chess again.

With Horatio it has been otherwise. My interest in him seemed altogether to disappear, but it had merely gone underground, waiting for another sign. This came when I was thirteen, during a history lesson, when I discovered that Horatio Nelson lost his mother *when he was nine years old*.

It came with the force of revelation, like an assault of light. All the surrounding circumstances were lit up by it, as if by the arc of a flare in the night. The usual darkness descends again, but the print is there for ever. My exact position in the classroom, the desk-top mutilated by generations of idle inscribers, the look of the blackboard, the gestures of the master's hands. These things were as present to me that afternoon last February as they had ever been. Undimmed, untarnished over the years, the lustre of the kinship so casually discovered then.

I felt the need now to look again at the Rigaud portrait, the picture my father had shown me on my last effective day as a chess-player, my first sight of Horatio's face. I got up, went through to the next room. The plate I had bought that morning was still lying there on the floor, but I left it where it was. I crossed to the wall where the portrait hung above a narrow cabinet containing objects commemorating his death: a black silk bookmark with the date of Trafalgar on it, a piece of Staffordshire pottery that showed him dying in the arms of two officers, a model of his funeral car that I made myself when I got interested in Horatio again, after my illness.

The original portrait of course is in the National Maritime Museum at Greenwich, a three-quarter-length oil by John Francis Rigaud. My picture was a photograph, blown up to poster size, mounted and framed. Horatio was an eighteen-year-old lieutenant when it was begun. It was commissioned by his commanding officer, William Locker, who must have seen his distinction even at that age. Before it was quite finished Horatio had to sail for the West Indies. He didn't return until 1780, three years later, still desperately ill with the Yellow Jack fever that nearly killed him and destroyed his youthful bloom for ever. But Rigaud changed nothing in the face, merely touched in the background and added the insignia of Horatio's new rank – he was a captain by now, one of the youngest in the navy.

I stood before the portrait for a time I did not measure. He had been through the shadow of death, but the painter had allowed no hint of mortality. No sickness, no lines of pain mar the confidence of his face. His sword is planted before him, his hands rest on the hilt. In the background, painted on his return, a view of Fort San Juan in Nicaragua, scene of the ill-starred expedition of the year before.

Disasters, fevers, the great victories and the heroic death, all this was before him, undreamed of, when this impervious face was painted. Twenty years away his crushing defeat of the French at Aboukir Bay, the triumphant entry into Naples, the gratitude of monarchs, the songs and the praise and the abundant love of Emma, Lady Hamilton. Twenty years away his dealings with the Neapolitan Jacobins, which day by day, with oppressed spirits, I was striving to disentangle.

Thoughts of this period in Horatio's life brought the usual vague distress to my mind. I was still standing there, before the portrait, but no longer looking at it. My eyes fell on the papier mâché bust of him standing not far away, more or less in the middle of the floor. It was larger than life-size, three feet high and crudely painted, the eyes jet-black and wide open, the cheeks rouged, hectic-looking; but there was a curve of power and authority in the mouth that I liked. I had seen it in the jumbled interior of a curio shop in Camden as I was passing by, and I had gone in and bought it and brought it home in a taxi, muffled up in brown paper. Only a month or so before – I would not have done it in my father's time. Now I found myself looking fixedly at him, at the straight line of the cocked hat that shadowed his eyes, the garish stars and medals on his chest, the gilt letters running along the base. I could not read them at this distance but I knew what they said: ENGLAND EXPECTS THAT EVERY MAN WILL DO HIS DUTY.

Sublime message, surely the most famous naval signal ever given. Greeted with cheers by every ship in the fleet. Then came the last message he ever gave, his favourite, number 16, the signal for close action, which remained at the top-gallant masthead of HMS *Victory* until it was shot away . . .

The trance of admiration that was descending on me was disturbed by the ringing of the front-door bell. I looked at my watch: it was exactly seven o'clock. I knew at once that it must be Avon Secretarial Services in the person of Miss Lily, who came twice a week, Tuesdays and Fridays, to help me with my manuscript, no small task, as I was constantly revising the earlier sections. I could not use a computer myself. My illness had left me with an abiding fear of screens. Twenty years ago, but I had not been able to overcome it. Not mirrors or clear reflecting surfaces, I had no fear of those, but opaque electronic screens from which faces might emerge. Faces with eyes . . .

I had known of course that she was coming. But what surprised and rather frightened me was the realization that nearly three hours had gone by that could not really be accounted for. Since the dusk of the battle and of this winter evening in London, since the separation of the fleets, as I sat by my operations-table and stood before the portrait, this mass of time had accumulated and then dissolved away.

As I mounted the basement steps and went along the passage to the front door, I felt some return of the terror of that morning. Twinges, no more. But somehow it was always later than I thought, I was constantly striving to keep abreast. So much, so very much, depended on that, keeping abreast, keeping the lines parallel.

3

Miss Lily was always on time. I had taken to calling her that, not to her face, only in my mind, though she had none of the aspects conventionally associated with the flower, she wasn't languorous at all or scented much or markedly virginal, she was a steady person, in her early thirties, and her name was Lilian Butler. She had been coming for three months by then and she had never been late. This punctuality was one of the things I liked best about her; without strict timing our lives are formless. However, Miss Lily was inquisitive and that was a drawback.

There she was, on the doorstep, her little red car parked in the street below. Slung over her shoulder the case that contained computer and printer. 'You've been going up those stairs too quick,' she said to me when I opened the door. Even after such a short acquaintance she allowed herself remarks like that. I must have been breathing rather heavily and she had seen it. How could I explain to her that it was not a question of haste? I could never publicly admit to anxiety, any more than I could show tears or give vent to anger. And how did she know I had been down there, in the basement? Only from my breathing? It didn't seem much to go on. It was as if she had somehow been spying on me. She had never been down there, no one had, I always kept it locked.

We went straight to the room I call my study, which adjoins the sitting-room on the ground floor. The room where I sleep is on this floor too. The house is tall and narrow, late Victorian, like all six houses in this short row off England's Lane. It has four floors if you include the basement, but I rarely used the two upper ones.

It was warm in the room and Miss Lily was clearly grateful for the warmth. Her nose was shiny from the cold air of night and she rubbed her hands together as if they were chilled, though she could only have been out of the car a couple of minutes. It occurred to me, not for the first time, that her circulation might not be so good. 'It takes ages for that car to warm up,' she said, as she saw me looking at her. 'I get here just when it's starting.' She only has to come from Camden.

I went to hang up her coat in the little entrance hall. When I returned she was already seated at the table she uses for these typing sessions. The screen and keyboard and printer were there before her, all connected up and ready to go; the case she keeps them in was stowed neatly behind her, against the wall. All this in the time it had taken me to walk a few paces and hang up the coat on one of the pegs! Not only that, she was sitting there somehow expectantly, as if she had been installed for some time and was wondering where I had got to. I saw that somehow I had fallen behind again. How had I spent the time? Had I studied the pegs, trying to decide which one was appropriate for Miss Lily's dark brown, nylon-fur coat? Had some reorganization been necessary to make space for it? Had I examined the coat itself, the loop at the collar perhaps, to find a clue there as to the right peg or the right way of hanging it? I could not remember. The time was lost, it had sifted away from me.

To disguise the disturbance these thoughts occasioned me, I began to pace about the room, something I often did in any case while dictating pages of my book to Miss Lily. It was for the sake of this dictation that I had employed her. I was constantly revising sections of the book already done, those dealing with Horatio's early life, his marriage and his career up to his great victory at the Battle of the Nile in 1798, his arrival in Naples in the September of that year, his rescue of the royal family and the beginning of his love-affair with Lady Hamilton, the wife of the ambassador, in February 1799.

This process of revision had intensified since I had reached the impasse of that June. My text was tangled with handwritten emendations, insertions, crossings-out. No one but I could have deciphered it. Miss Lily's help had been invaluable, she was patient and efficient and – until that same evening – ventured no comments of her own. She also represented a notable piece of self-conquest on my part. I had hesitated for several weeks before taking the step of applying to Avon Secretarial Services, whose advertisement I had seen by pure chance one afternoon while waiting to have my hair cut. It was a difficult decision to make. I was always reluctant to change my routine, apply to strangers. But I needed someone and there was really no choice. In the end I took the bull by the horns and phoned. Avon Secretarial Services turned out to be just one person and that was Miss Lily.

So far it had been a success, we had worked well together. It was rather expensive at £15 an hour; but I could easily afford it, my father's death had left Monty and me quite comfortably off. And I considered the money well spent. After such torments of indecision about engaging her, I did not want to lose her services now. We would continue together, or so I thought. With her help I would extricate Horatio with honour from the languors and horrors of Naples, I would accompany him through the final years, to his splendid death and sumptuous funeral. My book would be the best account of Horatio ever to appear in print, a profound study of the man and a lasting tribute to the hero.

This evening, however, I could not begin. I made no move to get my papers from the drawer in the desk where I kept them. The restlessness that had been possessing me, the sense of displacement, of tracks obliterated and time somehow running out of control, kept me moving about the room. I found myself speaking in an unaccustomed way to Miss Lily, more freely and directly than I had ever done before, more personally too – talking about Horatio was like talking about myself.

I talked about the battle of Cape St Vincent, which I had just been enacting, and its aftermath and in particular about the exchange of letters between Horatio and his wife Fanny after the news of the victory had reached her. 'Fame had come to him at last,' I said. 'At the age of thirty-eight he was a national hero, the whole country was ringing with his praises. Difficult to imagine now, but people were really afraid of French invasion. There was intense rejoicing when the news came, but Fanny didn't find much to say. His father wrote to him, full of pride, he was wintering in Bath when he heard the news, he had to go back to his lodgings to hide his tears.'

Quite unexpectedly, at this mention of the old man, my voice broke a little and I felt a faint prickling behind the eyes. I have always been easily touched to tears and I have always been ashamed of it, it goes counter to my upbringing and the precepts of my father, but the assault always comes before the defences can be assembled. Was he ever seen to weep? Horatio, yes, on occasion; my father, naturally, never.

I had turned away from Miss Lily's gaze and now fell silent for some moments, trying to think of instances. I hoped she had noticed nothing. It was weakness on my part, yes, but I had found it moving, that pride in his son, those private tears.

'Why was he wintering in Bath?' Miss Lily said.

'His Norfolk parsonage would have been freezing in winter. Anyway, the main point is that everyone was singing Horatio's praises, everyone but her. All she could do was express her own fear and anxiety. That was not the note to strike with a man like him.'

'You call him by his first name.'

'Yes, yes, I do. An old habit.'

Miss Lily permitted herself a smile. She has a wide mouth, rather pale, sharp at the edges, with a general tendency to curve upwards. 'It seems funny,' she said, 'when you think that he's long gone.'

'Gone?' I said. 'Horatio Nelson is not gone, what an idea. He lives in the memory and gratitude of the whole nation.'

'Well, I'm British enough,' Miss Lily said, this being the first of many cryptic remarks she was to make during our various conversations. I was still not sure what she intended by it when she spoke again: 'But if her fear was for him, for her husband?'

'What use was her fear to him?' I was beginning now to regret having opened my mind to Miss Lily, it was obvious that she understood nothing about the nature of heroism. 'He told her what he expected of her in a letter after the battle,' I said.

'What he expected of her?'

'Yes,' I said, and I quoted from the letter – much of Horatio's correspondence I know by heart: *All do me the justice I feel I deserve. You will receive pleasure from the share I had in making it a most brilliant day, the most so of any that I know of in the annals of England.*

I allowed a short silence for this to sink in. Then I said, 'There you are, there you have it, that is clear enough, I think.'

'Quite clear,' Miss Lily said. 'He wanted her to praise him.'

'He says that he expected her to be pleased at his success.' Her obtuseness was beginning to annoy me. 'Let us see how she replies.'

I went to the shelf where I keep the collections of his correspondence and took down Geoffrey Rawson's compilation of 1949 as being shorter and easier to handle than most. I found Fanny's letter in a few moments and read it aloud to Miss Lily, deliberately dwelling on the more plaintive phrases: *Thank God you are well . . . My anxiety was far beyond my powers of expression . . . Altogether, my dearest husband, my sufferings were great . . .*

This read, I looked rather closely at Miss Lily. 'She has a hero for a husband and that is how she writes to him.'

However, she returned my gaze firmly and I could tell that she was not convinced, that she was siding with Fanny. Her eyes are brown and soft in expression but very steady in their gaze. I could feel my annoyance with her turning into rage. 'She couldn't give him what he needed,' I said, 'she let him down.'

'Well, after all, she grew up in the West Indies. That was where they met, wasn't it?'

'Yes, they met on Nevis. But what has that got – '

'You said yourself that the parsonage would've been freezing in the winter.'

'Parsonage?' Later I was to become more used to Miss Lily's oblique approach to things, so strangely at odds with the directness of her gaze. But now I was bewildered. And my anger grew.

'You probably think I'm taking too much on myself. I knew hardly anything about him, about Lord Nelson, when we started this work. History was never my strong point in any case. I've got secretarial skills, that's about all you can say. Most of my work isn't historical, it's more contemporary.'

'I don't know what you are driving at with this reference to the parsonage.'

'She would have been used to something warmer, wouldn't she? As I see it, he left her there alone, or with just her father-in-law for company, I mean disregarding him being a hero and all that side of it, either in a freezing parsonage in Norfolk or in lodgings somewhere she had not chosen to be. Draughty places, those old houses.' I saw her hunch herself a little and clutch at her elbows; she was putting herself in Fanny's place. 'And I grew up in this country,' she said. 'He doesn't write to ask her if she is keeping warm enough or anything like that. I mean, it was the middle of February. He was all right, wasn't he, he was down there in the south . . .'

'All right? Good God. He had received a shrapnel wound in the battle that opened his forehead to the skull. He was suffering from attacks of breathlessness due to stress and fatigue, he had – '

'She was alone, she was frightened for him. You would think he would know what it's like to be frightened.'

'But he did,' I said. 'He never showed fear himself, but he understood it in others, and he was always gentle with those who – '

'But that is among men, isn't it?'

I had no idea what she meant by this, but I could not escape the feeling that she was getting the upper hand in this discussion. And she was daring to criticize him, Horatio. The skin on my face felt tight with the efforts I was making not to let my fury show. I was afraid it would show in my eyes, which tend to get suffused with blood when I am upset. I moved round behind her to the other side of the table, where she could not see me without swivelling right round in her chair. The screen was facing me now, but I took care not to look at it. At a distance of about three feet I found myself studying the back of Miss Lily's head. Her dark brown hair was caught up behind in a pony-tail, exposing the nape of her neck, naked, palest cream in colour, surprisingly sturdy-looking, with a tender, faintly gleaming down on it, just below the hair-line. Her ear-lobes looked pink and waxy seen from this angle, somehow improbable, ruby-coloured drops of glass dangled from them and seemed to shiver in the light. Words continued to issue from the front part of this head: 'It's just like Scott of the Antarctic, he left his wife alone for months and years while he went looking for the South Pole . . .'

One moment the words were there, in the space before her. Then, quite suddenly, the sound of them diminished, receded. A sort of throbbing hush descended on me as if something had been pressed over my ears. I was still looking intently at Miss Lily's undefended nape and the shape of her skull under the hair. Then she turned in her chair a little, as if to glance round. I had a moment of giddiness and the hush was broken, sounds started coming again, occupying all the room. I moved round to the side of the table. I felt no anger at all now, only a sort of surprise.

'I read about it in the paper,' Miss Lily said.

'I'm sorry,' I said, 'what was it you read about?'

'This rumour that she had an affair while he was away in the frozen wastes. His son was asked about it and he said it was absolutely untrue and slanderous because his mother wasn't that sort of woman. What sort of woman did he mean?'

Her voice had risen. I looked at her face and saw that she was flushed. 'What did he *mean*?'

This sudden annoyance over an issue so trivial seemed absurd to me and went a good way to restoring my feeling of being

27

altogether on a higher plane than Miss Lily. I could not understand how I had allowed myself to get so upset. After all, from Avon Secretarial Services what could one expect? She was light-years from appreciating that for a bright angel like Horatio praise was manna, it was essential nourishment, essential combustion, he fed and blazed, like the sun. No good trying to explain this to her, she was still talking about the wretched explorer. Where did Scott come into it, a person only remembered for the manner of his death? Scott was not a hero. Heroes *succeed*.

'He probably didn't know what he meant himself,' she said, more quietly. 'Years ago I read it and it always sticks in my mind.'

I decided to let her go early. It was too late now to start dictating. Besides, the mood was wrong. This time, when I went to get her coat, the parallels stayed in place: she was still busy when I returned, putting her things into the bag. I waited until we were at the door. Then, quite casually, I put the question to her: 'How did you know I had been in the basement?'

'In the basement?' She looked puzzled but this could well have been a pretence.

'When you arrived this evening, when I came to answer the bell, you said I had come up the stairs too quickly. I have been wondering . . . how did you know I had come up the stairs? Was it just because I seemed out of breath?'

'Oh, that,' she said. 'Well, yes, you did seem a bit breathless as a matter of fact, but I would have known anyway. These dark evenings, before you come to answer the door you always put the light on in the passage and anyone standing on the top step outside, if they look up at the glass panel over the door, they can see a sort of shadow passing over it. If the shadow comes from the right – my right as I'm standing there – it means you must have come up from the basement. If it comes from the other side, you've been in your study or the sitting-room.'

She was standing immediately below me, on the bottom step. Light from the passage behind fell upon her face. She was smiling as she looked up at me. Not a broad smile, just a sort of deepening of her usual expression. 'How funny you should remember,' she said. She seemed pleased, I couldn't quite see why.

'You are quite a Sherlock Holmes,' I said. 'Female version, I mean.' I realized now, as I looked down at her, that Miss Lily had been tested back there in my study, that she had passed and that her success had changed things between us.

4

After Miss Lily had gone, I found in the fridge a covered dish which proved on investigation to contain ravioli with a filling of spinach and cream cheese, which I then remembered buying at a delicatessen near Chalk Farm Station two – or perhaps three – days earlier. I sniffed it but could detect no trace of taint. Cold from the fridge like that it didn't taste of anything much. I washed it down with some claret, about half a bottle, all I had left.

After the various upsets of the day I felt exhausted, but I had no inclination to sleep, in spite of the wine. I returned to my study and began to leaf through the loose pages of my manuscript, coming soon – as invariably happened in those days – to Horatio's fateful arrival at Naples in September 1798 and subsequent events, in particular those of the following June, from the 10th to the 30th. I was enmeshed in those twenty summer days.

The preliminary events are not in dispute. I knew them by heart, without needing to look at the pages before me. Horatio arrives in Naples on the 22nd of September, some two months after his resounding victory over the French at the Battle of the Nile. He is given a hero's welcome by King Ferdinand, the Bourbon ruler of the Two Sicilies, and his queen Maria Carolina, who regard him as their saviour. They are terrified of the French and with reason – Queen Marie Antoinette, Maria Carolina's sister, had been guillotined in Paris five years previously. Horatio, though gratified by his reception, is far from well. He is still suffering from battle-stress and the effects of a bad head wound received during the action. He needs rest and nursing, and this is provided by Lady Hamilton, the wife of the British ambassador to Naples, Sir William Hamilton, connoisseur and collector, thirty-five years her senior.

The danger of a French invasion by land is not over, in fact it grows daily greater. Their armies have occupied northern and central Italy, they have taken Rome, expelled the Pope and declared the city a republic. There is a treaty in existence between France and the Kingdom of the Two Sicilies. However, from Rome to Naples is only a few days' march, too close for comfort. Horatio, supported by the Queen, urges the irresolute Ferdinand to assume command of the Neapolitan army and march on Rome as defender of the faith against the atheist French. After much hesitation he is prevailed upon to do so. At the head of thirty thousand troops, under the direction of the Bavarian general, Baron Karl Mack von Leiberich, he sets off.

What an army. Described by Mack as the finest in Europe, it consists mainly of peasants in uniform with an admixture of bandits and released convicts. Mack himself proves both obstinate and hesitant, not the best of combinations in a general. The King shares with his soldiers a strong distaste for personal risk.

At first there are successes. The French withdraw to concentrate their forces. Rome is recovered, Ferdinand rides in triumph through the streets, mounted on a white horse, accompanied by dragoons in glittering uniform. But then comes the counterattack, the Neapolitans break and run, both officers and men, Mack conducts a disorderly retreat, the King bolts back to Naples in civilian disguise, groaning with fear, beseeching his aides not to desert him.

Horatio, it has to be said that your advice was disastrous. The King is humiliated, Naples is left defenceless, the French have been given a pretext for breaking the treaty. The Kingdom of the Two Sicilies will be plunged into civil war, the Royal Family obliged to quit the mainland, flee to Palermo in order to avoid falling into the hands of the French.

Not Horatio's fault, of course. I was intent on making that absolutely clear in my book. Other biographers have called it a blunder, but this is to misunderstand completely his character and temperament. Attack came naturally to him, he was all fire. How could a man so noble of soul comprehend the baseness of his instruments, a king who had nothing of the kingly, a commander who could not command, an army that melted away?

He is now all that stands between the Royal Family and the advancing French. The ships are ready to embark the monarchs if need be. He has already vowed British support to the Queen, now he is drawn into a personal promise not to desert her. A very different thing . . . I had noted the reference, it was there on the page before me, taken from a letter to his wife, Fanny, dated the 11th of December 1798: *The poor Queen has again made me promise not to quit her or her Family, until brighter prospects appear than do at present.*

This promise was troubling to me. Why did you make it? Why did you tie yourself down in that way? Your orders from the Admiralty were to protect the whole Adriatic coast as well as Naples and Sicily and to supervise the blockade of Malta, then in French hands.

Ten days later the situation has become impossible. The French are approaching Naples and there are many who will welcome them with open arms, the educated classes, the liberal aristocracy, united in their hatred of Bourbon cruelty and oppression, ardently possessed with the spirit of reform and republican ideas.

On the night of the 21st of December the Royal Family is embarked, together with the Hamiltons and various Neapolitan notables. Bad weather prevents them from sailing until the 23rd. At 2 a.m. on the morning of Boxing Day they anchor at Palermo. It is here, in the following February, that Horatio and Emma become lovers. And it is here that the news is received from Naples that the French army has taken the city, aided by the Neapolitan republicans, crushing an uprising of the *lazzaroni*, the fearsome Naples mob, who are devoted to their King and Queen. The royalist forces have been expelled from the castles of Sant'Elmo, Nuovo and dell'Ovo and a republic, known as the Parthenopean Republic, has been set up.

Meanwhile King Ferdinand is approached in Palermo by Cardinal Fabrizio Ruffo, a warrior–cleric of ancient lineage, who offers to go to Calabria, where his family's estates are, appeal to the patriotism and religious faith of the peasantry and lead them in a holy war to recover Naples for the monarchy. The offer is accepted, Ruffo enlists a force of Calabrese irregulars, murderous, ill disciplined, avid for loot. Holding this horde by force of personality under precarious control, he marches on Naples.

This Christian Army of the Holy Faith, as Ruffo calls it, has astonishingly rapid success. By the end of May the French have been forced to withdraw, leaving only a garrison in the castle of Sant'Elmo to support the Neapolitan republican militia, patriots as they regard themselves, traitors as Horatio regards them – who now take refuge from the bloodthirsty vengeance of the *lazzaroni* in the fortified castles of Nuovo and dell'Ovo.

So far, so bad. I took up my papers again. We were approaching the last week of June, the days that were causing me so much perplexity. By now Naples is in chaos. Ruffo's troops are out of control, plundering, raping and killing unchecked. Mobs of *lazzaroni* are roaming the streets, murdering and mutilating anyone, man or woman, suspected of Jacobin sympathies. For the details of this terrible period I was mainly relying on the account of Constance Giglioli, who quotes an eyewitness, Giuseppe di Lorenzo. I glanced over his words now in the calm of my study, which, however, still seemed to have something of Miss Lily's argumentative presence in it. *Heads and mutilated limbs were scattered in the street corners . . . A great number of victims were shot, one after the other . . . This done those butchers, not caring whether they were alive or dead, proceeded to cut off their heads, some of them were borne in procession on the ends of long poles and others served them to play with, rolling them along the ground like balls.*

It is to avoid an indefinite continuation of this bloodshed that Cardinal Ruffo, on the 23rd of June, makes terms with the enemy. He accepts the surrender of the French garrison and their Neapolitan allies in the city's forts. The French will be shipped home, the Neapolitans given the option of either accompanying them or returning to their homes under a general amnesty. The treaty is also signed, in the name of His Britannic Majesty George III, by the senior British officer in Naples, a certain Captain Foote, Horatio having sailed to the west coast of Sicily in an attempt to intercept the French fleet. The other co-signatories are Baillie and Achmet, for Russia and Turkey respectively.

A regular treaty then, signed by accredited representatives of all the forces opposed to the French. Horatio, when he hears of it on the 24th, is violently opposed, not to the terms offered the French but to an amnesty for the Neapolitan Jacobins. There are heated arguments. The cardinal has given his word, the treaty must be honoured. For Horatio the republicans are vile traitors who have supported an invading force. They must surrender unconditionally and throw themselves on the royal mercy.

Could they have had any faith in this? Surely they must have known what to expect. Maria Carolina was frightened and ferocious, Ferdinand's vindictiveness was notorious. Yet, on the afternoon of the 26th, the rebels came out of their forts. The fate that befell them was predictably atrocious.

So why did they do it? In this question lay all my trouble. It was as far from solution that February night as it had been when I first stumbled on it three months before. Until I found an answer, an *acceptable* answer, I could not proceed. I had been over the events hour by hour, as far as I had been able to find reliable authority for them, especially the forty-eight hours between Horatio's arrival in Naples and the rebels' quitting of the forts. I had puzzled so long and so earnestly that it had all gathered to a sort of bruise in my mind; touched even gently it would throb and hurt me, driving me always to seek refuge in the less ambiguous triumphs of his career.

Refuge I found now, as I sat there, in thoughts of his splendid arrival in the city, just ten months before, the conqueror, still a sea-being, still untouched by this corrupt and sensual place. Already, off Stromboli, in early September, his squadron has been joined by the *Mutine*, bringing from Naples the first letters of congratulation on his victory. Sir John Acton, the Prime Minister of Naples, expresses the felicitations of Ferdinand and Maria Carolina addressed to the Saviour of Europe. Sir William Hamilton, on behalf of himself and his wife Emma, addresses him as 'bosom friend'. *You have now made yourself, my dear Nelson, immortal.* In fact, the acquaintance at that point was slight, they had met briefly five years previously when Horatio was a young captain, still whole and unmutilated. Since then there had been Corsica and the blinding of his right eye, there had been his exploits at Cape St Vincent, the fiasco of Tenerife and the loss of his right arm. Now this astounding victory at Aboukir Bay.

In the same batch of letters are two from Emma. All of Naples is mad with joy, she is walking on air with pride at having been born in the same land as he, she is dressed from head to foot *alla Nelson* – even her shawl has blue and gold anchors all over it. She urges him to write or come soon. He has written already, expressing the hope that his mutilations will not make him the less welcome.

The British ships are sighted at dawn on the 22nd of September off the island of Capri. A Saturday. I had then never looked across that most famous of bays; but I had imagined it often, that dawn advent of the hero, that slow approach to the jubilant city. I knew what it would have been like to see it from the quayside, the faint sails in the half-light, now seen, now lost, drawing nearer as the light strengthens, silhouetted against the tawny cliffs of the island. Then sunrise, a single track of flame across the expanse of pale water . . .

Ten o'clock. The bay is a platter brimming with sunlight. Hundreds of pleasure boats have put off from the shore. I see their sails and hulls reflected in the water, shades of blue, scarlet, dark orange. The boats make ripples in the surface, but to my mind there is no gash of white; it is as if the colours themselves

35

have the power to cleave the water. Bands of musicians have come out to meet the ships. The orchestra of the San Carlo Opera, in a barge strung with red, white and blue bunting from stem to stern, plays 'God Save the King' and 'Rule, Britannia' and 'See the Conquering Hero'. The martial strains resound across the bay and carry to the approaching ships. The *Vanguard* responds with the boom of cannon.

The quayside is thronged with cheering people. We stand there at the prow. Tier upon tier of houses rise above us, pale yellow, rose pink, parchment colour, terracotta, rising into sun-hazed darker slopes of cypress and ilex. The balconies of the houses are festooned with flags, hung with baskets of carnations and roses. The ambassador's barge comes out to us, greeted by a salute of thirteen guns. They draw alongside. Lady Hamilton, all dressed *alla Nelson*, flies up the ladder-way. One of the most beautiful women of her time. She exclaims, 'Oh, God, is it possible?' She faints in my arm and falls to the deck.

A left-handed handshake from Hamilton, elderly, thin, distinguished. His words are not recorded. An hour later a further salute, twenty-one guns this time. Ferdinand IV, Ruler of the Two Sicilies, is approaching in his state galley, painted scarlet and gold, with spangled awnings. Some months away still the fiasco of his expedition, the ignominious flight. Perspiring in his black velvet and gold lace, he makes a speech of welcome. There is gratitude in that big-nosed face as he hails his 'Deliverer and Preserver'.

As the *Vanguard* moves in stately fashion towards the waiting city, we sit down to an elegant breakfast. Among the illustrious guests is Commodore Caracciolo, Bailli of the Order of Malta, admiral of the Neapolitan navy, who is in charge of the nautical education of the King's nine-year-old son, Leopold. He is only a few months away from court martial and death at our hands by public hanging as a traitor to his king.

As we step on shore, the air is full of fluttering wings. Hundreds of fishermen with captive doves in wicker cages have been standing at the quayside, waiting for just this moment. They raise the cages aloft, release their captives. As the white birds mount upwards, I try to follow their flight, but my eyes are dazzled by the brightness of the sky, the sunlight hazed with dust, the rain of petals. I am confused by the music and the shouting of the people. We gain our waiting carriage and go clattering away over the black lava paving stones, up towards the British Embassy, Palazzo Sessa, whose façade is draped with red, white and blue hangings.

Something brought me back from this, perhaps some sound outside. Sitting there in the calm light of my study, my eyes felt this daze, this bewildering assault of sunlight and movement. Half involuntarily, I glanced up at the ceiling as if to follow those beating wings, those floating petals. But there was only the Victorian stucco, crumbling here and there, of the cornice. Has any man, before or since, any conquering hero whatever, made such a triumphant appearance in such a magnificent setting?

I doubt it, really I doubt it. In the carriage, clattering up to the embassy, there is not much talk. Fascinating to my mind, that short journey. The whole situation, all that was to happen, already contained there, in the words and glances. Four people in close proximity: Horatio, Sir William, Lady Hamilton and Miss Cornelia Knight, the authoress, who had accompanied the Hamiltons in their barge and was to relate the details of this historic meeting in her autobiography. Three principals, then. First – always first – the hero, still sick, suffering from the prolonged anxiety of that long pursuit and the stress of the night-time battle in the hazardous shallows at the mouth of the Nile, lonely, in need of comfort, in need of the mother we lost so young; Emma, the blacksmith's daughter, exuberant, beautiful, excessive, ridden by follies, full of admiration for him, experienced in love; Sir William, aristocratic, cultivated, world-weary, aware of declining powers, prepared if need be, though perhaps not knowing it yet, to lend his wife or even give her, as she had been given by his nephew to him.

So we go clattering uphill in our open carriage, leaving the pleasure boats and the white birds and the thronged quayside behind us, up to the Hamilton residence, easily recognizable at a distance by those vivid hangings of scarlet, white and blue. After arriving, some hours of repose. While we are resting, darkness falls. The three thousand lamps that have been set in the façade of the palazzo all spring to life and the words 'Nelson of the Nile' blaze out over the city.

We take our places at the dinner-table. A distinguished gathering. Among the blue uniforms are those of Troubridge and Ball, constant companions of those Naples days. Your two favourite captains. It was they who carried the note to Ruffo that June morning the following year, the note that seemed to promise so much, that brought the Jacobins out of their forts. Your note. I didn't want to think about this; I wanted to hold on to the scene of our triumph, there in the candlelight, honoured guest, perhaps unsettled by the steadiness of things after so long at sea, perhaps confused by the beauty of full-bodied Emma and the slimmer versions of her that looked down from the walls in a multitude of guises and postures, copies acquired by Sir William before the original was securely his: teenage rosebud Emma in a black hat and pink silk gown; Emma as a Bacchante, auburn tresses in artful disarray, flimsy draperies loose about her; Emma as Saint Cecilia, robed in white, palms closed in prayer, eyes looking heavenwards.

Your eyes were bombarded with Emma. Tired eyes but not too tired to be beguiled. Were there glances already? Was there already something you wanted to repress or deny? Is that why you said you preferred Emma as a saint? Is that why you found occasion to say, with emphasis, there at the table, that the happiest day of your life was not the victory at the Nile but the day you married Lady Nelson?

Your room was on the upper floor. It had a broad semicircular window looking southwards over the bay towards Capri. The entire opposite wall was covered with mirrors. You could see the pale disc of the moon rise from the fiery mouth of the volcano as if exhaled upwards. Below, on the silver water, the ruddy torchlights of the small boats, fishing for tuna. And all this again, this blending of ruddy and pale, reflected in every detail in the glass of the wall. And when, in the days of your sickness, the hot September afternoons when you were feverish and she came to tend you, to see to your comfort, as she moved about the bedside you would see the lines of her body through the light summer clothes. And every movement, the turn of her shoulders, the sway of her hips, would be reflected in the glass. Repeated reflections like a repeated caress. Sweetness of the loins under the bedclothes . . .

All this was to come. But how strange it must have seemed to you as you lay alone there on the first night, in that room of multiple reflections. It was the first time in six months that you had slept away from your ship.

5

That night my sleep was broken by dreams. As so often he was with me and there was the accustomed sense of mourning or lamentation, the massed sense of it and somehow the grain of it in the air. I never see his face clearly. I see it only in glimpses, in obscured light, a fleeting impression of the mouth, the brows, the line of the jaw. I am always strongly aware of his presence, shadowy, indistinct but immensely potent. He knows I am there, he expects certain things from me, but I am not sure what. This time we were together on that ill-fated expedition up the San Juan River in Nicaragua.

I had been reading Tom Pocock's account of it – the fullest there is. Horatio saw a good deal of action on land, a fact that is sometimes forgotten. In January of 1780, as a 21-year-old captain in command of the *Hinchingbrooke*, a frigate of 28 guns, he was ordered away from the West Indies to assist the army by landing a force at the mouth of the River San Juan, which rises in Lake Nicaragua and flows into the Caribbean Sea. This was the naval part of a grandiose plan to transport troops up the river, storm the Spanish forts that controlled the upper reaches and take possession of the lake, thus at one stroke cutting Spanish America in half.

What had not been much studied by the Army High Command, if at all, was how to get troops totally unacquainted with tropical rain-forest, along with their artillery and essential supplies, through the hundred miles of the river's course. No one knew the position of the enemy strong-points. No one knew what conditions were like in the interior. Apart from local Indians, nobody was thought to have navigated the river since the days of the buccaneers, a century previously. Horatio's task was to escort a convoy of troopships to the river-mouth and wait there on guard till they returned.

There were, however, problems. None of the five hundred or so officers and men that had been assembled had the smallest experience of river navigation; many of them were already sickening and should have been in hospital, instead of preparing for active service. And the preparations had taken too long, the dry season was already two months old; the river was so low that boats often had to be unloaded and hauled by men wading in the shallows. Now enter Horatio. He does not believe that the soldiers can manage it unaided. So what does he do? As always, he is practical, unhesitating, prompt without rashness. He offers to leave his ship at the river-mouth and lead the way with two of her boats and fifty of her crew. Major Polson, the commanding officer, is delighted to accept.

Offered like that, on his own initiative, fifty men! It impressed me when I first knew of it and I had thought often about it since. Even here, even at so young an age, he showed the angelic nature, he disobeyed or at least exceeded his orders, which were simply to await the troops' return. *I'll give you myself and fifty men.* It was the same for him, I tried to explain to Miss Lily when we were revising this section later – in May, I think. He went with them, he led them, he took the same risks. The fangs of the cotton-snake, the sucking of the vampire bats, the hammer-stroke of the sun by day and the noxious damps of night. And the diseases, I said, above all the diseases – malaria, bloody flux, black vomit. Before they reached the enemy, before they even knew where the enemy were, a third of the expeditionary force was already dying. Miss Lily couldn't see it – there is a lot she doesn't understand and never will. It wasn't the same for him, she said, it was his idea, not theirs. By that time she was accustomed to make remarks, whether invited or not. What had they to gain? she said, with that very clear and candid look of hers. What was there in it for them? A typical Miss Lily question, difficult to answer and at the same time quite beside the point. Those men had no destiny, I told her, tried to tell her. Horatio had. Destiny is possessed by very few.

Fifty miles upriver, fifteen terrible days; then the first sign of the enemy, a small outpost on an island in midstream. Horatio's sailors take the battery by storm, he leading them barefoot, his shoes having got stuck in the mud. Two days later, just below the lake, they come upon a powerful fort, called by the Spanish Castel San Juan. Horatio urges an immediate assault by storm – when did he ever counsel delay? But the castle is in a strong defensive position, above the fiercest rapids in the river. Major Polson waits to land his men, he waits to take the surrounding heights and position his batteries, he waits for reinforcements to arrive. And while he waits the clouds build up, the rains break. The forest steams, malaria kills the men in droves.

After a siege of eleven days the fortress surrenders. The surviving Spanish are in even worse case than the besiegers, gaunt, starving, in rags, living in low sheds made of putrid animal skins. A stink of death hangs over this place, this possession so much suffered for, so much longed for. Spanish and British are now united in misery. The rains have swollen the river to a torrent, the expeditionary force is trapped there in the jungle, unable to get through to the lake. There, in the mud of the river bank or among the wet leaves, they continue to die.

And Horatio, by a miracle is not there! He is not there to see the taking of this stronghold and its disease-ridden garrison. If he had remained, he would have died, beyond a doubt, choked on his vomit like so many. He had acute poisoning after drinking from a pool infected by the sap of the manchineel tree; he had contracted yellow fever, fatal in most cases; it is likely he had dysentery as well. Yes, he would have died . . . At the very last moment, before it became impossible for any boat, even a canoe, to struggle up against the flood, a message came from Admiral Parker, his commander-in-chief. Horatio was recalled, he was to make his way down to the sea again, hand the *Hinching-*

brooke over to his friend Collingwood, return to Jamaica and take command of the *Janus*, a bigger and better frigate, with 44 guns. Not luck, destiny, I said to Miss Lily, but it was a waste of time trying to explain such distinctions to her. Those fifty men, she said, what became of them? They all died, I told her.

Make his way down to the sea again. Of all the phrases contained in his orders that one had stayed in my mind. The sea was life, the land was death, these were the parallels on which my book was constructed. His mutilations were suffered on land, a fact I regard as highly symbolic. But that was not the reason these words had stayed with me. It is a question of dates. Horatio's reprieve came on the 28th of April and that was the date I first started seeing Penhas. True, I was younger by a year, I was only twenty; but that is not important. The date is the same and for both of us it meant a return to life.

Horatio set out that same day. He could not walk unaided, he had to be helped on to the boat. As those swirling, muddy currents carried him towards the sea, I was seeking help from Penhas, who belonged to the same London club as my father and was a psychiatrist. I am aware of the time difference, in Nicaragua it would have been several hours earlier than in London. But Horatio's journey to the sea took four days and four nights; it is the *parallel* that has to be kept in mind – that full river was still carrying him over shoals and shallows when I began the first of my conversations with Penhas. And it was Penhas who brought me back to him, to Horatio, whose hope lay in the sea, just as mine – guided by Penhas – lay in him.

Of course, this was not apparent to either Penhas or myself on that first meeting between us, which was more in the nature of getting acquainted. I had been dreading this meeting as at the time I dreaded everything not entirely familiar, which in practice meant everything but the four walls of my room.

It was the end of my second year at Cambridge, where I was reading philosophy. I had been working very hard. I had to give up my rooms in college and find lodgings in the town. Possible reasons. How can one know? It is difficult to know the moment when the world starts to change aspect. It was mainly a matter of suspicion getting out of hand. Twenty-two years ago now. The progression of my illness has become vague to me in its detail, at first merely a daily sense of surviving, of reaching bed-time unscathed – coming through a tutorial, a chance meeting in a café or pub, even, later, just a wave of greeting across the street or a nod to some acquaintance in the library. The days bristled with encounters and my fear of them grew, extending to glances from strangers, especially certain faces, certain eyes. Unpredictable, uncontrollable, always just round the corner, the power to smash my life. Fear of eyes kept me from sleeping. Then, one morning I was unable to leave my room. I dragged a cupboard across the door. When they began knocking and calling I remember pressing back against the wall farthest from the door, pressing hard with my back against the wall – I remember the pain of it. They had to break in and I soiled myself while they were doing it.

At home in London, here in this house, in my familiar room, the fear receded, but I knew it waited for me outside. I kept my door locked. Monty talked to me and so did my father – it was my father who wanted me to see Penhas. I had been schooled to trust my father's judgement and in his judgement what I needed was this fellow member of his club. Even so I must have been somewhat better by then or I could not have been persuaded.

Penhas was in his fifties, aquiline of feature, with a short beard lighter in colour than the hair on his head, sombre dark eyes and a smile of disconcerting charm. Some faces grow indistinct in our minds as the years pass but his has never done so, nor the slow, emphatic gestures he made with his hands as he talked. He talked a great deal. I have often heard since that the psychiatrist's function is mainly to listen, but this was not true of Penhas, at least not at the beginning. He told me a great deal about certain things that had befallen him when he was just my age. He was a Sephardic Jew whose parents had gone from Spain to Turkey in the years before the Second World War. The family had an agency for imported machine-tools in Izmir, but this collapsed, leaving them in poverty. Penhas wanted to get back to Spain and set off in 1952 with almost no money in his pocket. All sorts of things happened to him on the way. He had begged in the streets and snatched washing off a line and even rooted about in rubbish bins. But the stories I afterwards remembered most vividly were the stealing of the bicycle and the adventure with the high-class prostitute, the *poule de luxe*, as Penhas always called her, reverting to French for this salacious interlude.

Both these stories contained a moral lesson in Penhas's view, but the lesson of the bicycle was easier to see. In some hilly region, footsore and penniless, he had seen two bicycles standing outside a lonely farmhouse, one very old and battered, the other quite new. He had stolen one of them. Which one did I think? 'The new one,' I said, because it was expected, but he shook his head. No, he had taken the other. Now came the lesson: in thievery, as in all else, there were degrees of gravity. This, rather obvious in itself, led to the more important point: the vital need to make distinctions. Sanity depends on our ability to make distinctions, Penhas was fond of saying. The bicycle he took was falling to pieces. The reason he stole the washing was to wrap it round the wheels, the tyres having rotted off. He had done a thousand kilometres on this contraption, he told me.

The *poule de luxe* episode must have happened before this. It seems she took a fancy to Penhas, took him to live with her in her luxury apartment, which he had to vacate whenever there were clients, maintained him for some unspecified period of time – a period he brought to a close by leaving at dawn with the contents of her purse. As I say, the lesson in this case was not so clear to me. It had to do with clarity. Incompatible missions, Penhas said. Hers was to pursue her profession, his was to get to Spain. Sanity depends on clear perceptions of incompatibility.

His adventures were interesting to hear about, and when I did begin talking to Penhas it was not so much a matter of admitting or confessing anything but of trying to invent a personality for myself capable of responding to the confidences he had made me – the confidences of a fellow twenty-year-old. I think now that this was his deliberate purpose. Otherwise, how could it have been that I knew so much about these youthful escapades of his but nothing at all about his later life, his metamorphosis into a psychiatrist with an office in Brook Street, W1, speaking carefully perfect English and a member of the same club as my father, about whose doings at twenty I knew nothing at all? I could not match his exploits with any of my own; but I could more than match them with Horatio's.

So it was that in the presence of this talkative psychiatrist I found him again. He had been there all the time but underground, obscured by the stress of A-levels and my studies at the university. In the course of time I told Penhas about the chess game, the two faces side by side in my father's book, the luminous moment of my discovery that Horatio and I had lost our mothers at the same age. I told him about my history teacher, the redoubtable Grigson. I told him about the scrapbooks and the model ships.

Once this was avowed, there was no going back. Penhas fastened on it. With gentle questions he led me along. For months he was the only person I really talked to. I told him about my earlier conviction that there existed some intimate link between this great man's life and mine. Penhas encouraged me. He never reacted immediately. Things I said would lie dormant between us, sometimes for several meetings. Meanwhile, though he never admitted so much, he did some studying on his own. His knowledge of eighteenth-century sea-battles visibly increased. He even began to use nautical terminology.

'Think of the mystery of the man, use him as a source of meditation.'

'What mystery?'

'The mystery of his courage. Think of him there, in the heat of the action, on the quarter-deck. Think of the tendency to fear there must have been. Men are more likely to be mastered by

46

fear when they are fully conscious of the risks they are running. Everyone else would be too busy manning the guns, and so on. Only the officers on the quarter-deck had to stand still and be shot at. Think of that quarter-deck. At the forward end, looking across the waist towards the forecastle, there was only an open rail. That is where your Horatio stood. Think of him there, dressed impeccably, full uniform, cocked hat, silk stockings, buckled shoes. Immaculate. Unoccupied, fully aware of his danger, carnage all around him. Like a rock, Charles, like a rock. That is the way, that is the way forward, Horatio is your lifeline, stay with him, he will get you out and about. Join the Nelson Club, there must be one – in London there is a club for everything under the sun, if you can run it to earth. I'll get my secretary to find the address.'

This was towards the end of my treatment. I remember it quite well, an afternoon in late summer. I remember the gesture of his hands as he spoke, a downward movement, with the palms facing inwards, about eighteen inches apart, as though sketching two sides of a box. Dark eyes with their look of sombre sincerity. Sunlight filtered through thin curtains, white or beige. Two parallel lines, the sides of a box. *Horatio is your lifeline.*

There is a club, Penhas was right. It is called the Nelson Club and has premises in Bloomsbury. But I did not become a member then, in spite of his advice. In fact I did not join until much later. At the time I was not up to joining anything. I did not return to university. For quite some time I could not easily be persuaded to leave the house. Neither Penhas nor anyone else succeeded in explaining how it had come about, how it was that I had stumbled into such terror. It might as well have been some viral infection, like jaundice for example. You are dreadfully familiar with the symptoms, but you don't know why it happened, why it happened to you. However, I stayed with Horatio, who did not know fear, and he with me; we have been together ever since.

The fifty lives he had offered were wretchedly consumed. Many thousands more were to go the same way before Dalling,

47

the governor of Jamaica, and Lord George Germain, the colonial secretary, were to abandon the dream of possessing Lake Nicaragua and opening a route to the Pacific. There was no expeditionary force left by this time. Since the previous February two thousand troops had been sent to Nicaragua, of whom less than a hundred survived, and they were wrecked in health. More than a thousand sailors died in their ships. These are details that make Horatio's escape more wonderful and I liked to dwell on them.

The final act of this tragic farce was curiously fitting. When, finally, the survivors made their way downriver (the boat they left in was called the *Lord Germain*, after the man who in the remote purlieus of Whitehall dreamed up this costly enterprise), the rearguard of Light Dragoons was left behind with orders to blow up the bastions of the fort before abandoning it. Of these soldiers, recruited in the quayside bars and brothels of Jamaica, a motley assortment of Portuguese, Italians, Negroes and a few British, nothing more is known. Perhaps the charges were too weak, or the bastions too strong, or they were surprised by the Spanish before they could complete the work. Presumably they died there. All that is known for certain is that by the end of the year the Spanish flag was again flying over the Castle of San Juan. The jungle closed over the corpses just as the discreet silence of government closed over the expedition itself.

How fortunate for Horatio that he was not present at the final stages of this fiasco. Now that is luck, I said to Miss Lily. I was still trying to make her see the difference. He was not associated with the defeat. Because, you see, he had advocated immediate assault by storm, but Polson had chosen to wait. Waiting proved disastrous, so Horatio emerged with credit, his superiors were favourably impressed. Had young Nelson been listened to, they said, the castle would have been taken, the lake attained and the healthy uplands of Nicaragua occupied before the onset of the rains. It was never put to the test of course. That is what we mean by luck, I told her. Reputation enhanced, skeletonic, dressed in his captain's uniform, blue, white and gold, he was borne swiftly away, down to the open sea. Heroes have both, I said, they have luck *and* destiny.

However, I did not, that night last February, dream of open skies and sunlit seas and the passage of Horatio to life again, but of that nightmare journey upriver with the fifty doomed men of the frigate *Hinchingbrooke*, the stream narrowing as the forest pressed dense and close on either side. There was no turning back. Horatio at the prow with his narrow back turned to me, I behind him in the same boat. He looks round once, his face is noseless, eyeless, mouthless, just a pale shape of flesh beneath the sharp wings of his captain's hat, but I know it is at me he is looking, we are about to face something terrible together. From the banks on either side a massed sound of lamentation, sorrow falling on us like rain. The river takes a bend and we come upon the Spanish stronghold, fortress of the dead and the dying, open gates, litter of corpses, crawling survivors, the swarming glint of flies. The sound of mourning grows wilder, it fills the air. Suddenly I am alone, he is no longer with me . . .

I woke from this sweating. I was not Horatio in the dream, he abandoned me, I did not take his place. Otherwise, how could I dream of the besieged in their putrid prison, something he never saw? An echo of the Holocaust, filmed images of the heaped dead, the walking dying, central experience of our century, whether we lived through it or not, pit into which all our nightmares flow?

For a long time I lay awake in the darkness. The intensity of the dream – that mingling of horror and grief – kept my mind on a gloomy track. I thought again of those dying dragoons, lost between the lake and the sea, fumbling to blow up the fort. No one will ever know what became of them. That much, at least, we know about Jervis's decapitated marine. Perhaps he was no farther than a foot away. The grotesque *suddenness* of that death, no gasp or cry. And soundless in effect, amid all that din of battle. Only the brief song of the missile, then the splatter of blood and brain over the face and chest of the crusty old admiral. Why did he call for an orange? To demonstrate unconcern? Or did some stuff splash into his mouth? Probable, yes, though naturally beyond the touch of proof. It must have been a shock. There would have been an intake of breath, an involuntary gasp of surprise. Even so seasoned a campaigner ... Yes, the viscid substance of the marine's death, some of it entered his mouth and he called for an orange to get rid of the taste. Naturally, he stayed on the quarter-deck till victory was assured, stained with the marine's blood and bits of his brain tissue and spinal marrow and the soft, fatty substances that had sheathed his nerves.

Somewhere that soldier's name will be recorded, though I have never found it; also, just possibly, as an incident in some more general account, how he was standing at the moment of his death, whether loading or firing, and so on. But of course his name does not matter, what he was doing does not matter, he provided an occasion for his admiral, at the height of the battle, to call for an orange. Jervis acquired an extra name, he was created Earl St Vincent. And Horatio, hero of the day, became Sir Horatio, Knight of the Bath ...

Sea-battle, in those days, so peculiarly designed for mutilations and maimings. A hail of missiles. Shrapnel from the cannon-shot, razor-edged projectiles from sliced and splintered timbers, whizzed through the crowded decks. Selective, however – death not a reaper but a sort of crazed sniper, here a face shorn off, there a leg carried away. Men rarely died in swathes. Sometimes, of course, when a ship was raked fore and aft - this was the fire Horatio had to suffer at Trafalgar, when he drove into the French line at right angles. But death in daily dress was the gouger, the slicer, lord of eviscerations and lopped limbs. And he, my Horatio, pacing back and forth on the quarter-deck, pausing to observe the progress of the battle, stars and ribbons prominent on his breast, showing no haste, showing no fear, as if he were out on a Sunday morning stroll, looking at birds or clouds through his telescope. What sublime conquest of self he gave proof of, not once, but over and over, what shining bravery and quality of command. Nerves of steel, a courage not merely of endurance – that alone is not the hero's brand – but possessing that fierce patience of the fighter who waits to deliver the killing stroke. *The mystery of his courage.* Admiration, the old admiration, flooded over me as I lay there. Ever since my talks with Penhas I had loved him for this sauntering in the midst of terrible damage. The ugly dream receded and I felt again that prickle of tears, so common with me then and now.

My own first experience of death was on a Sunday morning, during a stroll in the country. It came in the form of one sick rabbit which my father stamped on. I was five years old – it is one of my earliest memories. My brother Monty was with us, he is three years older. We were out on a country walk with my father. This was in Surrey, where we lived then – it was two years later that we came to live here, in this house. We were walking along a footpath, not very wide, clay-coloured, dusty – I suppose there had been no rain for some time. Open, heathy country. I have worked out that it was a Sunday; we were generally taken for walks on a Sunday morning if the weather were fine enough, while my mother, unaided on this day of the week, saw to the lunch.

We met the rabbit, or it met us – it was coming from the opposite direction, hopping slowly towards us along the edge of the path, not seeming disabled or distressed, not at first, though slower than you would expect a rabbit to be in the open and in full view. When we were quite close it stopped and I saw the gummy bulge of its eyes and I knew there was something badly wrong with this rabbit. Its head was too big. At the last moment, when we were almost upon it, fear supervened, it made an effort to get away, leaving the path and going off perhaps three yards into the grass. Then it stopped again. I saw now that the rabbit was trembling all over. I looked at my father's face to see what we were to make of this business, but there was no expression on his face at all. A last impression of the bloated head, the swollen, suppurating eyes. Then my father, without a word, stepped off the path, approached the rabbit, raised his right knee well above the horizontal and stamped down with force – a single, plunging motion. Then he briskly but thoroughly wiped his shoe in the grass.

Strange how clearly I could remember these actions in their exact sequence, yet had no certain recollection of the dead rabbit, nothing I could be sure belonged to the time. Images of pulped or squashed rabbits visited my mind frequently enough afterwards and still sometimes do, but I can never be sure they are authentic. The stamping and the wiping I remember well, however, the grey flannel trouser-leg, two or three inches of greenish sock, the stout, cherry-brown brogue; this last could not have been much below my eye-level at the time, when raised to stamping height – he was a tall man. He looked at us and I remember his face. We have put the poor beast out of its misery, he said.

I don't know what I felt about this or what I feel now. We crave a dominant note, we seek in memory for the single element, one stain to colour the whole. But the tints do not blend, the colour eludes us. There was no balance in the thing. The dream-like preliminaries, the loping, lolloping rabbit, my father's casual stepping aside, the violence of the plunging shoe, that brisk rubbing in the grass.

We have put the poor beast out of its misery. He included Monty and me in that decisive act. It was true, he had done a merciful thing. A paradox too difficult for a child to appreciate, the intention of mercy expressed in a gesture so seemingly brutal. And then there was the look on his face, a certain look of alertness, almost eagerness, as he scanned our faces to see if the lesson had gone home.

That is the earliest memory I have of my father's face; the latest is the face of his death, that settling of stillness, as if he had answered his own question. But what lesson was it that he was seeking to bring home to us? This is the nature of reality, this is what the world is like, a place of suffering and pain which a man must confront with decision? Something like pleasure on his face, a sort of brightness; not at killing the rabbit, I don't think he took the smallest pleasure in that; but at the stern message implicit in it. He was observing his sons' faces, driving home a moral, making a useful dent on the soft minds of Monty and me. The memory is all violence now, like the springing of a trap in a silent place; the moral side of it has been diluted. In later years my father seemed often to be held in that same incommunicable woe of the rabbit. Not his eyes, not the alertness of his glance, that was unimpaired . . .

I did not want to think about this. Horatio was my refuge, as so often. I felt the impulse to look again at the face of his father. For some minutes I lay there, summoning resolve. Then I got up, put on my heavy dressing-gown and went along to the kitchen, with the idea of making some tea and taking it down to the basement.

6

It was not yet light and very cold. I always turn the heating off before going to bed, it makes the air too dry and gives me headaches. Besides, a cold bedroom is more manly, or so I was brought up to believe. Apart from anything else, it's a long-standing habit and habit is law, habit is safety; without habits we would just flop around and die. I put the heating back on now, however, and began to make the tea.

By then it was taking me a long time to make tea. In fact everything seemed to take longer and longer. I urgently wanted to look at Edmund Nelson's face but things had to be done in order, I knew I couldn't take short-cuts. I had given up cooking because it took up too much time, all the pondering what to buy and getting lost in supermarkets. And there had been times when it conflicted with some important date in the Horatio calendar – I celebrated all the key events of his life. I didn't mind giving it up, there is no framework in it, no procedure, as an activity it is messy, amorphous, clogged with alternatives. Mrs Watson would have cooked for me, at least on the days that she came; but I didn't want that, it was too much of an involvement.

Run the cold water for ninety seconds to flush out the pipes, kettle two thirds full, warm the pot, two level teaspoons of Darjeeling, catch the kettle at the precise moment it rises to the boil, on no account must it bubble or oxygen is lost and then you have to start all over again. Pour from a height of eight inches – I had made a pencil mark on the wall. Tea-cosy. Allow to stand a full three minutes. Strainer at the ready, resting on its blue saucer. I believe in procedures. When our world comes crashing down about our ears, when this planet chokes in its own fumes or stings itself to death like a demented scorpion, it will be owing to neglected procedures. Horatio knew the importance of procedures, none better.

I have my own mug, blue and white, with a thin band of silver going round the top. It has my monogram on it, in a panel of pale blue, two curly C's twining together, Charles Cleasby. It was a present from my mother when I was six years old, one of a number of things given to me when I came home from hospital after my appendix operation. It seemed to me miraculous that she should have found a mug with just my initials on it, among all the initials and all the children in the world. Only years later, long after she had left us, did it occur to me that she might have had them specially put on. I had been drinking my tea out of that mug for thirty-five years. Apart from the rug in the sitting-room it was all of her I had left.

No milk – I never touch milk. One cube of Demerara sugar. Mug in hand, I went down to the basement. I went through to the small middle room that lies between my collection of Nelson exhibits and the ops-room with the model ships. This was my picture gallery, mainly reproductions – original portraits are naturally difficult to obtain even if one could afford them, though I had some good paintings of sailing ships, among them one by John Nathan, RA, of HMS *Victory* with sails loosed for drying at Spithead.

Fanny Nelson was there, the wronged wife; and Emma Hamilton, the adored mistress; and Sir William Hamilton, the complaisant husband; and Horatio's uncle, Captain Maurice Suckling, who gave him his first chance, and Jervis, he of the orange, and Collingwood, who supported Horatio so loyally at the Battle of Cape St Vincent, and Hardy, who kissed him when he was dying. Horatio himself was not to be found on these walls. I hung all the likenesses of him that I had collected in the exhibits-room; he looked down over the cabinets and showcases that commemorated his wonderful life.

I stood before the portrait of Edmund Nelson, sipping my tea, warming my hands on the mug. He was seventy-eight when Beechey painted this likeness of him. Less than two years to live. A long, fair-browed, narrow face, lugubrious, scraped close to the bone with age, resigned, yes, but not serene. The tones of the painting are sombre, his black habit merges into the dark sepia of the background, his two-tailed clerical stock is tucked close up to his bony chin. Submission in the face, feeling suppressed, something feminine. Not quite the face you would expect in a Norfolk parson of yeoman stock . . . My father's face quite different, all straight lines: square jaw, sheer planes at the temples, level eyes and brows, large, regular teeth – the stem of his pipe had bite-marks on it.

The man who begot me, the man who begot Horatio – in death they had become contemporaries, as all the dead are. In the face before me now there was no trace of the angelic, no hint of breaking the line. Duty his creed, as it was his son's, but like many of the virtues we extol this can take forms active or passive. The Reverend Nelson's was the latter sort, finding its reward in sufferance. Not so Horatio, for whom duty was a seeking-out, a fulfilment in fame.

His was the ambition of genius. But it was the lesson of obligation, of doing what one is called upon to do, that the father passed down. What Horatio made of it was his own. *Thank God I have done my duty.* Probably the last words anyone heard him say, as he lay dying in the dimness below decks at Trafalgar. The surgeon that attended him and recorded the last hours of his life heard him murmur these words some minutes before the voice was lost for ever. Duty done, victory achieved – it was the same thing for him, the duty lay in the achievement. And so it is with me, I am the same, in spite of appearances. My doubts and fears, these were his purifying discharge. A medal has two faces, my face was hidden against his breast.

Still looking closely at that eroded face, I thought of the stories of Horatio's childhood that have passed down to us. Courage, leadership, indomitable will, all so precociously shown by this slightly built, pale-faced boy. How, one Norfolk winter, he battled through great drifts of snow to get to school, urging on his faltering – and much more robust – elder brother, because they had promised their father to do their utmost. *Remember, brother, it was left to our honour.* How, at an even tenderer age, he wandered away, got lost in the woods as darkness fell, was found after long search, sitting by the side of an impassable stream. Surprising that fear did not bring you home, they said. *Fear? I never saw fear. What is it?*

Useless to look for clear outlines in this twilight of infancy. These were anecdotes told after his glorious death, after he had become the saviour of his country, memories embroidered into legend. The life of a hero is a grafted tree, rooted in fact, branched with hearsay. And Horatio Nelson is the English hero, he has no rival. No threat of rivals in the future either – this country will never produce heroes again.

Equally useless to judge by faces. This mild-faced man I was looking at now was capable, when roused, of seizing a house-breaker by the collar and throwing him bodily out of the house. Horatio and his brothers and sisters, when old enough to sit at table, were forbidden to touch with their backs the backs of the chairs. Weak sight was not deemed a reason for spectacles. Yet the rector did not strike his parishioners as a man of forceful character, and he considered himself to be lacking in firmness. 'Tremulous over trifles and easily put in a fuss', to use his own words. Always something strange in the progenitors of genius . . . Self-denial imposed on a sensuous and emotional nature, was this the key to both father and son? Quite suddenly, while still formulating the question, I felt that same gathering of tears behind the eyes, but they were more urgent now, I knew that if I allowed my features to relax I would blub in good earnest. I kept my face stiff and fought it off, knowing the cause quite well. It was the grief of never grasping, never fully knowing. Horatio had occupied my life, I knew more about him than anyone else because I was his heir, I had inherited his being. The conviction

57

of this had grown stronger in the years that had passed since my chats with Penhas; it had been fed by both study and intuition. But still I could not reach to the essential part, the mystery of his courage.

I did not then, that February night, as I clutched my mug and resisted the tears, see myself as an angel like him, a creature of radiant violence. That came later. At the time I thought of myself merely as a repository of his essence, a sort of memorial urn. But I knew that the same forces had moulded us both, thoughts of his childhood led me always back into the labyrinth of my own. For him the lesson had been duty. What lesson did my father give to me, what guiding principle? *Put things out of their misery.* That look of alertness, a brightness on his face. My father was a watcher. Not, I think now, I permit myself to think now, a very kind one. Selective, highly so. Unobservant of many things, unseeing, locked in some cold trance of self-absorption, nevertheless he watched our faces. My mother would hesitate in replying to him, beginning in one way and changing to another, and he would watch her with that same expression, a sort of expectancy, a hope of entertainment, in which there was also, when I think of it now, the ironic certainty of disappointment. Afterwards, long after she had gone, it came to me that she must have been afraid of him, as Monty and I were, though I cannot remember him ever raising his voice.

I looked at my watch: ten minutes past four on the morning after the great victory of Cape St Vincent. Did Horatio manage to get some sleep in these morning hours? So much can never be known to us, whether he woke or slept, what he thought of in this aftermath of his triumph. The night before the battle he had not slept at all, and in the action itself he was wounded by a shell-splinter which, though he described it as of no consequence, gave him acute pain for some days afterwards and must have made sleep difficult. He was still awake at 2 a.m. to receive the note of casualties aboard his ship – sixty dead and wounded. We know that he wrote to his friend Collingwood later that same morning to thank him for his support in the engagement. Perhaps in the space between he was able to snatch some hours of sleep.

The old man was in modest lodgings in Bath when the news came. He and Fanny were spending the winter there, the Norfolk parsonage too miserably uncomfortable now in cold weather for his age and frailty. In February, Horatio's promotion to Rear-Admiral was posted up, and his father, in the innocence of joy, posted an immediate letter to him – *My dear Rear-Admiral.* Then, less than two weeks later, came the news of Cape St Vincent. The rector was in the street when he heard it, heard of his son's part in it. He was obliged to return in haste to his lodgings so as to hide his tears. *The height of glory to which your professional judgement, united with a proper sense of bravery, guarded by Providence, few sons, dear child, attain to, and fewer fathers live to see . . .*

I know these words of his by heart. They sounded in my mind as I stood there. Orotund in phrasing, but no mistaking the pride. My father had no pride in me, or at least he never showed any. I suppose I never gave him cause, I was not good at the right things. I was good with my hands, even when quite small, good at making things. For a brief season I shone at chess. Then at fifteen a certain sort of order came into my mind, things began clicking into place, I started to do well at school. But these were not the right things. I think now that for my father there were no right things, but as a child I tried to find out what they were. I suffered when I failed and must have shown it. Better not to show, better to conceal, much better – perhaps that was the lesson, the guiding principle my father gave me.

All the same, it was showing that brought me to Horatio: that and my father's need, I suppose it was a need, to chasten and subdue. I remembered it again as I stood before this meek-faced father, remembered the forced jocularity of that Treasury colleague defeated at chess by a child, remembered the strangeness of my father's displeasure and his words. *Look at these people here, they had some reason to be pleased with themselves.* And the two portraits side by side, the ravaged, dark-suited statesman and the dashing captain in the splendour of full-dress uniform. No comparison, then or now. But there was a shadow on the splendour now, one that I could not dispel, and it came to me in the words of Cardinal Ruffo's secretary Sacchinelli, who wrote a biography of his employer after the latter's death. *The violation was at sea.* He was talking about the violation of the treaty with the Neapolitan republicans.

How could anything Horatio did at sea be wrong? Written years after the events, of course, and partial to Ruffo; but in the silence of that early morning the words were loud in my mind, seeming to defy argument, like a warning bell in a threatened town. No, not at sea. It was in the city that the plan was made and the harm done. Naples seemed to me more than anything else like a carnivorous plant that I had seen years before on a television wildlife programme, in the days when I still watched television, a wide-mouthed, pinkish flower, like a frilly trumpet, with a pool of some sweet substance in the depths of it, into which unwary flies went slithering down to be dissolved and devoured. Quite unexpectedly, as it seemed from one day to the next, I had lost the bright track of Horatio's life, slithered down into this scented, tainted well of Naples. I felt in danger of dissolving there, ending up as a mere particle of nutriment for this monstrous host of a city, so flaunting and gross and beautiful, which so much changed Horatio's life.

I should have left the basement then, before Sacchinelli's words could work their poison; but I waited long enough to feel the return of nausea, the sense of being caught in the sticky gum of a city I had never seen. Fear followed this close behind, fear of my need and my solitude, made sharper by the vastness and promise of the night outside, where some bird had started singing in the darkness, fear of the eyes and the face before me, from which I could not look away. They were mild no longer, they watched me, they were my father's eyes.

I was saved by a sudden thought of Miss Lily, whose eyes were calm and somehow dwelling on things but not watchful at all.

She had felt sorry for Fanny in that cold parsonage with no one to hold her in his arms. *Better to be warm in bed* . . . The matter-of-fact voice with its dying falls of Essex stayed in my mind as I left the basement, shuffled in my slippers back up the stairs to my room. Slight edge of protest in it, as if borders unquestioned by the decent were constantly being impinged upon, infringed. What borders? Once more in bed I tried for some time to determine this. There was a slide of light now, very faint, on the plaster mouldings on the wall above the window. With the approach of dawn the eccentric birds of England's Lane had stopped singing. I passed into sleep without being able to decide what it was that for Miss Lily made life fall short.

7

On the Wednesday of the week following, I went in the evening to the Nelson Club, as I do most weeks. Wednesday evenings are open evenings at the Club, there is usually someone giving a talk and members can invite guests or bring their wives – the membership is entirely male, to the best of my knowledge no woman has ever enrolled, though I have heard talk of an Emma Hamilton Club with premises in Battersea, which boasts a large female membership. There is no Fanny Nelson Club, of course. Who would want to identify with the wronged wife?

I had been a member of this club for eight years now. Making up my mind to join had involved me in much travail, three months of painful hesitation elapsed before I felt able to take the plunge. In fact, becoming a member of the Nelson Club and engaging Avon Secretarial Services were the two most decisive steps I had taken in years, perhaps since choosing to confide in Penhas.

I didn't go there for the company, far from it. I could well have done without that, but I was always hoping to learn something more about him, the smallest fact can be illuminating when it is added to others. It could be anything. Generally, of course, I was disappointed. That evening a man called Robbins, a long-standing member of the Club, was due to give a talk on the system of signalling by means of coloured flags, devised by Admiral Sir Home Riggs Popham and introduced into the navy in 1803, not long before Trafalgar.

The premises are on the top floor of a tall, narrow-fronted house off Gray's Inn Road above an obscure publisher of devotional literature. There is no lift, the stairs are uncarpeted and the banisters have a rickety feel to them; but there is a small licensed bar, open on Wednesday and Saturday evenings, a reading-room where you can find the publications of the Navy Records Society and back copies of the *Nelson Despatch* and the *Trafalgar Chronicle*, and a lecture-room that can accommodate an audience of seventy or so – it is rare indeed to have that many.

They open the bar at half past six. It was about ten to seven when I arrived, and there was no one there but Hugo, the barman, and a morose, sleepy-looking man called Jimson, sitting on his own at the far end. I was feeling very much on edge, having struggled for hours that day and the one before to disentangle the events of June 1799 in Naples and establish a strict chronology, especially for the period spanning Horatio's arrival in the city on the afternoon of the 24th, the quitting of their forts by the rebels on the 26th and their arrest and imprisonment on the 28th. It all lay here, in these few fateful days. If I could only get the times right, fix the moments at which things had been said and done, surely I could clear him of blame. How wonderful to be the one to free him from the shadow that has been hanging over him so long. Nearly two hundred years, ever since Robert Southey's scathing verdict of 1812. Those terrible words of his came frequently to my mind these days: . . . *no alternative but to record the disgraceful story with sorrow and with shame* . . .

I asked for a glass of red wine, with the vague idea of fortifying myself, restoring the corpuscles. It came from a Spanish bottle and was roughish but not unpleasant. While I was paying for it, a couple called Barber came in and stood beside me at the bar.

'Here we are again,' Barber said. 'Half of the draught lager for me, please, Hugo, and a Bloody Mary for Barbara. You ready for Popham's flags?'

This question was put to Jimson, who, however, did not reply. Barber smiled at me and shook his head. He is a shortish, balding chirpy man with a beakish nose and a thin mouth and a habit of tapping his feet. Upon meeting his eyes and his smile, I at once looked away. For years now I have not been able to sustain eye-contact for more than a few seconds and I found the close proximity of the Barbers distinctly oppressive, especially in a place so nearly empty – I can endure much better the closeness of people in a crowd. I was looking straight before me when he spoke again.

'Your turn coming up soon, old boy, isn't it?'

'Not for some weeks yet,' I said. I was sure he already knew the exact date of my talk, which was Wednesday, the 9th of April. They had asked me to do it on the 2nd, but that is the date of the Battle of Copenhagen, last of his great victories before Trafalgar, and I wanted to be at home for it, at my table, with nothing to distract me. 'It is up on the notice board,' I said. Thinking about it made me nervous – it was my first talk in eight years of membership.

'What is it about again?' Mrs Barber asked, and tilted her head a little, like a thrush on a lawn – she is bird-like too, they are both bird-like people. The question irritated me, though of course I showed no sign. There was no interest in it, only a sort of social reflex, she was keeping the conversation going.

' "Two Episodes in the Making of a Hero",' I said.

'Ooh!' Mrs Barber straightened her head from its tilt with an exaggerated suddenness, clearly derisive in intention. Why did she come to these meetings? I wondered – not for the first time. What possible interest could she have in Popham's system of naval signalling? Anyone might think she would be glad to see the back of Barber for a while. But no, she always came with him.

A short silence followed this exclamation of hers. To the oppression of their nearness was added that of their mockery. I have no friends in the Club. People are jealous of me, they envy my intimate knowledge of his life. I never boast of this, but there is nothing I can do about the aura it creates about me.

'Don't much care for the title,' Jimson said, speaking for the first time, as if emerging from some unhappy sleep. 'Heroes are born, not made.'

'Quite right, good point,' Barber said, eager to ally himself against me.

'Well, that is true of idiots,' I said.

'I beg your pardon?' Jimson's eyelids fluttered, he was rising to an unprecedented state of wakefulness. It came to me that he had misunderstood, he thought I was calling him an idiot. I felt an impulse to prolong this impression.

'What's the point you're seeking to make, old boy?' Barber said. 'We low-brows need things spelling out.'

What could they know about heroes? Jimson was interested in eighteenth-century naval dockyards; Barber dabbled in Horatio's life, as many do, but had no essential knowledge of him. I felt indifferent now to their hostility. 'Fools, cretins, morons, blockheads,' I said, and paused long enough for them to suspect that I might be ending here, with these terms of abuse. Then I went on: 'These are born, not made. You can't refine on stupidity, can you? But the true hero has to go through the fire, he has to be purified, he has to shed his dross.'

My own words moved me, they came close to my feelings about him, too close – I could feel my hands trembling slightly. I rested them on the bar, I don't think anybody noticed. I glanced towards his portrait on the wall behind Hugo, high above the glass shelves and the rows of bottles, one of the earliest of the many likenesses of him painted by Lemuel Abbot.

'What about humble heroes, then?' Hugo said from behind the bar. 'People you've never heard of that do something really brave.'

Hugo is somewhere round the thirty mark and has a narrow, long-nosed face, rather sensitive. He has a gold band passing through the pierced lobe of his left ear. He is not a member, at least he wasn't then, he just came to do the bar twice a week. What he did with the rest of his time I had no idea.

'Or what about the people that devote their lives to others?' he said now. 'You know, asking for nothing, spirit of service and all that.'

'Hear, hear, good point,' Barber said.

'I have nothing against them. They are not heroes, that's all. Humble hero is a contradiction in terms. Heroes are public figures, they represent the nation.'

Jimson was beginning to say something indignant about lowly privates who won the VC, he wanted to bring it all down to obscure people, but at this point I withdrew from the conversation, I turned away and rested my elbows on the bar and began to look more steadily at the portrait, which was deeply familiar, a rather good copy of the famous one commissioned by Horatio's friend William Locker, and painted during the autumn of 1797 while Horatio was convalescing at Greenwich after the amputation of his right arm above the elbow. The stump had not healed yet, he was still in much pain from it.

Sparse grey hair swept back, mouth resigned to the maiming, the right eye not much showing its damage, though virtually sightless by now, three years after the injury on Corsica. A face bleak with pain and the knowledge of glory. He would be scarred a year later by a wound on the forehead at the Battle of the Nile, but otherwise this face would not change in the eight years remaining to him. It would, however, change greatly in the versions of him made by Lemuel Abbot, who died insane in 1803. Abbot did at least forty subsequent portraits of Horatio, slowly slipping into idiocy as he did so. In fact, Horatio was his main source of income during this long decline. Versions were painted for Lady Nelson and Collingwood and many others. In these later Abbot portraits Horatio loses the severe and drawn expression of a man who has suffered much and made a conquest of suffering. His looks become gentler, better tempered, like a ruddy, benevolent farmer at first, then gradually plumper, softer, more vacuous. Like Abbot's brain, it occurred to me now. I have always been fascinated by parallel tracks and this was an almost perfect example. Forty likenesses over the years. Horatio's face softening back into infancy along with Abbot's brain.

Oppressed by this thought, which in some way seemed disloyal to him, I turned my eyes away from the portrait. The bar was more crowded now, though I had not been aware of people coming in. I expected to see Jimson and the Barbers, but there was no sign of them. Standing beside me now was Kismet Walters. My glass of wine was still half full. Through the open door I saw people passing down the passage towards the lecture-room, among them the President of the Club, a tall, slow-moving man named Pratt-Smithers. I had again the feeling that time had slipped away from me, I had somehow fallen behind.

'Heroism is a form of pure energy,' I said to Kismet Walters, and he instantly and fervently agreed, nodding his head so forcibly that his white hair – still thick though he is well into his sixties – flopped over his forehead. He is the only member of the Club who comes remotely near to sharing my feelings for Horatio, but he is a dangerous ally because his notions are very simple, some might say crude. His nickname, which no one ever uses in his hearing, comes from his lifelong denial that Horatio ever said 'Kiss me, Hardy' when he lay dying below decks at Trafalgar. Walters regards such a request as out of keeping with the heroic character, altogether too unmanly. According to Walters, what Horatio actually said was '*Kismet*, Hardy', this being the Arabic word for 'destiny'. Basing himself on this premise, he has spent twenty-five years accumulating evidence that Horatio was early attracted to the faith of Islam, was in fact a secret convert and made incognito trips to Cairo on three separate occasions for audiences with the Sharif. He is intending some day to publish the results of this research.

'Fuelled by faith,' he said now. 'A hero has to *believe*.' He reared his head back and fixed me with his small blue eyes. 'Valhalla,' he said.

'Right enough.' I finished my wine in one go. 'It's nearly half past,' I said. 'Shall we go in and hear what Robbins has to say?'

There were a respectable number of people in there, about thirty-five, I estimated – not too many empty seats. Robbins had fixed up a blackboard so that he could illustrate with coloured chalks the way the system worked, how the same coloured flags or pennants were used for the numbers 0 to 9 and for the letters of the alphabet 1 to 26, and how each ship had a code book in which common words or phrases were allotted numbers from 26 upwards. Where possible the ships used these standard forms; any other words had to be spelled out with a flag for each letter. The flags were hoisted to the upper yardarms or the mastheads, wherever they could be seen by the ships they were addressing.

Robbins had faults as a speaker, he was hesitant in delivery and tended to repeat himself; but the miraculous nature of this new form of communication came through all the same, to me at least. He quoted the young Henry Blackwood, commanding the leading frigate, *Euryalus*, in the build-up to Trafalgar, within four miles of the enemy and nearly sixty from Horatio's flagship, yet still, as he later wrote to his wife, 'talking to Lord Nelson by means of Popham's signals'. In that slow approach, as the British fleet closed in and the French under Villeneuve tried first to wriggle through the Straits of Gibraltar for the safety of Toulon, and then made a run for Cadiz, it was the frigates that kept Horatio informed – using Popham's system. And in that last, most famous message to the fleet, the word *expects* was substituted for *confides* because it was in the code book and the other wasn't, and could therefore be signalled with only one flag instead of eight.

It was after half past eight when the talk finished. I did not return to the bar or speak to anyone, I got my coat and went straight downstairs and out on to the street. It was a cold night, very clear. In spite of the streetlights the sky looked black and stars were visible in it. I went across Mecklenburgh Square with the intention of making my way to King's Cross and getting the Tube home. However, when I came out on to Gray's Inn Road, without pausing to think about it I turned south towards the river.

At the moment it seemed no more than an impulse, though of an unusual kind for me, perhaps no more than a desire to prolong the evening. But by the time I was crossing Holborn and starting down Chancery Lane, I knew exactly where I was going and why. For the first time, consciously and deliberately, I was following in his footsteps. Of course, it was wrong, it was the wrong time of the year. It should have been December. But I was troubled in spirit, there was this obstinate shadow over our relationship, I needed to do it then, I had to violate the calendar.

December 1800. Those closing weeks of the year saw the end of his marriage. The Naples days were over for Horatio, that strange interlude in the unreal city where his passion for Emma grew at a landsman's rhythm in gaudy nights and slow mornings, along with his allegiance to the implacable Queen Maria Carolina. Over for the Hamiltons too. Sir William was recalled to London and never returned. The three came home together in close amity, the husband, the lover and the mistress–wife, arriving at Yarmouth in early November and reaching London three days later. News of the scandalous liaison, conducted under the husband's roof with his apparent blessing, had preceded them.

It was in London that the historic meeting took place between Fanny and Emma, with Horatio introducing his mistress to his wife. Emma had been carrying his child for six months but her amplitude of form and the loose clothes she wore perhaps concealed this. Fanny, the soul of provincial gentility, angular, reticent and dutiful; Emma, flamboyant and insecure, her Lancashire accent still there after all the years in Naples. Two different sorts of women, divided by temperament and by the traditional roles forced upon them. Each saw in the other her fears and prejudices realized. Below the civilities of the occasion a palpable detestation that was never to waver. He must have seen it, the instant, inevitable dislike. What else could he have hoped for? Whatever dream of harmony he had, perhaps the hope that the amity of three could merge into one of four, must have gone for good that afternoon, as he watched them together, with the wind bellowing outside and the rain lashing the windows – it was a day of drenching storm with gales uprooting trees in Kensington

Gardens and St James's Park. The place of that meeting has long gone, vanished without trace, Nerot's Hotel on the south side of King Street, where the St James's Theatre later stood and office blocks now rear up their undistinguished façades.

According to James Harrison, one of his first biographers, late one night some three weeks after this bleak encounter, Horatio left the rented house in Dover Street where he was living with Fanny and walked for hours through the streets, quite alone. He went eastward along the Strand and Fleet Street as far as St Paul's, then down to Blackfriars Bridge, then back via the Embankment and Soho. Slightly built, maimed, wasted in looks, quite unrecognized. Miles of walking in the dead of night.

I came on to Fleet Street and turned eastward. Now I was on his actual route. The streets were quieter in the vicinity of the City. I had the feeling that I was stepping in time with him, my heavier footfalls and his lighter ones making a single rhythm. I knew with absolute certainty where he had lingered, where he had hurried. When I paused at the corner of Pilgrim Street I knew he had done exactly the same, that he had looked at these same gaunt, unlighted buildings against this same black sky. I knew what his thoughts had been that night – he had been possessed by the strange discrepancy between his private and his public life.

The most celebrated Englishman of his time, victor of Cape St Vincent and the Nile, scourge of the hated French, destroyer of Bonaparte's designs on Egypt and India. From the moment of his arrival in Yarmouth squads of cavalry escorted him throughout the county. In Ipswich the crowd took the horses from their traces and drew his carriage in triumph through the town. In London he was cheered wherever he went, admiring throngs followed his every step. If it was known that he intended to go to the theatre every seat in the house would be instantly sold, he would enter his box to the strains of 'See the Conquering Hero' from the theatre orchestra. By day there was business at the Admiralty and the Navy Office, the evenings were occupied with banquets, presentations, receptions in his honour. He had taken his seat in the House of Lords – he was a peer now, Baron Nelson of the Nile.

Such adulation has seldom befallen mortal man. But at home within the walls of number 17 Dover Street there was tension and distress. This same evening of our lonely walk, or so I believe, he had earlier insisted that the Hamiltons should be invited to dine. He could never accept defeat, it was not in his nature. Emma was advanced in pregnancy, a fact which may or may not have been known to Fanny. During the meal she felt ill and left the table. Rebuked by Horatio for neglecting their guest, Fanny went after her. There followed a painful parody of that mutual goodwill he must still have been hoping for: the dutiful wife held the basin while the pregnant mistress vomited into it.

Had he witnessed this scene before he set out? As I crossed Ludgate Circus I felt suddenly convinced that he had. Harrison does not give us the date but I believe it was on that same night, after the Hamiltons had returned home to Grosvenor Square, after Fanny had gone to bed. It was this grotesque episode that threw him into despair, set him walking the night streets. He expected the fear and antagonism of the women to melt in the warm breath of his enterprise, as the odds had melted at Cape St Vincent and would again at Trafalgar. Sure mark of the hero, this believing so completely in the transforming power of his desire.

It was well after ten now and Ludgate Hill was all but deserted. The banks and business houses were darkly cavernous within their Corinthian porticoes, waiting for the next day's tide. I felt footsore, I was not used to so much walking, but I was happy to be so close to him in understanding and sympathy. I stood looking up at the dome of St Paul's, followed the struggling white of pigeons caught up there in some remote alarm, fluttering in the milky shafts of the floodlights. I had the brief impression that they were trapped in the light itself, the rays were like bars.

In the crypt of this great church he lies entombed, this is where they brought him, after the Painted Hall at Greenwich where he lay in state, after the room in the Admiralty where he rested overnight before the funeral service. No one before him, in the whole history of England, ever had such a splendid funeral. Thinking of this, and of his nearness and farness, I felt the air around and above me thicken with mourning, that massed cry of lamentation I experienced in my dreams came raining down from the cathedral and the buildings all around – it came like gentle rain, not sound, enveloping, all-pervasive, like rain.

How long this grief endured I could not tell. It was broken by an unkempt man who appeared from some dark place beyond the churchyard and came up to me and asked me for money. He was old and smelled very bad and he did not look at me. I put a pound into his hand, taking care not to touch him.

I walked the whole way back with Horatio, all the way to Dover Street. I was afraid of the streets so late but I did it. I was tempted briefly to give it up when I reached Trafalgar Square, and take a taxi home. I was tired out and, as I say, afraid. Moreover, it seemed fitting to leave him there with his pigeons and lions, standing on his tremendous column at the farthest reach of the light, too high to be really seen from the common level, endlessly scanning the Thames, keeping his eye on Big Ben. But the parallels had to be kept up. I went on, I went all the way back with him.

8

Miss Lily's attitude towards me had changed significantly in the two weeks since our disagreement over Horatio's treatment of Fanny, as had mine towards her. She had survived something that night and it had brought her into a privileged zone. I could not think of her now merely as someone I was employing, not when I had looked with such passionate interest at the back of her skull. She registered the change, of course, though she could hardly have known the reason, and it made her bolder. She became somehow more personal, she felt free to interject, to express opinions. To the danger of her sleuthing was now added this irritant of her judgements. Then on Tuesday, the 11th of March, she came bearing a circular tin with a design in tartan around the top. Her manner seemed less positive than usual. 'These are for you,' she said.

The weather was still cold and Miss Lily presented her usual chilled appearance. It was an accident, the date, she didn't know or had forgotten that this was Horatio's wedding-day. Or so she was to maintain. I opened the tin and found to my astonishment that it was full of biscuits.

'Shortbread,' Miss Lily said. 'They're home-made.' She was looking at me in a way that seemed almost apprehensive. Miss Lily is not pretty but she has unusual eyes, a deep, soft brown and very steady, somehow undefended-looking, like a cow's – they seem to have no means of concealment or retreat. But they are not timid, far from it, they do not flinch away. Miss Lily notes things. This gaze of hers, helpless and perceptive at the same time, makes it difficult to know whether what you see there is a disturbance of her feelings or a reflected disturbance of your own.

'I put them in that tin,' she said. 'Just to have something to carry them in, nothing to do with Scotland.'

I was sure at this point that she had schemed to make an effect by timing this gift of biscuits to coincide with his wedding-day. I was on the point of handing back the tin, telling her I never ate biscuits, which was actually true since it never occurred to me to buy them. I almost began to say this, then held back at the last moment. The fact is that I hate people giving me things under any circumstances, it is demeaning, it subjects you. But to show this openly looks like weakness. Something of an impasse. So I held back, I said nothing, I just looked at her.

This I was able to do as she was for the moment distracted, she was burrowing in her capacious handbag for something, a hankie as it turned out, so I had a short period of grace in which to regard her undetected. Tonight she was wearing her hair loose and she had on a dark blue woollen jumper and a rather narrow-fitting grey skirt which came down to just above the knees. She usually wore loose, smocky sorts of things, but the jumper, without being very tight, showed Miss Lily's straight shoulders and the shape of her breasts. There was something I recognized as characteristic in her movements as she searched in the bag, a sort of total intensity of purpose, as if for these few moments nothing else existed in the world. She looked up and caught my eye on her. 'I made a good lot,' she said, 'and I thought, you know, why not take some round, he probably doesn't get home-made shortbread all that often.'

'Well, that is quite true, he doesn't,' I said. 'The right day for gifts, in any case, on the anniversary of his wedding-day.'

'I didn't know you had been married.'

'Two hundred and ten years ago today he married Frances Nisbet at Nevis in the West Indies.'

'Oh, you were talking about him.' A silence followed, during which Miss Lily seemed to be considering or absorbing something. Then she said, 'I didn't know.'

'The whole thing is in my book. You have typed it out at my

74

dictation and we have revised it at least once since then. Perhaps you knew subconsciously?'

Miss Lily had flushed, though this might have been owing to the warmth of the room. 'People use that word a lot, don't they?' she said. 'In my opinion, you either know something or you don't, and I didn't. I knew they were married on Nevis, but I'd forgotten the date.'

Of course if she truly hadn't known, it made the symbolism of the timing stronger. This gift to me, Horatio's sharer . . . 'Easy to forget dates,' I said. 'He met her first in the May of 1785 when he was commander of the 28-gun frigate *Boreas* and posted to the West Indies.'

She was some months his senior, widow of a surgeon, with a young son, Josiah. Slender and delicate, a daughter of colonial society, her father a senior judge on the island, her uncle president of the Council. A product of her time and class, parasol-wielding, tea-dispensing, intensely proper. Not original or forceful or very clever but loyal and devoted. The other woman, who was not proper at all, was waiting in the wings. She would wait without knowing for thirteen years to release the joys and torments lacking in his marriage and to share in his fame. Seven years younger than the victim-wife, outstandingly beautiful, the daughter of an illiterate blacksmith named Henry Lyon, London maidservant at the age of thirteen, then some years of modelling and occasional whoring. At sixteen she was the mistress of a wealthy young baronet who cast her out when she got pregnant. When Horatio met Fanny on the island of Nevis, Emma Hart, as she called herself then, was living in a house on the Edgware Road, installed there by Charles Greville, second son of the Earl of Warwick and the nephew of Sir William Hamilton, at that time British ambassador to Naples. Later, wanting to marry well and recoup his fortunes, Greville passed Emma on to this elderly uncle, who had seen her on a visit to London and been smitten.

The graphs of these lives are fascinating to me, the parallels, the convergencies and collisions. In the centre the glittering thread of Horatio's life, with these others running alongside, above and below, some lightly touching the thread, some giving it a twitch, some clinging. That May, when Horatio met his wife-to-be, Emma was sitting for portraits to Romney, who painted her in a bewildering variety of attitudes; Hardy, who was to give the dying Horatio his last kiss, was a sixteen-year-old midshipman in the Channel Fleet; Arthur Wellesley, later Duke of Wellington, had just been taken out of Eton on grounds of invincible stupidity; Napoleon Bonaparte was a sulky cadet at the Military School in Paris.

I did not speak to Miss Lily of these presences hovering over his wedding-day. In fact, we did not talk much more about Horatio's wedding. I mentioned – while still clutching the tartan tin – that his 'people', the crew of the *Boreas*, gave him a silver watch, which they had clubbed together to buy. 'A very handsome gift,' I said, 'they didn't have much money, you know. But then, he was always greatly loved.'

Miss Lily made no reply to this. She had never seemed much impressed by this quality of Horatio's, charisma we would call it today, the devotion he inspired in crew after crew, the way his men would follow him wherever he led and be ready to lay down their lives for him, this great gift – for we must call it that – which I so much admired and which so moved me, seemed to leave Miss Lily quite cold. Perhaps a question of gender. All the same, in some obscure way I was disappointed. I wanted her to see how wonderful Horatio was. She smiled now, but it was not a smile that occupied much of her face. 'Well,' she said, 'it's his wedding anniversary, not yours, you can't expect silver watches.'

I could have said much to that: nothing that ever happened to Horatio did not also happen to me. I had stood with him that Sunday morning in the great drawing-room of Montpelier House, the president's mansion, where they were married, I had stood beside Fanny, who wore a gown of Irish lace. She was given away by Prince William Henry, son of King George III, a personal friend. Toasts and speeches, to which we replied with grace and wit and a likeable sincerity. Arm in arm down the steps of polished teak, out into brilliant sunshine. Behind us the immaculate house with its white wood gables and verandas. Arm in arm on the flawless lawns, kept trim and vivid by generations of faithful blacks. We assemble in the shade of the great silk-cotton tree. Popping corks. We are surrounded by well-wishers, all dressed in light colours, the men in satin suits, the ladies in summer dresses, smiling in the tinted shade of parasols. Beyond the terraced gardens and the parkland, as far as the eye can see, the smooth green sweep of the sugar-cane fields . . .

'Nothing left of it now,' I said. 'Someone was talking about it at the Club.'

'Left of what?'

'The house they got married in, where Fanny lived with her uncle. Nothing left but a pair of stone gateposts. Thank you very much for the biscuits, I look forward to having them with my tea in the mornings.' I resolved as I spoke to find some way of reciprocating this gift and so cancelling it out, something on my part stronger, more lordly. For the moment, however, no ideas came to me.

I remember some degree of tension developing between us later on, during our session of work. I sensed that Miss Lily was dissatisfied, or disappointed rather, because I was proposing to bypass, for the time being, Horatio's sojourn in Naples and Palermo, the period between September 1798 and June 1800. I told her I was not ready to deal with it, there were so many revisions of one sort or another, I could not even dictate it, I would have to make a fair copy. The real reason was that I could not yet determine the part Horatio had played in the surrender of the Neapolitan republicans, could not yet find a path for him out of that marsh. I knew that Miss Lily, though it was not in her character to admit it, had been looking forward to dealing with this period of his life. She did not care so much about Horatio's triumphs at sea, to my mind the most essential part of him; but she took a close interest in his life on land. And of all Horatio's land experience, his stay in the Kingdom of the Two Sicilies was by far the most colourful and dramatic, comprising his hero's welcome in Naples, the love-affair with Emma blossoming in the hothouse of the Bourbon Court, the *ménage à trois* that resulted, the flight of the royal family as the French closed in, Horatio's dealings with the republican rebels and much else besides. And here was I, proposing to go round it and resume in the June of 1800, the date of Horatio's recall to England.

As I say, I could not tell her the true reason, could not explain how important it was for me to preserve his name and reputation, how the remotest suggestion of deceit on his part filled me with a sort of dread, as if it called my own existence into doubt, as if my being depended on his truth. However, we were able to go as far as the triumphant arrival, one of my favourite passages so far in the book. He anchored in the bay on the 22nd of September, just a week from his fortieth birthday, after a voyage of thirteen hundred miles from the mouth of the Nile. I had decided to include extracts from Horatio's letter of the 25th of September, written to Fanny, in which he describes his arrival and the meeting with the Hamiltons. My own comments were interspersed with these extracts, so the whole thing had to be dictated:

Alongside came my honoured friends: the scene was terribly affecting; up flew her ladyship, and exclaiming, 'Oh God, is it possible?' she fell into my arm more dead than —

'Did you say "arm"?' Miss Lily said. 'Oh, yes, I see, he only had one by this time, didn't he?' She giggled a bit. 'Sorry.'

I made no reply to this but observed a pause before continuing in order to mark my disapproval of the interruption. *I hope some day to have the pleasure of introducing you to Lady Hamilton, she is one of the very best women in this world. How few could have made the turn she has. She is an honour to her sex . . .*

I paused again here as I wished to insert some speculations which I had written the evening before about Fanny's reactions to these words. It was typical of Horatio's frank and enthusiastic nature that he should write in such terms to a wife so conventional, so far away and lonely, who must have known Emma's fame as a beauty, must have known too about her earlier career as mistress to the rich.

'One wonders,' I began, 'what Lady Nelson would privately have made of – '

But Miss Lily was not typing. She was sitting inactive at the keyboard. After a moment she turned to me with an expression of perplexity I knew at once to be false. She said, 'What does that mean, an honour to her sex?'

Now this was not, strictly speaking, a legitimate question for Miss Lily to ask, it did not arise from any difficulty in carrying out her task of typing. That she should ask it at all – and even more that I should attempt to answer it – was a mark of the changed relations between us and her talent for taking over the ground.

'He was paying her a compliment,' I said. 'He thought she did credit to her sex.'

'No, but what does it *mean*?' Her face wore the same expression as when she had talked about Scott of the Antarctic.

I tried again: 'He thought her a fine example of woman-hood.'

'Nelson was a fine example of manhood, I suppose.'

The grotesqueness of this understatement almost made me laugh aloud. 'Only the finest this nation has ever produced or ever will.'

'Could someone, writing about him, have said he was an honour to his sex?'

I thought for a moment, Miss Lily's eyes intently on me. 'Well, not in so many words . . .'

'It is words we are talking about, isn't it? Could it mean he was brave or had a good character or that there was something special about him like he was very strong or – ' Miss Lily's indignation wavered a bit. 'Something physical,' she said. 'Could it be that?'

79

'No, I don't think so.' I was growing weary of this conversation, for which, after all, I was paying at the rate of £15 an hour.

'It isn't what you would call logical, that's all I am saying,' Miss Lily said.

'It meant something to Horatio and that is the point at issue, in my opinion. You have to think historically.' But this was something, I had already discovered, that Miss Lily never did. She used the past tense, but she had no sense of the past at all. Everything and everybody lived in a perpetual present in her mind.

She looked at me now in silence for a moment or two, compressing her lips as if considering how to reply. The expression gave an unaccustomed severity to her face, slightly increasing the prominence of her cheek-bones, thinning out the rather full lower lip. 'Well,' she said, 'instead of talking about honour to her sex and so forth he should have had the sense to see that she was just making a big scene of it. How long had she known he was on the way, three or four weeks, wasn't it? She had plenty of time to get the act together.'

'Perhaps we could move on?' I said. I spoke rather coldly. It was true of course that Horatio was simple-hearted and devoid of guile, but I didn't like Miss Lily's tone, it reflected on his intelligence. She was not much taken with Emma, that was obvious — but I didn't want to lose more time discussing the matter, I was keen to make the two-year hop, to reach the haven of June 1800, the departure from Naples. All the same, we had not proceeded far when there was another interruption. I was dictating a passage very much altered and revised, describing the return to England of Horatio and the Hamiltons. A strange trio they must have seemed to those who met them at this time: the admiral so wizened, so decked with stars and medals, returning to popular applause and establishment disfavour; Sir William not far from his end, his face like parchment, his liver in ruins after thirty-six years at the Naples Court; Emma large and flaunting and noisy, heavier now but beautiful still, facing an uncertain future in England, on affectionate terms with both husband and lover, as were these with each other. *Tria juncta in uno*, they called themselves; three joined in one. The motto of the Order of the Bath, to which both men belonged. Emma's phrase, perhaps. Horatio could never have said it, he was joined with no one, ever, he was unique. He travelled with them, yes, so much is true. As a trio they did not make a good impression, at least not on their compatriots. I was obliged to admit this, though it pained me he could be so misjudged. It was not any fault of his. He was on land, he was in travesty. And he was envied. In my book I was intending to quote a passage from General Sir John Moore's diary as typical of this prejudice against him. In the summer of 1800, in Leghorn, Moore made a brief note: *Sir William and Lady Hamilton were there attending the Queen of Naples. Lord Nelson was there attending on Lady Hamilton. He is covered with stars, ribbons and medals, more like a Prince of the Opera than the Conqueror of the Nile. It is really melancholy to see a brave and good man, who has deserved well of his country, cutting so pitiful a figure.*

Moore did not remark on the strangest fact of all: Rear-Admiral Lord Nelson of the Nile and of Burnham Thorpe was returning home *overland*. It was a decision that had always perplexed me. An admiral recalled after famous victories, his flagship waiting in the bay . . . I was arriving at this point now, in my dictation:

'In Nelson's life, as in all lives, there were concurrent paths, lines running in parallel, each characterized by a cluster of attributes particular to itself, appearing simple in stated form but complex and subtle in suggestion. The obvious broad division in Nelson's case was between sea-life and land-life. At sea he was himself, he was performing the task for which he was gloriously fitted; on land he sometimes faltered, his faculties lost the concentration of genius they possessed at sea. Why then, in that June of 1800, did he choose to return home by land? Was it for the pregnant Emma's sake, because she was unwilling to face the long voyage?

Had Sir William some business to see to on the way? Or was it that Nelson himself was anxious to postpone – '

But Miss Lily had paused again. Without looking at me – she was regarding the screen of her computer – she said, 'I've a good idea why they went by land.'

I became aware of needing patience, a considerable store of it. 'Have you?'

'It was the obvious choice, really. I mean, they were a travelling show by this time, weren't they?'

'What on earth do you mean?'

'Everybody knew about them in advance, wherever they went. So the more places they went to the better, that's all I am saying. From the point of view of the spectacle, that is. It was like a tour. I mean, they took risks going by land, didn't they? Napoleon had just defeated the Austrians at the Battle of Marengo. He was invading Italy again. Their carriage passed within a mile of the French outposts. It would've been much safer by sea, but that way they wouldn't have been able to put on the show, would they? Trieste, across Slovenia, then through the Alps to Klagenfurt and Vienna, then Prague and Dresden, then all those little courts in Germany, all the way to Hamburg. Everywhere they went, fireworks, bands playing, spectators by the thousand. I mean, it's obvious, isn't it? It was a show, they were stars, that's all I'm saying.'

For some moments, hearing her say these things about Horatio, hearing her compare this greatest of men to a travelling player, I felt a mixture of fury and distress that I was afraid might have drained the blood from my face. I turned away from her in a pretence of looking at the shelves of books, as if in search of some reference. I could not read the titles, agitation blurred my sight. But I felt no urge to move round behind her, no impulse to renew that terrible scrutiny. All I wanted was to hide my feelings. She was immune and somehow she knew it. I cannot describe my sense of this more exactly. It was as if she had got inside my guard.

However, something else came now into mind, the disturbance in my feelings settled into a kind of curiosity. Still with my face turned away, I said, 'How is it that you know so much about the circumstances of the journey, the route they took and so forth? We haven't done this part before.'

'I got a book out of the library.'

At this I turned to face her. She was sitting quite composed, her hands resting quietly on either side of the keyboard. 'What book?' I asked her.

'It's about the three of them, Nelson and the Hamiltons. It's by a man called Russell.'

'I know the book. I've got it here.' I made a gesture towards the shelves. I was touched, deeply, inordinately, that Miss Lily had shown this interest, had taken the trouble to borrow this book from the library. My rage was forgotten. 'Quite good,' I said, 'a bit on the chatty side.'

'That's what I like about it.' She smiled suddenly, her first real smile of the whole evening. It occurred to me now that her sharpness of tone, her tendency to interrupt, those disrespectful remarks about Horatio, might simply have been due to wounded feelings, at my seeming to doubt her word in the matter of his wedding date. (I was wrong about this, as it turned out. She continued to argue and interrupt on a regular basis.)

I don't know how it happened, an accidental combination of circumstances, the smile, this moment of perception coming after my rage, a desire to trump the shortbread biscuits: before I knew it I was asking Miss Lily if she would like to come to Portsmouth one of these days to visit HMS *Victory*, Horatio's flagship, now permanently docked there.

'Well, that would be nice.' Miss Lily's eyes were bright and helplessly steady and somehow relentless. 'Get a bit of sea-air,' she said. 'It would have to be a Saturday.'

9

Almost as soon as Miss Lily had gone I fell prey to doubts about the wisdom of this Portsmouth offer. The typing sessions were one thing, they were limited in duration, specific in function, easily controllable – though Miss Lily was showing alarming signs now of breaking through the fences. The trip to Portsmouth was a very different matter, it involved a whole day, we would be thrown together, obliged to converse, to look at each other, in a train, in a café, without the protection of the desk, the book-shelves, my dictating voice. The prospect made me feel nervous.

On the other hand, there was a certain excitement in the idea and an element of self-congratulation – I had acted spontaneously, I had taken a leap. As I thought more about it, this aspect came uppermost. All in all, I decided, it had been a Nelsonian gesture, putting me albeit briefly on a plane with him. Of course, he was an angel, he was a creature of free, untrammelled action, in him impulse and decision were fused together, sheathed in the same fire. But for him too there were periods of monotony, of a constricting sameness; the weeks and months of blockading duties, the long pursuit of an elusive enemy over immensities of ocean.

And there were the periods on land, that time of travesty in Naples and Palermo, the long years of enforced inactivity on half-pay in Norfolk. I thought about these Norfolk years now as I sat on in my study, which was still somehow not quite empty of Miss Lily. How you must have hated it. Twenty-eight years old, just married, distinguished service in home waters, the West Indies, North America. Clear already that you were a commander of no ordinary gifts. Zealous, energetic, fearless in combat, a superb seaman. You had influential patrons – essential for any rapid advancement in the navy at that time. And yet you found yourself placed on half-pay and living with your wife in your father's parsonage in the village of Burnham Thorpe in Norfolk, where you were born, which you left at twelve to go to sea. And you remained there, beached up, for more than five years.

Who the ill-wishers were, the nature of the emnity – presumably it was among the Lords of the Admiralty – are questions difficult now to determine. In fact no one will ever answer them fully, though I had tried to address them in my book. Of course, it was a period of relative peace and low naval employment. The American war of independence was over, the French revolutionary war had not yet begun. A brief lull in the almost incessant fighting of the century. All the same, lesser men got ships. He himself never understood the matter. While stationed in the Leeward Islands he had made enemies, he had insisted on enforcing the Navigation Act, by the terms of which American ships could not trade in the British Colonies. He had ordered the seizure of ships attempting to break the embargo, and this had caused financial loss to a number of influential people and led to quarrels with the governor, Sir Thomas Shirley. Perhaps his friendship with Prince William did him harm, the Prince had enemies in high places and was not always on good terms with his father, George III. However this may be, when Horatio, that devoted servant of kings, applied for help to Lord Hood, whose patronage had been promised, he was told that no request could be made to the Admiralty on his behalf for a ship, *as the King was impressed with an unfavourable opinion of him.*

This was in 1790, halfway through your exile. It must have been a heavy blow, this royal disapproval. Worse was to befall you ten years later on your return to London after what Miss Lily so perversely referred to as the travelling show, when you were deep in disfavour. At a royal levee, King George snubbed you publicly, addressing a brief remark to you, then turning his back when you started to reply. On that occasion, ironically, you had arrived decked out with the gifts of kings, the gold medal for Cape St Vincent, the Star of the Bath, the Sicilian Order conferred by King Ferdinand and a resplendent aigrette, or plume of triumph, from the Grand Seignior of Turkey, which had thirteen strands of diamonds, one for each of the French warships taken or destroyed at the Nile, and in the middle a radiant star turning on its centre by means of concealed clockwork. This glittering plumage, with its spinning centre, you wore in your hat . . .

Unkindness from kings cut you deeply. You needed a higher power, divinely appointed, to seal and sanctify your courage and achievement, to bestow the decorations which you hung about your person, signs of favour, marks of status. Perhaps that is why you detested rebels and revolutionaries so much — they had violated the principle of authority and authentication which gave your whole existence its meaning. And I was with you there, as in all else, every inch of the way: without recognized authority there is no concept of the sacred, a Nelson cannot be born.

You hated the French even before they rose in revolt, even before they killed their king. You got that from your mother. Catherine Nelson talked fiercely against the French. For the whole of your infancy the two nations were locked in bitter combat from Quebec to Bengal. Was it this fierce mother that made you believe so in legality, in vested powers? I believe in these things too but my mother wasn't fierce, she admired Gandhi, she practised yoga, a word that disturbed my childhood with painful questions, not fearful, nothing about her inspired fear in me, she was always gentle, she touched things as if to avoid hurting them, even things that couldn't feel. But I could not discover what this yoga was and never saw her do it, the door was always locked. I knew the rug she used, she left it there on the floor, it was thin and made of cotton and had a twining pattern of dark pink and pale blue tendrils. When she left us she took it with her. Now I have a clearer mental picture of this rug than I have of her face. There were no photographs, they disappeared overnight, my father destroyed them all. I thought for years he had put them away somewhere, but when I went through his things after his death there were none to be found.

A total belief in constituted authority, that's how you made enemies. You were applying the law, you were doing your duty, how could you be at fault? I would have done the same, absolutely.

It was very quiet in my study as I sat there, thinking these thoughts, communing with him. In that short terrace where my house is, just off England's Lane, the sound of traffic is barely audible, more like a graining of the silence than a sound, something you easily get used to. I felt very close to him that night, I had the feeling of *confirmation*, like a current of power.

He was innocent and open-hearted. Miss Lily did not understand this when she criticized his letter. Only an innocent man could have written to an insecure wife in the terms he did, extolling the virtues and attractions of a famous beauty and former courtesan, who was there on the spot, swooning in his embrace. The swoon was real enough, I forgot to tell Miss Lily that, Emma was quite bruised by the fall.

No, you were innocently set on describing the nature of your triumph, of your glory . . . or didn't you care?

This thought, intensely disagreeable, swooped on me before I could block it. Of course he would have cared, that was not the point. But did he *see*? Enthusiasm, generosity of judgement, these are merely terms, they can mean more than one thing. Was it that Horatio didn't see other people as existing in a space separate from his own, that he couldn't admit into his mind the possibility of different minds? Not opinions, he was used to differing over the conduct of battles, but sensibilities, other ways of feeling things.

The silence in my room had lost its comfort, it had become stark, there was no refuge in it. So often lately, since my father's death, I had been undermined by unworthy thoughts of this kind; proof, not of any defect in Horatio, but of my own corrupted nature. It was a poison that spread, and the centre of the discharge was Naples. I was struggling against darkness now, this madness of judgement that opened the gulf between us, broke the current of power. I felt that constriction in my breathing and the throbbing somewhere behind the eyes that always accompany my agitation. Then the room was again bright and clear about me. I could feel the beat of my heart but my breathing came easier. I had realized my error. I had been upsetting myself over irrelevant issues. You had every virtue that could be reconciled with the mission and destiny of a hero. Probably too I had been unconsciously confusing your physically impaired sight with moral blindness, a great blunder – there was no doubt of course that your eyesight was deteriorating; even before the wound, while you were still 'on the beach' in Norfolk, from the inner corner of each eye a membranous substance was beginning to cover the ball. If you had lived to be old, you would have died blind.

Released from the nightmare of doubt, I turned my mind to the January of 1793, which was when the call came. This was one of my favourite episodes in his career, I used often to dwell on it. On the 26th the news comes from Paris: Louis XVI has gone to the block before a jubilant populace. Even as the royal head rolls into the basket, life changes for Horatio, his long exile is over, his days as petty squire draw to a close. It is the beginning of that twelve-year struggle with revolutionary France which was to bring him to the heights of achievement and renown. That same day there is a despatch from the Admiralty: he is appointed to command HMS *Agamemnon*, 64 guns. At the beginning of February, France declares war on Britain. Four days later Horatio leaves Burnham Thorpe for London, never to return.

What an amazing change of fortune. As yet no one knows his name. All his great battles are before him. He is thirty-four years old, emerging from obscurity with all his energy and ambition, still whole and unmutilated, at the height of his powers and in the prime of life. The ship they have given us is in the prime of life too – twelve years old. She is sheathed in copper to reduce the drag of accumulated weed and shellfish. Standard practice by then. But the *Agamemnon* is one of the first ships to have her plating secured by copper bolts instead of iron to avoid electrolysis. Technically her 64 guns are too few for a rating of ship-of-the-line, but her sailing qualities more than make up for this. That February, as he sets about commissioning her at Chatham, Horatio is taking possession of a warship that for her size is one of the fastest and strongest in the world.

Thinking of this, the power and promise of it, the mettle of the man and the ship, I felt again the prickle of tears, companion of my solitude. I was with him as he trod a quarter-deck for the first time in five years, amid the odours of river water and tar and raw hemp and wet planks, with him as he went down to his cabin, opened the new logbook with its binding of black leather, saw in its unmarked pages his days of opportunity ahead.

There is a lot to be done before we are ready for sailing, the hold has to be trimmed, a new foremast and bowsprit have to be fitted, stores to be loaded, working clothes and hammocks to be issued to the crew. By the middle of April she is ready. She waits in the Downs roadstead for a convoy she is to escort down-Channel to Portsmouth. I see her, swinging at her anchor, tugging at her cables – the ship as impatient to be gone as her captain. The ancestral foe across the water . . . It was the beginning of his true life, the phase of glory.

With this image, the slim figure pacing the deck, the scent of battle borne to his nostrils through the Channel mists, I took myself off to bed. A few pages of John Keegan's *Battle at Sea* and I was ready for sleep. I passed into first sleep easily enough in those months, but almost always woke in the early morning and then could not sleep again. Waking me this time was one of my sorrow dreams, as I was in the habit of calling them. The ground floor of an old house, ruinous and empty, with wooden floors that echoed to the steps. From somewhere above me a voice raised in lamentation, high-pitched, throat-formed sounds, over-whelmingly lonely and desolate, as if from some far edge of the world. As always, the sorrow seemed tangible, physical, like rain;

and the rain had a light of its own, whitish, slightly phosphores-
cent. It came down through the house, enveloping but not
touching me. The voice was known to me but I resisted the
knowledge. Then the divisions between the levels of the house
melted away and I saw in a sort of sliding diagonal vista the slope
of attic ceilings and a figure with its back to me, sitting on a bed.
High-collared coat, narrow shoulders, some suggestion of a wig.
Then I was in the same room, the figure had fallen silent, the
head was beginning to turn slowly towards me. I made a clattering
escape downwards and away, a sensation like running downhill
in a landslide, a debris of metal or wood moving under my feet.
I slid and scrambled down, away from the turning head, the
terrible prospect of meeting the eyes. This clattering descent
drowned other sounds. However, it was not the panic of being
pursued that I woke to but the anguish of that screaming grief
and the fear that lay below it, a fear that kept me lying rigidly
there, as if waiting for an assault in the dark – fear of grief itself,
fear of the loss foretold.

10

I slept again when the light came. But all next day and the one following I felt the shadow of that dream over me, a sense of foreboding and at the same time a sort of restlessness, a feeling of impending change. This mood was broken on the 13th of the month, when – as always – I celebrated the engagement known as Hotham's Action. March 1795, an important date, I had always considered it. Though hardly more than a skirmish compared to his great battles of later, it was the occasion when Horatio first showed signs of angelic promptings, his capacity for breaking free, breaking the line.

Two years and some weeks have passed since Horatio was treading the decks of his new ship at Chatham and just over eight months since the injury to his right eye at Calvi during the Corsican campaign. On this side, by now, he is virtually blind – he can distinguish light from darkness but not much more than that. Still in command of the *Agamemnon*, he is with the Mediterranean Fleet under Admiral William Hotham, engaged in the blockade of Toulon – there is a danger that the French may break out and attempt to retake Corsica.

Difficult to say precisely when a sea-battle begins. There is the vast arena, the seeking out, the sighting, the chase, the first shots. I date Hotham's Action from the 8th of March, a Sunday evening, six days before fighting was joined. Horatio is at anchor at Leghorn, writing home to Fanny. He is interrupted, there is no time for more than a hasty close. *I have only to pray God to bless you.*

This interruption can only have been the order to put out to sea. Hotham had received intelligence that the French under

Rear-Admiral Pierre Martin had left Toulon with 15 sail-of-the-line. Their intention: to cover a troop convoy bound for the invasion of Corsica. Two days later, on the morning of the 10th, the French ships are sighted. Hotham, with 14 British warships and one Neapolitan, gives the signal for a general chase. It is the first fleet engagement of Horatio's career, but he has to wait for the action he craves; the enemy is elusive and the weather fickle.

Impossible here, of course in this unvarying light, on this glinting sea of my table, to reproduce that uncanny weather, mists that lifted and fell, dwindling breezes, shifting hazes on a horizon of phantom clouds and phantom sails. It is during this time that the ardent Horatio, on fire to get to grips with the foe, adds a postscript to his letter: *My character and good name are in my own keeping . . . Life with disgrace is dreadful. A glorious death is to be envied.*

I quoted those words to Miss Lily one evening – I think it was after this. They had always been important words for me. I first heard them from my history teacher when I was fourteen. 'Not very reassuring for Fanny,' she said. That was her only response. A perfect statement of the heroic creed, and that was all she could find to say. *Not very reassuring for Fanny.* She reduced the whole thing to the reactions of a limited person like Fanny Nelson. I tried to point this out to her at the time, how absurd it was, but she wouldn't see it. Not couldn't, wouldn't. 'Well, he was writing to her, wasn't he?' she said. 'I mean, he was writing to *her,* not one of his mates. She would've been worried enough already. Did he have to talk about dying?'

I felt a sort of pity for Miss Lily as I was setting out the ships, because in uttering these words she had shown herself to be just as limited as Fanny. But I soon forgot this as I began to concentrate on the action. It was a brush rather than a full-scale engagement, though the French losses were high, at least eight hundred dead. I did not set out the whole line, only the ships immediately concerned: on the French side, the *Ça Ira,* the *Censeur, Sans*

Culotte and *Jean Bart*; on the English side, the frigate *Inconstant*, Horatio in the *Agamemnon* and Hotham's flagship, the *Britannia*.

7.45 by my watch. In anxiety not to fail with the timing, I had set the alarm for seven that morning, but I had not needed it, I had been awake since four. It was 8 a.m. when Horatio saw his chance and that is for me the beginning of the action. At daybreak the enemy have been sighted, three or four leagues to the south-west, approximately a yard on my table here. The French are refusing battle, they are running southward with the wind, pursued by the English fleet on a parallel line. Hotham, in the *Britannia*, breaks the red flag for action stations. The sound of drumming is heard on all the English ships, bulkheads and screens and movable furniture are stowed away, the galley fires doused, the gun-decks watered and sanded. The ships' companies bind their heads, cast off their shoes, strip to the waist – cooler working at the guns and easier for the surgeons to operate on wounds not infected by dirty cloth. The surgeons themselves wait with their knives and saws and swabs down in the orlop, below the waterline. Sleeves rolled up well above the elbows . . .

Six minutes from the first drum-beat to readiness for battle. Now, exactly now, 8 a.m. on this morning of the 13th, Horatio, well ahead in the speedy *Agamemnon*, sees a French 80-gun ship, afterwards identified as the *Ça Ira*, fall foul of another, sees them collide, draw apart again, sees that the *Ça Ira* has had her fore and main topsails carried away – they lie trailing over her starboard side. At once she begins to lose way, she is detached from the main body. Here she is, here I place her, lying astern of the French line.

For all their stateliness and the beauty of their sail, these fleets were like fierce hunting packs, constantly famished. To fall out, to be isolated, to be sick or disabled, meant mortal danger. First to go for her is the leading frigate, the *Inconstant*, at the head of the English line. But the *Ça Ira* is a heavily armoured ship, she can't run but she can still bite. The frigate is savaged, she reels away. Now comes Horatio's moment. He swings out of the line and

93

stands towards the disabled ship. She has now been taken in tow by a frigate, which is attempting to draw her away westward. The *Sans Culotte* and the *Jean Bart* have come in to protect her. I place them here, on her weather bow, at gunshot distance.

Horatio bears down on her. Still in tow, she gives him a raking fire as he approaches. He is intending to wait till the ships touch before ordering the broadside, but this fire from her stern is so accurate and damaging that he cannot wait so long. At a distance of a hundred yards, less than an inch on my table, he gives the order: the helm of the *Agamemnon* is put a-starboard and as she falls off he gives the *Ça Ira* a full broadside, raking her from stern to stem, each gun double-shotted. Almost every shot goes home. Immediately the broadside is discharged he puts the helm a-port and stands after her again. For the best part of two hours this manoeuvre is repeated. He stands after her, falls away to starboard, pounds her with a broadside, stands after her again. The Frenchman, big enough to put the *Agamemnon* in her hold, is still under tow, she cannot get round to return the broadsides. The carnage among her crew is terrible, her masts and rigging are in ruins, but most of her guns are still serviceable.

Now the towing frigate succeeds in getting her round, at last she can bring her broadside to bear, use her heavier guns to pulverize her tormentor. But their setting is misjudged, they are too much elevated. Horatio runs on boldly, the enemy shots fly over him. He is ready to fight the Frenchman broadside to broadside. And it is now, at this crucial stage, that the cautious Hotham hoists the signal of recall.

Nothing could better illustrate the difference in temper between these two commanders: the angelic extremist and the prudent half-measures man. Believe me, I know what you must have felt that day, I understand your frustration.

Next day, the 14th of March, after a brief but violent action, the wrecked *Ça Ira* and the 74-gun ship that was now attempting to tow her to safety, the *Censeur*, were both taken by the British. As soon as the French ships struck their colours, Horatio – always prompt to seize the occasion – went aboard the admiral's flagship to urge an immediate pursuit. They could leave their prizes under a guard of frigates, with bold action they could destroy the French fleet altogether . . .

I saw them in fancy that March morning, as I had seen them often before, in private colloquy together on the quarter-deck of the *Britannia*, the stolid Hotham, not much heat there despite the name, and the slight, eager Horatio with his strange dead eye – the pupil of the right eye was much enlarged now, diffused in shape and immovable, almost covering the blue of the iris. When another life is closely knit into the fabric of one's own, certain pictures are favoured by the frequency with which they occur to the mind, though this frequency seems arbitrary and is impossible to explain. From boyhood I have seen those two pacing together as the firing grows slacker and the French ships crowd all possible sail to westward, making for the shelter of Toulon. Hotham is looking straight before him, Horatio is gesturing, glancing from time to time at his commander's face. The cursed French, they could still be cut off, they are demoralized, what a victory it would be for the Crown. He is vehement, too much so probably, in view of the difference in rank. And the admiral's measured reply: 'We must be contented, we have done very well.'

This in its way was true. Corsica was temporarily saved, two French warships had been captured. But Horatio expressed his feelings privately in a letter home some two weeks later. If we had taken ten sail, he said, and allowed the eleventh to escape, I could never have called it well done. Here, in a nutshell, the whole thesis of my book, the ultimate statement of heroic ambition. Always reaching higher, seeking greater achievement, always wanting the odds to be greater. In that same letter words printed on my mind for many years now: *My disposition cannot bear tame and slow measures.* Neither can mine. In spite of all appearance to the contrary, in spite of my obscure life, I knew that he and I were at one, we were like diamond and carbon.

The moment is all, he knew that, none better. Circumstances

had favoured him in this brush with the French, giving him the opportunity to distinguish himself, to be the only commander to go singly into action, a thing very rare in fleet engagements. And he had a fast ship, he was well ahead in the line. But it was he, and he alone, who seized the moment, made it his own. Hotham's Action, they call it; but it will always ring with Horatio's name.

Again the words of the letter came back to me, first heard from the man who taught us history when I was in the fifth form, the man I had talked about in my sessions with Penhas. His name was Grigson. He was broad and short and he had wiry, reddish hair that would not lie back, it stood up straight from his forehead like bristles. He wore rimless glasses, behind which his eyes were a warm orangy colour, like marmalade. I remember him well. He was a Nelson lover too, the first I had ever met. Also, he was a brilliant teacher. Copper-nob, his nickname among us. He had a habit of rather tense-seeming gesture, quick cutting or chopping motions of the hands. He would sit before us and talk, not from behind the desk – he brought the chair and sat in front of us, almost among us. Grigson had no problems with discipline, he was strong-voiced and challenging in his gaze and there was a suggestion of contained violence about him, in those abrupt movements of his hands. No one dared to show a flicker of derision, even when he fell into the moralizing vein, which was fairly often – it was moralized history he gave us, a course of events determined by character, good or bad. If Napoleon had been a different kind of man, if he had been a true patriot as Horatio Nelson was, and not set on personal glory, he would have struck at England's heart in 1798, when the way was open, by landing an army in Ireland, which was in revolt and ready to welcome him with open arms, instead of sacrificing that same army to his grandiose dreams of Oriental conquest. Genius, perhaps. But what price genius in a mere adventurer? And he was Corsican into the bargain, which, Grigson implied, was in moral terms a grave disadvantage to start with. Nelson, in that situation, would have put King and Country first, he would have gone for the jugular.

I thought then that Grigson was right and I think so now. He had notes in a quarto-size red folder, which rested on his knees as he sat there. There was a gesture he made, both hands brought sharply down, a foot or so apart, in a sort of double chopping motion, to indicate the red file in his lap. *Here is your Grade A in O-level history.*

He kept the flame alive. I was already making my model ships by then, I started that at thirteen; and I kept a scrapbook in which I put anything to do with fighting ships before the age of steam. But Grigson gave my passion for Horatio an adult endorsement. In a certain way this was fortuitous, it depended on the power he was able to exert. Had it been possible to make fun of Grigson or disrupt his lessons or behave disrespectfully towards him, his view of Nelson and the importance of character would have gone up in smoke along with everything else about him. Inconceivable now of course, but then . . . In adolescence we are easily swayed. If Grigson had been a different kind of man, I might have lost Horatio. But he sat among us and controlled us and drove the message home. *This great Englishman, I use that word advisedly, boys, no admixture of the Celt there, generations of Norfolk yeomen, he was English to the core . . .*

And a mind knife-like in its penetration, a heart inspired by selfless devotion to duty, a spirit that knew no fear. The embodiment of the genius of his country. How I drank in those words. Grigson was the most stimulating and exciting teacher I ever had. He quoted from Horatio's letters and despatches and sometimes dictated short extracts for us to memorize and repro-duce in essays. *My character and good name are in my own keeping . . . Remember that, boys, always remember that.*

He was wonderful on the battles, he went through every phase on the blackboard. But there was nothing in all he said that could help me now in my quandary over Naples and the part Horatio played there. Grigson made no reference at all to this episode, nor to the involvement with Emma Hamilton, nor to the separation from Fanny, nor to anything to do with his domestic existence. Grigson was a devotee, for him Horatio was an ethereal being, all fire and air, no nether parts.

Quite suddenly, thinking of this, I was swept by despair at the protracted hold-up with my book and my problems with the business in Naples. Somewhere, I was convinced, there was the clinching piece of evidence that would set everything to rights. But supposing I could not find it? We would both be left floundering there, in that quagmire. *My disposition cannot bear tame and slow measures.* On an impulse, standing there in the quiet of my operations-room, with Hotham's Action over and only the dead to dispose of and the decks to swab clear of blood, I uttered these words of his aloud. My voice sounded hollow to me, quite unreal. How would he have pronounced them? I knew nothing of his voice, whether it was harsh or soft, high-pitched or deep. He would have kept the burr of rural Norfolk, people did not try to gentrify their accents in those days. East Anglian, then, but softer than the urban south-east, perhaps a bit slower. I tried the same sentence again. It sounded more like Essex than Norfolk. I needed more text, only by some more continuous reading could I get any closer.

I left the ships there on the table and went upstairs to my study. I took down J. K. Laughton's edition of the letters and despatches, opened it at random and began to read aloud.

As to myself, upon the general question, that if a man does not do his utmost in time of action, I think but one punishment ought to be inflicted. Not that I take a man's merit from his list of dead and wounded . . .

I was self-conscious at first, but I persisted. I wanted to find his voice. Then, as I settled into the reading, my intentions of mimicry were somehow cancelled out. The sounds I began to make were not a stranger's but they were not mine either. And they were not the accents of rural Norfolk. The voice that came was slightly metallic, with a slur on the dental consonants

98

caused by the tongue being held too close to the roof of the mouth.

It was not his voice, how could it be? It was not a friendly voice at all. It ended by frightening me.

I could not stay in the study after this. I thought of going back down to the basement and perhaps rearranging some of the cabinets, always a soothing occupation. But I suddenly felt enormously weary, so much so that I could hardly keep on my feet. I was averaging no more than four hours sleep at night during all that period. For some time now I had been sleeping at odd times of the day, a habit quite new to me.

I went along the passage to the living-room and sat in the big old armchair, the one I always used, dark green in colour and very capacious. I wrapped myself in the patchwork rug that my mother made, which I always kept over the back of the chair. I saw her making this rug. I suppose I was three years old or perhaps four. She had her own room where she did this kind of work and I was allowed in there. She used odds and ends of different coloured wool to make the squares, any colour at all, it didn't seem to matter. Use enough colours and they will not clash, she said. The table was heaped with bright remnants.

I found this rug some time after she was gone. It was in a spare bedroom, rolled in a cotton bag, in the big drawer at the bottom of the wardrobe. I think my father put it away there, or told the housekeeper to do so. There was a housekeeper then, a Mrs Bryce. I suppose I was eleven when I found it, one day during the summer holidays. In those August afternoons I would sometimes go to the bedroom, get out the rug and spread it on the bed. I would take off my clothes: shoes, jacket, trousers, shirt, underclothes – socks always last for some reason. It always had to be in the same order. When I was naked I would creep under the rug until it came over my head, but in such a way that I did not disturb the edges at the sides or foot. If I failed in this, I would have to spread the rug out and try again. I would lie there on my back, quite still, in the dimness under the rug. I would feel the warmth spread over me and with the warmth there seemed to come the scent of my mother. No one ever found out about this and after the beginning of the new term I never did it again. Now, when the rug was warm, I still sometimes imagined I could catch the scent of her in it.

I slept long, perhaps two hours. When I woke it was late afternoon, the light was already fading. I was not conscious of having dreamed, but I had woken with some vague feeling of horror, and as I sat there this became clearer and colder, and I knew it had concerned the *Ça Ira* and the terrible damage she had suffered, a disabled beast, cut off from the pack, wallowing there with her heavy cannon that she could not bring to bear, while Horatio savaged her hind-parts, rent her and bled her. Images of the slaughter on her decks came to me, the sounds of it, always the same sounds, crash of shot in the timbers, keening of shrapnel, the shrieks of the men on the raked decks, cheers from our English lads as they gave the crappos a good drubbing. Shrieks and cheers again mingling . . .

I sat there as the room grew darker around me, trying to break free from these thoughts. After all, war was war, it had been a triumph, Horatio had acted with great gallantry and panache. It was the next day that the *Ça Ira* was taken. She was too much hurt to repair her masts in the night and make good her escape. She waited there, bleeding into the sea. All through the night her surgeons worked in the after cockpit, sweating in the close heat, fighting to win the race against gangrene, sawing and slicing on the improvised operation-table in a stench of blood and sawdust and rum, with buckets for the amputated parts and a brazier to warm the blades, lessen the shock of the cold steel.

And then, with her masts gone and most of her guns out of action, at five minutes past ten next morning, she surrendered. Andrews, the name of the lieutenant that Horatio sent aboard her to take possession. He would have needed a strong stomach, walking about on those decks. Three hundred and fifty dead and wounded, getting on for half her total complement. And on the *Agamemnon*, in the whole engagement, thirteen men slightly wounded, no dead. We were right to hail it as a triumph, to thank the Almighty for his manifold favours, as we did that following Sunday, holding services on the decks of the ships. Horatio did his duty and came out with credit. *Thank God I have done my duty.* His last words . . .

Upon this thought, quite unbidden, there again came into my mind the verdict of the Poet Laureate of the day, Robert Southey, most famous of all his biographers, on the events in Naples in 1799 – the sticking point of my book. *A stain upon the memory of Nelson, and the honour of England.* I had always discounted this judgement. Southey was influenced by the views of Charles James Fox and the Whig politicians, he listened to the malicious innuendoes of republican sympathizers, he actually allowed himself to believe that Horatio had tricked the Neapolitan Jacobins into quitting their forts under promise of safe-conduct, only to have them arrested and handed over to the vengeance of Ferdinand and Maria Carolina.

Horatio could never have stooped to such a thing, his nature was too noble, he was the incarnation of the spirit of fair play, that profoundly British virtue, for which we are known far and wide. But the slanders had persisted, maintained an evil life on their own, in spite of his many champions. Buried somewhere in this great heap of argument, two centuries old by now, was the bright fragment that would clear his name. How glorious to be the one to find it, to see it glint like gold among the husks of old polemic. My name would be joined with his for as long as his deeds were remembered. Charles Cleasby, the vindicator of Horatio Nelson.

I got up to put on the standard lamp behind the chair. But Southey's unjust words remained in my mind, despite the light that came flooding. I decided to check the reference once again.

Pointless, I was completely familiar with the words, but there was a semblance of purpose in it and anything was better than sitting on there, a passive prey to his vilifiers. I was worried about returning to my study so soon because of that inimical voice. I entered the room somewhat apprehensively, but everything seemed quiet and accustomed in there. I found the passage almost at once: *To palliate it would be in vain; to justify it would be wicked: there is no alternative, for one who will not make himself a participator in guilt, but to record the disgraceful story with sorrow and with shame.*

Strong words indeed, and beautifully put, however misguided. The most robust response I had so far found was Laughton's in the preface to his selection of Horatio's letters and despatches, which came out in 1886: *Southey was wrong. There is another alternative. We neither palliate, nor justify, nor record; we deny. The story is a base and venomous falsehood.*

My heart warmed to this sturdy and patriotic rebuttal by the then Professor of Modern History at King's College, London. Historians were more personal and more passionate in those days. I was sure that Laughton was in the right of it but unfortunately he calls no witnesses, he refuses to admit any evidence outside of Horatio's own words, as contained in his letters and despatches. The reasoning is therefore circular. Of course it is right, in a way, that it should be circular. After all, Nelson is in a special category as our quintessential hero and quintessential national representative. We British do not extol cunning as a virtue, but courage and honour. Horatio is the soul of honour, he tells the truth under all circumstances, therefore his own reports of the business are to be believed without reservation, therefore Southey's verdict is false.

Certainly, Horatio's words are there and he never wavered in them. There is his letter to Alex Stephens written nearly four years later, in the February of 1803: *I very happily arrived at Naples, and prevented such an infamous transaction from taking place; therefore, when the Rebels surrendered, they came out of the Castles as they ought, without any honours of War, and trusting to the judgement of their Sovereign.*

This is clear enough but lacking in detail. The transaction he was referring to is the treaty with the rebels signed before his arrival. The crux of the thing is in the last few words. Did these people, when they came out of their forts, think that they were going to be shipped to France in accordance with the treaty, or did they think they were going to be handed over to their Sicilian Majesties? That is the argument, that is the form it has taken; but for me there was no argument at all: to believe that they didn't know what they were coming out to is to believe that Horatio was first a party to fraud and afterwards covered it up by lying. No one could believe that who knew him as I did. The difficulty did not lie in knowing what to believe but in finding the proof of his innocence.

He is not helped by those of his defenders who try to gloss over the business or even, in their generous sympathy, actually misrepresent the facts. Carola Oman is a case in point. A surprising thing, to my mind, that it should be a woman to write one of the best lives of Horatio this century. First published in 1947, containing much new material, it is a detailed and vivid picture of the man. Yet coming to his dealings in Naples on the morning of the 26th of June 1799 this is what she writes: *Sir William Hamilton sent the Cardinal a hasty assurance that Lord Nelson would do nothing, pending instructions from Palermo, to break the Armistice, a statement which Nelson . . . later confirmed in his own hand.*

This confirmation in Horatio's own hand I had not so far found, nor, as far as I knew, had anyone else. The ambassador's note, however, does exist: *Lord Nelson begs me to assure your Eminence that he is resolved to do nothing that can break the Armistice which your Eminence has accorded to the Castles of Naples.*

That is the whole text. Nothing about pending instructions, nothing about Palermo. Palermo, of course, was where the King and the Queen were, having fled to Sicily from the advancing French. What led Carola Oman, so generally scrupulous, to insert that phrase into her text as if it were an integral part of Hamilton's note? She would have had that note before her, as did I. It is hard not to conclude that she was taking for granted the very thing she should have been trying to prove, that these people knew when they came out of the forts that the fulfilling of the treaty depended on the endorsement of their offended sovereigns – an endorsement not yet received.

A being of such shining honesty as Horatio is not to be defended by sleight of hand. Nor is it to be done by glaring omission. In the most recent biography I had read, that of Christopher Hibbert, published in 1994, in a total of almost five hundred pages, only five lines are devoted to the 26th of June 1799, surely one of the most important days in Nelson's entire life. Hibbert refers to the rebel garrisons, emerging under the treaty, as refugees, which suggests that they were already outside of the forts before the intention was formed to arrest them, which completely begs the question of why they left the forts in the first place. As I sat there that March evening, as darkness settled over the stricken *Ça Ira*, I was swept – once again – by the ardent desire to clear him, free him for ever, from the bungling of his friends as well as from the malice of his foes. Everything lay there, in those few days of June. The clue was there if I could find it. I fell to pondering the sequence of events yet again.

Already, by the 25th, relations between Horatio and Cardinal Ruffo are breaking down. For hours the two of them argue, face to face in Horatio's cabin on the *Vanguard*, in the hot June weather, the cardinal speaking French, the admiral English, and the ambassador interpreting. Emma in the background, dressed in white, with a broad-brimmed hat. Perhaps she throws in the occasional few words in her mixture of Lancashire and Neapolitan. She peers through the bay window of the cabin to see if there is anyone she knows in the pleasure boats out in the bay.

The dispute continues. Horatio does not hate Italians in the way he hates the French, but he regards them as immoral and lacking in the military virtues. He distrusts Ruffo as a devious, and probably treacherous, cleric. To Ruffo he seems irascible, overbearing, ignorant of the real situation in Naples. Horatio refuses to accept the treaty that Ruffo, as commander of the royalist forces, has signed in King Ferdinand's name. The rebels are traitors, they must surrender unconditionally and be delivered to the justice of their sovereign. Ruffo insists that the treaty to which he has put his name should be honoured. The people in the forts are misguided patriots. The best way to heal the wounds of civil war is to be lenient with the vanquished.

This treaty, the heart of the dispute, has been signed not only by Ruffo but, in the name of George III, by Captain Foote, the senior British officer in Naples at the time, and by the representatives of the Russian and Turkish detachments, in other words by the whole allied command. By its terms the castles are to be handed over to the allied troops and the people composing the garrisons are to take their choice of being carried with their property under safe-conduct to Toulon, or of remaining unmolested in the city.

Neither will give way. Horatio works the stump of his arm, a habit of his when irritated or impatient, Ruffo displays an amazing virtuosity of gesture. Voices rise and tempers fray. Ruffo quits the ship in disgust. Horatio writes a 'Declaration' which is handed in to the forts at daybreak on the 26th: *Rear-Admiral Lord Nelson, KB, Commander of his Britannic Majesty's Fleet in the Bay of Naples, acquaints the Rebellious Subjects of His Sicilian Majesty . . . that he will not permit them to embark or quit those places. They must surrender themselves to His Majesty's Royal mercy.*

This they show no smallest sign of doing. Noteworthy, this use of the word *embark*. It seems here to mean depart, sail, leave for Toulon. Later it came to bear a more restricted meaning.

By now the situation is extremely dangerous. The English fleet is drawn up in line of battle in the bay, ready to bombard the forts. The guns of the French garrison in the Castle of St Elmo are ready to reply. The republican rebels in their forts lack cannon and shot, but they are desperate, and there is enough explosive in the magazines to blow themselves sky high and half the city with them. Ruffo has made it clear that if Horatio breaks the armistice he will give no assistance with either men or guns. Not only that: he will withdraw his forces from the positions they have occupied, leaving the English to conquer the enemy with their own forces.

In spite of all this Horatio sends in his 'Declaration'. Thereupon the cardinal, believing that the English are preparing an assault, sends in a note warning the garrisons that the allied troops will now retire to their original positions. This sudden withdrawal causes immediate consternation and terror in the city. People stream out of Naples in their thousands, fearing a general bombardment is about to begin. Rumours circulate that the besieged Jacobins have torn up the steps over the powder magazines so as to be able, in the last extremity, to throw in a match. This seems to suggest, if it is true, that they were not thinking of surrender, not yet at least.

Now, at this most critical of moments, there occurs that sudden change in Horatio's attitude, which no documents have yet been found to explain. By ten o'clock on the morning of the 26th, Ruffo had in his hands that hasty note of Sir William Hamilton's to which Carola Oman so misleadingly refers. It is brought by two of Horatio's captains, Troubridge and Ball. In the cardinal's presence these two either write or dictate a further declaration:

Captains Troubridge and Ball have authority on the part of Lord Nelson to declare to his Eminence that his Lordship will not oppose the embarkation of the rebels and of the people who compose the garrison of the Castles of Nuovo and dell'Ovo.

There it is again: *embarkation.* They were embarked, so much is certain. That same afternoon they came out of their forts, carrying with them the personal effects they were intending to take to France. But they did not sail. They waited there, in the harbour, under the eyes of the English ships, crowded together on the small transports, men, women and children – for many of the men had been joined by their families. Then, on the morning of the 28th, the expected letters were received from Palermo:

Horatio was officially authorized to act. The transports were brought under the English guns and the people aboard them made prisoners.

You detested the French, that much is beyond doubt. I remembered your solemn words of advice to a young midshipman: *You must hate a Frenchman as if he were the devil*. You also detested rebels and these were rebels doubly detestable, they had leagued themselves with the French. But you would never have allowed that to sway you from the path of honour. You, more than any other Englishman who ever lived, epitomize our great past, you are the standard-bearer to this more tarnished age, you gave your life, you cleared the seas of our enemies for a century to come. Was there a distinction in your mind between embarking and sailing? Could you have thought those people in the forts would come out only to be embarked and not to sail? That hasty note, it was written by Sir William Hamilton and sent by him to Ruffo. It was written in French, a language of which you were largely ignorant. Could this foxy diplomat have deliberately omitted something you intended him to include, something to make that crucial distinction clear? But if so, where was the proof? And how can one explain the subsequent declaration, made in your name by Captains Troubridge and Ball, in which you repeated the undertaking not to oppose the embarkation? Was it possible for Ruffo to take this document in any other sense than as an agreement on your part to allow the treaty to be put into effect?

I was now at the heart of the problem that had held up my book and exhausted my mind for more than two months by that time. And I was no nearer a solution that March evening than I had been at the outset. I was beginning to feel the usual nausea of defeat, that slackening and slipping away of the mind, that seemed like a foretaste of death. Always worse, compounded by all the previous failures . . . Quite suddenly I remembered Miss Lily's words: *It was a show, they were stars*. Ludicrously inappropriate to talk about Horatio in that way. But perhaps, in the absence of any other sort of evidence, some clue to the truth of those June days could be found in the personages involved, in the interplay of character. A cast of six: the two protagonists in conflict, Horatio and Ruffo; the diplomatic go-between, Hamilton; the confidante and messenger of the Queen, Emma; and their Sicilian Majesties, in whose name these actions were taken, Ferdinand IV and Maria Carolina. I could make a brief sketch of each in turn and see what light was cast, if any. Not a path of events, a maze of personality. There can be more than one way into a maze and which you have chosen doesn't matter once you are in it. I started with the diplomat.

Sir William Hamilton. Sixty-eight years old at this time, tall and lean, slightly stooped, either from scholarly activities or the many years of elaborate courtesies at the Neapolitan Court, a man of distinguished appearance, with an aquiline nose and an air of intelligence and refinement. Son of Lord Archibald Hamilton, grandson of the third Duke of Hamilton, he had served for some years as an officer in the Third Foot Guards and had been — very briefly — Member of Parliament for Midhurst. Younger son of a younger son, he had no money of his own, a state of things he remedied in 1758 by marrying an heiress, through whom he obtained an estate in Wales worth about £8,000 a year. In 1764 he joined the diplomatic service, a career for which by background and manners he was well fitted. The delicate state of his wife's health made Naples, with its sea-air and warm climate, a natural choice. The marriage, by all accounts, was happy. The first Lady Hamilton died in 1782, and in the following year, returning to England with her embalmed body for burial, he met the extremely beautiful young woman who was his nephew's mistress. She called herself Emma Hart at this time and was to become the second Lady Hamilton and Horatio's great love. (I had been fascinated to learn that he met her at the same hotel, Nerot's in St James's, where eighteen years later Fanny and Emma were to endure the mutual dislike of their first encounter.)

That September of 1798 when Horatio, the victor of the Nile, came sailing into the bay, Hamilton had been British Envoy Extraordinary and Minister Plenipotentiary to the Court of Naples for thirty-six years. A man of elegant manners, all were agreed. A keen sportsman, hunting companion of King Ferdinand – they slaughtered thousands of quail and woodcock together. A more than competent musician. He played the cello and kept his own band of musicians. He made experiments with electricity, kept a tame monkey and planted an English garden in the grounds of the royal palace at Caserta. William Beckford said of him: 'The first of connoisseurs – not only in the fine arts, but in the science of human felicity.' *The best dancer at the Neapolitan Court, it was said, though his dancing days were drawing to a close by then, must have been, he was feeling his age, his liver was in bad shape. Too many banquets. The wild and voluptuous Sicilian dance, the tarantella, which was all the rage, was probably beyond him. Emma, still only thirty-three, danced it wonderfully well . . . From February of the following year, the Year of the Jacobins, Horatio and Emma were sleeping together, as regularly as Horatio's duties would allow.*

I paused at this point to pace about the room for a while. No clue in the bare facts of anyone's life. A typical product of his time and class. He seems not to have believed in anything much. Prejudices and opinions, yes, but no very firm principles. He wanted to pass his days agreeably. And yet in one or two important ways he wasn't typical at all. What really distinguished him was his very refined taste. Connoisseur, collector of classical antiquities, expert vulcanologist . . . He had one of the best collections of antique vases in private hands. And he was tolerant to an extraordinary degree. Victorian biographers deny that he knew of the adultery, deny that there was any adultery. But all the evidence goes to show that there was and that he did. Not only knew, but fully accepted it, lived in the knowledge of it, unruffled and benign. All three lived under the same roof, they saw each other every day. Emma had been passed on to him, perhaps he was ready to pass her on in his turn, feeling himself too old, too tired? A woman, of whatever class, was always a commodity. And for a collector, of course, anything could be passed on, people as well as objects. Just a matter of rearrangement. I remembered reading somewhere that when he returned to London in 1800, his days of foreign service over for ever, the house he took in Piccadilly had garden statuary that outraged his taste. It gave him a headache just to look at it. He could not live in the house until he had got rid of it all and put there in its place an antique statue of the Nile.

Nowhere any evidence that this exquisite sensibility suffered through thirty-six years at the corrupt and devious Court of Naples. Presumably there was nothing in this to outrage him, moral outrage probably not much in his line. A collector acquires things, sets them out, finds the right arrangement. If it doesn't look good here, we shift it there. I had quoted in my book some lines from a letter of his that very well illustrated this readiness to shift things. Written to Sir John Acton, prime minister to the Bourbon Court, the Queen's adviser and former lover, perhaps the most powerful man in the kingdom: *However, after good reflection, Lord Nelson authorized me to write to his Eminence yesterday morning early to certify to him that he would do nothing to break the Armistice . . . That produced the best possible effect . . . If one can't do exactly what one wishes, one must act for the best; and that is what Lord Nelson has done; I hope therefore that the result will be approved by their Sicilian Majesties . . .*

That is a shifty letter. What does it mean? Acton would have known, presumably. This was the 27th of June, when the rebels had already been embarked. *If one can't do exactly what one wishes, one must act for the best.* In what way did you act for the best? What you wanted is clear enough: you wanted unconditional surrender. And all the rest of your life you maintained that that was what it had been. What can Hamilton be talking about? The assurance was given, Naples was restored to calm, the Jacobins came out and embarked on their transports. Two days later they were seized, the transports were converted into floating prisons.

Yes, there is no doubt that Hamilton was shifty. Highly diplomatic, to call it by a gentler name. He even, in a later despatch to Lord Grenville at the Foreign Office, says that the Jacobins were already on the transports on the 14th of June, already there before you arrived, and that there was an urgent need to arrest them because they were about to set sail! No question of subterfuge, no question of what the garrisons were led to believe. So he became the first in that long line of obfuscators that extends to the present day, those who have smirched you, who was all truth, by their lack of it. Grenville could not have believed it in any case. His view of Hamilton's conduct comes out clearly enough in his letter to the new ambassador in Palermo, asking him to explain to Sir William, *without reserve* the utter impossibility of his going back to Naples in any public situation. Though this, of course, may be due more to disapproval of an ambassador sharing his wife with an admiral at a foreign court.

In the stress of these thoughts I fell to pacing from bookshelf to wall. Approach the bookshelf, choose a book. This evening it was Harold Acton's *The Bourbons of Naples*. Choose a word in the title. You can choose any word but, once you have chosen, you must keep to it. I chose *Bourbons*. Forefinger of the right hand, touch the word, then straight across, six paces, touch the wall with both palms flat against it, thumbs horizontal but they mustn't touch. Then six paces back to the shelves, touch the word again. Very soothing. The only other thing about Hamilton that came to my mind that evening, as I went through my paces, was the fact that he had recently suffered a grievous loss. Earlier that year he had heard that the *Colossus*, bound for England with his entire collection of classical treasures aboard her, the cherished hoard of a long career, had been wrecked off the Scilly Isles. Nothing of the cargo was saved but the corpse of Admiral Lord Shouldham, preserved in spirits. The kind of thing to break the heart of an elderly aesthete; a dead admiral pointlessly saved, his precious collection lost in the depths. Did he somehow hold the Jacobins responsible? Habitual cynicism, embittered by such a loss, might have made him vindictive . . .

I went back to my desk, settled down to write again. Who next? Who but the detested adversary, the man behind the treaty?

Cardinal Fabrizio Ruffo. Fifty-five years old at the time of these events, active and vigorous. Member of an ancient, princely family, inheritor of vast feudal estates in his native Calabria. In his younger days a prominent member of Roman high society. (He was descended from the Roman family of Colonna on his mother's side.) For a while he was the lover of the Marchesa Girolama Lepri, notorious for her promiscuity. This was a profligate, licentious, profoundly corrupt society. By all accounts Ruffo was entirely at home in it. Horatio calls him a 'swelled-up priest', but he had never taken orders. His cardinal's hat had been bestowed on him when he retired from the post of treasurer-general to the Vatican – some say in order to get rid of him after a suspected misappropriation of funds. Slander probably, a man like that would not have lacked for enemies . . . Of all the nobles and Court hangers-on that fled with their Majesties to Palermo, he is the only one to show spirit. With the blessing of Ferdinand and Maria Carolina – though without their material assistance – he leaves Sicily on the 27th of January 1799, four days after the proclamation of the republic in Naples. His declared object: to promote and lead a counter-revolution, drive out the French, suppress the republican rebels, restore the Kingdom of Naples to Ferdinand.

At the beginning of February he lands in Calabria with only eight followers and proclaims a holy war to rid the kingdom of foreign atheists. Within a few weeks seventeen thousand fierce and undisciplined irregulars have flocked to his standard. This horde, the Christian Army of the Holy Faith, as Ruffo calls it, set off from Naples bearing the Sicilian Royal Standard and spreading terror as they advance. Their numbers are swelled by bands of brigands and by some thousands of convicts released from Sicilian jails.

Success is rapid. By the beginning of June the French have withdrawn, leaving only a garrison in the castle of Sant'Elmo. On the 14th Ruffo lets loose his Christian Army on Naples. No, that is to misrepresent him, he can no longer hold them back. The Jacobin rebel militia take refuge in their two forts of Nuovo and dell'Ovo. Ruffo's troops give themselves up to slaughter and pillage. They are joined by the street people of Naples, called the lazzaroni, a ragged army many thousand strong, fiercely loyal to the King. Anyone suspected of Jacobin sympathies – and it is enough to be respectably dressed – are hauled off to the main square and butchered on the spot.

I paused at this point to consider the situation now facing the victorious Ruffo. The city is in chaos. His troops openly defy his attempts to restrain them. A visiting German author, August von Kotzebue, describes the terror of those days in his *Travels through Italy*. One or two extracts were there in my book.

The lazzaroni roasted men in the streets and begged money of the passers-by to purchase bread to their roast meat. Many of them carried in their pockets fingers, ears, etc. which they had cut off; and if they met a person they looked upon as a patriot, they triumphantly exhibited their bloody spoils . . . All who wore cropped hair fell victim to the mob. False tails were procured but the people ran behind anyone that passed, pulling him by the tail, and if it came off, it was all over with the wearer . . .

Touch the word, six paces, palms against the cool wall. Naples given over to a festival of blood. People dragged out of their houses, on any pretext or none, men, women and children, and hacked to death on the streets. The slaughter went on through the night, lit by the flames from buildings set on fire by the looters or by incendiary bombs from the besieged republicans in their forts.

What was Ruffo to do? He was not burdened by principle, any more than Hamilton – in fact these two had a great deal in common. The aesthete and the pragmatist, both deep-dyed. Not much difference. The cardinal's main purpose in all this, from the very beginning, had been to secure Bourbon gratitude and the rewards he hoped would follow. He was cynical, opportunistic, completely egotistical. His whole career goes to show this. But above all he was very, very realistic and therefore entirely unheroic, light-years away from an angelic nature like Horatio's.

This was the main difference but there was another. I wanted to be fair to Ruffo, to try to see things as he would have seen them that afternoon as he sat arguing there and the rage mounted. Otherwise there was no point in assembling these people, there could be no exit from this maze of personality, I would just go walking round and round in it. Ruffo was a royalist because the power of the great families was guaranteed by the monarchy. But he had no devotion to the Bourbon cause or to any other. The thing that really marked him out was that he was an Italian, and Calabrese at that, Naples was his city. He cared what happened to her and to her people. A Spanish king, an Austrian queen, a prime minister half English and half French, a British ambassador . . . So he makes the treaty, knowing it will not be welcomed in Palermo, but believing himself to be authorized, as vicar-general and Ferdinand's accredited representative, to act on his own initiative. The objective is gained, he sees no point in further bloodshed. But the others do, they are intent on punishment, especially the fearful and vindictive Maria Carolina, from whom in one way or another they all take their tone. Yes, even you, Horatio.

Then, on that morning of the 26th, after all the quarrelling, there comes the volte-face. Ruffo finds in his hands, first Hamilton's hasty assurance, then the declaration delivered by the captains – which they refuse to sign. *His Lordship will not oppose the embarkation.*

And in fact you did not. Now comes the question: if on someone's part there was an intention to deceive, who in fact was deceived? Was it Ruffo? Domenico Sacchinelli, the cardinal's secretary, in his account of the events of that morning, says that his employer suspected something was wrong: *The Cardinal, although he suspected there might be here some treachery, not wishing to wrangle with those two captains, took no further measure beyond deputing the Minister Micheroux to accompany those two captains to the Castles to arrange with the republican commanders the execution of the articles agreed upon . . .*

Why should he suspect treachery? Not because the captains refused to sign, there was no reason for them to sign, they were the transmitters, not the authors. Surely then because of the equivocal tone. In that case, why didn't he demand further clarification? Why, above all, did he send to Micheroux, together with the ambiguous documents he had received, a letter in his own hand stating that Lord Nelson *had consented to carry out the capitulation*, a clear exaggeration of their import? Did he believe what he wrote or merely pretend to believe it? Perhaps he didn't suspect anything at all? Sacchinelli was writing many years later, working from notes and memories. He was on a pension from the Bourbon Court, he wanted to shift the blame to the English for the terrible things that happened afterwards.

In this business, wherever one pressed, a dark syrup of treachery came oozing round the edges. But whose? Whose was the mind, whose were the glances? The rebels came out to atrocious deaths. Was it Emma? The thought sent me back to my desk again. Difficult to write briefly about Emma; there was so much of her, and so much of it was folly. Her beauty, her vulgarity, her extraordinary spelling, her capacity to absorb and deal out flattery . . . However, there was no play without her, the attempt had to be made.

Emma, Lady Hamilton. Born in 1765 to a colliery blacksmith and his wife on the Wirral Peninsular in Cheshire. Baptized in the name of Emy Lyon. No birth certificate yet found. Father signed his marriage certificate with a cross. The hamlet where she was born one of the most wretched and squalid in the land, a collection of hovels lived in by the colliers who worked in the nearby pit. Difficult to imagine, even in those times, more miserably deprived beginnings to life.

Emma was spirited and notably beautiful and she got out. At twelve she was employed as an under-housemaid in the home of a Chester surgeon. A year or two later she found a place in London as a maidservant. At the age of sixteen she gave birth to an illegitimate child, having been abandoned in pregnancy by the young baronet who was keeping her. She subsequently fell into the hands of the Hon. Charles Greville, whose mistress she became. She loved and admired this cold-eyed young man, second son of the Earl of Warwick, and was deeply hurt when, wanting to marry money, he packed her off to Naples, into the hands of his uncle, Sir William.

She was stricken, yes – she had thought Greville returned her love. But she must have known already, must have known from her earliest years, that she was a commodity. And the move turned out lucky for her.

There wouldn't have been much for her in England, once her looks had gone. In Naples, beauty and spirit again combining, she first captivated the ageing ambassador, then became indispensable to him. In 1791 he made her his wife. So she got out twice – she was an escapee. (Her third great escape, drunk and destitute in Calais, ten years after Trafalgar, was out of this world altogether.)

When Horatio's sails appeared on the horizon that September day, he was nearly forty, she was thirty-three. For eight years she had been a celebrated figure at the Bourbon Court, intimate friend of the Queen, hostess to a wealthy and glamorous international society.

I paused on this. Thoughts of Emma excited me almost always. She was fond of dressing up, and in my imaginings she had worn many kinds of attire and often none at all. But I wanted that evening to control all stirring in the loins. I was intent, not on putting her beauties together in that synthesis of touch upon touch until only the last, the lightest touch is needed, a patient and precarious process that I knew well. No, I was set on analysis, I wanted to isolate some element in her that might help me to understand the part she had played in those June days.

She had become flaunting and splendid and in a way powerful, with many favours in her gift. But to have known want and degradation, to have known yourself for a commodity, these are things that can never be effaced. Kindness will seem like love; love will get confused with gratitude. I remembered an early letter of hers to her benefactor, Sir William, and I got up from my desk to find it.

My friend, my All, my Good, my kind Home in one, you are to me eating, drinking and cloathing, my comforter in distress. Then why shall I not love you?

It is all there. This was what lay behind her habit of flattery, both the practice and the appetite. The mutual assurance of being safe, being necessary, being admired. Like preening among birds that have come to a sheltered place in the course of some perilous migration. For full effect it had to be reciprocal . . .

Finger on the gilt letters. *Bourbons*. Six paces, palms against the wall, thumbs mustn't touch. Miss it once and you have to start all over again with a different book. Emma's love for Greville was not reciprocated, though she thought it was. Sir William was kinder but not much different in spirit. Besides, he was drying out. The Queen, she loved the Queen, they wrote to each other every day, even when they were both in Naples. Emma would write to Maria Carolina in moments of exaltation, with no intention of sending the words to her. It was a form of praying. Like the words she wrote on the envelope of one of the Queen's letters: *Yes, I will serve her with my heart and soul. My blood if necessary shall flow for her. Emma will prove to Maria Carolina that a humble-born Englishwoman can serve a Queen with zeal and true love, even at the risk of her life.*

There was no risk to Emma's life. She always saw herself as the heroine, Miss Lily had been right in that. But once again she believed that her love was reciprocated. She was surely mistaken in this. Maria Carolina was a member of the great Hapsburg dynasty, rulers of Austria-Hungary, allied by blood or marriage with practically all the crowned heads of Europe. She would have grown up in the art of self-preservation and the exercise of power. Monarchs rarely reciprocate devotion from commoners. They take it for their due and use it for their ends. Emma was the deputy and mouthpiece of this woman, who hated the French and all liberal sentiment, who feared the loss of her life and throne, who needed Horatio's total support in eliminating opposition in Naples, and who knew that Horatio was deeply in love with her devoted messenger.

She was there with them that day, in the cabin of the *Foudroyant*, while Horatio and the cardinal argued together, while the differences between them widened and the dislike grew. As I continued to pace back and forth, never faltering, never missing, soothed by the simple but exact repetition of gestures and steps, I could see them there, in their particular places.

Horatio walks up and down, working the stump of his arm. Such a poor remnant, it seems strange it could move at all. The cardinal sits at one end of the table, he is richly dressed and wears a black velvet skull-cap. He interrupts, he gestures. The treaty must be respected. Horatio raises his voice. He is being contradicted aboard his own ship, in his own cabin. He stops to slam his left hand down on the table. The treaty must be scrapped. Hamilton stands midway between them in close-fitting white trousers and a cutaway coat, peering down that high-bridged nose of his, softening the tones as he translates. Emma takes no direct part, but she is very much there, she is the Queen's special agent. She is constantly on the move – she could never keep still for long. She listens to everything. How she hates this wily priest who wants to offer terms to the vile republicans. She is in a dress of white muslin with a fringed sash. Her hat, broad-brimmed, trimmed with red ribbons and crowned with ostrich plumes, lies discarded on the table.

Through the great bay window of the cabin, stretching the whole width of the ship, they can see the lights of Naples and the flames and smoke of riot, they can hear the occasional crash of shots, perhaps the screams of raped or mutilated victims carry across the bay. Among the warships the bobbing lamps of dozens of small boats, offering to sell fish to the sailors. The barges of the nobility have seen a hasty change of flag since Horatio's arrival. The tricolour of the republic has been hauled down; they fly the white standard of the Bourbons now. From these barges, through the soft summer air, come the strains of 'Rule, Britannia' – the fiddlers have played it so often in these two days that they know it by heart.

Emma moves constantly against the lamplight in her fever of duty and importance. That perfect moulding of the brows and mouth. She passes from one side to the other, across the whole width of the window. Between the lamps of the cabin and the deepening indigo of night outside, her limbs glow through the thin stuff of the dress. With every movement, every slightest turn, the muslin touches and defines her – the beautiful shoulders, deep breasts, strong hips. The dress is high-waisted, in the fashion of the time, emphasizing the long thighs, the curve of the abdomen as it dips to the shadowed cleft below, the exquisite concavity in the small of the back, the swell of the buttocks. Back and forward, wall to wall she goes, she cannot keep still. She leans to look through the window, she waves, she has seen someone she knows on one of the gilded, high-prowed barges. Her dress at the front falls away from her body, only a little, enough to see the sway of her breasts, to know they are unconfined. She is wearing only the lightest of garments underneath. Stripped away, thrown aside easily.

We know, even in the rage that possesses us at the cardinal's obduracy, we know she is waiting. Back and forth, between the lamplight and the lights of the murderous city, waiting for us. She is entirely ours, entirely ready. When this discussion ends, as it will, in frustration and ill-temper, she will still be there for us, she will wash the cramp away in a gush of love. What greater pleasure than the sureness of love waiting? Across the window, from side to side, a promise in every movement . . . Later, when the yellow-looking Sir William has retired to his chamber, she will come to ours. She will still be in the same dress, she will kneel, she will lift it up over her head, she is wearing nothing under it. She kneels above us. She will take us in her hand, she will lower her warm mouth to us . . .

12

I wrote no more character sketches that evening; Emma's visit drained me. I slept better for it, however. Next day was a Friday, I spent most of it examining what information I had been able to collect as to Horatio's state of health during those Naples days. He had received a bad wound at Aboukir Bay, a piece of shrapnel had opened his forehead above the right eye, blinding him with blood, so that he thought at first the sudden darkness was a presage of death. This came after weeks of intense uncertainty and strain while he ranged the Mediterranean trying to find the pusillanimous French and bring them to battle. After the victory he suffered from headaches and nausea and had frequently the sensation of a metal belt being tightened across his chest, constricting his breathing. When he arrived at Naples he had been continuously at sea for six months.

Could a case be made out for temporary disturbance of personality, some medical condition that made him peculiarly vulnerable – to Naples, to Emma? A blow to the forehead, almost certainly concussive, might damage the frontal lobes of the brain, disturb the judgement, loosen inhibitions . . .

I grew absorbed in this and did not ask myself until much later in the day – halfway through the afternoon – what I was really engaged in, what I was trying to do. Immediately I did so I felt hot with shame. I had vowed to clear his name, not to seek excuses for him, not to explain everything away on spurious medical grounds.

I had forgotten about lunch and now began to feel hungry. There was not much to eat, however. I had by this time lost all system in my shopping. I could no longer be bothered to make lists. Sometimes there was too much and things went bad; some-times there was hardly anything. Bread and cheese was all there was that afternoon, and half a Mars bar. There was a cauliflower in the plastic box at the bottom of the fridge but it was half liquefied, I had to throw it away. The bread needed to be thawed out in the oven. In those days I used to buy sliced loaves, several at a time, and keep them in the freezer. The cheese tasted all right, perhaps slightly stale. In any case, by this time I was feeling depressed and not in a mood to register gastronomic subtleties. Afterwards I tried to sleep under my mother's rug but I was too tense. The same questions revolved in my mind, scraps of quotations asserted their terrible familiarity, the usual clusters of doubts and misgivings forming immediately round them, like scavenger fish converging on scraps of offal cast into the sea.

To make things worse I was beginning now to feel distinctly nervous about my forthcoming talk at the Nelson Club, due to be delivered on the evening of the 9th of April – the day, incidentally, on which Horatio, not yet eighteen, passed his examination for lieutenant and was appointed to HMS *Lowestoffe* for service in the West Indies. I wanted my talk to be a success, to have impact, to be something people remembered and talked about afterwards, an important contribution to the understanding of Horatio's life. I intended subsequently to submit it for publica-tion in *Mariner's World*.

At seven in the evening Miss Lily arrived, punctual to the minute, as always. She was carrying a large bunch of daffodils. In the rather dim light of my hall the trumpets of flower and the fleshy stems looked strange and savage.

'Dad put the bulbs in, years ago now,' she said, with that sort of slight irrelevance, or excess of information, which was somehow typical of her, as if she were disarming some protest in advance. 'We've a bit of a garden at the back, they keep coming through year after year. It doesn't matter what the weeds are like, they push up through, nothing stops them.'

She paused, looking at me solemnly over the nodding heads

of the flowers. Her mouth was different. Then I saw she was wearing lipstick, something I had not known her do before – I would have noticed it sooner, but for the flowers. 'Nothing is stronger than a daffodil,' she said. 'I think they'd find their way through concrete.'

'Your father is keen on gardening, then?' I was constrained to keep on with the conversation, not knowing how to greet these clamorous intruders, afraid of a pause in which I would have to make some response. A distant memory of some similar gift tugged at my mind, a memory of helplessness and dismay.

'Dad died eight years ago, that's what I am getting at. He died eight years ago and he put the bulbs in, I don't know, maybe nine or ten years before he died. That's seventeen years or so these daffs have been coming out, and they've spread, they're all over the place now. No, we live with my mum. Or she lives with us, rather – it's my house.'

I had noticed the 'we' and wondered, not for the first time, if Miss Lily shared her bed with someone. Was there someone who watched her move about, back and forth, with that absolute trust in her love? She wore no ring but that meant nothing. 'Well,' I said, 'it is really very kind of you.'

'I thought they might brighten the place up a bit. You know, now that the weather is better.' While I was still puzzling over this she said, 'I'll just go and get something to put them in.'

Barely pausing to deposit her computer, still in its case, against the wall, asking for no directions, she went rapidly down the passage and turned without hesitation into the kitchen, where to the best of my knowledge she had never set foot before. I was left standing there in the hall, in the narrow space between the door and the tall Oriental jar I used for my umbrella.

I felt I should join her in the kitchen but hesitated. It seemed a risky thing to me. Too intimate, searching together in that small space for something to put the flowers in. More to the point, I thought, to look for something to put Miss Lily in; it was she that needed containing, far more than the daffodils. I still could not quite believe she had gone marching in like that. There was, however, in spite of my incredulity, a strange feeling of peace at the idea of being in the kitchen with her. I remained where I was, not for long, perhaps a minute or two. The silence seemed intense. I was aware of the small complex of cracks in the wall above the door, like a delta, and the shiny black handle of my umbrella, leaning out of the jar. I began to make my way down the passage. Faint sounds of movement came from the kitchen. I made no sound at all as I approached, I was wearing slippers, but this was an accidental circumstance – I had no intention of creeping up on her. At the doorway I stopped short. Miss Lily had taken a kitchen chair and was standing on it with her back to me, reaching up into one of the overhead cupboards. She did not know I was there. Her black skirt ended some way above the knee and as she reached into the cupboard the hem rose an inch or two. I saw that her legs, though sturdy, were well shaped, even beautiful, full at the calf and narrow at the ankle; also that she had on black tights decorated with a sort of diamond pattern; also that she had no shoes on, she had slipped them off before climbing on to the chair, but for the thin integument of the tights she was barefoot.

I did not stay there longer than the time needed to register these impressions. I retreated to the sitting-room and waited there, near the open door, so I would know when she passed. She saw me as she came down the passage, stopped at the threshold for a moment, then came through. She had the flowers in a green glass vase with fluted edges, which I knew from my childhood days when my mother used to put flowers in it. It had not been used for a long time – I would not have remembered where it was.

'I had to stand on a chair,' Miss Lily said. She was smiling with pleasure as she bore the daffodils before her, holding the vase chest-high. She moved about the room with complete assurance, not as if it were strange to her at all. She set the vase down on a small round table in one corner. 'There,' she said. 'They look nice there, don't they?'

All this had taken up some time. 'They do, yes,' I said. 'Shall we go along to the study and sort of get started?' There might have been some edge to my voice, I don't know. I had felt a sudden impatience at this dalliance. Miss Lily looked at me more closely. 'You're very pale,' she said. 'You don't look well to me. You should try and get out more.'

'Get out more?' I said. 'I've been in Naples all day.'

She did not smile much at this. 'There's such a thing as too much studying,' she said as we made our way towards the study. She looked round at me and nodded seriously. 'A bit of fresh air and a good brisk walk never did anybody any harm.' She sounded as if she might at any moment thrust a cap on my head and wrap me in a scarf and send me out for a turn round the block. It was really too much. I am not a child, I felt like saying. Secretarial services are what I need. But of course that would have hurt her – I did not want to hurt Miss Lily.

And so, a good quarter of an hour late, we began the evening's work. As I have said, I was getting nervous about my talk. I had decided to set my book aside for the time being so as to prepare the talk well in advance. I hate being hurried, it always results in the neglect of something essential and it was a relief, in a way, to suspend work on the book, postpone the problems of Naples. I had already written a first draft in pencil and corrected this in black ink, my invariable procedure: pencil, correct in black, dictate, typescript, correct in red, dictate. Already, even at this early stage, my pages were a mass of alterations and insertions. I was eager to dictate it all to Miss Lily so that I could then start revising on the typescript. Type gives us a whole new experience of the text, refreshing the eye, stimulating the critical faculty. Those who don't first labour in longhand never get this boost.

I intended to base my talk upon two episodes in the early life of Horatio, absolutely crucial in my view to his development as a hero, as *the* English hero, *no slightest admixture of the Celt there, he came from generations of Norfolk yeomen.* These episodes took place in 1771 and 1775 respectively. The earlier one concerned the first days of his naval career, when he joined the *Raisonnable*, a 64-gun ship taken from the French twelve years before and captained now by his uncle, Sir Maurice Suckling. Wanting to render this episode as vividly as possible, I had decided to recast parts of it in the present tense. I began my dictation as soon as Miss Lily was ready:

'It is March 1771. His father, the Reverend Edmund, has accompanied him from Norfolk to London, to the inn from which the coaches leave for Chatham. There, in the yard of the inn, father and son say goodbye, with sage advice on one side and earnest promises on the other. Now the boy is quite alone. He is twelve years old, small for his age, delicate in appearance.

'The coach goes jolting along – it is a six-hour journey to Chatham, time enough to ponder the future. Perhaps he wonders if he has after all made a mistake. But to admit the possibility of mistake was not much in his nature, nor is it in the nature of heroes generally, they know they have been singled out, in the furnace of their destiny mistakes are either consumed away or transmuted to the intentions of providence.

'When he arrives at Chatham he asks people at the staging inn for directions, but no one has so much as heard of the ship. Carrying his baggage, he makes his way down cobbled streets to the docks . . .'

By a coincidence which to my mind far transcended chance, the *Victory* was also lying in the Medway at this time. In seeking his first ship Horatio passed close to his last, his death-ship, which had been commissioned in the year of his birth. I was tempted to include mention of this pattern of timings, in which I too, as his parallel-walker, was involved. But I decided against, it could not be done briefly, it would have disturbed the balance.

'Still lugging his valise, he asks passing sailors if they know where the *Raisonnable* lies. One of them points. The boy strains his eyes. Across the grey, wind-scourged water of the Medway he makes out the ship lying at her moorings. But now comes the real problem: how can he get to her? There are no boats. The ship is too far away for him to attract the attention of anyone on board. For a time that seems endless he waits there in the icy wind, completely helpless and forlorn.'

At this point, as I was dictating my text to Miss Lily, there came to me a sensation not altogether unfamiliar but more pronounced that evening than ever before: my voice, the quality and sound of it, had become more present to my mind than the words it was saying, the meaning it was seeking to convey. From being a strand of sound edged with silence it was filling the whole room, there were no borders to it, it was not my voice at all but someone else's, someone whose borders of silence lay elsewhere. I saw Miss Lily's hands pause, move away from the keys and come to rest at either side of the keyboard. I looked at her hands – this was an evening for noticing things about Miss Lily. Strong hands but not ill shaped. Like the rest of her. I came back to myself at the sight of them and in the momentary blankness of this return I felt a sudden rush of pity for Horatio and myself and all the lost children. But pity for him was wrong, I had never felt it before, he was not to be pitied. In that lonely moment, under that hostile sky, the steel of resolution had entered the child's heart. It was an essential moment in the heroic career. Miss Lily had not looked up. With a sense of having got away undetected, I resumed my dictating:

'Finally a passing officer takes pity on him and arranges for a boat to carry him across the river. For the first of many times he climbs aboard a warship. Step by step, as he climbs the companion-ladder, he is entering a new world. He is a child, it is natural that a sort of dread should descend on him, he does not know what will be required. However, the captain is his uncle after all. Uncle Maurice will guide and advise him.

'But Uncle Maurice is not on board; he is not expected for some days. No one has heard of the new midshipman, no one shows the slightest interest in him. He waits for someone to take notice of him, tell him where he should go, what he should do. Eventually he is told to carry his luggage down the two steep ladders that lead to the midshipmen's berth on the orlop deck. Here all seems chaos and confusion to him. It is dark down here, below the waterline, the beams are low and there is a smell of tar and damp rope. Someone shows him how to sling a hammock, how to stow away his things.

'For the rest of that day and all the next he walks the deck. The weather could hardly be worse – "fresh gales with squally weather and snow", according to the ship's log. No one pays any attention to him. He walks about on the tilting deck, he looks across the choppy waters towards where London lies and beyond that Norfolk.

'Then at last, to much ceremony of saluting and a great shrilling of bosuns' whistles, Captain Suckling comes on board. With his appearance everything changes, the ship takes on life and purpose. He summons his nephew aft to the great cabin. This is on the upper deck, where only the captain can have his quarters. The tallest man can walk upright here and it is flooded with light. The wide bow windows occupy the whole width of the ship, beautifully framed in scrolled wood, elegantly curving, giving broad views across the river. From the dark, cramped, malodorous place where he has been peering and creeping below, the boy mounts into space and light . . .'

I paused here, and Miss Lily paused with me, and for some while there was silence. I was not yet satisfied with this passage. I wanted to convey the contrast somehow more vividly – as vividly as it was present to my own mind. For in this contrast lay the whole meaning. The chintz and mahogany of that beautifully appointed cabin, furnished in masculine style but with great elegance, the great swathes of light, the order and the calm. The strangely different uncle, metamorphosed from the country squire the boy knew, resplendent in his blue, gold-trimmed uniform. Uncle Maurice was transfigured, he was a god, he had come aboard and breathed life, he lived up here in the pure ether. As the diminutive Horatio listened to his uncle explaining the workings of the ship, he understood the meaning of power and godhead. It was the first lesson of his naval career and one he never forgot.

I was about to resume when Miss Lily spoke, breaking the silence. 'That was really interesting, if you don't mind me saying so. I could just see that poor lonely boy, walking about in the chilly wind, not having the least notion what to do with himself. My brother used to live near Gravesend, it can get bitter down there, I hope he had a good coat on.'

Her imagination, as usual, had been stirred by the drama of weather. But had she got the essential point, I wondered, the being summoned into light, that crucial early experience of the privilege that went with command? It irked me that she should seem so sorry for him – it reminded me of my own earlier moment of weakness.

'They took hardship better in those days,' I said. 'They were tougher, more enduring. They didn't expect to be cosseted as people do now. There was no Granny State to shelter them from the cradle to the grave.'

'Cradle to the grave? You been on the South Bank lately, round Waterloo Bridge? You won't see much of Granny there, unless it's her that gives them the cardboard boxes. Anyway, I wouldn't have liked it, I do know that.' She grimaced in saying this and wrinkled her nose, a sign of serious emphasis. I didn't know if she meant the period as a whole or just Horatio's experience. 'Why didn't he just go and find some corner where he could sit down?' she said, 'somewhere out of the wind?'

'He didn't want to appear idle. Character was character in those days.'

'I can't see the point of suffering for nothing. If he'd kept out of the wind I would have thought more of him. They cut pieces off him, didn't they?'

'Well, the surgeons had to take off his arm after the failure of the attack on Tenerife, and then there was the eye, but that – '

'I don't mean pieces of his body, I mean pieces of himself as a person.'

'I don't understand what you are getting at.'

'He was an orphan, wasn't he? His mother died when he was nine and he was only twelve when he went away to sea. After they parted that day in London his father never knew him again as a child, it was years before they met again, he was grown-up by then. You can't take a boy away from home and the world he has grown up in without him losing some bits of himself. I don't know whether you'd call it cutting pieces off or just sort of putting him in a narrow place where he couldn't grow.'

Miss Lily paused. I saw the rise and fall of her breathing. She was impassioned. 'He was hemmed in, that's all I'm saying,' she said.

Avon Secretarial Services, from Camden, were remarking on the narrowness of Horatio Nelson's life. It was so absurd that I could not feel angry. In fact I think I smiled. 'A narrow place, was it? Horatio served five months as a midshipman on the *Raisonnable*, then he sailed as captain's servant on a West Indiaman bound for the Caribbean archipelago. He went from Florida and Yucatán to Venezuela, then to the Bahamas and the Antilles Islands. He saw birds of paradise and coral snakes and armadillos. He saw forests of palm. When he returned, still only fourteen, he piloted a longboat on the Thames, transporting stores from the Pool to the Delta, learning to deal with cross-currents and shoals. In the following year he took part in an expedition to the Arctic, where he saw polar bears and fields of ice and the sun at midnight. Then he joined HMS *Seahorse* and went to the East Indies with her, from Bengal to Bushire. And he was still only sixteen. Would you really call that a hemmed-in life, Miss Lily?'

I had become excited in my turn, stirred as always by these gorgeous travels. 'If he was hemmed-in, what are we?'

'What was it you called me?' Miss Lily was smiling slightly but looked at the same time rather perplexed. I realized then that I had made a slip. 'I'm sorry,' I said, 'that's what I call you when I think about you, it just came out.'

'When you think about me?'

'You know, when you need to think about someone or something you generally give it a name. Might be Socrates or dialectical materialism or Manchester United. Your name in my mind was always Miss Lily.' As I was saying this I realized in a confused kind of way why I wanted her to see what a wonderful person Horatio was, how marvellous his life had been. He and I were so close, she could not admire Horatio without admiring me . . .

Miss Lily's expression changed, her smile faded. I had the impression that my confusion of feeling was reflected in her eyes, which continued to look steadily at me. Not experienced on her part, simply reflected. 'Well,' she said, 'I'm not going to call you Mr Charles.'

'Charles will do.'

My face felt hot. I could not remember when I had last invited anyone to call me by my first name. It was Miss Lily who brought things back to order. 'What he didn't have was a normal life, that's all I'm saying,' she said. 'By the way, I meant to ask you, what is a midshipman exactly?'

I was aware that this was a sort of diversion, but I was grateful for it. I explained that midshipmen were junior ratings, mainly intending to be officers, that they lived together in the cramped and crowded quarters of the orlop, that they were of all ages from children of ten or eleven to full-grown men, the raw material of the officer class.

Miss Lily listened carefully enough, but her comments, when they came, only served to prove how tenacious she was in argument. 'That's exactly what I was getting at,' she said. 'I didn't mean narrow in the physical sense. I meant emotional. He was narrowed down in his emotions. Stands to reason really, doesn't it? If you're pushed out too soon, certain kinds of feelings aren't much use to you any more, so they sort of get lost. Must have been the same with all those boys, those that went to be midshipmen, it just isn't normal.'

'That's how the navy got its officers, the ship was the school. That was the system and it worked – it gave us Camperdown and the Battle of the Saints and the Glorious First of June. Above all, it gave us Trafalgar, it gave us supremacy at sea into the twentieth century.'

'Be that as it may,' Miss Lily said. 'I can't help thinking it sort of blunted them. I'm glad my Bobby doesn't need to go through it.'

'Your Bobby?'

'That's my little boy. He's just twelve. The same age Nelson was when he went to sea.'

'I didn't know you had a child.'

Miss Lily glanced away as if momentarily distracted. 'It didn't come up before.'

I was quite staggered by this news, which was somehow completely unexpected. 'You must have been very young when you had him.'

'I brought him up myself,' she said, as if this fully solved the question of youth. 'Me and mum. His father pushed off at an early stage, which was just as well, in my opinion – and I even thought so at the time. I was wondering, Bobby is ever so interested in ships and battles. He's been doing a project on Nelson at school. When I told him, you know, that we're going to Portsmouth to see the *Victory*, I could tell he really wanted to go. He didn't say much but I could tell. It would be so good for him, to have a man to show him round . . .'

And so it was decided. Still in a state of mild shock at the news of Bobby's existence, I agreed on a date for the Portsmouth trip. We would go – the three of us – on the first Sunday after my talk.

13

During those years my Aprils always began with a battle, third in that great quartet of his victories I enacted on my table, the 2nd of April 1801, the Battle of Copenhagen, last of his triumphs before Trafalgar. He had been appointed second-in-command of the Channel Fleet at the beginning of the year with the rank of vice-admiral. Tempting to think there was some motive of humanity on the part of the Lords of the Admiralty in this appointment, which cut short the misery of his marital break-up, allowing him to escape – without seeming to be running away – from the public scandal of his affair with Emma and the cruel caricatures by now so frequently appearing in the London papers, where the trio were depicted together, Sir William the desiccated connoisseur, surveying the world through his lorgnette, Emma fat and billowing and given to dramatic Attitudes, Horatio grizzled and thin, with one eye and one arm missing. *Travelling players* . . . He was grotesque, Horatio was grotesque in that company. I accepted it, I had accepted it for years, it had never made any difference between us, I set it down to his angelic disorder on land. What else would an angel seem, out of his element, portrayed by mediocre men, but grotesque?

A great relief it must have been to escape from these devastating lampoons. But there was reason enough in the appointment, without looking for kindness in it. England by now was fighting for her life, for her very existence. With Napoleon's defeat of the Austrians at Marengo the anti-French alliance had collapsed, we stood quite alone, with a great fleet preparing against us in the Baltic ports and a new army of invasion gathering across the Channel. Not until 1941 was this country again to be in such danger.

Once more he comes to the rescue, so slight, so maimed, what an overwhelming debt he has laid on us! At the beginning of February he learns that he will be sailing for the Baltic in an operation designed to discourage the Scandinavian states from allying themselves with France and Russia and closing their ports to English shipping. These are not traditional enemies, but the crazed Tzar Paul, shortly to be assassinated, is besotted with Napoleon and has leagued Russia with him. And he, the scoundrelly Corsican, diabolical bogeyman to generations of our ancestors in infancy, has come to a logical conclusion – the cursed French, they are never short of logic. England rules the seas, yes, well then, we will make the seas useless to her, we will close the Baltic ports to her trade. Grain and timber: without the one she cannot feed her people, without the other she cannot build masts for her ships.

First move on our side is to threaten the Danes. Perhaps a show of force will be enough. The commander-in-chief, Admiral Sir Hyde Parker, who has played safe all his life, is a good enough man for that; but they have Horatio as second-in-command, knowing – as everyone in the service knows – that where he goes victory goes with him. A fortunate appointment because the show of force is not enough, the Danes reject our terms, they are set on resistance, they prepare to defend their city.

I had to start quite early in the morning. The first shots were not fired until shortly after 10 a.m., but the signal was given at 9.30, and there was a long approach before that. The battle in any case took quite a while to lay out because it involved the Danish land defences. I was slower even than usual that morning because I had lain awake most of the night, then fallen asleep at about five. The alarm went off as usual but I could not come to the surface, I lay between sleeping and waking till after eight, then panicked at the idea of being late for the battle and went down to the basement carrying my coffee with me – I did not even stop to heat the milk.

I had everything I needed, I had modelled the Danish shoreline years before in compressed paper, exactly to scale, the inlet into the harbour of Copenhagen, the headland with the formidable Trekroner battery defending the approaches. I had the shore guns too, small-scale models made in lead, which I had bought at Wrights in Holborn. The shape of the Middle Ground I had first traced and then cut out of thick cardboard, which I had left its natural sand colour.

It is this tapering lozenge of sand-coloured cardboard, this Middle Ground, that constitutes the main difficulty for the attackers. I take care to place it in exact position. It lies here, sharp end to the south, between the Danish shore batteries and the Swedish coastline, dividing the straits into two channels, the western or inner one narrower and shallower, heavily defended by the floating batteries, which I put in place now to the south of the city. Here they are, one after the other, moored broadside on. Formidable obstacles to any approach from the south. However to approach by the outer, more easily navigable channel means bringing the English ships under devastating fire from the guns of the Trekroner fortress guarding the harbour.

Horatio is all on fire to attack, his superior hesitates, prevaricates – he will not risk the heavier ships in those shallow waters. Once again that classic combination of prudent principal and risk-taking second; only at Horatio's last battle will this conflict be resolved and all power rest in the hands of the risk-taker. But he has more on his mind now than impatience with Sir Hyde Parker. He has received word from London that Emma has been delivered of a baby daughter, whom she will call Horatia. He is a father for the first time and wild with joy. Also, and at the same time, he is tormented by jealousy. The Prince of Wales has ogled Emma at a reception, and Horatio fears she may fall prey to the wiles of this practised lecher. He even suspects Sir William – his devoted friend – of acting the pander out of deference to royalty.

Sir Hyde Parker continues irresolute. He summons one conference after another. He cannot decide whether to fight or not.

Horatio sums up his feelings in a letter home: *If a man considers whether he is to fight, when he has the power in his own hands, it is certain that his opinion is against fighting . . .*

Finally, he has his way: they will attack from the south, approaching by the narrower channel, avoiding the Trekroner guns. He shifts his flag into the shallower-draught *Elephant* and takes command of about half the fleet: 12 sail-of-the-line with shallow draught, a squadron of frigates, some bomb-ketches and fire-ships. He will make a direct attack on the city. Hyde Parker remains with his heavy ships, here, six miles to the north, eighteen inches on my table.

The wind turns fair, veers to the south. On this day 196 years ago, at just this time in the morning, the first signal flew from the *Elephant's* halyards: weigh anchor and make sail. With this order the action begins. The English ships under topsails move majestically into the attack. I place them in their order of sail, the *Edgar* leading. The plan is simple: they will pass down the enemy line, concentrating their fire, battering the moored gunships into silence one by one.

The opening phase is disastrous. The *Agamemnon*, which should have followed the *Edgar*, fails to do so, she cannot weather the shoals, here she is at the entrance to the channel, signalling her inability to proceed. Then the *Bellona* goes aground on the east side of the Middle Ground. The *Russell*, mistakenly following her in the smoke of battle, suffers the same fate. I place them together here, one just south of the other, almost touching. Horatio's 12 ships are reduced to 9. However, he keeps the signal to advance flying, the remaining ships take up position, the action becomes general. It is a static, murderous battle now, with great slaughter on both sides, a series of thunderous, half-blind duels at cable-length range. On the main deck of the *Monarch*, immediately ahead of Horatio, not a man is left standing the whole length of the ship. Our gun-crews, as always, are superbly trained and disciplined; but the ships are on the light side because of the shoals and the Danish floating batteries are strongly built, low-lying; some of their guns are 44-pounders, heavier than anything on our side. A thousand dead and wounded on the English side, in the first three hours of fighting.

My *Monarch* rested on her glinting artificial sea, with no sound, no motion other than what I gave her. As far from the bloody pandemonium of those decks as my body was from risk of wounds . . .

Just at this moment, in the midst of these thoughts, I had a terrible sensation of having been wounded myself, somewhere low in the leg or in the foot. There was no pain but I could feel the wetness of the blood. For a moment I braced myself for the pain to come. But the wetness was cold, too cold for blood. When I looked down I saw that I was standing with one slippered foot in water, the other just out of it. A stream about two feet wide was running from under the door.

I was forced to abandon Horatio in the midst of the battle, the issue still in doubt, something I had never done before. The water was flowing in a shallow stream down the basement passage, fortunately not spreading much as the floor slanted slightly towards the skirting board. It was coming from above, shining and murmuring in a sort of ecstasy as it dropped down the stairs. When I went up I found the kitchen floor completely submerged, water was brimming over the sink and splashing down. In my sleepy haste I had left the cold tap running and somehow the sink had got clogged.

Slippers and socks and trouser-bottoms were now completely soaked. I splodged my way to the sink, turned off the tap, scrabbled to clear the paste of bread crumbs and coffee grounds from the plughole. A bucket and mop were the only answer. For some nightmarish moments I waded here and there, trying to remember where Mrs Watson kept them. I found them in the cupboard adjoining the pantry. Then I began swabbing – a task that was to take up all my afternoon and most of my evening.

Mop and squeeze, mop and squeeze. I was still in the kitchen at 1 p.m. when Sir Hyde Parker began to grow alarmed – or

137

rather, when the state of alarm he had been in from the beginning began to intensify – and he sent his historic signal of recall. Quite understandable, in a way. From six miles off he couldn't see much – a thick pall of smoke lay over the battle. He could hear the thunder of the guns, apparently unabated. He could make out the distress signals flying from the grounded ships. He was an old man and he subscribed to the old maxims – one of which said that ships could not stand and fight against fortifications. In his heart he did not believe Horatio could carry the day. So he sent signal number 39, the signal of recall.

At this historic moment, one of the highlights of Horatio's career, I was still miserably mopping and squeezing. I hadn't even got as far as the basement stairs. My feet were soaked. Nevertheless, on this day of his triumph I fixed my mind on him, I gave him his due of homage. He sees the signal, of course. What is his first reaction? He asks if his own signal is still in place, his favourite, the signal for close action. He is told that it is. *Mind you keep it so.* Then he turns to Captain Foley at his side – Foley, superb seaman and pilot, his battle companion at the Nile. *You know, Foley, I have only one eye – I have a right to be blind sometimes.* He puts the telescope to his blind eye. *I really do not see the signal!*

This is the moment when legend is born. The path of the hero cannot be smooth; he must show disregard for all restraints of prudence, he must not stop short; he must always struggle to thrust aside impediment, to break through into pure freedom, absolute success. Those around him on board the ship never forgot this moment: the lieutenant who brought him the news of the signal, Foley to whom the words were said, Colonel Stewart, the commander of marines, who recorded them for posterity. And so they have come to generation after generation of British schoolchildren, as they came to me. The quintessential act of heroic insubordination, the ultimate rejection of half-measures. And he, the hero, he understood completely the value of that gesture, the moment when acting the part and realizing the self meet and blend together. And to use his infirmity to

138

reinforce his strength! *I really do not see the signal.* Wonderful, wonderful. At 1.40 p.m., when these words were uttered, I stood with mop suspended, quite still there in the kitchen, observing a minute's silence.

However, fear somehow entered this silence, or foreboding rather, making it difficult to sustain: I had not been properly present in these moments of his triumph, I had failed in my role of witness and shadow. There would be a price to pay. Again that yearning for freedom came to me. I thought then it was *his* freedom I wanted, all fear conquered. Some day, and perhaps soon, I would prove worthy of him. I vowed it as I stood there. But then I began to worry about my wet feet, I was afraid I might catch cold and be unable to deliver my talk, only a week away now. The kitchen floor was still wet but no longer awash. I went to my bedroom and changed my socks. I had no idea which of my shoes might be waterproof or whether any of them were, but I put on the stoutest I had. Then I went back to my mopping.

It was nearly eight in the evening before I got things back in some sort of order and by that time I was tired out. In my anxiety to deal with the flood I had neglected to eat. The Italian takeaway on Haverstock Hill had a delivery service, and I phoned them and ordered a pizza margarita, which came very promptly – it took twenty-two minutes from the phone-call to the ring at the door. I had some claret with it. Sitting in my study afterwards, I felt reasonably at peace, to begin with at least.

I was thinking about the battle as it had developed after Horatio's inspired disobedience. The firing had begun to slacken off after an hour or so. By about four in the afternoon most of the Danish gunships were smoking wrecks. Their dead and wounded amounted to more than two thousand. But they still had not capitulated, still maintained a sporadic fire on our ships. It was now that Horatio showed the other essential side of the untrammelled angel, to courage and panache is added the ruthless will to victory. He sent for writing materials. Spreading the paper on the wooden casing over the rudder-head, he wrote a message to the Crown Prince Frederick. He would spare the Danes if no longer resisting, but if resistance were continued he would be obliged to set on fire all the floating batteries he had taken, *without having the power of saving the men who had defended them.*

And he would have done it! He would have sent his fire-ships in among the defenceless hulks and burned the whole line, men and ships together. And if this had not been enough to bring them to a ceasefire, he would have pounded into ruins the beautiful city of Copenhagen, whose steep-pitched roofs and copper-green spires were clearly visible to him.

The Danes knew it was no bluff; their remaining guns fell silent. After a week of negotiations an armistice was signed, Denmark was detached from her alliance with Russia. By an irony of history, one of those parallel courses I always found so fascinating, none of all this was necessary, none of those thousands of dead and maimed need have received a scratch. Unknown to either Danes or English at the time, an event had taken place that made the bloodshed and the bargaining equally superfluous. A week before the battle a group of Russian officers, who had dined rather too well, made their way to the Mikailovsky Palace and strangled the lunatic Tzar Paul, choking the life out of the Scandinavian alliance at the same time.

But this, in a sense, was beside the point. Horatio would have done it, he would have burned Copenhagen to the ground if necessary. There was only one portrait of him I had seen which reflected this capacity for extreme measures, that painted by Heinrich Füger, Court painter of Austria. Both Emma and Horatio sat to him in his Vienna studio in the course of their return from Naples to England in 1800. By training he was a miniaturist but failing eyesight had obliged him to take up the larger scale.

I felt an urge to look at this portrait again. The only form in which I had it was as a colour-plate in *The Nelson Companion*. I found the book on the shelf and took it over to my table. This was covered with papers – notes about Horatio in Naples in 1799, discarded sheets from my forthcoming talk at the Club. I pushed them aside, feeling distaste at these reminders of my labours. I felt again that longing for freedom, for the removal of my doubts. To be his chronicler was not enough, it never had been . . .

I found the portrait, brought the arm of the lamp closer down to it. He is in full-dress uniform and encrusted with silver and gold: gold collar, gold facings and epaulettes, the silver rays and gold suns of his three Orders – the Bath, St Ferdinand, the Turkish Crescent – pinned to his breast on the left side, with the three gold discs of his naval medals one below the other down his front.

I stared at his face, under the strong light. Füger had caught something no other artist had, perhaps because of his training as a miniaturist, a technique that requires close observation. Not caught, *detected*: there was a ruthlessness here, a capacity for intense concentration. But it was a borrowed face, it was not his . . . Eyes a greenish-brown, an expression cold, pitiless, but not as though native to him – it was induced, laid on his face. The cruelty was something he was bleakly resigned to, as he was resigned to his role. Not the travelling player now. This was Horatio in the part of killer.

Always a mistake to look at anything too long. Already in childhood I knew this. In the days of my illness it was a kind of frightening game. Any object can become dangerous when detached by the violence of the eyes from everything else in the world. A pencil, a rubber-band, a light switch. And how much more the pictured human face – and his, of all faces! I looked too long at this face of a necessary killer and I felt my being dissolved in his stronger one, I felt the terror of this necessity, there was a darkness at the edges of my vision. I raised my hand to my face, but I could feel nothing that made this face my own. I shut my eyes and clutched at the front of my jacket and felt the rough tweed and knew it was mine. I closed the book without glancing again at the picture. I stood there at the table for a time that seemed short but may not have been, striving to keep my eyes unfocused. By degrees I came to myself again, a self that was clammy: I had been sweating all over my body and the sweat was cold.

14

As I have said, Miss Lily had broken through into a zone of immunity, she had crossed the line. I still felt hostility when she spoke against Horatio, but there had been no impulses of violence after that first. She had changed too in these few months. She had taken to reading about him, she argued, she stayed on longer than the two hours without charging me extra. Her hair was longer and she wore it in a softer style, in a fringe over the forehead. Now that the weather was milder she had lost that shiny look and her skin seemed paler. I looked forward now to the evenings when she came. I even looked forward to getting her view of things, limited as this invariably was. By that time I had begun to neglect my appearance rather, but on Tuesdays and Fridays, knowing she was coming in the evening, I made a point of washing and shaving and cleaning my nails.

However, she seriously annoyed me that Friday evening, two days after Copenhagen, by what she said about his conduct during the battle. Where she had got it from I don't know. I had been repeating the story of how he clapped the telescope to his blind eye. One of the great moments in our island story. The impulse, the improvisation –

'Well,' she said, 'there are them that say the importance of this incident has been very much exaggerated.'

'Exaggerated? How can it be exaggerated?' She sounded as if she had lifted the words straight from some book, they were not like her words at all.

'There is reason to believe that this Parker had a private understanding with Nelson that if he hoisted the signal at a certain point it was to be considered optional.'

'Are you saying it was all arranged in advance?'

'I'm not saying anything, I'm just remarking.'

'And Foley and the others?'

'They were all in the know.'

By this time I had begun to experience the usual symptoms of rage: a sense of impaired vision, a feeling that the skin of my face was too tight. But the unusual and surprising thing was that I did not try to hide this from Miss Lily, did not turn away or make any diversionary gesture. That evening, with Miss Lily, I broke my lifelong habit of concealment.

'And the telescope?' I said. 'That putting the telescope to his blind eye? Just playing to the gallery, according to you.'

I saw her eyes widen, become somehow more alert, more watchful. But she went on looking at me steadily enough.

'It's not according to me. That's what they say about it, that he knew beforehand.'

Whatever blood had been left in my face must have drained away at this. 'What they say? *What they say*? How can you repeat such lies? Do you realize what you are doing? You are adding to the slanders about him, you are joining the ranks – '

I had to pause to control my voice. My vision was narrowed to her face, the dark hair over the brows, the soft, undefended-looking, obstinate eyes, the wide mouth with its sharp corners.

'You are joining in the conspiracy against him,' I said, too loudly for that small room. 'Two hundred years it's been going on. It's the same people that talk about his conduct in Naples in 1799, trying to make out that he committed a fraud there.'

'What people are those?'

Her tone had not changed; she was still looking closely at me. This steadiness had a chastening effect, my voice was more under control when I answered. 'Those who cannot bear to think that anyone so great could ever have existed, who always have to undermine him, to take the lowest view of everything he did. This man who saved our country from the vile French, who had a lion's heart inside his frail body . . .'

Uttering this praise of him my voice broke a little. I turned away from Miss Lily and began to shuffle with the papers on my table but stopped almost at once because my hands were trembling.

There was silence for some moments, then she said, 'You only say the French are vile because you know he didn't like them. I know it means a lot to you, Charles, and it's a very good thing to have a hobby, but he was only a man, that's all I'm saying. Don't take offence, but I think myself that you're too wrapped up in him. As far as I can see, nobody knows the truth of that telescope business and nobody ever will. You can think one thing or another. I mean to say, there are lots of things like that, aren't there? I know it isn't my place to say it, but you really need a bit more variety in your life.'

Variety, when I had his life to look at!

'I know we're going out on Sunday,' she said. 'But it's still Nelson, isn't it?'

When I turned back towards her, I found her eyes fixed on me with a serious and quite unmistakable solicitude. That she was in her own way concerned about me I had sometimes felt before. Misguided, of course, I was managing well enough. But I understood now for the first time that the way she expressed this concern was by undermining Horatio. She wanted me to think less of him, but this did not put her among the ranks of his slanderers because she did it for my sake. In this brief moment of humility I saw – glimpsed rather – how much less selfish Miss Lily was than I, who had wanted her to admire Horatio, not for her sake but my own, so I could share with him, bask in the same sunshine . . .

The mood, as I say, did not last long, but a certain obscure prospect of change had come with it and the last of my anger was cleared away. And then I broke my second rule, I told a story detrimental to myself, I told her of my frantic mopping while Horatio thundered at the gates of Copenhagen and she laughed. I laughed too – I remember that I laughed too.

She was not much interested in his battles, not even Trafalgar. She seemed to see no more in them than a perverse expenditure of human life, all the courage and patriotism and fighting spirit counted for nothing, or she turned it into a cause for pity. As I say, her view was limited. She hadn't much in the way of idealism. But she took a great interest in Horatio's private life and particularly in his relationship with Emma Hamilton, whom most of the time she didn't really care for.

'That woman,' she said, 'she played on his jealousy. She didn't care that he was about to risk the lives of all those men.'

I could not help smiling at this. I had been telling her about Horatio's state of mind on the eve of Copenhagen, that strange mixture of feelings: impatience for battle, joy of fatherhood, torments of jealousy. 'The risk to his men's lives was not the foremost consideration,' I said.

'If it wasn't, it should have been. What was there in it for them?'

'Horatio didn't ask them to take any risk he wasn't prepared to take himself.'

'We've had this conversation before. He shared the risks, I don't say he didn't. But he didn't share the rewards. If he lived he got richer and more famous, if they lived they stayed the same.'

I felt my smile wearing thin. It was always the same problem with her; she simplified the issues to such an absurd degree that there was no way of explaining anything to her.

'You can't say there isn't a difference there,' she said. 'Anyway, she exploited his love, this woman he thought such an honour to her sex.'

How did she know about it? We hadn't got to that point yet in my book. A question not worth asking – I knew by now that my book was no longer her sole source of information.

'I've been reading their correspondence,' she said, as if after all I had asked. 'They go to a reception in London, the three of them, the Hamiltons and him. The Prince of Wales is there, he sees her and he fancies her, he always liked them on the large

146

side. So he makes eyes at her. Nelson notices this and afterwards he takes it up with her. She tells him there's nothing in it, she can't help it if the Prince likes the look of her, but that's as far as it goes.'

Her face was settling already into the expression, dogged and exalted at the same time, that it always wore when she was giving vent to feelings of disapproval.

'Strange to think,' I said, 'that William Pitt the Younger was also there, together with most of his cabinet. Horatio came face to face with him that same evening.'

This was an attempt to sidetrack Miss Lily, but of course it failed, because she had no idea of the significance this meeting had in my mind, she did not know the story of the chess-game and the two figures side by side in my father's book. It came to me now, with the force of some exciting, illicit impulse, that I could actually tell Miss Lily this story, as I had once told it to Penhas, I could try to explain how important it had been to me, that wound I had received in the moment of victory, the choice between the statesman and the sailor, the early lesson in conceal-ment. I hesitated, the moment passed; but temptation once admitted leaves us never quite the same; I was to remember that urge to confide in her and how it came to me like something sinful. For the moment, I contented myself with a statement of fact: 'It wasn't a reception exactly. It was a very grand dinner-party at the house of Alexander Davison, in St James's Square.'

'Who was he?'

'He was Horatio's prize-agent.'

'What's a prize-agent?'

'That is the man who managed the prize-money falling due to the people who fought in a battle. Some of the enemy ships taken might be carrying valuable cargoes. Occasionally they might be carrying hugely valuable cargoes. There was a system of prizes. The total value was divided in strict proportion. The commander of the ship got one quarter, the lieutenants got one eighth, and so on.'

'So they just sort of shared out the booty?'

'You could put it like that, I suppose.'

'How much did the men get, the ordinary seamen?'

'It depended on how many there were. There was always one quarter left after all the rest had been shared out.'

'Sounds like blood-money to me.'

'Horatio didn't fight for money. He fought for his country.'

'Be that as it may, it wouldn't have come amiss on top of his pay, that's all I'm saying. Anyway, where the party took place is neither here nor there. The Prince of Wales takes a fancy to her and she makes sure her lover knows it. As soon as he goes to sea again she starts tormenting him. The Prince keeps cropping up in her letters. She is taking care not to go where the Prince is likely to be. The Prince is doing his best to seduce her, but so far she has managed to escape him. Then, against her will, Sir William invites him under their roof. She has her duty as hostess, what can she do? And so on. Letter after letter. That reception or dinner-party or whatever it was happened in November and she's still keeping it warm the following March. He's sitting in his boat, miles from anywhere, going through hell.'

'Ship, not boat.'

'I can read her like a book.'

'Well, she wasn't young any more, her looks were going, she was worried about the future.'

'Who isn't? I mean, if we made that an excuse for everything . . .'

Miss Lily was obviously not herself destined to be a fading beauty, and I privately thought this was why she was so unsympathetic towards Emma, but naturally I did not say so. Instead I suggested it might be time we got on with some work.

My talk was only five days off now and I was still not satisfied with what I had written. I crossed out and rewrote and crossed out again in a progression that was beginning to seem infinite. Everything took longer than expected. Miss Lily grew weary of these endless corrections. 'I know you're a perfectionist,' she said, 'but there is a limit.'

A limit was precisely what I couldn't reach, there being virtually no limit to the ways that words can combine. Under the stress of all this an old nervous habit had reasserted itself, a tendency, slight and I hoped unremarkable, to gulp a little, make from time to time a sort of involuntary swallowing, the teeth meeting in a very faint click, I think only audible to me. It was a strange reflexive motion of the throat, perhaps belonging to the remote diluvian past of the species, like snapping at some wavering insect that had come too close.

I had rewritten part of the second of my two episodes in 'The Making of a Hero', the one which occurred in 1775 when Horatio was seventeen, and marked the real end of youth for him. He had been serving as midshipman on board the *Seahorse* on a voyage to the East Indies, a voyage of marvels – they had rounded the Cape, stood along the northern edge of the Roaring Forties, steered north for Madras and Calcutta, then up the Persian Gulf to Basra and back to Trincomalee in Ceylon.

From boyhood, from my first interest in Horatio, I had followed every step of the way in my school atlas, imagining the brilliant light, the sea tilting up to meet a voracious moon, deserts of red sand, the swollen waters of great rivers, stork-legged people who lived in flooded places, fiery tigers, crocodiles like floating logs. The scattered fragments of my reading and imagining, all came together in that voyage of the *Seahorse*. Thoughts of my mother too. It was for India that she left us. Somewhere on that continent my mother is or was. Just as I was Horatio's witness and his shadow over this wide gap of time, so the process could work in reverse. Perhaps Horatio saw a woman in a blue robe on temple steps across wide muddy waters against the sky of swooning whiteness . . .

All my childish knowledge of brutality was in that voyage too. Horatio had been to the Arctic and the tropics, but this was his first fighting-ship on active service, and the captain, George

Farmer, was a noted disciplinarian. On three hundred occasions, each meticulously recorded in the ship's log, a man was stripped to the waist, lashed to the gratings and flogged with the thonged whip known as the cat-o'-nine-tails. Two or three times a week. Horatio would have witnessed these floggings.

The voyage ended for him in December 1775 somewhere south of Bombay with an attack of malaria. It was his first and it nearly killed him. He was transferred to the *Dolphin*, the only available ship, to be carried home – England was thought to be his one chance of recovery. But the *Dolphin* didn't sail till the following March, with Horatio still confined to his hammock, still at death's door.

'His famous luck,' I said to Miss Lily. But luck was the wrong word, I knew that even if she didn't. 'If they had sailed immediately he would have died, the voyage would have taken five or six months, he could not have lasted out.'

It was a storm that saved him. The first days were calm, the ship made slow way, with light breezes puffing her sails. I wanted to convey the quality of this calm, the slow heave of the sea, the sick boy's hammock swaying with the sway of the ship, the moaning complaint of the timbers, the moving shadows of the rigging, the shadow of death on him as he lay there. A famous ship, the *Dolphin*, though he would not have cared just then; the first ship ever to sail twice round the world.

Then, in early April, the storm struck with tremendous violence, choking the scuppers so that the decks flooded, splitting sails, carrying away the lighter yards and springing the heavier ones from their slings. Already enfeebled and sick, helpless in this nightmare tumult, the young Horatio came very close to his end. But now, just in time, Table Mountain is sighted across the surging waters, they reach the shelter of the Cape, the *Dolphin* anchors at Simon's Town for repairs. These take a month, a month of fresh air and wholesome food for Horatio after the stifling humidity of the Indian coast – a month that saved his life.

All these preliminaries I wanted to include, as being essential to the drama. But the formative experience came afterwards, somewhere in the Atlantic on the way home. He was returning to health by this time, but still extremely weak and listless. He thought much of the future and in this depressed state his prospects seemed bleak.

'I've decided to put it all in the first person,' I said to Miss Lily. 'I want to use his own words as far as possible – I don't know why I didn't think of it to begin with.'

Miss Lily turned to me a face of concern. 'You're changing it again, for the umpteenth time. You're making yourself ill over it. There comes a point when you have to say enough is enough, it's as good as I can make it.'

'I have to do it justice. I have to quote him in his own words. This was a conversion experience, a call to vocation.' I gulped, lowered my head in an attempt at concealment, heard the tiny click of my teeth. 'There he is,' I said, 'standing on deck or perhaps in his quarters below. He has been in the valley of the shadow. Then the long convalescence, the body is recovering, but there is still that darkness in the mind. The future seems to hold nothing for him. What does he say? *I could discover no means of reaching the object of my ambition . . .* Then comes the deliverance, the vision, he sees a radiant golden orb suspended in the air before him, actually there before him physically. In that moment he understands his destiny, he is a boy no longer. I want to put it in his own words. *A glow of patriotism was kindled within me and presented my King and country as my patron. My mind exalted in the idea. Well then, I exclaimed, I will be a hero! And confiding in Providence I will brave every danger.*'

I paused on this. I felt suddenly exalted myself. It seemed to me that some streaming of that radiance, a fainter impression of that shining orb, lay now between Miss Lily and me. 'There you are,' I said, 'there you have it. The vocation of hero, solemnly vowed and undertaken. That radiant vision stayed with him all his life, it must be stressed in my talk.'

However, I saw no slightest look of exaltation on Miss Lily's face. 'I don't believe in this orb,' she said. 'It was a long time afterwards when he wrote about it, twenty years, something like that. I mean, things get embroidered, don't they? Besides, your country can't be a patron, it has to be a person. And King George III was off his head and the Prince of Wales turned out to be nothing but a playboy and overweight with it. Nelson thought he was after Emma, but he probably wasn't at all. *God strike him blind if he looks at you*, that's what Nelson wrote to her.'

It was the first time she actually quoted his words to me. Of course I ought to have known that she would be incapable of seeing the meaning of this transcendent moment in his life, patriotism experienced as religious impulse in this clergyman's son. She was unable, constitutionally unable, to shift from the concrete to the abstract, unable to see that it was not this or that embodiment of kingship that mattered, but the dedication to an ideal of service. It was really so obvious that it wasn't worth arguing about. I said, 'I want to follow it up with some general remarks about the symbolism of the orb. Held in the hand of a monarch, it signifies his sovereignty over the world. It was first used by the Roman emperors. In religious art it is held by Christ as Salvator Mundi, the Saviour of the World.'

'He must have been lonely, that's all I can say.'

'Who?' I was bewildered by this interjection, which seemed not to relate to anything I was saying. 'Do you mean Christ?'

'I mean him, Nelson. He must have been terribly lonely, it wasn't natural.'

There was pity in her voice – she was presuming to pity him. Even worse, when I glanced at her face I had the impression I was being included in the same intolerable embrace.

15

The night before I was due to give my talk I slept very little. I lay awake for hours in the dark, thinking of the April deaths. In our calendar, Horatio's and mine, April is the month of deaths. It was in April 1802 that Horatio's father died, the Reverend Edmund Nelson, pride in his son's career darkened by distress at the wreck of the marriage, Fanny's unhappiness, the scandal of the affair with Emma. A year later, again in April, Sir William Hamilton breathed his last, desiccated and sad, in his house in Piccadilly. In Emma's arms, holding Horatio's hand, he faded away 'like an inch of candle'. The trio was dissolved, the pretence of Horatio as a sort of permanent guest went with it, there were just the two lovers, they could not stay under the same roof after this death. Horatio's own end was not far away; it was in April, two years later, that he set out on his death-chase, the pursuit of the French fleet that would culminate in Trafalgar.

It was in April that my father died, last April, a year ago. On a hospital bed, in a private room, his life haemorrhaged away. It was a process he would have condemned as illogical if he had been able to gather himself; the tumour was not a killer by nature but became so in effect when they removed it.

Where did the blood go? There was no outward mark of it on him, no slightest spot or faintest smear. Again, as I lay there in the dark, the question returned, I felt the same horrified incredulity at thoughts of the blood pooling slowly within the wasted vessel of my father's body. And again, to fend off the horror, I thought about the light on the April afternoon when he died. It was that impartial light that comes through thinly curtained windows on dull or cloudy days and lies without discrimination over everything. I tried again to remember where the windows were in that room and where the bed lay; and again it seemed strange and in a way outrageous that a scene so stamped on my mind in its essence should be in its particular details quite beyond recall. Perhaps it was my own blankness of memory that made the light that afternoon seem in retrospect so blank, so unselective. There was a fan-shaped window over the door, glazed white . . .

Periodically my father's eyes would open and his hands would pluck at the coverlet, the white coverlet, yes. For perhaps half a minute he would keep this up. Then the eyes would close and the hands would be still again, as if halted by some abrupt reflection, something occurring behind the mask of the face, something that needed to be processed carefully, in utter impassivity and stillness. Whatever the conclusions arrived at, they were not communicated to my brother Monty and me as we sat there on either side of the bed. Chairs with chrome frames, yes, their gleaming softened in that light. After some minutes the eyes would open and stare upward, the little fretting movements of the bloodless hands would begin again, as if in search of some fresh food for thought.

It was strange, and I was tempted afterwards to mention it to Monty but never did, how in these intervals of ambiguous stillness, which seemed like grave reflection but might have been something else altogether, heralds of his death in any case, how then, at the edge, our father seemed most himself, most in command. He had always ruled us by not demonstrating anything and he kept it up to the end, almost to the end. But it was not the kind of thing Monty and I could ever have talked about.

He takes after our father in looks, the same long face and prominent square chin, the same straight cast of brow, eyes dark and rather deep-set. Perhaps it was this that made him the preferred one, a doubtful blessing – more was expected. Such a resemblance is a good start, father possibly reasoned, a boy with those looks may do something. Monty was not thought clever at school, but he is hard-working and he understands about money

– like father in this too. He makes a fair amount of it working in the City as an investment consultant for the Japanese. He likes men. My looks are different, I am fair and blue-eyed, more like my mother, at least as I remember her. I have no photographs, all likenesses of her vanished, it seemed overnight, after she left.

Awkwardly, in that flat light of mid-afternoon, on the edge of our chairs on either side, we watched him dying. We were not told he was dying, no one there in the hospital said so. An Irish nurse bustled in from time to time to check the suspended bottle. She must have known, all of them must have known, that his life was leaking away.

For a few minutes, not long before he died, there was a change. He became feverish, a certain warmth – not colour – came to his face. He set up a sort of muttering, accompanied by fumbling movements of one hand, his right hand, yes, he attempted to point at the air before him or at the opposite wall. He was indicating something or asking for something, but we could not understand at first what it was. He struggled to raise himself and we helped him. His eyes were wide open and full of urgency. He was staring across the room, at the curtained recess in the white wall. 'Trousers,' he said, in a voice that was clear but quite unrecognizable as his. 'Get them for me.'

He paused for a moment, still pointing. Then his hand moved up to his face in a gesture of secrecy and caution. 'Don't tell *her*,' he said. 'She won't see, do it now, get my trousers.'

He wanted to escape from his death, which without trousers he could not attempt. He had not asked us for help ever before; appropriate, of course, that it came in the form of an order. My brother and I both made a movement to obey. Even then, in his weakness and delirium, his notion of reality was stronger than ours, his vision of himself as trousered escapee impressed itself on us. 'Quick,' he said, in that stranger's voice, 'You must be quick.'

We started up, both of us, momentarily ready to be his means of escape. And it came into my mind then, in that briefest of moments, before I remembered the limits of his power, the

155

question forced itself on me: did I want him back in trousers, home again, back beside the billiard table which I was already envisaging with its glinting cover of baize and glass as our ocean, Horatio's and mine?

This pang of hesitation was terrible, the moment of it has haunted my mind ever since. Did I want him to die? I saw Monty settle back in his chair and wondered whether he too had been blighted by this doubt. I wonder still.

When we made no move to get his trousers, my father's face became sorrowing and then quite blank. He lay back and soon afterwards he died. The moment was quite undetectable. We had been looking at the lifeless face for several minutes when the nurse came in, touched him, went out again and came back with a doctor, who told us he had passed over.

There was a strange element of reversal in it, this command of my father's to be rescued from hospital. It echoed a distant time when he had come to a hospital to rescue me. I did not think of the connection on that afternoon of his death, but it had come often to my mind in the months following and it came again that night as I lay sleepless in a darkness that was filling with voices.

I was six years old. Before my chess days, before the pictures in the book, long before I knew that Horatio and I were the same age when we lost our mothers. I had been in hospital for two weeks, after an operation to remove my appendix. I hated the hospital and wanted terribly to go home. However, adept at concealment even then, I had shown no sign of these feelings to anyone there, any of the nurses, any of the other children on the ward. I was washed and combed and ready, but they had not made me dress in outdoor clothes; I waited for him in pyjamas and dressing-gown – a new, smart one, I remember it still. I was without trousers, in other words. Probably because of the car, I think now; I was to be taken home in the car. But at the time this did not occur to me. The notion of betrayal came early to me. The fact that I was still in hospital clothes made me suspect that they didn't really mean to let me go.

He seemed from another world when he came for me, god-like. In that place of pale walls and floors, glazed and glimmering to my memory, he was alien and sombre with his dark hair and eyes, his long, navy-blue overcoat and maroon scarf. The clothes he wore that day made an impression on me that has never faded. He was triumphantly trousered then. His long, big-chinned face with the sociable smile on it.

Some words with the nurses while I stood waiting. They were impressed – there was a flutter of interest round him. Then he looked at me. 'Ready to go?'

How I responded to this I don't know. No more than a nod perhaps, or some shy assent – in company he made me shy. Response enough, in any case, to reveal my state of mind to him. He was always very noticing of troubled states.

'Perhaps you'd rather stay?' He looked at the nurses. 'You would keep him, I daresay, wouldn't you?'

'Only too pleased. Quite a little charmer. He's made conquests everywhere. Won't you stay with us, dear?'

I didn't know, I was too young to see, or perhaps my precocious suspicion of treachery prevented me from seeing, that this was not meant seriously, that grown-ups bait children in a pretence of joking, with words not really addressed to the child at all but to themselves, to one another, to celebrate their superior worldliness and wisdom. I thought they meant it. I thought he would go away again without me, leave me in that awful place. I did not know what I could say to stop him without betraying my fear, without hurting the nurses' feelings. And on my father's face that same expression when he glanced at me, the one I knew already, not really amused, I never saw amusement on his face, but alert, interested – he was *studying* me. Perhaps it was born then, my fear of eyes . . .

Only a moment or two, I suppose, the time that I stood there, speechless and lost, in my new dressing-gown, dark blue with silver stitching round the pockets and a silver cord belt. Then the tone of the laughter changed, my father picked me up and carried me in triumph out to the car – his triumph, not mine. Thirty-six years later, in the indifferent light of a hospital room, he mutters and points and yearns for his trousers.

My brother and I have met only once since the funeral and that was to settle some matters arising out of the plan we had made together for me to buy him out of his half of the house. I was arranging to do this by using some of my share of the money placed in trust for us by our mother's father, who died when I was ten and Monty thirteen. The balance of the capital was still enough for me to live on, more than enough.

He came on a Saturday afternoon, the 18th of May. I was down in the basement when he rang the bell, drinking red wine and rearranging some of the cabinets. I had lost no time in having cabinets fitted to house the pieces I valued most, the nineteenth-century long-case clock with a picture of HMS *Victory* on the face, the set of Wedgwood vases in coloured jasper made in 1905 to celebrate the centenary of Trafalgar, a Liverpool creamware soup tureen with tinted portraits of him in the panels. The other pieces I kept on open shelves set round the walls. What a joy it had been to get these things out of the boxes they had lived in so long, set them out where they could be seen.

I remember the date of Monty's visit quite well – it was on the 18th of May 1803 that Horatio, newly appointed Commander-in-Chief Mediterranean, hoisted his flag in the *Victory*. I was having a glass of claret down there in the basement to mark the occasion. I was working my way through a stock of it that my father had been obliged to leave behind.

I got a terrible shock when I opened the door. I thought for a moment that it was my father walking in, come back to resume residence, take over the basement. Monty had grown a narrow moustache on the exact model of father's, he had parted his hair near the middle in just the same way. He was wearing an old-fashioned brown tweed suit with broad lapels, which I recognized as having belonged to father. The shirt looked old-fashioned too. Monty had kept all his clothes, down to socks and underwear, or

158

so I now suspected; and in a final bid for approval he was dressing up in them.

The strangest thing of all was that I made no comment about this and neither did he. We had not been in the habit of confiding in each other, not of late years, not since my illness. Seeing him impersonating our father like that made me seriously doubt his mental balance. Certainly not a person to show one's Nelson collection to. I had never shown it to anyone, as a matter of fact. I always kept the basement double-locked.

Penhas was at the funeral, rather surprisingly – no personal invitation had been sent to him. A notice had been sent to his and my father's club, the Athenaeum, he might have seen that, or perhaps been told of it – he was not really a viable club-member any longer, though I did not realize this until we talked together.

He was sitting towards the rear of the church with a woman beside him in a stiff-looking black hat. After the first surprise it seemed somehow natural that he should have come. I had not seen him in the years since my illness, but I had always thought of him as belonging to my life rather than to my father's; I don't think they had ever been particularly close. To me he had been, if not a friend exactly, for a while, in a way, a fellow twenty-year-old. In his efforts to help me he had told me stories about his youth, brought himself to an age with me. It was he, after all, who had put me back on the rails, held out to me the lifeline of Horatio. I felt sure he had come to the funeral for my sake, out of professional concern, to see how I was bearing up.

This feeling was confirmed afterwards, after the delivery of my father's body to the flames, when I found them both waiting outside in the uncertain spring sunshine, the woman still beside him, taller than he and straight as a ramrod. We shook hands. He did not introduce the woman, she introduced herself – her name was Elizabeth White. It was she, not he, who expressed their condolences. Even before he spoke it was clear that Penhas was greatly changed. The short imperial beard was still in place, quite grey now. The eyes were as I remembered them, dark and depthless – the first eyes I was able to sustain when I was beginning to recover. But the rest of the face had departed, so to speak, from the sombreness of the eyes. The features were relaxed and oddly puffy, the mouth looked softer and thicker and it wore a half-smile, inappropriate for a funeral. The whole face was blurred somehow, as if it had been sponged over.

'He wanted to come,' Mrs White said. 'He wouldn't take no for an answer.'

'Well, nothing is for ever,' Penhas said. His voice still had the careful modulations of a foreigner, but it was slower and thicker than I remembered. 'There was the *poule de luxe*, do you remember her? Living on the earnings of a high-ball lady. *Born, worn*. She kept us in funds for nearly . . . How long was it?' Very swiftly and adroitly, almost imperceptibly, he winked at me. 'She has a most amazing repertoire, that woman, she is a professional contoonist, made of India-blubber. *Rubber*. God, the things she gets up to.'

'Now then, keep the party clean,' Mrs White said. She gave me a look of grim patience. I had thought for a wild moment that Penhas might be referring to her, though her appearance made this improbable. Then I understood that she was a nurse or attendant of some kind.

'That was in Stralsburg,' Penhas said. 'No, wait a minute . . .' The smile disappeared and his face became anxious and intent. '*Salzburg, Stralsburg, Strassburg . . .*'

There were other people I should speak to, Monty had already gone back to the house to receive those of my father's relatives and closer acquaintants due to foregather there. I was beginning to express my thanks, beginning to withdraw, but Penhas – who I don't think had a total sense of where he actually was – began to tell me the story of the bicycles, how somewhere in a hilly region north of Bolzero or Bulzano, footsore and penniless, on his way to Spain, he had seen two bicycles standing outside a lonely farmhouse, one very old and battered, the other brand new. He had stolen one of them. Which one, did I think?

'No idea,' I said. I didn't want to spoil his story.

'I took the old one. I was not a high-trade thief, you see. *Grade.*'

'Sanity depends on making distinctions,' I said, couldn't help saying.

Penhas nodded, his smile broadened and little webs of saliva stretched at the corners of his mouth. He seemed to be attempting, with that sponged-over face, the same expression, ironic and sly, that he had worn twenty years before when he told me the story of the bicycles.

I spoke on an impulse, a thing very rare with me. 'You are not someone who steals, Mr Penhas, you are a giver, you gave me Horatio, you brought me back to normal life.'

'Horatio?'

'Horatio Nelson.'

There was no faintest look of recollection on his face. He had no idea at all what I was talking about. Whatever had brought him it was not the professional follow-up to an interesting case. I thought I knew now what it was. He had not come here for me at all but for himself, to grope, through the mist that was descending on him, for the self he had been when he told me the stories, bold and adventurous in a way I had never been, with Spain and the world before him.

'Horatio?' he said. 'Sheer affectation. Why not Horace?'

Mrs White took him by the arm. 'Time to call it a day.' She smiled for the first time, a smile incongruously cheerful. 'Homeward bound.'

Penhas gave me a look, perhaps of complicity, the fathomless eyes seeming to cast sadness over the ruins of the face and mind. Then obediently, without farewells, he allowed himself to be led away. I watched them walk down the path to the chapel gate. He had a walk that was at once shambling and quick. Mrs White kept close beside him, a head taller, regimental-looking in her black hat.

I was left with my memories of the story, the theft of shirts and knickers from a clothes line, the binding of the bare rims of the wheels with them, the epic journey on this rattling steed. Somewhere south of Avignon, in difficult terrain, it finally gave up the ghost.

Perhaps after all I was wrong, I thought now, perhaps Penhas had told these stories to scores of people since . . . Such questions occupied me as I lay through the hours of darkness thinking of the April deaths, actual and foreshadowed. Towards dawn I heard the resident blackbird strike up in the small drenched garden behind the house. It sang the story of faces, Penhas's spongy and sly, my father's transfigured by eagerness for his trousers, Horatio's pale and noble in the allegorical painting by Benjamin West, where the dead hero's body, unmarked by blood or wounds, is raised by Neptune and Victory into the arms of mourning Britannia.

Other birds joined in, the song became a chorus of lamentation, like the rain of grief I sometimes experienced in my dreams, which was both sound and touch. I felt something of the oppressive sorrow that comes on waking from such dreams and then a return of the terrible restlessness that afflicted me all through that spring and summer, the sense that my life was changing, that something would be required of me. My body had tensed – with resistance, with acceptance, with a kind of fear. Then, quite casually, with a typical absence of fuss, Miss Lily came into my mind and I remembered a conversation we had had about April, how I had quoted to her the lines of T. S. Eliot, in which he says that April is the cruellest month. Quoting poetry to Miss Lily! Three months ago I would not have dreamed of such a thing. I thought of the lines again now; they come, appropriately enough, at the beginning of 'The Burial of the Dead' in *The Waste Land*:

> April is the cruellest month, breeding
> Lilacs out of the dead land, mixing
> Memory and desire . . .

Famous lines. Miss Lily considered for a while, compressing her lips and slightly tilting her head, as she did when focusing on something dubious. Then she made a quick, decisive movement of the shoulders. 'No,' she said, 'he's got it quite wrong. I know poets have to follow their inspiration, but if he had stopped to think he would have seen that the cruellest month is November, because you know that winter is just round the corner.'

Accusing that most sober and cerebral poet of ill-considered haste! All her hatred of cold weather in those words, and something more: a literalness of mind that now, remembering it, seeing her convinced face, made me smile broadly in the dark. Poor Miss Lily.

16

I spent most of the next day going over my talk, resisting the temptation to make further changes – it was too late for that now. The day began fine but in the afternoon the sky clouded over and towards five o'clock it started to rain, something less than a downpour but much more than a drizzle, very steady and remorseless.

When I left the house it was still raining at the same steady pace. I thought briefly of a taxi, but my habit of economy prevailed. Armed with raincoat and umbrella, I walked to Belsize Park station, took the Tube to Russell Square and cut through behind St Pancras to the Club premises.

In my anxiety not to be late I had left home earlier than necessary and it was still not quite seven when I arrived, a good half-hour before the talk was due to begin. Ample time for a drink, a glass of red wine to steady me, give poise to my body and timbre to my voice. Only one, however . . .

Hugo was there as usual and gave me good-evening in his thin, rather nasal tones. He is conscious I think that his voice lacks natural bonhomie and tries to make up for this, infusing warmth into it by drawing out the vowels, making him sound stagy at times, to me at least.

There were only three people in the bar but I thought nothing of this at the time, no premonition came to me. It was early, after all. Afterwards it was to occur to me that there was cause for misgiving right from the start, not so much in the small number of people but in who they were. Kismet Walters was there and Robbins, the expert on naval signals in the age of sail, and a pallid man named Summerfield, a great admirer of Admiral Cornwallis, the commander of the Channel Fleet at the time of Trafalgar. Now the point about these three was that, despite being very different one from the other in their personalities and opinions, they were all absolute regulars, people who passed probably the greater part of their leisure time on the Club premises, invariably present at talks and slide-shows, snoozing away odd hours in the reading-room or browsing through the compilations of the Naval Records Society and back numbers of the *Mariner's Mirror*. In short, they were people who would have been there *in any case*.

As I say, the significance of this did not come home to me at first. Having decided in advance against a second glass, I took this one slowly. I had to be careful not to cloud my mind; I needed clarity for the numerous questions I was sure my talk would provoke. I encountered Horatio's regard in the Abbot portrait up on the wall behind the bar, that face of suppressed pain. Something about the eyes I had never noticed before, they seemed to look inwards as if in search of a self that was deserting, absconding, leaving him to the pain of his wounds and the loneliness of the stars on his chest. *They cut pieces off him, didn't they?*

It was anxiety about my approaching talk that gave me these negative thoughts about him, I knew that a bright angel never looks inwards, though dark angels may. Introspection makes for hesitation and divided counsels. No, consistency of word and deed, magnanimity, fearlessness, self-command, these are the heroic virtues. Honour, in a word . . . A shaft of anguish struck me. Naples, 1799. Just one week from your arrival in the city to the embarkation of the rebels. Just one week in a lifetime. *The violation was at sea.* Of course, Sacchinelli was biased, Ruffo was his employer, he wanted to show him in a good light . . .

I could feel that my palms were sweating. I had the folder containing the pages of my talk held closely under my left arm. I saw Hugo's movements duplicated in the mirror behind the bar. He caught my eye and gave me his slightly rabbity smile.

It was twenty past seven. I had again the impression that time had somehow accelerated, gone ahead of me. These thoughts, which had seemed of the briefest, had occupied twenty minutes. Naples, it was Naples that had slowed me down . . . There were six people in the bar now. Summerfield came over to me and said he was looking forward to my talk, but this was just a prelude and a pretext; he wanted to tell me about a talk that he himself was due to deliver on the subject, inevitably, of Cornwallis.

'The point is, you see,' he said, 'and it can't be repeated often enough, that without Cornwallis, Nelson's victories would not have been possible. Nelson gets all the credit, no one ever praises Cornwallis, he is the unsung hero, but if it hadn't been for the blockade of Brest between 1803 and 1805, Napoleon would have been landing troops in Kent long before Nelson got to grips with Villeneuve at Trafalgar.' Summerfield's eyes, so pale as to be almost colourless, were wide with sincerity. 'In my talk I intend to set the record straight,' he said.

As always, I sprang to Horatio's defence. 'Wars are won by winning battles.'

'Listen, what was the navy trying to do from 1803 onwards? Basically, I mean basically, what were we trying to do?'

'Destroy the French fleet, break French naval power, drive them from the seas.'

Summerfield shook his head. 'You are talking in Nelsonian terms. You are conditioned, like everyone else in this club. What we were doing was trying to prevent a French invasion. The true hero of Trafalgar is therefore Cornwallis, who kept them bottled up in Brittany for the best part of two years.'

Even in my growing agitation at the poor turnout, I could not help thinking it strange that a man would join the Nelson Club and spend much of his time on its premises when the main focus of his interest was not Nelson at all, but an obscure admiral named Cornwallis, an effective blockader no doubt, but that was about all – no glamour, no hint of the angelic. Not for the first time it occurred to me that the Club numbered too many cranks among

166

its members. 'Well,' I said, 'the obvious thing to do is go off and found a Cornwallis Club.'

The Club president, Pratt-Smithers, now came in, accompanied by a man with a short white beard and an abstracted way of looking about him as if he were not quite sure of being in the right place. This was the guest for the evening. Members were allowed to bring guests but quite often someone was invited in the name of the Club as a whole; and Pratt-Smithers, who knew nothing much about Horatio but liked running things, tried to bring in people who might be good for some publicity or might help to increase the membership. This one, it seemed, was a writer who had just published a long novel about the eighteenth-century African slave trade. I hadn't read it. Until that moment I hadn't heard of it, or him – I am not a man for fiction.

'Absolutely monumental,' Pratt-Smithers said now, apparently referring to this novel.

The novelist had a slightly crooked smile and large grey eyes behind thin-rimmed glasses. The eyes were mournful in spite of the smile and the glasses were very old – the metal of the frame was tarnished green here and there. I didn't much take to this man, he didn't look the sort who would take pride in our country's great past, and that's a fundamental division of categories with me, those capable of patriotism and those not.

'Scotch, please, no ice, no nothing,' he said to Hugo, in a voice that contained traces of north-east England. Waiting for it, he squinted vaguely round the bar. 'This all the audience?' Not tremendously tactful. I had a feeling it wasn't his first drink of the evening.

'Oh, there'll be others,' Pratt-Smithers said. 'Not everyone comes to the bar, you know, some people wait in the auditorium.' He smiled at me and I knew what the smile was saying. *This is the most miserable turnout for any talk in the history of the club.* 'It's a rainy night,' he said. 'Puts people off, some people.'

'Auditorium?' Summerfield looked bewildered. 'We were just talking about Cornwallis.'

'Friend of yours?' the novelist said.

Summerfield is a solitary character, easily thrown out. First there had been the unusual word, then this dreadful ignorance. Looking if possible paler than ever, he made a rather abrupt movement of the head, jerking it sideways, then back to the front again. The novelist followed this jerking motion with his eyes. Summerfield had seemed to indicate the area behind the bar.

'That's him, is it?' The novelist was looking at the Abbot painting. 'Naval man, I see, yes.'

'Good God, man,' I said, 'that's Nelson.' It was all I could do to keep my voice steady. I couldn't yet quite believe, not altogether, that the membership as a whole could have boycotted my talk. I knew it, yes, but I resisted the knowledge. Perhaps I had slipped out of parallel again, gone too far ahead somehow ... The sounds in the bar seemed to die away and a sort of ringing hush came to my ears. I was still clutching my file, pressing it close against my side, under my left arm. I felt some pain at this pressure now from the hard edges of the folder.

'Time we were going in, I think,' Pratt-Smithers said. 'Ah, you're having another.'

This was said to the novelist, who it seemed had asked for another whisky, which Hugo was now passing to him. He disposed of it with a fair turn of speed, but it was twenty minutes to eight by the time we got into the lecture-room.

Not until I was there at the table, facing my audience of seven scattered persons in a room with seating for seventy, with the carafe of water and the clean glass before me and Pratt-Smithers's introductory remarks sounding in my ears, not until then did I finally accept it: they had deliberately stayed away. The rain was not the reason, though of course it was the reason they would give.

In that moment, while I was still arranging my papers before me, everything came together, everything made sense. I knew this was a plan that had been concerted against me. They had been waiting several weeks – for this occasion of my talk –

168

to deal the blow. A faint feeling of sickness accompanied this realization, but there was no surprise in it. Ever since joining the Club I had known that my better understanding of Horatio was resented by the common run of the members. Brilliance of any kind infuriates the mediocre. It was the same with Horatio. When he broke the line at Cape St Vincent and so secured the victory, there were those who urged Jervis to reprimand him for disobeying orders.

If this was a plot against me, and I now felt certain it was, then the people who had actually come were obviously suspect too, among them there must be spies whose sole purpose it was to observe my reactions and report back. Otherwise, where would be the satisfaction? There and then I made my resolution and it was one worthy of him: I would show no sign of disappointment, I would give my talk, I would deliver it with clarity and force, I would speak to this small, spy-riddled group as I would have done if the room had been packed to overflowing. I owed it to him, I owed it to myself. *Never show what you feel.* My father's lesson.

And I kept to it. I redeemed the occasion for us both, I made it my own and his. I relaxed my shoulders, I lightened my glance. I heard my voice in that almost empty room, reading the sentences I had put together with such careful toil. The two essential elements, vision and conversion. The lonely boy at the dockside, his vision of divinity in the person of his metamorphosed uncle, in that light and spacious cabin of his first warship; then the conversion, the radiant orb, the culminating phrase: *Well, then, I will be a hero.*

As I spoke I glanced at the faces, wondering who were the spies. No one could be excluded, not the president or the guest, not Hugo, who had left the bar and come to sit at the back of the room, not even Summerfield or Kismet Walters. Any or all of them might be in the enemy camp. But I did not falter. I was defending him as well as myself, I was saving his dignity with my own. The hero carries human dignity for all those who cannot.

Horatio's role and mine – I felt closer to him that evening than perhaps I had ever felt before.

Of course such exertions take their toll. When I sat down again at the table and reached for the water glass, I saw that my hand was shaking and realized that this would be obvious to anyone who saw me try to drink. I retracted the hand with studied slowness, as if I had thought again.

Pratt-Smithers was now on his feet, inviting questions. There was a short interval of silence and then the visiting novelist raised his hand. 'It would be interesting to know,' he said, 'whether Nelson ever had a black woman?'

This was the question, this was the level of interest my talk had aroused. Contempt for question and questioner steadied me now, the trembling ceased. I poured out water and drank, without a clink or a spill. I allowed myself a slight smile. 'You are suggesting that that would be a third stage in the making of a hero?'

'No, no.' He sounded on the defensive – I had scored a hit with this counter-question. 'No, but he spent a lot of time in the West Indies in his younger days, didn't he? I mean, I know he was a hero and all that, but youth will have its fling – he was only about twenty. The climate favoured it, there was an abundance of woman slaves, a hundred thousand or so in Jamaica alone, no shortage of choice . . .'

I remembered it now, his novel was about the slave trade. Clearly an obsessive type. 'There is no evidence for anything of the sort,' I said. 'One can always speculate, if that is what one likes doing.' In the midst of saying this it came into my mind, with the force of a decision already made, that I would resign from the Club.

There were no more questions. Pratt-Smithers uttered some thanks and I was released. I made at once for the door but not in any abrupt or unceremonious manner. Appearances had to be kept up. Pratt-Smithers suggested a drink with himself and guest, who it seemed wanted to pursue the question of Horatio's sexual activities on Jamaica. This was more than I could stomach and I declined, though politely enough, as I hope and think. Naturally I said nothing about my decision to resign, otherwise it might have seemed I was acting out of pique rather than responding to a mortal insult. I was eager to get away. Kismet Walters was bearing down, doubtless intent on telling me about his latest researches into Horatio's secret links with the world of Islam.

'I thought your talk was really good, first rate,' Hugo said to me as I was passing through into the corridor that led to the stairs. He came close to me in the manoeuvrings at the door. He moved his narrow shoulders as if uneasy in the confined space. I saw his eyes, moist blue and full of seeming sympathy, quite close to my own. 'I'm ever so sorry at the poor attendance,' he said. 'Shame it's such a rainy night.'

I could not be sure whether this was meant sincerely, so I said nothing, merely nodded. Next moment I was out and down the stairs, into the street. Once I was on the pavement, however, under cover of night and anonymity, my composure began to crack. It was something like the experience of having drunk too much and been constrained to conceal it, show no sign; then the release into solitude, the cooler air – one begins to stagger and lurch.

This I did now in spirit, so much so that I went the wrong way, turning left into Doughty Street. Before long, without quite knowing how, I was in the unfamiliar region south of St Pancras. The rain had stopped but the pavements were still wet, they gleamed in the reflected lights of cars and street lamps. I must have lost the best part of an hour wandering here, but I was not much aware of time passing. Then, quite by chance, I found myself back in Mecklenburgh Square, which was completely deserted.

I knew the way now but I did not want to turn towards home. Nothing awaited me there but the evening's end, the final acknowledgement of failure and fiasco. I walked round the small square several times, past the locked gates and the spiked railings. From the darkness on my left, beyond the railing, came the smell of wet leaves and mould and some vague fragrance of flowers. But the trees and bushes inside were indeterminate, massed together in the dark. I had the sense, frequent in night-time London in these regions of quiet squares, of walking at the limits of the light, as if I were on the bright rim of a dark bowl and the light merely served the essential darkness, made it denser, less accessible, created a territory separate enough, extensive enough – or so it seems at night – for rapine or oblivion.

An impulse came to me to climb the railings, get through somehow into the darkness beyond, enter that darkness and stay in it for ever, absorbed, annihilated, unseen and unseeing in the thickest part of the bushes. All my persecutors I could escape in that way, all my problems with Horatio in that nightmare city. In fact, even Horatio would be extinguished, in that darkness beyond the railings he would die with me. For some terrible moments I wanted this, wanted to climb in there and put an end to us both. Then a car went round the square, making a soft hiss on the wet road, a small sound but it startled me, like a reminder or a warning. I turned and began to walk back towards Guilford Street. With calmer feelings came a renewed sense of my isolation. It was impossible to pretend to myself that I was unhurt. From time to time, as I walked, the smart of tears came to my eyes.

I heard my name called, and when I stopped and turned I saw, but not immediately, that it was Hugo, unfamiliar in a mackintosh. I had only ever seen him in the rather skimpy clothes he wore when behind the bar, tight waistcoats, shirts with narrow collars, that sort of thing. We had passed each other, it seemed, and he had recognized me at the last moment and called after me.

'You don't usually go this way,' he said.

'Well, no. I felt like a bit of exercise, so I decided to take a turn or two round the square before making for home.'

We stood there a moment or two without saying anything more, and I was about to resume my way before the silence grew too protracted, and in fact may even have taken a step or two, preliminary to bidding Hugo a cheery goodnight, when he said,

'I live quite near, just round the corner. Would you like to come for a coffee or something?'

I had actually started to refuse this offer, I think, when something – perhaps no more than a renewed wish to postpone my lonely and defeated homecoming – made me change my words in mid-career, shape them to a stumbling acceptance. And so we went together back to the square again and along the western side of it.

'Very handy, living so near the Club,' Hugo said as we went along. 'Ten minutes after leaving home I can be behind the bar.'

He had a basement flat just off Great Ormond Street, not far from the hospital. He took my coat and umbrella and hung them up in the narrow hallway. I sat on a sofa with pink and white stripes while Hugo made the coffee, a process I could watch from moment to moment, as the tiny kitchen was built on an open plan with only a counter separating it from the room where I was sitting. The lower part of Hugo was cut off by the counter, his head and shoulders were sometimes visible, sometimes not, depending on whether he was standing straight or reaching down for something.

A sense of wonder possessed me as I sat there, conversing intermittently, glimpsing Hugo in sections, his glinting earring, his furry-looking hair – he wore his hair very close-cropped – his rust-coloured pullover, narrow-fitting and short as all Hugo's clothes seemed to be.

'I think it's a real shame so few people came to your talk,' he said, as he put the coffee things on the counter. 'They missed something, they missed an experience.'

It irked me, this further reference to the fiasco of my talk; it brought back my earlier doubts as to where Hugo stood in the matter. Was he probing the wound to elicit winces and whimpers so he could then carry tales back? It was important to give nothing away.

'Well, it was a rainy evening,' I said. 'Besides, the talk is what

173

it is, I mean, it is as good or bad as it was before I gave it, irrespective of the audience.'

I wasn't quite sure what I meant by this, but Hugo widened his eyes at me and nodded seriously. He was sitting opposite in an armchair upholstered in some velvety red material – there was a lot of red in this room. A faint, sweetish smell, like incense, hung in the air, and on the wall behind him there was a poster, a picture of a man with fine-drawn features, rather androgynous-looking. His hair was matted with some silvery dust and his suit glittered with tiny spangles like coarse sugar. In the background a dark sky thickly scattered with stars.

'Well, my word,' Hugo said, 'I call that a really mature attitude.'

Away from the softer lighting of the bar, Hugo looked older, nearer my own age, rather than in his middle twenties as I had thought. The earring and the short bristle of the hair and the clothes like those of an adolescent growing too fast had all contributed to this impression, as did his habit of twitching his shoulders from time to time, as if in some impatience with his own body.

'Take your jacket off if you feel too hot,' he said now. 'I keep the heating full-on, it's my only extravagance.'

'I'm all right like this,' I said. It was indeed very hot in the room and the predominance of red made it seem hotter still. I felt a wave of nostalgia for that cold breath that had reached me through the railing of the square and the promise of oblivion that had come with it.

'I love the heat,' Hugo said. 'I should have been born in the tropics. I like to go round, you know, in just light clothes. Sometimes, in the summer, I don't bother with clothes at all. It's very private here, no one can see in.'

I said nothing to this. Hugo waited some moments, then said, 'Rise above it, that's what we've got to do. Like he did.'

'Who's that?'

'Him, Lord Nelson.'

This seemed a very strange thing to say about Horatio, who

did not need to rise above anything because he was above already. What could Hugo mean, what could he be referring to? I was about to ask him when he started speaking again.

'Rise above it, that's the only way. Take my case now, I've only got these two evenings at the bar, and on Saturdays and Sunday afternoons I work in a bookshop in Covent Garden. I have to manage on that, for the time being. There was someone sharing with me, but he walked out two weeks ago. Just up and left without a word and took a looking-glass that used to belong to my grandmother, framed in silver and mother-of-pearl, a family heirloom you might say.'

'Can't you get it back from him?'

'He didn't leave a forwarding address, did he?' Hugo gave a twitch to his right shoulder. 'What a creature,' he said. 'After two years and a bit. I don't know why I'm talking to you like this, I just feel you're a very understanding person.'

He paused on this and again seemed to wait. Silence lengthened in the room. My eyes were confused by the heat, the pink sheen of the sofa, the spangled figure on the wall. I was troubled by the blank television screen on my right, a lurking presence whose gaze I could only avoid encountering by being careful not to glance that way.

Hugo shifted in his chair. 'Well, anyway,' he said, 'one has one's value as a human being, they can't take that away, can they? I'm a bit of a psychologist and working behind a bar gives you scope for it, if you know what I mean. Of course you have to have intuition. I'm very rarely wrong about people. You always struck me as a free spirit. First time I saw you, I thought to myself, here's someone who knows his way about, someone who's seen a thing or two, been in some odd corners. Someone not easily shocked. A man of the world in the true sense of that term. Some of those others, you'd think they had spent their entire lives with only Nelson for company.'

I was conscious now of the beginnings of a headache. 'Who is that chap with the silver hair and spangly suit?' I asked.

'Who do you mean?'

'The man on the wall behind you.'

Hugo smiled a little as if he thought I was joking. Then, as he looked at me, his face lost all expression. 'You don't know who that is?'

'No idea, I'm afraid.'

'That's David Bowie.'

'He's a pop-star, isn't he?'

Hugo shook his head slightly as if seeking to dislodge some small object. 'I don't believe we're having this conversation,' he said. 'David Bowie is much more than a pop-star, he's a wonderful actor and a superlative singer, he's the media star of our time, he's the person I would most have wanted to be. He's just like me, he has the same attitudes that I have, he's non-aggressive, he believes in cosmic harmony and animal rights.'

'You can't really tell whether he is a man or a woman, can you? Why is he wearing that sugary, shiny stuff all over him?'

'That's stardust, David Bowie belongs among the stars.'

This was a fairly sickening thing to say in any case, but there was something in the inflection that brought about a return of my suspicions. I thought back quickly over his earlier remarks and it seemed to me now that I could see a pattern in them. What had he meant by saying that Horatio had to rise above it? *Rise above what?*

'I've got everything of his.' Hugo gestured towards a low, open-fronted cabinet against the wall near the sofa where I was sitting. 'Would you like to hear something?'

'Are you trying to make a convert of me?'

Hugo seemed not to hear this. He got up, crossed to the wall beside me and crouched before the cabinet. 'What shall it be?' he said, crouching there at the side of the sofa, close beside me, tilting his head and stretching his neck to see along the row of CDs. His pullover had ridden up over his narrow waist, showing some inches of dark red shirt. His eyes were invisible to me. There was the back of his head, his neat ears, the left one with its gold band, there was the pale, undefended nape of his neck. Higher, up towards the crown, a glaze of pinkish skin showed through the sparse hair. Hugo was balding.

Pity for his early baldness, for the pathetic inadequacy of his starry icon, made this dwelling on him more terrible, more monstrous. He was too close to my eyes. Sensation, sound, the hot colours of the place, the lingering smell of joss-sticks, all merged in that helpless scrutiny of the frail skull. I was impaled on my own regard, my eyes were pierced to an even narrower focus, the slight bump above the hair-line, just before the more pronounced convexity of the occipital bone. A ridge rather than a bump. It had the dull shine of an eggshell under the hair . . .

Then he straightened up, moved away. 'Got to begin somewhere,' he said. 'Let's try this.' He put in the disc, then turned towards me. He was smiling, I suppose in anticipation of the music. But it seemed to me that his face changed when he met my eyes. A moment later a sound of lamentation filled the room, a voice that resonated with shuddering falls, as if the recording had been made in some remote and echoing cavern far from human eyes. It was like all the sorrow of my dreams. I was sweating heavily and I felt giddy. I spoke loudly through the music, explaining to Hugo that it was late, that I had to leave. He seemed not to understand.

I went quickly into the hallway, found my coat and umbrella, and fled up the steps into the street.

17

Miss Lily came as usual on Friday evening. She was hardly through the door when she began asking me about the talk. 'I was thinking about you,' she said. 'How did it go?'

'Very well.'

'I saw that it was raining and I wondered, you know, if it would put people off.'

'No, no, they came all the same.' A modest smile. 'The place was pretty packed.'

'Did you get some good questions?'

I had a brief recollection of the novelist's raised hand. 'One or two, yes. It was a mixed bag, you know. But there was a fair degree of interest, I think I can say that.'

'And so there should have been.'

Miss Lily said this with considerable emphasis. I looked at her, not for long – I never look long at faces – but long enough to see that she really meant it, she really was glad at the thought of my success. Her face was bright with pleasure. And I thought, if the talk is a success in her mind, then so am I and all that work is rewarded – rewarded by the look on her face. I felt a certain impediment in my throat and tried to swallow it down but it stayed. I busied myself with papers for some moments. Then I said, 'I couldn't have got it together without your help.'

It was an effort to say this, to overcome the humiliation of gratitude. When I glanced at Miss Lily again, the pleasure was still there on her face but it was different, more serious, there was that deepening of expression I had noticed before. It came to me that there was beauty in her face and something more, she possessed without effort the dignity I strove to protect in Horatio and in myself. It was disturbing, that I should see myself as striving to protect what he possessed so that I could possess it too. Hugo's face came into my mind, rabbity-looking somehow, with the eyes wide apart, rather protuberant. His look that changed as the music began. *You have to rise above it.* Only the evening before, but it was remote already, like something in somebody else's life.

'We'd better get going,' I said. I was still trying to circumvent the problems of Naples 1799, at least temporarily, by jumping ahead to the following year, when Horatio and the Hamiltons, after their long journey home, with the cruises, the sittings to painters, the sojourns at foreign courts – the 'roadshow', as Miss Lily persisted in calling it – finally arrived in London.

In a way she was right, I had to admit that. They were performers whether they wanted to be or not. Even when they were back in England the show went on – it had to, because the spectators were always waiting, the theatre was always crowded. The maimed admiral, the antiquated ambassador, the beautiful, corpulent dame they shared, the suffering, unoffending Fanny. Fame and scandal made them players. Everywhere they went reporters followed, every move they made was recorded in the daily press.

The rift between Fanny and Horatio was past mending now but they still appeared together in public. I wanted not merely to catalogue the events of those days but to convey the essence, catch the highlights and the low. However, the main job that evening was to correct a mistake I had made, a confusion between two separate visits to the theatre by the Nelson party in the same week. In fact, it was difficult to be certain about Horatio's activities during this period. Many of the newspaper reports of his attendance at public events were apocryphal, the managers of every show in London from Pidcocks Zoo to the Sans Souci in Leicester Square had found out that they could fill the house at short notice by putting it about that Lord Nelson would be in the audience that evening.

The first occasion was on the 18th of November, at the Covent

Garden Theatre, where the comedy *Life* was playing, followed by the spectacle *The Mouth of the Nile*, celebrating Horatio's victory. The theatre was packed to overflowing and Horatio's appearance in his box was greeted by prolonged applause. He had to take repeated bows before the curtain could go up. The cast sang 'Rule, Britannia'; the Reverend Edmund, Horatio's father, burst into tears; the hero then seated himself, with Emma on his right and Fanny on his left, and the play began.

'He had the mistress on his right, you notice, his disarmed side,' I said, by way of a joke, but Miss Lily did not think it funny. 'What a fuss, all that jumping up and down and bowing,' she said. 'I'm sorry for Fanny, that's all I can say. Why did he have to put her through all that?'

I made no reply to this typical piece of parochialism; I knew that if we started arguing now we would never get the passage corrected that evening. I had ascribed to the second occasion the dresses which the ladies had worn on this one. I wanted to put it right but still keep the description, because it seemed exactly to convey their different temperaments and situations: Emma flamboyant in a blue satin gown, fashionably high-waisted to conceal her pregnancy, and a headdress with a great plume of flowers, Fanny in simple white with a violet turban and one small white feather.

After the comedy, and before the spectacle, Munden came forward and sang a song specially written for Horatio:

> *May peace be the end of the strife we maintain,*
> *For our Freedom, our King, and our right to the main!*
> *We're content to shake hands; if they won't, why, what then!*
> *We must send out brave Nelson to thrash 'em again.*

Prolonged and deafening applause. Horatio jumps up again to bow his thanks. It takes two more choruses of 'Rule, Britannia' to restore order for the next piece, which being in Horatio's honour naturally brings the audience to its feet again with cheers and huzzas.

In short, a totally successful evening. The second occasion, which took place six days later, was less so. This was at the Theatre Royal in Drury Lane, the last occasion when Fanny and Horatio appeared together in public. The play was *Pizarro*, a melodrama by Kotzebue, touched up by Sheridan, with the celebrated John Kemble in the part of Rolla. It had been a great hit. Pizarro hats were in fashion for a whole season. In the box with the Nelsons were Emma and Sir William, the Reverend Edmund and a certain Princess Castelcicala. The party was greeted with loud cheers from every part of the house and a spirited rendering of 'Rule, Britannia'. Emma had been disappointed to learn that Mrs Siddons was not playing Elvira, but Mrs Powell was generally accounted a success in the part. Horatio appeared to be enjoying the play, he applauded vigorously throughout the first two acts.

'How did he applaud?' Miss Lily said, and she giggled a little. 'I mean, he couldn't clap, could he?'

'I've no idea. Probably he cheered or shouted.' This was said stiffly; I hated his being laughed at.

'Perhaps he just jingled his medals. I'm sorry, I shouldn't have said that, should I? The truth is, he brings out the worst in me.'

I looked at her in absolute amazement. The man who established British supremacy at sea for a century to come, who secured for us the tea gardens of India, the sugar islands of the Caribbean, one of the principal founders of the greatest maritime empire that the world has ever known, who made this country great and died for her in the end, this man brought out the worst in Miss Lily! I couldn't say anything, I could only stare – yes, stare, I even forgot my antipathy for the mutual regard. There were still the traces of laughter on her face. 'I'm sorry,' she said, 'I won't interrupt again.'

I took a deep breath and resumed:

'At the end of Act Three, Elvira, her pleas rejected by the cold and inhuman Pizarro, breaks into her impassioned vow of vengeance. *How a woman can love, Pizarro, thou hast known . . . How she can hate thou hast yet to learn . . .* Elvira is alone on the stage. The audience is spellbound. Her voice rises. *Thou, who on Panama's brow . . . Wave thy glittering sword . . . Come fearless man! Now meet the last and fellest peril of thy life, meet and survive — an injured woman's fury . . .*

'A piercing scream from the box. Lady Nelson has fainted. She has to be taken home. The curtain falls, but applause is hushed. All eyes are fixed on the box where the admiral sits immobile . . .'

'Do you mean to tell me,' Miss Lily said, 'that he just went on sitting there when his wife – I mean, she was his wife, wasn't she? – had just given a shriek and passed out? He had the use of his limbs, didn't he, those that were left? I mean, he could jump up and take his bow quick enough.'

'The trouble with you, Miss Lily,' I said – she drove me to frankness – 'the trouble with you is that you have no historical sense, none at all. As far as you are concerned everything is happening in a sort of eternal present. Horatio was a great hero, a great public figure. It was an age that valued decorum. He had always to think of the figure he was cutting.'

'Well, he cut a bad one there, that's all I'm saying.'

'There was a French word much in use at the time among the upper class, *bienséance*, propriety. You had always to keep up appearances.'

'That's what I'm saying, the appearance he kept up was a bad one. Besides, I think you go too far in the opposite direction.'

'What do you mean?'

'Well, I daresay you have got this historical sense, but you don't join up the past with the present. I mean, the present is where we are now, isn't it? If you did join it up you would see that Nelson is one of those people who think they are above everything. Whatever they do is all right because they are so popular. Like these footballers who play for England, or that punk group that smashed up the hotel, the Sex Pistols, gone without trace now, thank God, or someone like Woody Allen who goes and marries his adopted daughter when he's old enough to be her grandfather and does it in the middle of a film festival. Then he

182

complains that the journalists won't leave him alone. If enough people think you're great you can do anything, but it doesn't make you a better person.'

These comparisons were so absurd, it was all I could do to keep from laughing. 'We are in the Nelson decade,' I said. 'In a few years we will be commemorating the great victory of Trafalgar. The whole nation will remember Horatio with gratitude. There will probably be a two-minute silence for him at Plymouth. Do you really think that in two hundred years' time the nation will be remembering with gratitude the goals scored by some footballer or the films of Woody Allen?'

'They'll be cheering someone else. Some last longer than others but it comes to the same thing in the end. Anyway, there was something wrong with him. He must have known it was humiliating for Fanny, he wasn't stupid. Yet he insists on bringing her, he sits between them. I mean, it's pretty obvious why she fainted, isn't it?'

'Well, yes, she was an injured woman, but – '

'And that is what he couldn't forgive her,' she said triumphantly. 'She put him in the wrong and he couldn't be wrong, could he? That's why he was so cruel to her. I mean, think what she must have felt in that theatre. What happened after she fainted?'

'She was helped out by the Hamiltons and old Mr Nelson.'

'Did they come back?'

'No, it seems not.'

'So he sat there on his own till the end of the play? Charles, don't you think there's something terribly wrong with that?'

'No, I don't, as a matter of fact. You persist in looking at him as if he were any Tom, Dick or Harry. He was the idol of the people. Do you think that the break-up of his marriage was the only thing he had on his mind? He had money problems as well. He had lived far above his means in Naples. When he came back he had to sell half his holdings in stocks to pay off his debts. So he lost half of the interest. And he was involved in a court case with Lord St Vincent. Do you remember who he was?'

'I'm not likely to forget *him*. He was the one who called for an orange in the middle of a battle, when the soldier beside him had his head shot off.'

'That's him, yes. Two Spanish frigates had been taken the year before and the prize-money had gone to St Vincent, £14,000, a lot of money in those days. Horatio thought it should have gone to him, as he was senior officer in the Mediterranean at the time – St Vincent was in London. So you see he had quite a lot on his mind besides Fanny.'

'We all have our troubles,' Miss Lily said. 'But we still have to try to do the right thing.'

'He was in the situation, there was nothing else he could have done.'

Miss Lily looked at her watch, something she did openly only when she had decided that the session was over. 'That's what's so terrible about it,' she said. 'That's why he had to do all that fighting and killing, isn't it? That's how people come to get their heads blown off.'

A typical *non sequitur* on her part, though I lacked the energy by this time to take her up on it. When she had gone I stayed where I was in the study, thinking about the conversation. It had followed the form of nearly all our talks about Horatio. Miss Lily generally started by joking, then worked herself into a state of indignation and ended on a softer, more sympathetic note, which contained, however, some quality of darker hinting. For my part I always tried to be indulgent, to make allowances for her obvious inability to appreciate Horatio's genius. My closer understanding made me – as it made him – impervious to the sort of criticisms that she brought to bear. All the same, there was something troubling to me in the note of pity she struck so frequently these days. Troubling too, even more so, was the fact that I looked forward to Tuesdays and Fridays, looked forward to breathing the air Miss Lily brought with her . . .

As a refuge from these thoughts, I turned back to Horatio, to the December of that same year, when he and the Hamiltons were guests of William Beckford at his country estate in Wiltshire. Strange guests, a strange host – the incongruities of this visit had intrigued me for years, ever since I first read about it. Beckford had inherited great wealth from his merchant father, something like sixty million pounds in equivalent value today. At the age of five he had been given piano lessons by the child prodigy Mozart, aged eight. He was the author of the celebrated *Vathek*, classic among Gothic novels, a tale of gloomy splendour and bizarre invention. Eccentric, romantic, increasingly reclusive, he devoted most of his energies – and vast sums of money – to the construction of a Gothic 'abbey' on his estate, all turrets and crenellations, with an octagonal central tower that rose eventually to a height of nearly three hundred feet.

He invited them because they were celebrities – it is difficult to see what else they could have had in common. They were escorted from Salisbury by a detachment of cavalry. As they made their way up the drive to Beckford's mansion, a thirty-piece band played 'Rule, Britannia'. Beckford waited for them on the steps, accompanied by his pet monkey and a dwarf he had acquired in Portugal.

The highlight of the stay was a visit to the abbey, which took place after lunch on the 23rd. Also in the party were: Madame Banti, the opera singer, Benjamin West, the American painter, John Wolcot, a composer of satirical verses, and an architect named James Wyatt, who was helping Beckford in the design of his amazing Folly. Darkness was already falling when they climbed into their carriages and set off across the park through the gloomy avenues of trees. Their way was shown by lanterns hung from the branches. As they came in sight of the vast building, a hidden orchestra struck up a solemn march. The massive walls rose above them, and the great tower, still incomplete, was half lost in the darkness.

Once through the portals of the place we walk across the hall, a room so high that the light from the sconces did not reach the ceiling, then into the Cardinal's Room, hung with purple damask, where hooded servants silently take our cloaks and hats. We sit down to eat at an enormous refectory table covered with golden baskets of sweetmeats and flagons of spiced wine. Solemn music sounds from the gallery. But where is Emma? She is not there beside us.

Some moments of anxiety – her presence is necessary, indispensable. But Sir William does not seem perturbed. Then, from the far end of this vast, dim room, glimmering and vague at first, dressed in a simple white robe, she advances, very slowly. She is bearing a golden urn. Urbane, knowledgeable Sir William whispers behind his hand: 'Agrippina bearing the ashes of Germanicus.' We nod, as being well acquainted with this episode in Roman history.

Emma passes from pathos to pride, from sorrow to scorn, from rage to final triumph as she rouses the Romans to revenge the death of her husband. It is one of the most successful and memorable of her Attitudes. Her fellow guests, sitting in that strange room with its yellow hangings and candlelit statues and reliquaries, are moved to tears as they watch. Above them in the darkness rises the great tower. It is nearing completion – it will reach an amazing 276 feet. Seven years later it will collapse, destroying most of the building.

Scholars, poetasters, opera singers, journalists – you were the odd one out in that company, as you always were in any company on land. Sir William was a collector and bookish. His taste did not run to the Gothic, but he would have had much in common with Beckford. Emma was a natural actress and a talented singer, she won applause with her Attitudes, she sang duets with Madame Banti. But you? Victor of the Nile, Saviour of your Country, your brightness was eclipsed among them. Better so, better you were dimmed. As an angel you could not have endured such company. It was much like what you had come from, in Naples. *A country of fiddlers and poets, whores and scoundrels.* That is how you wrote of Naples on the morning after your fortieth birthday.

Those were the early days, before you were caught in the toils of the city.

As always, I had returned to Naples. Whatever the point of departure I always ended there. I had solved nothing by leaping with Horatio to a London theatre or a Gothic Folly. The doubts kept pace with me, however far ahead I went in his life – and only five years remained for him now. He took the city with him wherever he went and so did I, and so we both would until I could clear him.

18

Perhaps it was fear of drowning in the poisonous flower-trap of Naples that was responsible for the dream I had that night. Fear was my inseparable companion in one form or another – and it has many forms.

A pervasive presence in this dream was a woman called Pat whom I did not see but knew to be living in the desolate aftermath of an unhappy love-affair with the president, he too invisible. I was approaching Pat's ruined cottage, which I knew in my dream represented her ruined life. In the abandoned garden was an old Morris Minor, half submerged in water. The garden itself had sunk and flooded, and I found myself standing chest-high in black water, tepid, not unpleasant. A woman who was not Pat appeared beside me and told me to look at my legs. I succeeded somehow in getting one leg out of the water. It was naked and covered with black centipede shapes printed on the skin. I felt a horrified repugnance and knew that I had stayed too long in the water. Rising before me was a sort of stone column, not very tall. If I could climb that I could get out of the water. I had to embrace the column in order to climb. But the stones were loose, they crumbled in my hands, I kept slipping back. Surmounting the column, outlined against the sky, a figure leaning towards me, a shimmer of light on his chest. He leans towards me, but he does not offer to help. He is leaning to watch me, not to help me. He is faceless, some suggestion of wispy hair. He is wearing the same cocked hat, I feel the same terror as he brings his face nearer.

I woke from this sweating profusely and for some time afterwards I groaned to myself in the darkness. Thoughts of my dead father came into my mind and I was stricken with a sense of irreparable loss, as if something immensely valuable, irreplaceable, had slipped from my grasp and shattered beyond mending. It was myself I grieved for, what I might have been to him, I suppose I knew that then – it was the same grief that coloured my dreams, all-enveloping, too pervasive to be contained, an element of weather like mist or dew.

Memories spring without warning or bidding into the mind, near and far, real and fabricated, all weeds in the same garden. There was no definite moment of transition, no moment when you saw him cross the great divide. There should be a moment, there must be a moment. The one detectable change was when his face lost that cruelty of keenness, of questioning. He died then.

So many things realized too late, understood too long after. I thought he was concerned with truth. A May afternoon, late May, I was seven years old – it was the year after my stay at the hospital. Another of those country walks, but this time my mother was with us and it was in Cambridgeshire, where her parents lived.

Childhood memories so helplessly subject to tampering. So difficult not to take a chisel to them or a brush. Sure memory of it is only sunlight, of being first high up as we walked, then low down between the hawthorn bushes, my mother in a light blue summer coat, no hat, her hair loose, blown sometimes across her face. Later days of similar weather must have got into the picture, but to me the essence of May is concentrated in that afternoon of broken cloud and hazy sunshine, the silver gleam of the birches, the hawthorn blossom everywhere in profusion, pink and white, accompanying us along the path like a prodigal bride.

We had driven out to Devil's Dyke, to where the road crosses the dyke on the Newmarket Downs, not far from the racecourse. The footpath ran along the top of the dyke and it was high at first, you could see a long way across the downs on either side. To children from London the openness was exhilarating, the broad views, the vast sky criss-crossed with singing larks. The larks were stitching up the sky, so my mother said that day or another. Who had torn it? Some giant, I imagined. I am not sure, she said, perhaps it tears itself. But the larks are busy stitching it up. Smiling, flushed with the sun, her reddish-brown hair falling sometimes across her face. Blue eyes, like mine.

Then the dyke flattened down into wooded gullies, with clumps of alder and scrub-willow. Names not belonging to that day, learned later. The path was more winding, less clearly defined, there were possibilities of detours and short-cuts. My father set Monty and me on to a game of his own devising, in retrospect totally characteristic of him, a game of observing and competing and reporting. Perhaps he had seen that we were flagging. In any case, a good way of getting rid of us for a while. We were to go on ahead, take careful mental note of everything and return to make a full report.

It was seductive, to be an explorer, to break new ground before the adults, to be able, just for once, to tell them something they didn't know, couldn't know. I remember the excitement of running ahead. I kept close to Monty at first, thinking that if I looked where he looked I would see what he saw, a tactic wholly mistaken – I could not know what messages were being conveyed to him, and he, wanting to outshine me, offered no clues.

So I developed ambitions of my own and from the very beginning they were enormous. I wanted to have something outstanding to report. I wanted to find another pathway, one that nobody else knew about, a sort of secret alternative to the one we were on. Did it start there, the fascination of the parallel track, the private access, a life to run alongside my own life?

Down into those wooded hollows, plunging down, looking for the big scoop. Cardinal error, looking for what you hope to find rather than looking at what is there before you. My father would not have made that error, nor did Monty. I was lost in the confusion of detail, not knowing the names of things. Flowers, birdsong, broken sunlight.

Meanwhile my brother, sober and methodical, three years older, not distracted by grand designs, pursued his observations. When I saw him run back I ran after him, wanting somehow to share in the credit, but then I had nothing to report, I stood silent under a blank sky. Monty had seen: tracks of a dog, a big dog in a place where the ground was soft; he had seen a colony of ants in a dead tree; he had seen briar roses in the hedge. He brought back, concealed till the moment of presentation, a pheasant's tail-feather, a piece of the chalk on which the downs rested. *Good work, Monty. Try again, Charles – use your eyes, boy, you must learn to use your eyes.*

But my eyes were clotted with failure. My mother was smiling but she knew what I was feeling, she knew my distress. Did I know hers? So difficult, across this ocean of time, to see her, to know. She spoke very quietly to me, a little aside. Perhaps you will see some oxlips. The yellow flowers with leaves like primroses. Not among the trees, they grow on the banksides. They like the chalk, you know. My father could not hear but he saw, he guessed. *No special treatment, Dorothy. The boy must learn to use his eyes.* But I knew that with my eyes I could not win.

I knew there were creatures called moles and they fascinated me because they were black and blind and had a mysterious alternative life under the ground. What more triumphant thing than to see one in broad daylight? I reported that I had seen a mole.

My father's face at once took on a certain gleam. I think he understood from the beginning that I had made it up, but he didn't say so, he expressed no hint of scepticism, offered me no joking way of escape. That was not his way. No, he led me on with questions, friendly questions.

Gracious me, a mole. Did you hear that, Dorothy? What was it like?

I said it was little and velvety black and explained that it kept its nose close to the ground as it went along because it couldn't see very well.

What was it doing when you saw it?

191

I said it was just walking along, it was enjoying the sunshine after being in its dark burrow underground.

Is that all it was doing, just walking along?

Some hint of disappointment in my father's voice. My report was not dramatic enough. I said that I had seen it eating something.

Really? Now that is really interesting. What was it eating?

I think my mother attempted to intervene at this point. I have a vague memory of some words, an expression of remonstrance on her face as she looked at my father. But he was enjoying the game too much.

No, no, fair play. The boy must be allowed to make his report. What was it eating?

I said it was eating a piece of sandwich. It seemed reasonable – I had seen scraps of old picnics blown down there.

The trap was closed. My father's face lost its smile. *Moles don't eat sandwiches. Look me in the eye, Charles. You didn't see any mole at all, did you?*

I didn't see any mole, Monty said. I was in the same place that he was and I didn't see any mole.

You know how imaginative he is, my mother said. Don't be hard on him, he got carried away.

You told us a deliberate lie, didn't you? The whole thing was a lie.

Still that gleam of alertness about his face. Not anger, not reproach. He was *interested*, he was waiting for my confession. Then the moment of inspiration. No, I said, it wasn't a lie, it was a trick. His face changed as I spoke. This was unexpected, it was not part of the entertainment.

Come, you must learn to face up to things. Admit it was a lie and we'll say no more about it.

Not a lie, a trick, it was a TRICK.

I was afraid of him, in all his moods, but that afternoon I was afraid of humiliation more. This was the fear that made me obstinate, that gave me one of the few triumphs of my childhood. For I did not retract.

He was enraged. He had been ready to put the rabbit out of

its misery but if I would not admit to being a liar where was the rabbit? He made me walk back on my own, behind the others, in disgrace. *Until you own up, until you learn to face the music.* But I never did own up.

It was not that I thought him in the wrong or myself in the right. At the time I believed his anger was due to outraged principle, my failure to face the music and so on. Only much later did I come to understand the true nature of my offence: I had spoiled his game. But I knew even then, as I trailed behind the others, forlorn but unrepentant trickster, knew that I had held out against an adversary immensely more powerful on his own ground and I had done it by not yielding, not admitting – I had done it *by not showing*. I began to learn the lesson then: reveal yourself and you are lost, you are crushed. It is by concealment that we avoid the fate of the rabbit under the boot.

19

The following Sunday was the day of the Portsmouth trip, a prospect which had been troubling me intermittently ever since Miss Lily and I had made the arrangement, several weeks before. The whole thing had been complicated further by the inclusion of this son of hers, Bobby, whose existence I had not suspected when I first suggested the outing.

As I got ready that morning the same feeling descended on me that used to descend when I was returning to school at the close of the holidays. I had a special style of dressing then. Everything had to be done in a certain way so as to compensate for loneliness, disarm threats, make sure things would be all right. The basic principle was to do everything contrary to habit, right sock first, left sleeve first, shoe laces left over right. The more custom could be violated the safer you would be. Sometimes, in the years since then, I had been able to muffle my fears and doubts in this way. I did it again now, socks before trousers, trousers before shirt, left hand first into the shirt-sleeve.

I was there ten minutes early under the big clock at Waterloo Station. Exactly at eleven I saw them coming towards me, Miss Lily in a dark brown beret and a long suede coat, the boy in a padded anorak with various badges stitched to it and a red cap with a long peak. She smiled when she saw me, as if in relief. She looked quite unfamiliar, like a stranger at first, and I realized after a moment that this was because I had never seen her out of doors before – my top step could hardly be called out of doors. This was the world where people caught trains, had drinks together, looked in shop windows. 'This is Bobby,' she said. 'Bobby, this is Mr Cleasby.'

'Charles,' I said.

He was a pale boy, quite tall, with a bony face. He had his mother's wide mouth and a gaze just like hers, very clear and steady; but the eyes were lighter, rather an unusual colour, somewhere between green and hazel.

'I am glad you were able to come along,' I said. I smiled at him. I was managing this meeting really rather well.

'But you're not wearing a coat,' Miss Lily said to me, a remark that certainly belonged to the new, outside person she was now, rather than to Avon Secretarial Services. 'Not so much as a scarf,' she added in accents of dismay.

'I don't wear scarfs, I don't possess one,' I said, answering the smaller matter first. It was true that I had omitted to bring a coat with me, but I was wearing a woollen pullover and a tweed jacket and flannel trousers. And the morning had seemed mild enough. 'I am quite all right as I am,' I said.

Miss Lily seemed to doubt this – there was a tendency to pursing of the lips. 'You really don't take enough care of yourself. It might be chilly there, beside the sea. I mean, it's only April.'

I could not help feeling the irony of it. Horatio walked the decks in all weathers, enduring everything that sky and sea could visit upon him, from the tropics to the North Pole; and here were we, discussing the perils of an April day in Portsmouth. I made a sort of face at Bobby. 'Does your mother go on about scarfs to you too?'

'She does, yeah. Coats and hats as well. She feels cold so she thinks everyone else does.'

He spoke as if he were my age, or I were his.

'Don't you be cheeky,' Miss Lily said. She smiled at him and he smiled back and I saw that these were two people who got on well together.

'Well, we are made of sterner stuff, aren't we?' I said, man to man. I saw now that he was wearing a scarf, a blue and white one, tucked inside the collar of his anorak.

While I was waiting to get the tickets I fell to wondering what it really signified, that expression, to take care of yourself. Of course Miss Lily had meant nourishing food and wrapping yourself up. But that is not the self, only the body; harm is done to the self before we have a say in it; after that the choices are limited. It was in order to help me take care of myself that poor Penhas steered me back to Horatio.

When I turned back to them, I seemed to notice Miss Lily all over again. In that great glass hangar of a station, with its strange, bleak plenitude of light and strains of vaguely martial music, she looked bright-eyed and ready for anything in her jaunty beret. The other people I saw moving through those light-filled spaces seemed faint and somehow glaucous, leached of colour, but she was deepened. Bobby stood close beside her, solemn and still. For some reason he had turned his cap back to front – the long peak lay over the back of his neck. His eyes were on a dishevelled pigeon that had found its way in and was strutting about among the feet of passers-by.

Nothing much was said in the train. There were others in our compartment and the presence of strangers imposed a constraint on us, who were not much more than strangers ourselves. She was sitting opposite and sometimes our eyes met. Bobby fished out a folded magazine from his anorak pocket. It had a picture of a dinosaur on the outside and seemed to be mostly pictures inside too. We got sandwiches and tea and a Coke for Bobby from a trolley that passed down the corridor.

Portsmouth was distinctly chilly. A cold wind straight from the sea met us as we stepped from the station, striking through the poor defences of my jacket and pullover. My eyes watered. Naturally I denied any slightest discomfort when Miss Lily – inevitably – remarked on this nasty wind and asked me if I didn't feel perished. No, no, very bracing, very refreshing. It got even colder as we approached the harbour; Miss Lily tucked her chin into the collar of her coat; Bobby took some quick steps forward and then back as if casting for a scent. He was still wearing his cap the wrong way round.

It is not possible to go aboard HMS *Victory* and wander about as and when you want; you have to go in a group with a guide and these tours take place at regular times through the day. We had an hour to wait before the next one and I suggested a visit to the Naval Museum on the quayside. This houses the whole splendid story of our wars at sea, from the timbers of Henry V's flagship the *Grace Dieu*, to maps of naval operations in the Gulf War. But in view of the limited time we naturally made for the Nelson Gallery.

It was warmer in here but the sea light followed us, striking through the walls of glass that ran round the gallery on three sides – the same desolate light he must have seen on so many days, the light that lay around him as he waited that March day at Chatham to join his first ship. We mounted to the upper gallery, where the figureheads and pennants and cannon are displayed. I pointed out the ensigns and flags hanging there and explained to Miss Lily and Bobby what they stood for, whom they had belonged to. They always stirred my blood and quickened my imagination, not these naval standards only but all flags, all insignia of battle, the tattered banners of obscure regiments collecting dust in country churches, the monuments to the fallen in quiet squares, with their scrolled lists of the dead, the poignancy of these symbols wreathed in sacrifice and mourning.

Overhead and on the walls all round the emblems hung motionless. I pointed out the ensigns on their poles, the white ones and the red, some with the Union Jack set in the upper left-hand corner, some without. 'Do you know why that is?' I asked Bobby. He shook his head. His eyes seemed dazed, perhaps from the flooding of light through the huge plates of glass that surrounded us. 'They started to include the Union Jack after 1707,' I said. 'That was the date of Union with Scotland.'

I felt cheerful and happy explaining these things. The gallery was empty, we had it for the moment to ourselves. The things that had been plaguing me, my restlessness and foreboding, my failure so far to extricate him, haul him free from the swamps of Naples 1799, all this receded and I felt at peace. Moreover, the light had changed, a thin sunshine had struck through the cloud and through our glass walls and it fell here and there among the objects on show. Faint and pallid in itself, it brought brilliance to the painted figureheads, the pitted snouts of the cannon, the pink-faced uniformed effigies lining the gallery. I pointed out the Broad Pennant Horatio would have flown, as commander of a squadron, when he went into action at Cape St Vincent, and the two flags, one below the other, that made up his favourite signal, the first in vertical stripes of red, white and blue, the second a blue cross on a white background: *Engage the enemy more closely.*

'He was a great believer in close engagement.' I looked at Miss Lily as I said this, wanting her to share my feeling for the impetuous genius of Horatio, for the scenes of heroism that had taken place beneath these vivid emblems. However, she seemed no more than politely interested. It was when I glanced at Bobby that I saw where my true audience was. He was chewing some substance now, very slowly. There was no mistaking his interest in these flags. In that pale face of his, with its thin ridges of bone at the temples and cheeks, the greenish eyes were serious and intent. 'How close could they get?'

'They could still go on firing broadsides when they were practically touching.'

'But it is better to avoid fighting altogether,' Miss Lily said. 'Things can generally be settled by a bit of common sense and nobody gets hurt.'

'We couldn't have settled Napoleon's hash by any amount of common sense.'

'There's always somebody's hash to settle, isn't there? That's one thing that never changes. Might be the French, might be the man next door. It's the Bedouin syndrome.'

'What on earth is that?'

'Me against my brother, me and my brother against our cousin, my family against the rest of the tribe, my tribe against everyone who isn't Bedouin. That sums it all up for me, all these flags and things.'

'Common sense is the virtue of the common man,' I said, 'and that is one thing Horatio Nelson wasn't.' I was rather vexed with Miss Lily for these inappropriate remarks of hers among the emblems and engines of battle. 'Where did you pick up this Bedouin business?' I asked her.

'Heard it on the radio. Years ago now.' She was looking from Bobby to me with the expression of mild obstinacy that characterized her. 'It stayed in my mind,' she said. 'Because it's true, that's why.'

'We had a different style of fighting,' I said to Bobby. 'The French gunners preferred to fight at long distance, cutting away our masts and rigging and so disabling our ships. Our tactic was always to get in close, taking the enemy's fire at first, until we were near enough to do massive damage. *Lay a Frenchman close enough and you will always beat him.* One of our favourite sayings. And by God it is true. I got that saying from Locker.'

Bobby was still chewing, even more slowly now. 'Who's Locker?'

I looked smiling at Miss Lily, expecting her to answer. But she said nothing at all. Her face wore a slight frown, as if she were puzzled about something. This silence on her part struck me as distinctly odd. She must know who Locker was, I had referred to him several times in the earlier sections of my book. At this moment of uncertainty I was again aware of the sunlight, but now as a source of confusion, my mind wavered among real and fabricated things, the staring figureheads, the stiff models of midshipmen and marines, the woman and boy before me. I knew I had to be careful how I answered. 'Horatio's friend and mentor,' I said. 'He was captain of the frigate *Lowestoffe*, 32 guns, which Horatio joined in April '77 as an eighteen-year-old lieutenant. Locker was forty-six and they became lifelong friends. Horatio had a great gift for friendship.' I was aware of the difference as I said this; I had no friends at all. But of course it was the price one paid for being on the shadow side.

The time for our visit to the *Victory* was drawing near. We left the museum, walked back along the quay and joined the party waiting to go aboard, about a dozen people loosely grouped in the shadow of the mighty hull. No sign of a guide as yet.

She towered above us, fresh-painted in black and pale gold, stripped of sail but fully rigged, the Union Jack at her bow, the white ensign at her stern. I had seen her a number of times over the years but the sight thrilled me again now, the exact intervals of her gun ports, the scarlet and gilt of her figurehead, the fretted window-frames of the captain's cabin – his, Horatio's cabin. In this splendid ship the nation honours the time of her greatness, now gone for ever, when she was mistress of the seas, honours too her greatest hero, a man fashioned for heroism just as this great wooden ship with its tiers of guns was fashioned for destruction. Instruments both . . . *They cut pieces off him, didn't they?* Miss Lily's question came at me again, uninvited, deeply unwelcome. I was turning to her, perhaps with some vague idea of expunging the offence by the sight of the offender, when the guide appeared at the top of the companion-ladder – he had been lurking within all this time – and beckoned us to come up, recommending caution as he did so.

A motley crew we clearly were, now that we converged on the ladder and I was able to take more note. Two couples who looked married; a younger couple who might or might not have been, two stout elderly ladies with identical-looking grey perms in company with a younger, talkative man, perhaps a son or nephew; a woman, short and whiskery, with notebook and pencil at the ready; and a silent tall man on his own. In anoraks and overcoats and hats and scarfs they had come together on this cold day to pay their respects to Horatio. However, we were unfortunate in the constitution of this group, I sensed it from the start.

'Up you go,' the son or nephew said in jovial tones to the

ladies he was escorting. He glanced behind and gave the rest of us a wink. I hate these self-appointed jokers and professional jolly chaps. Urged on by him, the unwieldy permed ladies started up the ladder. They mounted with excruciating slowness, making the rest of us wait. At the top, in the confined space of the upper gun-deck, we reassembled in a ring round our guide. Some members of the group made exaggerated sounds of exertion, especially one of the older couples, who had already been infected by the joker. 'Mind your head, dear,' the husband said, as we ducked under the beams. 'You never know when you might need it.' It is always the case; you start off with one fool, then the spirit of emulation sets in and you end up with several.

The guide was a sandy-haired, square-faced man in a buttoned-up double-breasted blazer with coronet and shield stitched in blue and red on his breast pocket. 'Well, here we are on HMS *Victory*, Lord Nelson's flagship,' he said. 'I am intending to conduct the tour in English, if that's okay with everyone.'

'We was sort of hoping you would do it in French,' one of the perms said. Everyone laughed at this, except me and serious Bobby and the lady with the notebook. Miss Lily laughed with the others and I was sorry to see this.

This laughter, in which she shared, was the real beginning of my suffering that day, because the guide too, as we descended to the bowels of the ship from deck to deck, stooping lower and lower as head room diminished, he too turned out to be a comedian, delivering his commentary in a stale mix of joke and drama, no doubt derived from a hundred past tours. The joking was blasphemy, the drama was superfluous. On this ship where Horatio fought his last battle and took his last breath, all the imagination needs is the stimulus of facts.

In regard to these the guide was competent but not wholly reliable. He said Horatio was 'just turned twelve' when he joined the *Raisonnable* as midshipman, whereas in fact he was twelve years and three months when he was entered on the muster-roll and nearly twelve and a half when he actually joined the ship.

Then he told us that the firing-rate on board the *Victory* was a shot a minute, whereas in fact our gun-crews at their best could deliver a broadside every seventy-five seconds, the French needing almost twice as long, a crucial element in the ultimate victory.

Nor did he succeed very well in conveying to his audience, accustomed to central heating and refrigerated food and the privacy of bathrooms, the nature of daily life on board a ship like this, the suffocating promiscuity of the lower gun-deck where several hundred men, among them a good number of disturbed or violent persons, lived in a proximity from which there was no escape, sleeping in hammocks slung from the beams and eating at mess-tables put up between the guns. At sea, with the gun ports closed, it would be dark and hot, the air would be thick with the stench of unwashed humanity. And the latrines, only six of them, out in the open, in the bows, six 'seats of ease' for upwards of five hundred men . . .

In spite of the guide's shortcomings I did nothing to interrupt him, but now and again shook my head at Miss Lily. At one point, my forbearance growing thin, I drew her and Bobby a little apart, in a darker space between the guns, and began to mutter some of the essential facts. But Miss Lily was only half listening to me, she was trying at the same time to hear what the guide was saying. He was telling them about the procedure for burial at sea.

'They put two cannon-balls at the foot, to weigh the body down. Then the tailor is brought in and he stitches the corpse into the hammock, beginning with the feet. When he gets to the face – '

'Excuse me, how many guns were there on the ship?' This was the lady with the notebook, she was in a world of her own. It was the third time she had interrupted the guide with a question, severely factual, quite unrelated to the discourse of the moment and always timed to ruin some high point in the narrative.

'One hundred and four, madam. The *Victory* was a first-rate,

202

and a first-rate ship-of-the-line had to have a hundred guns as minimum.'

She wrote this down, peering at her notebook in the light from the open gun port, just as she had peered a short while previously when writing down the cost of the ship's construction, £63,000 in the money of the time, about fifty million today. What could she want with this information? She wore thick glasses and there was a whiskery glint about her jaws. It was pathetic, really.

I began my muttering again, trying to secure Miss Lily's interest, divert her attention from the guide. 'That piece of rope there, you see it is blackened at one end, it has been dipped in tar in order to harden it.'

'Why did they do that?' Bobby asked. In the half-light I saw his eyes fixed on me. Miss Lily had moved away. She was listening to the guide, who was still rambling on about sea burial:

'When he gets level with the nose, he puts his needle through it as a final test of life before stitching the canvas over the face. If the face twitches or the eyes water . . . I can give you a practical demonstration if you like. The hammock is here before us, I'll be the tailor. Any volunteers?'

Laughter. Again I see Miss Lily laughing among the others. She belongs in the crowd . . . The laughter is cut short by the lady with the notebook, who this time performs a service. 'How much canvas was used in the sails?'

'Madam, roughly four acres of canvas were needed to make the *Victory*'s sails.'

General expressions of astonishment. Bobby was still standing close and he was looking at me, not the guide. On an impulse hardly understood at the time I drew him further from the group, away from the light of the gun port. I began in low tones to tell him about the loading procedure, illustrating with gestures in the dimness the action of pushing a charge into the bore, then ramming it home, then jabbing a stiff wire down the vent to pierce the flannel cartridge before priming and firing.

It was strange, I forgot myself completely, acting this out for Bobby. I explained, in no more than a murmur, the mechanism of the flintlock, the spark that ignited the priming.

'Flintlock.' He lingered on the word. I saw the gleam of his eyes in the dimness. He was still wearing his cap back to front in that ridiculous fashion. 'Did the flint always make a spark? What happened if the flint didn't make the spark?'

'They used a piece of hemp as a match. There is a piece of it over here.'

We moved a little farther away. We were standing close together, speaking very quietly so as not to disturb the others. His face was turned up to me, very pale, glimmering slightly. He was looking towards the source of light, the open gun port and the 32-pounder cannon within it, resting massively there on its blocked wheels. It suddenly seemed to me that I knew Bobby's face from somewhere long ago, it was the face of someone I had once known well. I felt a certain threat to my balance as I stood there on that motionless deck, then something more, a feeling of urgency, an impulse to raise my voice, speak a loud warning. I had to go on talking, I could not look away from his face.

'This is a kind of shrine now. You must try to picture it as it was when the ship was in action, the heat and the din, the deck heaving, the guns roaring, the crews barefoot so as not to slip in the blood, the powder-monkeys running up with cartridges from the magazines.'

'They were boys, weren't they?'

'Boys like you. Younger than you. They had to be small and light to get up and down the ladders quickly. Men and boys alike wore bands around their heads to keep the sweat – '

'Protect their ears.'

'What?'

'I put it in my project. The teacher told us. They wore the bands over their ears instead of earplugs.'

'Quite right, your teacher is quite right. Not that cotton headbands were much good, the men would bleed from the ears

204

after the battle, quite copiously, yes, gushes of blood, did your teacher tell you that? No? Well, you can put something in your project that he doesn't know or at any rate doesn't say.'

'He says our sailors were the best in the world and we had better officers.'

I could not remember when I had last looked into another human face for as long as I had now looked into this boy's. Again I felt the impulse of warning, again I blunted it, held it off with speech, but in a voice not like my own.

'And then there are the types of shot, cannon-balls for damage to the body of the ship, chains to cut through the rigging, grapeshot for killing the crews . . .'

I could feel my larynx working and was aware of my mouth stretching and contracting but it was as if I were listening to someone else on a bad line. Then I suppose I stopped talking altogether, there was a sort of resonant hush, faint and steady, like a distant sea.

Through this the guide's voice came, from somewhere behind me. I wrenched my gaze from the boy's face, looked again at the tarred rope's end, the hemp match, the grapeshot in cloth bags, strangely like testicles, lying on their racks behind the thrusting black muzzle of the cannon: things placed here for display, for devotion. It was true what in my agitation I had said to Bobby. This was a shrine, a memorial to forms of warfare long superseded. Here, in the still heart of the ship, one knew it. The *Victory,* so painted and burnished, so scrupulously maintained, was dead.

'Three tons of metal on wheels,' the guide said behind me. 'Imagine the recoil of it, imagine what happened to the men in its way if once it got free.'

How much time had passed in this talk with Bobby I had no definite idea; not very much, I suppose – no one paid any attention to us when we moved back to rejoin the group. Miss Lily glanced at us and smiled. After some minutes more we went down to the cockpit in the orlop, where the dying Horatio was carried. And now at last there was unity among us and harmony of feeling, an absence of that coarse human propensity to belittle things, bring them down to our own mediocre level. No one was so grossly insensitive as to make jokes down here, not even that clown of a nephew or son.

He was carried down to die among the dying. Space was made for him in a narrow corner. The pallet he died on is still there and a low lamp is kept burning. He received his wound while the issue was still in doubt, but he was alive when they came to him with the news of the victory, the greatest British naval victory in history, the annihilation of the enemy that he had hoped for, prayed for. Some of the words of that last prayer he wrote before the battle ran through my mind: *May the great God, whom I worship, grant to my country and for the benefit of Europe in general a great and glorious victory . . .*

The prayer was answered. The Franco-Spanish fleet was destroyed, their dead and wounded five times ours – the French lost twice as many men by drowning alone as we lost in the whole action. A triumph to ease the pains of his wound, the approach of death. *Thank God I have done my duty.* As we stood there in silence, the spirit of devotion rose in me, as it always had in this place, finally setting to rest the disturbance I had felt earlier, whispering to Bobby on the dark gun-deck. I knew in that moment that I had been foolish and perverse to think this great ship was dead. Our small group, standing in awkward silence at the place where the hero died, was part of a vast annual pilgrimage. Millions of people had stood where we were standing in this obscure corner of the ship, far below the waterline. Millions . . . That was hardly to be called a death. He had not died, he never will, not while our country's great past is still remembered.

The tour finished on the quarter-deck at the point where he received his wound. How vast the world seemed after the closeness and darkness below decks, how vast it must have seemed to them on that morning of Trafalgar as they prepared for battle. We stood round the polished brass plaque, flush with the deck, marking his exact position when the ball struck him.

'Captain Hardy was walking with him,' the guide said. 'Hardy was a big man, a good foot taller than Nelson. More of a target, you might say. It's the luck of the draw, isn't it? They were walking side by side here on the quarter-deck. Ten paces forward, ten paces back.'

He took a few stiff paces to dramatize the event.

'They turned here, at the ladder-way. Then they started out towards the stern . . .'

With a sudden gesture he opened the palm of his right hand and showed us what he had been holding there: a lead ball, looking too small to do much harm, like a small marble that a child might play with.

'The admiral was struck by one of these.'

I thought this was a pretty cheap piece of showmanship, but there was no doubt it impressed the others, except the woman with the notebook, who was, as I have said, in a world of her own and about to prove it yet again. My feeling of hostility towards the guide returned when I saw them riveted on him, Miss Lily included. Paunchy, undistinguished-looking, not totally reliable as to the facts, he yet could command attention, hold the stage. He had seduced her away from me. But not Bobby . . .

'Entered by the left shoulder,' the guide said. He was still displaying the ball in the palm of his hand. 'Passed through one lung and lodged in – '

'Excuse me,' the woman with the notebook said, 'how much rope went into the rigging?'

A muttered exclamation from someone, I think the tall, lonely man, at this crassly inopportune question. The guide looked a bit glassy, as if he had taken a punch. However, he behaved well, I had to admit it. His big moment had been ruined, but he showed no more than a laborious politeness.

'Twenty-seven miles of rigging, madam, on HMS *Victory*. It lodged in the admiral's spine.'

On this anticlimactic note and with a chorus of thank-yous, the guided tour came to an end. I remember little more about the day. Bobby wanted a hamburger, so we went to a McDonald's and all had one. I enjoyed mine but I did not say much. I felt ill at ease and over-exposed among the shiny surfaces and bright colours. Miss Lily was chatty – it seemed she had enjoyed herself. But it was the other members of the group she talked mainly about, not Horatio; she had noticed all sorts of things about them which had quite escaped me, and formed opinions as to their occupations, material condition in life, character and degree of personal fulfilment. Bobby, I remember, ate with gusto, pale face intent over his plate, cap still back to front.

We had the compartment to ourselves during the train journey home. Miss Lily was still quite talkative. She had been affected by the drama of Horatio's last moments, but it was not so much the heroic sacrifice that moved her as the sad cutting short of a promising love.

'They could have had another twenty years together,' she said. 'He would have retired, they had already bought a house in the country. I haven't all that much time for Emma Hamilton, I mean she wasn't my sort, too much of a show-off. But think what she must have felt when the news came. She had no friends in England, she had no secure income, she had a young child to bring up on her own.'

Her mouth had thinned with feeling as she spoke. I could see that she was acknowledging something she felt she shared with Emma. I personally felt the situations to be distinctly different but this was not the moment to say so, not with Bobby sitting there.

'If they had really thought so much of him they would have carried out his last wishes for her,' Miss Lily said. 'I read all about it before we came here to Portsmouth. One of the last things he said was that he left Lady Hamilton and their daughter as a legacy to his country. He said it with his dying breath. It was the only thing he asked them for. And what did they do? They left her to die abroad, completely penniless.'

'She was a very extravagant woman,' I said. 'Her life in Naples hadn't exactly taught her restraint. She was addicted to gambling and in her later years she had what we would now call a drink problem.'

'And so?' She had flushed a little and was looking at me with that particular sort of steadiness that I recognized as the prelude to indignation.

'Well,' I said, 'she was a difficult woman to help.'

'Charles, don't mind me saying this, but you can be really dodgy sometimes when it comes to discussing things. What's the point of saying she was difficult to help when you know perfectly well that they didn't even try to help her? It was his dearest wish and they just let her go to the dogs and the child with her. They were ready to give him a big funeral and put up statues to him but not to recognize the woman he loved, the mother of his child. It was the same thing when he was dead as when he was alive. They went on cutting pieces off him. Don't you think there's something terribly wrong with that?'

Asking me to share a sense of wrongness was one of Miss Lily's favourite ploys in argument and I generally resisted on grounds of principle. But here, in the enclosed space of the compartment, with her earnest face so close before me, it was more than usually difficult. She had made progress in debate in these months, I had to admit that; she had become formidable.

'But really, don't you think so?' she said now. 'They didn't want to honour him as a man, that's all I'm saying. I mean, they didn't even let her attend his funeral, did they?'

It was Bobby who saved the day for me, relieved me from the need to answer, showing again that reverence for facts as opposed to sentiments that I had noticed in him earlier. 'What did they do with him?' he asked.

'Do with him?'

'How did they get him back? I mean, the *Victory* took a long time to get back home, didn't she? Did they put him in a coffin?'

'They had to preserve the body,' I said. 'They stripped him and put him in spirits.'

209

'What spirits?'

'Brandy, I think it was.'

I saw that a smile had appeared on Miss Lily's face, the curving smile I liked, with her mouth just sufficiently open to show the white edges of her teeth. Her indignation was forgotten.

'Cognac,' she said. 'Must have been French. There you are now, that's what you call a turn-up for the books. He hated the French so much and he was brought home pickled in a barrel of French brandy.'

Bobby's stare, its solemn character unaffected by his mother's levity, came back into my mind that night, when I was alone again at home. He was a boy for facts. One fact which the notebook woman had not elicited and the guide had forgotten to tell us, to my mind the most staggering of all, was that more than two thousand oak trees had gone into the making of the *Victory*'s hull, she was a floating forest. On that scale the British fleet at the battle of Trafalgar must have represented something like fifty thousand oaks, roughly two million years of oak tree life. Bobby was twelve, his sense of scale and number would be developed enough, I resolved to impart these facts to him when I saw him again so that he could incorporate them in his project.

This resolution made me think of his face and particularly his eyes, his awe in that dim place, my recognition of him as someone I had known and that strange paralysis of faculties which had descended on me. I had wanted the world to continue, I had wanted to shout a warning. But the memory of this was easy and calm now, it was like recalling an anecdote. Miss Lily had glanced at us when we rejoined the group, with an expression difficult to read, approval perhaps, two men getting together. Perhaps something else altogether.

The faces, mother's and son's, thinned away and I was left with a memory of that drab and disparate group standing round the memorial plaque. They saw Horatio as a being expressing their own humanity and aspirations. Totally wrong, of course. He was not an ordinary man translated into greatness by particular circumstances; he was a bright angel. He is unaccountable, un-judgeable by the standards of those who gather at the place of his death – except for me, except for me.

At 1.25 p.m. on the 21st of October 1805, a French sharp-shooter perched aloft in the topmast of the *Redoubtable* drew a bead on your starred and medalled breast. The ball struck you as you were about to take your third step from the companion-ladder towards the stern. It pierced your lung and broke your back and you fell silently to the deck. At that precise moment, all around you on the upper deck, and on the gun-decks below, men were screaming and dying. Only half an hour before, at almost exactly the same point, your secretary John Scott had been cut in two by a round shot. But it is your death that we commemorate, there is only one plaque. Many were crucified, but there is only one cross.

20

I let six weeks go by before resigning from the Club; time enough, I thought, for the decision to seem considered, deliberate. They were weeks of waiting, for what exactly I didn't know – certainly not for the moment when I would be writing to inform Pratt-Smithers of my decision to cancel my subscription. That had been my intention, worthy of Horatio himself in its unswerving firmness, from the moment I realized the implications of those empty seats.

I didn't attend the Club in the interval, I didn't want to see any of them again, and certainly not Hugo – I wanted no deepening of acquaintance there. A man who could work behind the bar in the Nelson Club, have Horatio's image constantly before him for two nights every week and then go and pin up an effeminate pop-star on his wall. He and I had survived something that night. It was enough.

No, the waiting went on, it continued after my resignation, though taking on some extra quality afterwards, some quality of dread, something that disturbed my nights rather than my days – these were still absorbed in the close study of that June week in Naples in 1799. I had not lost hope of being the one to clear his name. I was reading A. T. Mahan's account of those days, contained in his 1897 life of Nelson and in his subsequent articles in the *English Historical Review*, defending Horatio from charges of fraud. Mahan is the great champion of Horatio's honour and argues the case very strenuously and forcibly. Chief opponent among his contemporaries is F. P. Badham, a waspish close reasoner, dangerously precise in the matter of dates and times. These two, with names so similar, the impetuous and patriotic Mahan and the lucid, sardonic Badham, had come to seem like allegorical figures to me, Virtue and Vice personified.

This, as I say, kept my days busy. My paper had failed, I was resigning from the Club, but there was still my book. Miss Lily came as usual on Tuesday and Friday evenings. A week after our visit to Portsmouth she brought me a burgundy-coloured woollen scarf, which she had knitted herself. 'I had a lot of wool left over,' she said, 'just lying around, taking up space.' Bales of it, she implied. All her gifts were the result of some surplus, or so she said, and all described in the same way, hasty but not shy – she always looked straight at me when she spoke and I was finding myself, as time passed, more able to look firmly back at her, meet her eyes. Nowadays, we looked at each other when we spoke together.

'You said, you know, that you hadn't got one.'

As always I found thanks difficult. Besides, some part of me resented this attempt to change my habits. What I had actually said was that I never wore them. The scarf lay there, over the back of a chair, till the following Monday. Then, noticing it again, on an impulse, I picked it up and held it against my face.

I was thinking at that time about suggesting a trip to the Maritime Museum at Greenwich one Sunday afternoon. They have a whole section devoted to Horatio there. With the days getting warmer now it would be a pleasant outing. We could walk across the park or along the river and have tea somewhere in Greenwich. She could bring Bobby too, now that a precedent had been set. In any case I had a certain feeling of tenderness for him after those moments of communion between us on the lower gun-deck. But the days passed and I did not ask her, I found reasons for delay. Instead of taking the plunge I made more and more elaborate plans for a time when the plunge had been taken. We could go to Burnham Thorpe in Norfolk, Horatio's birthplace, and stay at the village inn, the Nelson Arms. On that occasion Bobby could be left with his gran. It would mean a weekend together . . .

With all this to occupy my mind the General Election and the Labour landslide went over my head. I did not know of it till the Friday evening, when Miss Lily told me. I had forgotten altogether it was voting-day, impaled as I was on the twin prongs of Mahan and Badham, trying to establish to my own satisfaction whether Cardinal Ruffo had indeed withdrawn the Russian troops from their advanced positions on the morning of the 26th of June 1799, as the ascerbic Badham maintained, whether he had merely threatened to do so, or whether there had been neither the act nor the threat, as generous Mahan appeared to be asserting. It was a crucial point: if there had been no threat, Horatio had been under no pressure, would not have needed to mask his purposes, trick the rebels into surrender so as to hand them over to their Bourbon king.

She was elated by the election results, but I didn't want to talk about it, I didn't find it interesting, I didn't know what any of them looked like. I still had the horror of blank screens which had been with me since my illness, so there was no television-set anywhere in the house; and for some months now I had not been bothering with newspapers. Miss Lily, of course, could not forbear to comment.

'Well, you are strange in some ways, Charles, that's all I'm saying. You wouldn't know Tony Blair if you passed him in the street, but you'd know an admiral that fell off his perch two hundred years ago.'

'He never fell off anything, he is immortal,' I said, but it was a waste of breath. She used habitual phrases and did not think beyond them; it did not occur to her that she was speaking of Horatio as if he were a dead canary.

That was about the sum of our political conversation. After that we resumed work. But the book was giving me less pleasure now. It is from around this time that I date the real beginnings of the dissatisfaction that would lead me in the end to suspend work on the book altogether. The further I went ahead with his life, the more my failure to clear up the Naples business weighed on me. It was in the May of 1803, on the 16th, that the Napoleonic War began, after the brief interval of peace afforded by the Treaty of Amiens signed the previous March. Two days later, as Commander-in-Chief Mediterranean, he hoisted his flag in HMS *Victory* and the run-up to Trafalgar began. How could I take him through these days of unparalleled glory while still leaving unresolved in his wake the question of his conduct in Naples? It was not a question of some violent excess or tempestuous love, such as could easily be accommodated in the heroic life. It was a question of cold-blooded falsehood and fraud. This would never do for the British. A wily hero might suit the Greeks, but we are a straightforward people, detesting perfidy in all its forms. No, he had to be cleared.

As the weeks passed, and the anniversary of the events themselves came closer and closer, I dashed myself repeatedly against these rocks of the past, made up of truth and lies and unsupported assertions, and fell back bruised. Mahan and Badham, allegorical twins, stalked mouthing and gesturing through my days and nights. Whether Ruffo had actually moved the troops was in a way immaterial; it would have been enough that Horatio believed he intended to do so. In fact, to withdraw them would have been the proper thing if Horatio was offering to break the treaty, because they had been moved to this favourable position on the 23rd at the request of the rebels themselves, in anticipation of their coming out, to protect them from the vengeance of the populace, the savage *lazzaroni*, one of the most bloodthirsty mobs in history, passionately faithful to King Ferdinand, murderously disposed towards his republican enemies. Natural and honourable then, if the treaty was to be abrogated, to restore the *status quo ante*. And Horatio *was* threatening to abrogate the treaty. There is his 'Declaration', sent into the forts on the morning of the 25th, signed by his own hand, in which he acquaints the rebels that he will not permit them to embark or quit those places, that they must surrender to his Majesty's royal mercy.

The following morning the cardinal despatched his ultimatum

215

to Horatio that he would withdraw the Russian troops and leave the English to conquer the enemy on their own. Or so Badham asserts – Mahan denies it. On that morning, the 26th, a Thursday, I woke at daybreak and the questions fastened on me again, buzzed in my ears like flies. Why would Ruffo write thus if he didn't believe Horatio was about to break the treaty? Even if, as Mahan maintains, there was no document at all, even if there was no more evidence than the resumé of the cardinal's intentions, made in retrospect by his secretary Sacchinelli, even so, would it not have put Horatio under pressure to seek some less direct way of repossessing the forts? There *was* a change of attitude on his part between the 25th and the 26th, no one denies that. He gave an assurance to Ruffo on the 26th that he would not oppose the embarkation of the rebels. This document exists. In Badham's view this was tantamount to an endorsement of the treaty as a whole, or so the rebels would have understood it – they would have believed they would be allowed to sail for France. In Mahan's view the document referred only to the embarkation and nothing further, and the rebels knew this perfectly well. The crux of the thing was there. *What were they given to understand?* Would they have come out only to sit and wait in the crowded transports? Wait for what?

His Majesty's royal mercy . . . It occurred to me now that I had not completed the cast of players. There was still the royal couple, Ferdinand and Maria Carolina. The prospect of some action came as a relief. I got out of bed, dressed in the dimness and went along to the kitchen, where I made tea, observing each stage in the process carefully. I took the teapot and my special mug with the double C on it into the study. Clean sheet, carefully sharpened pencil.

Ferdinand IV, King of Naples and Sicily. Born in 1751, the third son of Charles III of Spain. The eldest son was mad – he had to be restrained from assaulting any woman on sight; the second was feeble-minded, quite incapable of rule; Ferdinand was not mad, but from childhood on he was kept ignorant and simple so that the government of Naples could continue

*to be directed from Spain through Charles III's ministers. He grew up
without any call being made on his mind or judgement, his companions
were people of the lowest sort, and his speech was like theirs, the street-
language of Naples. At the age of seventeen he married Maria Carolina
of Austria, a woman far more intelligent and forceful than himself.*

*He was strong and active, and his cramped energies found release in
rough games, practical jokes, above all in hunting and fishing. Hunting
was his ruling passion, but it was hunting without risk. He would drag
his ministers with him for dawn-to-dusk sessions of slaughter. Standing
in a brick-built shooting box, he would wait for his keepers to drive the
game to him. He was a crack shot – a visiting diplomat recorded that in
a hundred shots the King only missed once. He was an expert fisherman
and sailor, and delighted to run races with boatmen out in the gulf.
Dressed as a fisherman, he would sell his catch on the market, haggling
over the price in Neapolitan dialect. The common people loved him, they
thought of him as one of them. Unprepossessing in appearance, with a
low forehead, a huge nose and a pendulous lower lip.*

*He had a rough, good humour when things were going smoothly, but
he hated anything to be required of him, any opposition or difficulty, any
mental effort. He avoided the trouble of having to sign documents by
giving one of his ministers, the Marquese Tannucci, a stamp with his
signature on it. He was never required to consult anything but his own
pleasures. His manners were gross, even for that age. Sir William
Hamilton, who was often in attendance on the King, relates in a letter
how Ferdinand, after a hearty meal, would lay a hand on his belly and
remark that having eaten well he now needed a good easing of his bowels.
He would choose some of those around him for the privilege of keeping
him company during the performance. Infantile, cowardly, vindictive when
crossed, totally lacking in conscience or compunction . . .*

Attacked by restlessness at this point, I got up and fell to my
usual pacing from bookshelves to wall. The title this time was *The
Wooden World* by N. A. M. Rodger, and the word was *Wooden*.
Finger on the letters, six paces, palms against the wall, thumbs
mustn't touch. This was the King of Naples and Sicily, this the
man who came out across the bay in his royal barge, sweating in

his black velvet and gold lace, to thank his one-armed, one-eyed saviour, the Hero of the Nile, on that September day in 1798, while the bands played and the white birds flew up from their cages into the sky. Infantile. That was the key. It was a ruined child that clambered aboard to make you that speech of welcome and thanks. It was a ruined child to whom you delivered the Neapolitan Jacobins. The past is littered with ruined children. *His Majesty's Royal mercy* . . . But that was not it either: it was not to him but to the Queen that they were really delivered. Her turn now, the last member of the cast.

Maria Carolina. Born 1752, daughter of the Austrian empress Maria Teresa. At sixteen she was married to Ferdinand, who was one year older. She bore him eighteen children, of whom eight survived. Her sister, Marie Antoinette, married Louis XVI of France and went to the guillotine some months after him, in October 1793, confirming Maria Carolina's fear and hatred of republicanism and all forms of liberal dissent, especially if they came with a French stamp on them. They had this in common, she and Horatio . . .

Devout and superstitious — she wrote prayers on scraps of paper and tucked them into her stays or sometimes swallowed them. In marked contrast to Ferdinand, she had regal manners, a grasp of European politics and the will to rule. On the birth of her first son in 1775 she claimed her right to sit in the Council of State and within a few months was the effective ruler of the kingdom. She was subject to violent swings of emotion. On the few occasions that Ferdinand attempted to oppose her will she screamed and raged at him and drove him to flight. On that day of your triumphant arrival in the Bay of Naples she was forty-five years old. She had never been regarded as a beauty. A glassy eye, a frozen look, the long Hapsburg jaw, a figure at once massive and gaunt. But she had a grand manner. You were impressed with her, touched by her dignity, and her distress at the danger from France, the common enemy. Truly a daughter of Maria Teresa, you said. What did you mean by that? You were moved because she placed her trust in you, the one man who could save her kingdom and her person. And she, what did she think of you, what did she really think?

The question gave me pause. There was no way of knowing. She needed the ships and the guns, the backing of Britain. Horatio was a hero, she flattered him – he was always susceptible to flattery, she would have known that. And in those June days of the following year which were giving me so much trouble she would have known something more. The admiral was deeply in love with the Lady Ambassadress, who was also her private ambassadress – a flatterer too and a hater of the French. Love, trust, flattery – not easy to disappoint the expectations of two such women, not when you share the hatred too.

Truly a daughter of Maria Teresa. Somewhere in my notes I had an extract of a letter of Hamilton's in which he spoke of this inheritance. After some minutes I found it: *It is well to own, and indeed the Emperor Joseph told me so himself when at Naples, that all the daughters of Maria Teresa had very tender hearts susceptible to sudden and violent impressions.*

A hysteric married too young to a ruined child, putting it in basic terms. This was the royal couple who enlisted your services and gained your devotion, to whose mercy the rebels were delivered. However obscure the circumstances in which they were prevailed upon to surrender, there is no doubt at all about what happened to them subsequently. They were embarked on the transports and kept there in the bay. On the 28th the letters Horatio had been waiting for arrived from the Court at Palermo, conferring full powers on him. Who had these powers before? A question raised by Badham. Presumably it was Ruffo.

Your first move was to order the boats with the rebels on board to be hauled under the guns of the warships. Some of the leaders were taken off and put in irons. The people who had left the forts during the truce were summoned to give themselves up on pain of death. Ruffo protested, then backed down, and with this all hopes for the rebels were at an end.

The King sailed in with his suite on the 10th of July and established his Court aboard your flagship, the *Foudroyant*. He held levees on the quarter-deck and amused himself by shooting passing seagulls. In the balmy evenings Emma would dress as Britannia and stand on the poop to sing to the assembled company, beginning, naturally with 'Rule, Britannia'.

The picture came irresistibly into my mind as I sat there. The warmth of the evening, the aromatic hillsides and the stinking city blending their scents together, wafting them across the bay; the shifting reflections in the water, with here and there dead floating gulls attesting the King's marksmanship; Emma resplendent on the poop in helmet and trident and billowing robe.

> *When Britain first, at Heaven's command,*
> *Arose from out the azure main,*
> *This was the charter of the land,*
> *And guardian angels sung this strain . . .*

The swelling notes must have filled the hearts of those on board and carried far across the bay – to the sailors of the British fleet in their hammocks, to the republicans in the cramped and insanitary prison ships where they had been confined for two weeks now, perhaps to the city itself, where the faithful *lazzaroni* were continuing to cut up, roast and eat suspected French sympathizers.

The royal justice began to operate soon after this. All through the summer the executions continued. Some went to the block; others, women as well as men, were hanged. It was these public hangings that were dreaded most because of the hideousness of the method. Thoughts of this fascinated and appalled me, I could not keep still, I had to get up and start my pacing again. This time the book was Keegan's *Battle at Sea* and the chosen word was the first one, *Battle*. But now, quite naturally and without being conscious of any choice, I found myself varying the procedure, touching the word with the forefinger of my *left* hand.

Most of the executions took place in the Piazza del Mercato, which I had never seen but imagined as vast and desolate, on a scale somehow with the number and manner of the deaths. The gallows was a tall post with one arm, which was reached by means of a ladder. The hangman bound the arms of the prisoner, blindfolded him and placed the rope round his neck. This done, he went first up the ladder, leading the prisoner by the rope. Blind, the rough hemp at your neck, tugged upward step by step, mounting to the sky, the terrible shouts of the populace in your ears. *Battle*. White word on a black spine. Left forefinger, six paces, palms against the wall, thumbs mustn't touch . . . Step by step, mounting the ladder. Close behind, bringing up the rear, the hangman's nimble assistant, known as *tirapiedi*, pull-feet. The hangman scrambles on to the crossbeam and makes the rope fast. He then makes a sign to his assistant, who pushes the prisoner off the ladder, adroitly catches him by the feet as he falls and swings with him into space. At the same moment the hangman lowers himself from the crossbeam and straddles the shoulders of the prisoner and the three of them swing back and forth like a circus act, applauded by the vast crowd. Back and forth, back and forth. Thumbs mustn't touch. This time, however, I stop, lean forward, lay my forehead against the cool wall, close my eyes. In my mind the picture of that dangling, three-headed beast, all in struggling movement. One riding above, one swinging below, the middle one choking, dying. Eleonora Pimentel Fonseca, the poetess, died like this, and Domenico Cirillo, the biologist, Fellow of the Royal Society, and Michele Natale, Bishop of Vico, and the philosopher Mario Pagano.

   You never faltered in the belief that you had acted justly, that their punishment was deserved. At least you did not falter in asserting this, and with you there could be no discrepancy between assertion and belief. You could not, surely you could not, have had any slightest sense that those who went to their deaths had been deceived, betrayed. Six times back and forth, and I could return to my desk. I wanted to look again at the letter you wrote to Lord Spencer that same July, in which you sum up your own sense of what you had achieved in Naples: *It will be my consolation that I have gained a kingdom, seated a faithful ally of His Majesty firmly on his throne, and restored happiness to millions . . .*

Certainly Ferdinand was grateful. On the 13th of August the Duke of Ascoli, one of the Gentlemen of the Bedchamber,came bearing a truly regal gift: the King's own sword. Made of gold, its hilt and blade set with diamonds, it is the sword Ferdinand was given by his father, Charles III, as a token of his duty to defend the kingdom, the same that Louis XIV gave his grandson Philip V when he succeeded to the throne of Spain. On the same day Prince Lucci writes informing us that we have been created Duke of Bronte with an estate at the foot of Etna worth £3,000 a year. Now we can sign ourselves Nelson and Bronte.

Then, not long after, there is the *fête champêtre*, held by the Court in Palermo, to celebrate the first anniversary of the arrival at Naples of the news of our great victory at the mouth of the Nile on the 3rd of September. This is the last and most splendid of the Court's tributes to us.

Evening, the garden of the royal palace lit with fairy lights, a select company of courtiers, foreign ministers and their suites, officers from the allied navies, British, Turkish and Russian. We are greeted on our arrival by the King and Queen and young Prince Leopold in his midshipman's uniform. I am wearing the new sword, Emma is breathtaking in a white gown with aigrette, earrings and bracelet of diamonds.

We begin with a magnificent fireworks display representing the battle of the Nile, culminating in the blowing up of the French flagship the *Orient* and the ceremonial burning of the tricolour. This we watch from a balcony with Emma on one side of me and Queen Maria Carolina on the other. In attendance are also the Turkish and Russian admirals. To the former, Cadir Bey, the Queen speaks a few words, pointing out to him how by this glorious victory I have saved his country and hers and all Europe. Cadir Bey smiles and bows. Then follows a cantata, specially composed for the occasion.

Long live the British Hero!
Long live great Nelson!

It is he who drove far from us all affliction.
It is he who gave peace to our troubled hearts.

Preserving a modest impassivity, I take my bow. Then come the
refreshments, ices and sweets. We saunter through the lamp-lit
lanes of the garden, Maria Carolina on my arm. Now comes the
climax of the evening. We pass between elegant pavilions. Before
us rises a Greek temple, magnificently illuminated. A flight of
steps leads up to a vestibule supported by columns. Inside, in a
blaze of light, three life-size wax figures: myself, Sir William and
Emma. I am in full dress, the ambassador in Windsor uniform
and Emma in white with a blue shawl embroidered with the
names of all the captains who took part with me in the battle.
Beyond, within the temple itself, is an altar surmounted by the
allegorical figure of Glory. There before it, in the centre of
the place, standing upright in a golden chariot, the figure of King
Ferdinand. Picked out in lamps, running all round the inside of
the temple above the columns: BRITANNIA RULES THE WAVES.

The orchestra plays 'God Save the King'. Little Prince Leopold
places a laurel wreath on my waxwork figure. He has to stand on
tiptoe to do it. I run forward up the steps. I kneel and kiss the
Prince's hand. The boy throws his arms round my neck, he
embraces me. I look into his face, it is a face I know, a face I have
seen somewhere, long ago. I try to shout a warning but can make
no sound . . .

The shock of this half-recognition brought me back from that
spectacular evening to the daylight of my room, the littered desk
before me. Why did he do it? It was not part of the programme,
it was an impulse, nobody expected it. The people cheered and
wept to see the maimed hero, so slight in frame, so haggard, kneel
before the boy. It was a sight no one there would ever forget –
this man who had saved the kingdom, kneeling.

No mention of it in *The Times* report. The fireworks, yes, the
paean of praise, the wax figures, Ferdinand in his chariot. All in
that tone of solemn satire the newspaper had made its own: the

beribboned admiral among the waxworks in the Temple of Fame. But no smallest reference to this one action that brought warmth and spontaneous feeling to the pomp of the proceedings, broke the mould. That was it, you shattered the programme, you found again the grace you had found at Cape St Vincent, *you broke the line.*

Leopold was wearing midshipman's uniform. Was it because you saw yourself in the child? On the quayside at Chatham that cold March day, staring across the grey water at your first ship?

It was too young. You acknowledged as much four years later at a dinner aboard the *Victory* celebrating the anniversary of the battle of Cape St Vincent. A young midshipman named Parsons finds himself, as the youngest present, seated on the right side of the withered admiral. He will write about it later: the stateroom flooded with Mediterranean sunshine, the gleam of silverware on the table, his awe at the proximity of his famous commander. He is too shy to look up during the meal, but when the cloth has been removed you turn to him, as custom demands. 'A glass of wine with you, Mr Parsons.' By way of opening the conversation you remark on his youth: 'You entered the service at a very early age to have been in the action off Cape St Vincent.' Parsons speaks his first words: 'Eleven years, my Lord.' He sees the smile vanish from the admiral's face and hears the muttered words: 'Too young, much too young.'

That September evening, when they cheered and wept to see you kneel, plaudits of a different sort were rising heavenward in Naples. There on the lamp-lit square they were celebrating the three-headed beast that dangled and swung below the arm of the gallows. One after the other, day after day, week after week, republicans of a short-lived republic.

You never doubted that right was with you. Perhaps sometimes privately? How can we know? Publicly you never wavered. *When the rebels surrendered, they came out from the castles as they ought, without the honours of war and trusting to the judgement of their sovereigns.* You wrote that in 1803, four years later. I know what

Miss Lily would say, she would say you couldn't forgive them, that you dealt with them in the same way that you dealt with Fanny, you were still sitting up there, immobile, in your theatre box, while she suffered and they died. *He couldn't be wrong, could he?* Strange how her remarks, which I generally at first thought flippant or ill informed, lingered in the mind, persisted and strengthened, took over the ground, just as she herself, her whole person, had done in my thoughts of her.

21

I continued my wrestling with the facts of those Naples days, or versions of the facts rather, though there was a growing sickness now in this travail, the sickness of anticipated knowledge or anticipated defeat. I think I must already have known then, as June drew to a close and summer green thickened the hedges of the gardens, known in my heart that this issue would not be listed among the victories, for Horatio or me. I was trying to set him securely in bluff and hearty Mahan's embrace, save him from the clutches of spiteful Badham, who addressed the preface to his *Nelson and Ruffo* from the Reform Club in Pall Mall in October 1904, a creature for whom preserving Horatio's honour mattered little.

When Miss Lily arrived on Friday evening, the 27th of June (the day Ruffo, under the illusion or in the pretence that the treaty was to be honoured, celebrated his Mass of Thanksgiving at the Carmine church in Naples), I was utterly weary with all these speculations. Moreover, I had neglected to eat that day, although, knowing she was coming, I had shaved and made an effort to tidy myself up. The house was not in good order. Mrs Watson, perhaps demoralized by the fact that I avoided communicating with her except in the form of notes, was not doing such a thorough job as she had in my father's time, there was a dustiness and unkemptness about the place, which I was sure Miss Lily noticed, though so far she had not remarked upon it.

This evening she took one look at me and asked whether I felt all right. 'You look exhausted,' she said.

'No, I am quite all right.' However, I stood up rather too suddenly in order to get to some papers. A blackness came before my eyes, I staggered slightly and put a hand against the wall to support myself. I felt her hand under my forearm, had the sense of a strong support.

'What is it?' she said. There was alarm in her voice.

'Just a dizzy spell. I'm all right now.'

'Are you sure?' Her hand was still there under my arm. I felt the warmth of it. 'Why don't you sit down for a while?'

'I tell you, I'm all right.' Her hand was gone but I felt the warmth of it still. 'Can we get on?' I said.

But of course I had reckoned without her obstinacy. 'I do think you ought to just sit down and take it easy for a bit. You would have fallen just now, if it hadn't been for the wall and me holding you up.'

Once you have shown weakness it is very hard to resist advice of this kind; there is somehow a psychological weight against you. She was trying to get power over me, I knew that. All the same, I capitulated; I made for the armchair and sat down in it. She remained standing before me, inquisitorial.

'Does it happen often, dizzy spells like that? I was frightened for a moment, I thought you were going to fall.'

'Just lately, now and again.'

Black specks before the eyes, sparse in the first moments, massing swiftly to form the darkness that threatened my balance. I did not go into these details with Miss Lily – the less you give away the better. But about Horatio's ailments I could talk.

'He suffered from something similar,' I said, 'in Naples and Palermo, after the Battle of the Nile. Giddy spells. Also palpitations and attacks of breathlessness. As if a girth were buckled tight over his breast, as he described it. These are all symptoms of Da Costa's Syndrome.'

'And what may that be?' Miss Lily spoke in the tone she reserved for abstract concepts.

'It's a disordered action of the heart. Sometimes called Soldier's Heart because there were so many cases during the First World War.'

'Are you telling me you've got a heart condition?' Her voice had sharpened, it sounded like reproach, strangely comforting to me.

'No, no, Horatio was afraid it was heart-disease at the time, but modern medical opinion gives it out as disorder of the heart due to prolonged anxiety and physical strain. Don't forget, it was only five months after the Battle of the Nile. That was a great victory, but it had taken weeks to find the French and bring them to action. His hours of sleep were short during all that time. He got a bad head wound in the battle, he thought at first his end had come. Then there was the affair with Emma, he was still under the Hamiltons' roof, he was still writing home to Fanny, there must have been a lot of guilt. And think of the responsibility. He was the commanding officer. Napoleon was already in Egypt with an army, en route for India. The fate of our Empire was in the balance, everything hung on this one man, thin, slight, maimed already in the service of – '

'He probably wasn't very used to the food,' Miss Lily said. 'I mean to say, southern Italy. The food is very rich, isn't it? Especially in those days. They hadn't been alerted to the danger of animal fats. Ignorance is bliss, you might say, but it can't have been good for them, can it?'

'Good God,' I said, 'we are talking about his heart and mind, not his stomach.'

'They're all pretty well tied up together. Anyway, you can't have this Costa thing, you haven't been in any wars. I don't suppose you have been hobnobbing with any ambassadors' wives either.'

In saying this Miss Lily looked at me with the teasing expression which had been more and more common with her lately. I was at a disadvantage, sitting there – I did not know how to reply. Her words constituted another proof, if one were needed, of her pedestrian way of looking at things. Had I not gone with Horatio every step of the way? I had felt his anguish at the cowardly tactics of the French. I had suffered his head wound, felt the warm blood slide over my eyes, blinding me. I had lived through his hero's welcome, his rescue of the royal pair, the love of the motherless boy for the sensual, ample woman. Was I not during these very days living through the terrible temptations of power, his negotiations with Ruffo and the Neapolitan Jacobins?

'I expect you haven't been eating so well yourself,' she said now. 'What did you have for lunch?'

I did not want to reply to this, not thinking it her business; but she waited, with her eyes fixed on me. It was only then I realized that I had omitted to eat anything that day.

'A sandwich,' I said. 'Cheese sandwich.' It was the first thing that came into my head, and at once I was carried back to the time before my mother left, that distant May afternoon, the walk along the dyke, the splendid profusion of the hawthorn flower. *Moles don't eat sandwiches. Look me in the eye, Charles . . .*

But I didn't fear Miss Lily's eyes. 'Cheese and cress,' I said.

'You're so absent-minded, you could be talking about yesterday or the day before or last week. I've known Bobby have them, dizzy spells, when he skimps his lunch at school, but he's still growing, and I don't think you are, are you? Well, we'll just have to see what there is.'

Her expression had softened talking about Bobby, but I could see that she was fixed on some purpose. 'What do you mean?' I said.

She gave two or three brisk nods. 'I'll just go and have a look.'

I asked her where she was going, but she went out of the room without replying. After a few minutes she was back again.

'Must have been a bought sandwich if you had one at all, there isn't a scrap of either cheese or bread anywhere to be found. Cress I didn't bother to look for.'

'Well, it was a bought one.'

She looked at me with a scepticism that she took no trouble to conceal. 'All I can find,' she said, 'in the way of foodstuffs is four eggs that are not in a carton so we don't know their date of

229

birth, a cauliflower that has seen better days and some potatoes in a string bag. Oh yes, and a bit of margarine.'

She paused on this. I had understood now that she was proposing to do something with these poor remnants. She was waiting for me to agree or object or perhaps even to suggest, as an alternative, that we should go out to eat. But I did not want to be with other people; I wanted the two of us to be together quietly. So sudden and strong was the attraction of this idea that I was afraid to speak, afraid of giving myself away. But I think silence betrayed me just as much, or else it was something in my face. After a moment she said, 'Well, it'll have to do, won't it?'

The upshot was that instead of going ahead with the book that evening we ate together in the kitchen. The eggs were all right still. Miss Lily broke them one by one into a cup to make sure. The central parts of the cauliflower were eatable, the potatoes virtually pristine, we had them steamed. There was just enough margarine to make an omelette. I still had a stock of claret and I fetched a bottle up from the basement passage where I kept it.

She sat opposite me across the kitchen-table. As we ate and drank I felt glad and relieved to be released from the book for a while. It was a kind of holiday and I knew I could not have had it on my own, could not have had it without her. There was no one else. Monty was no good, we had not been on close terms for years, not since we were children in fact. And now that he was dressing up in our dead father's clothes . . . There was something wrong with him, he needed some central interest in his life.

No, there was no one else. I was aware that this gratitude I felt was illogical in a way. She was kind but it was a constant kindness, not just for me. She was merely existing, being herself. I looked across the table at her; I was able, though briefly, to look into her eyes. The June weather had brought an olive tint to her face and throat – not that the days had been so sunny, but she had the sort of complexion that is deepened by warmth. She was wearing a white shirt, open at the neck. She was in that moment the sum of all the moments of her being as these had gathered for me, as I had known her, from the first time she had come to my door, Avon Secretarial Services in person. Her jokes, her rages, the perennial surplus from which she made her gifts, the limited sympathies which made her fail to understand Horatio, her championing of dim Fanny, her belief in wrapping up well . . .

As we ate and the wine went down, she talked about the circumstances of her life, something she had done rarely before and then only briefly. I had grown unused to conversation and there seemed to me an extraordinary immediacy in everything she said, they were the things on her mind, the things that affected her from day to day. She had been overcharged for repairs to her car and intended to take it up with them, they might think women didn't know much about engines but they would learn better, she had done a car-maintenance course at evening-class. Bobby was something of a problem at school, not that he was a bad boy but he was dreamy, half the time he was in a world of his own, sometimes his teachers got cross with him, he answered a different question from the one they were asking, they thought he was trying to be funny. She had been to the school, the class-teacher said it was only a phase. He was very good at designing things and drawing, where he got that from she didn't know, she wasn't any good at it.

'Perhaps from his father?' I said, a bold stroke but I was curious.

Miss Lily did not seem to be put out. 'Not him,' she said. 'He might have been interested in someone behind a bar drawing him a pint. Actually he wasn't so much of a beer-drinker as far as I remember. Scotch would have been more his style, malt of course, and a choice of wines with dinner. He had a lot of money. This will sound funny but he was a totally ideal person to me. For a while.'

'How was that?'

'He was fifteen years older, divorced, rather good-looking. He was used to running the show. Like I say, he always had plenty of money. He had his own firm and he employed quite a lot

231

of people. I suppose he told me how many – it was the sort of thing he would have told me – but I can't remember now. The boyfriend I had at the time worked for him, that's how we met, I was waiting for my boyfriend outside the office. I was just turned eighteen. I used to watch a lot of soaps, especially the ones where everybody seemed rich. All those glamorous people with such eventful lives. I used to love those programmes, I never missed. There was one called *Dynasty* which I specially liked. My own life wasn't glamorous or eventful, I was working in an office, typing out invoices. Then, when I met this man he seemed to belong to that other world. It wasn't that I thought *Dynasty* was the real world, but I thought there was a real world that was like *Dynasty*. Know what I mean?'

'I think so, yes.'

'His name was Alex. Perfect, isn't it? I was never a beauty but I was attractive – I spent more time on myself in those days. I was lively too. He sent me flowers all the time. He had a Porsche. He took me to expensive places. He was like a hero to me.'

'Like a knight in shining armour.'

'Shining Armani, more like it. I thought, you know, this is it, this is the real thing, this is what I was meant for. When I got pregnant the flowers stopped coming. He told me to get an abortion. If I didn't I would have to go it alone, he wouldn't help. An abortion would have been the reasonable thing, but I couldn't do it, I just couldn't. I mean the reasonable thing then, at the time. When I look at my Bobby now it's just unthinkable. I had the baby on my own – mum and dad helped, they were great. Then when Bobby was born this man had a change of heart. He'd be ready to help if I'd sign papers acknowledging him as the father. He would pay the rent on a flat. He was full of enthusiasm and paternal pride – it was a boy, you see. He was going to be a beautiful parent. "I'll buy him a speedboat," he said to me. That was what did for him. A speedboat! There was the little kid, a tiny baby with all his need for care and love, and there was this fool who was his father talking about speedboats. See what I mean? It was just what somebody in *Dynasty* would have said. But things were different now. This was a real baby and I was a real mother. I told him to make himself scarce. I never took a penny from him and I never watched *Dynasty* again. I never watch soaps now, except for *Coronation Street*.'

I listened spellbound to this story, which Miss Lily told without rancour or bitterness of any kind. She didn't mention any man currently in her life, though perhaps there was one. I didn't want to think about that. She lived in a world different from mine, not more eventful exactly – after all I had Horatio – but somehow more spacious and hazardous. I wanted to reciprocate, find something from my own experience that might engage her interest. For some time nothing came to mind; then I hit upon it.

'It is really quite extraordinary,' I said, 'the shift there has been in the course of this century in the tone of Nelson biographies. Right up to the 1930s there was a concern to show him as he was, a truly noble character. Not all his biographers of course, but nearly all' – I was thinking here of bilious Badham.

'How do you mean?'

'Well, there was a concern to show him as *good*. Not only brave, not only a naval commander of genius, but virtuous too. The Victorians denied the adultery with Emma because they didn't think it proper behaviour for the hero of Trafalgar. That's going too far, we haven't got the hang-ups they had, but I take the old-fashioned view myself. His modern biographers don't seem to care one way or the other. Here we have the national hero and they skate over the question of whether he was good or not, in the sense of truthful and honourable. They simply don't seem to care.'

'Well, we have gone down in the world, haven't we? Nelson has gone down with us, I suppose. We don't think we're so great any more, so we don't need to make him out to be so great.'

'But that is terrible, it is degenerate.' I felt the usual distress at this belittlement of him, this abject surrender of a glorious past.

'You would think it would work the other way,' I said. 'Here is someone who should make us proud to be British. Where has the pride gone?'

'It hasn't gone anywhere, as far as I'm concerned. It was never there in the first place. I'm not proud to be British any more than I would be proud to be a Hottentot. There's such a thing as luck, I grant you that, Hottentots might have less going for them in the way of secondary education and supplementary benefits. But I honestly don't see where the pride comes in. How can you be proud of an accident?'

This was so wrong-headed and even perverse that for some moments I could not find the words to reply. 'Where you are born is a matter of chance,' I said at last, 'no one would deny that, but from that moment onwards you accumulate impressions, form attachments, grow familiar with certain habits of thought and speech, certain great events in the past of your people. Horatio Nelson looms large in our past, he established our supremacy at sea for a century to come, he saved us from the vile French. Imagine what would have happened if it had gone the other way at Trafalgar and that rabble had come sailing up the Thames. That is what I meant by saying he should make us proud to be British.'

Miss Lily paused a moment, then said, 'Charles, I know you'd like me to admire him as much as you do and I take that as a compliment, but I can't. It's no good pretending. I can see he had his good points, but I wouldn't like my Bobby to turn out the way he did, just shaped for one purpose. There is more to life than shooting broadsides at the French, that's all I'm saying. As I see it, they took him away at twelve and sort of processed him. That midshipman business was a way of processing people. As far as I can see, they've been processing him ever since. Why couldn't they say, Well, yes, he was a great admiral and a very brave man and yes, he was generous and warm-hearted, and he won a sweeping victory in the hour of his country's need, but he was narrow-minded and eaten up with vanity and could never admit he was in the wrong. He was a person, in other words. But no, they had to make him into a great man.'

'You can't talk about him as an ordinary man. He wasn't an ordinary man. He was a great hero. And I don't believe he was processed either. You are seeing things in the light of the present. As usual. You are ignoring the nature of eighteenth-century society. You talk as if he had a lot of choice. He was well connected on his mother's side, but he couldn't expect much help there – on land at least. He inherited no fortune. He wasn't bookish, he didn't want to be a parson like his father. One step down and it would have been minor civil servant or farm bailiff.'

'But that's the whole point. That made it easier for them.'

'How do you mean?'

'The less choice he had, the easier they could brainwash him.'

'Who on earth are the "they" you keep talking about?'

'Them that stood to gain. Anyway, we were talking about being proud and he really doesn't make me proud at all. Being proud means not lowering yourself. Same thing applies to me and you and Nelson and everybody. I was left with Bobby but I kept my head up. I've had to bring him up on my own, trying to make ends meet, working freelance so I could be home when he got in from school. If he turns out well, maybe I can be proud of that. No, I've said it before, I can't help it, he puts my back up, Nelson, that is, he was always so ready to get people killed. If you look at it one way, he was a sort of serial killer. I like men who are gentle and kind and try not to hurt anyone. Women too, for that matter.'

She paused again, then said in a deeper tone, 'People like you, Charles. You can put it down to the wine if you want but there's something I've been meaning to say to you for a long time now. I mean, I know you are very bound up with him and it's a good thing for a man to have a hobby, but I have to say that you're just about as different from Admiral Lord Horatio Nelson as a person could possibly be.'

I was quite unprepared for this. She had spoken with such

conviction, it was almost like a blow. My first impulse was to get up, move to where she could not see me. She was wrong, of course, I was Horatio's other self, the shadow side, the reverse of the medal, I could not lose him without losing myself. But she was saying that she liked me, that I belonged among the people she liked. It came to me in my confusion that perhaps these contradictions were only apparent. After all, Miss Lily had nothing much in common with theatrical, beautiful, self-deluding Emma; but sometimes, in my thoughts and dreams, their bodies had blended . . .

I sat there in silence, without looking at her. I wanted to say that I liked her too, liked the sort of person she was, liked her looks and the way she talked to me, even when it made me angry. But I could not frame the words.

Into this silence came more words from her, words I hardly took in at first, in the confusion of my feelings. She had meant to tell me as soon as she arrived, but with one thing and another and me taking that funny turn . . . just out of the blue, the offer had come, she would have to leave Bobby with his gran to begin with, she couldn't take him out of school.

On her face the look of a person in serious argument, wanting to convince. 'I'm hoping they'll let him come up for the holidays, it would be so good for him to get out of London for a bit.'

I had the strange, familiar feeling of blood leaving the face. 'You can't go away, there is the book,' I said, as if it were something she had overlooked.

'It's only for ten weeks,' she said.

'But you can't.' Even to myself I sounded like a child.

'I've been thinking about it. If you like, I could find someone to replace me while I'm away.'

'No,' I said, 'I don't want anyone else.'

'I have to fend for myself, you know, Charles. I've always had to. I can't afford to refuse a thing like this, the money is so good and everything found.'

'When are you going?'

'The 7th of July, a week on Monday. It's a residential course in business management at Matlock in Derbyshire. I'll be doing the secretarial work – I was recommended for it. I can come next week as usual if you like.'

'No, you'll have things to do, preparations to make and so on. We'd better say goodbye tonight.'

I had spoken on impulse but I knew it was best. I could not bear the thought of passing another week in the shadow of her leaving. Seeing her, talking to her, knowing all the time . . .

'It's not goodbye,' she said.

'Of course I'll pay for next week's sessions anyway.'

'I wasn't thinking of that.'

'It's only fair – I'm the one that says you shouldn't come.'

The week in question was the first week of July and as I paid by the month I had to make a cheque out. This gave me time to gather myself together. I had accepted now that she was going away; the thing was to find some sure means of bringing her back.

'I've enjoyed it so much,' she said, 'working together on the book. It's one of the most interesting jobs I've ever had, it's started me off reading about him and that whole period, I never thought I would get so interested in history, I didn't take to it much at school. And it's entirely because you talked to me, Charles, you weren't just the employer, you asked my opinion.'

I couldn't really remember asking her opinion all that often; she had never much needed to be asked. There must be some way I could make sure she would come back, something I could tempt her with. Then in a flash it came to me: *Francesco Caracciolo.*

'We have to deal with Caracciolo next,' I said. 'When you come back, that is. I am beginning to believe he will provide some essential clues to the problem of Horatio's dealings with the Neapolitan Jacobins in 1799.'

This was calculated to please her. She had always been more interested in Horatio's doings in this murky city than in any other period of his life whatever, and had been distinctly put out when we sidestepped it.

'I don't think we've mentioned him yet in the book,' she said.

'No.' In fact I had been delaying his introduction because he showed Horatio in what some – and especially Badham – had thought to be a bad light.

'Who was he?'

'He was an admiral in the Neapolitan navy who went over to the Jacobin side and took part in the rebellion against King Ferdinand. They set up a republic, the Parthenopean Republic, it was called, very short-lived, it was born and died within a few months in 1799. It came into being when the King and Queen fled to Sicily and it was propped up by the French – they occupied Naples for a few weeks. When they withdrew the republic collapsed. We haven't dealt with this period in the book yet because I can't quite get it straight in my head. Horatio played a very important part in negotiating the surrender of the rebels, but this Caracciolo wasn't among them when they came out from their forts. He had gone into hiding on his uncle's estate. He was arrested and brought in handcuffs to the *Foudroyant*, Horatio's flagship.'

'What had he done exactly? I'll just wash up these few things while you're talking. No, there's hardly anything – you just stay where you are.'

So I went on sitting there at the table and watched her wash up the things and talked about Francesco Caracciolo, raising my voice a little to compete with the clatter.

'What had he done? What hadn't he done? He had rebelled against his lawful sovereign and accepted command of a rebel fleet. He had made gunboat attacks on British and royal Neapolitan ships. He had fired on the frigate *Minerva* and damaged her. The *Minerva* had been his own flagship, he was firing on his own colours, enough in itself for a capital charge.'

'What did they do with him?'

She had her back to me standing there at the sink. She reached to put the dishes in the rack overhead and I saw the arch of her back. An inch or so of shirt had escaped from the waistband of her trousers. Some strands of dark brown hair had worked loose from the coil at the back of her head, the light brought out glints of copper in them. She was going away. A feeling of grief rose within me, like a slow tide. I did not believe she would come back.

'He was arrested by Ruffo's men and handed over to Horatio, who convened a court martial that same morning. It took them two hours to bring in a death sentence by a four-to-two majority. The verdict was reported to Horatio, and he ordered the execution to be carried out at five that afternoon. Caracciolo was hanged in full view of the fleet from the yardarm of the *Minerva*, which he had once commanded. He remained hanging there till sunset. Then they cut the rope and let him fall into the bay.'

Miss Lily turned towards me. The washing-up was finished. 'Who ordered that to be done?'

'Horatio. He wasn't present at the trial, though.'

'He didn't need to be, did he? Do you mean to say he had this man tried, condemned and executed all in the course of a few hours?'

'He was absolutely right, in my opinion. Naples was still full of unrest. He wanted to make an example.'

'Well, he certainly did that. But what was it an example of? How to hang people in a hurry? He was supposed to believe in God, wasn't he?'

This was one of the fairly frequent occasions when the precise import of Miss Lily's words was not immediately clear to me. But she seemed to need no answer to her question. Perhaps I had succeeded in interesting her in Caracciolo, I couldn't really tell; but it was clear that she didn't view Horatio any more favourably than before.

It was nearly eleven by the kitchen clock. She was getting ready to go. I could think of nothing now to delay it. In silence I followed her to the study, watched her collect her bag with the computer, accompanied her to the door.

She smiled up from the lower step as she had so often done before. 'It's been a nice evening, hasn't it?' she said. 'Don't work too hard and don't worry. Take some time off in the summer, go for a trip somewhere. We'll catch up on the book when I get back.'

'I thought we might go to the Maritime Museum at Greenwich when you get back,' I said. 'They've got a whole section devoted to Horatio. We could walk through the park and maybe have tea somewhere in Greenwich. Bobby could come too, if he liked the idea.'

'That sounds nice,' she said. She sounded as if she meant it. She was going away, I sensed she was sorry for me, sorry to be leaving me alone in the house. I had a momentary, desolate feeling of advantage. This would be a good time to mention the trip to Burnham Thorpe, Horatio's birthplace, a weekend together and Bobby left at home. But before I could speak, while I was still gathering my nerve, Miss Lily did something she had never done before, she came back up the steps and kissed me on the cheek, the right cheek. I felt the brief warmth of her lips and the warmth of her face against mine.

22

I tried for a while to go on with the book but I added nothing more of significance after she had gone. I had come to depend on these dictating sessions more than I realized, and not only for the material help: I had come to take her interest, though generally expressed in interruptions, as a gauge of the interest of the book, a sort of guarantee. Without her, almost at once, I began to falter, lose confidence. Insensibly, without my being aware of it, Miss Lily had insinuated herself into the very grain and texture of the work; her presence, her voice, were everywhere in it, winding and coiling through. I knew by the middle of July that I would not be able to continue until she came back. I still hoped she would come back.

I spent my days reading and rereading the conflicting versions of Horatio's conduct in Naples in 1799. As I had remarked to Miss Lily, the more closely argued of these dated from late Victorian times, concern for his honour having declined more or less to zero level in this cynical age of ours. On the defending side there was a phalanx of robust, deep-voiced males: A. T. Mahan, naval historian, forty years service in the American navy, his staunch supporter Professor J. K. Laughton of London University and H. C. Gutteridge, late scholar of King's College, Cambridge, a more Jesuitical type. The other side was more feline in character: F. P. Badham, about whom I knew only that he addressed his prefaces from the Reform Club in Pall Mall, Constance Giglioli, née Stocker, who was married to an Italian botanist and lived many years in Italy, and various Italian sources, not translated and therefore out of my reach – out of the reach too, as it appeared, of Mahan, Laughton and Gutteridge.

This controversy, at once passionate and remote, was a maze which I entered and wandered about in every day after the ritual making of the tea. I would pour out the tea in the kitchen into my monogrammed mug and carry it through on the black and red japanned tray I always used, together with six biscuits, always six – I had taken to buying the sort of biscuit called wholemeal digestive, as being a convenient form of food and also pleasant to dip into the tea.

I could feel myself getting slower and slower. Everything took longer. I often felt impelled to stop what I was reading, and start again from the top of the page or the beginning of the chapter. Somewhere, embedded in the texts I was reading, lay the glinting nugget that would clear his name, set him beyond the snipings of malice for ever. I was dogged by the appalling fear that I would miss it, somehow skim over it. Hours went by in the contemplation of a paragraph, sometimes only a sentence. This one of Gutteridge's, from the introduction to his *Nelson and the Neapolitan Jacobins*, occupied a whole morning: *The chief object of the present volume is not to continue the controversy, but rather to bring together the mass of evidence which deals with the point, and to reduce it to a form in which it will be accessible to the English reader, who may therein find the refutation of these charges.*

I sought refutation too, but this sentence, from whatever direction I approached it, had a strange opacity about it, almost mystical in nature. The original pile, the mass of evidence, could obviously not be assembled within the covers of a single book; there was simply too much of it. So the reduction had been carried out beforehand. How could I know by what means it had been done? Abridgement, summary, excision, exclusion? And what particular attributes could a form have, by whatever means reduced, that would make it accessible to an English reader rather than, say, a Chinaman? He was writing in English, of course, but he surely couldn't mean that. Was he implying that the English have some faculty of understanding denied to others?

Or was he implying the opposite, that the English are so dense that only simplified forms can be accessible to them? Was it simply an appeal to shared prejudice? Could he really hope to put an end to controversy in such a way? What, in short, did H. C. Gutteridge *mean*?

He gave me headaches but he was merely a satellite. It was the two protagonists, Mahan and Badham, that stalked through my days and nights. By now they had acquired definite physical characteristics. Touch by touch, detail by detail, these two long-dead Nelson scholars, so opposed in their views and the tones of their discourse, had assumed form and shape in my mind. Mahan was bluff and hearty, large of frame, with blue eyes; he had sandy-coloured hair, rather bushy at the temples and those wrinkles around the eyes that come from scanning far horizons. He had a slightly shambling, careless gait and a sprawling fashion with his legs when he sat down; he was expansive and open-handed, always the first to pay for the round. Badham was thin and sparse and yellowish, and he wore rimless glasses that reflected the light; his mouth was like a cut in a lemon and he had a prominent Adam's apple; he was neat and precise in all his movements and very quick-stepping and he spoke Italian and wore thin black leather gloves. Their voices too were quite different. Mahan's was manly and energetic, interspersed with easy laughter; Badham's was metallic, slightly nasal, and though he sometimes showed a malignant glee he never laughed.

Mahan's view of the Naples episode accorded fully with his generous nature. Basically, he took Horatio's word for it. Incapable himself of treachery and falsehood, he could not believe it of a man he admired so much, any more than I could. He accepted Horatio's declaration that the rebels came out in the full knowledge that the treaty was annulled. Badham, on the other hand, subjected to close analysis – he was generally a disagreeably analytical character – Horatio's assurance that he would not oppose the embarkation of the rebels, maintaining that the distinction between embarking and sailing was never made clear to them, and that this was a deliberate fraud on Horatio's part, designed to winkle them out.

The whole moral world was here, in these two pure, irreducible representatives of the polarity that haunts our lives. Every day that July, in the silence of my study, good and evil did battle. Good was steadier, less coherent; evil more flickering, more lucid. I thought at the time they were contending for Horatio . . .

They disagreed about Caracciolo also – natural enough, they disagreed about everything. In Mahan's view, he was a traitor to his king under circumstances of particular flagrancy and richly deserved his fate. Badham, seconded by Constance Giglioli, pointed to the unseemly haste of the proceedings and to irregularities in the trial, the fact that no witnesses were called for the defence. An absurd objection, stout Laughton says; what need of witnesses when his guilt was so patently clear?

I had not told Miss Lily about the grisly aftermath of Caracciolo's hanging, whether to spare her or myself I didn't know. Since the age of fourteen or so I had been troubled by the horror of it. At sunset the rope was cut and his body was allowed to fall into the bay. Two days later King Ferdinand returned to Naples but the city was still in turmoil so he took up his quarters on Horatio's flagship and amused himself by shooting seagulls. Early one morning a fisherman reported that Prince Caracciolo had risen from the sea and was coming home to Naples. The King went up on deck, scanned the horizon with his telescope. Midshipman Parsons, standing near by, saw him turn white and drop the telescope and heard him utter an exclamation of horror. Looking in the same direction, Parsons saw the corpse of Caracciolo standing upright, half out of the water. His face was turned towards them, swollen and discoloured, the eyes started from their sockets by strangulation. He was bobbing up and down on the current and seemed to be heading for the shore. One among the retinue of priests on board, quicker-witted than his fellows, said that the Admiral Caracciolo knew he had offended

244

the King and could not rest. This helped Ferdinand to rally from his fear, and after a while he began to joke about it and say that the corpse had come to beg his forgiveness.

Whether the staring, bobbing, hideously bloated corpse stayed long in the King's mind or Horatio's, no one can say. It had certainly stayed in mine over the years, pegged there by a single, astounding fact: the admiral had risen and floated with a weight of two hundred and fifty pounds attached to him. There was no doubt of this. A boat was sent to tow the corpse ashore, where it found a shallow grave in the sand. The boat brought back the shots that had been tied to him and Captain Hardy weighed them. The ropes by which they had been fastened still had scraps of the admiral's skin on them.

Perhaps I was more than usually prone at this time to dwell on such thoughts. July is the month of maimings and disfigurements and outrages to the body. It was on the 12th of July 1794, when he was thirty-five, that he suffered the wound to his eye. On land, not at sea. Seven o'clock in the morning. I always made sure I was up and about well before this on the 12th, so I could give him his due of silent remembrance before I started with the tea.

I sat at my desk and made the shape of the island with my left hand – it helped me to concentrate. Corsica is shaped like a pointing hand, I had first seen this on my school atlas. The index finger is the peninsula of Cape Corsica, which points northwards. At the base of this pointing finger, on opposite sides of the knuckle, are Bastia to the east and Saint-Florent to the west, twelve miles apart. And thirty miles away, somewhere near the second knuckle of the little finger, lies Calvi. Blockaded by the British and harassed by the Corsicans on land, the French occupying troops had retreated to these three strongholds.

A combined sea and land attack was decided on. Having lost Toulon, we needed an alternative base and Corsica answered the purpose. Bastia had a good harbour and it was well placed for attacks on French shipping and for the defence of Italy. However,

Saint-Florent had to be taken first. One night in February, lying off Bastia, you saw the mountains behind the town lit up with a red glow and you knew then that Saint-Florent had been taken and the ships in the harbour set ablaze. You had both your eyes still, when you saw these fires of victory . . .

As always, you were eager to attack. You were set on taking Bastia by storm. But General Dundas, commander of the land forces, would not give you troops. Visionary and rash, he called the enterprise. Once again prudence and daring were confronted. So you landed with two hundred and fifty of your faithful crew from the *Agamemnon* and hoisted 24-pound cannon to the rocky ridges above the citadel, dragging them from rock to rock with the ship's tackle, a labour of enormous, almost superhuman difficulty. The men would not have toiled so for anyone but you.

We did this together, Miss Lily and I, it is all in the book. While still making the shape of the island with my hand, I remembered her voice, her face. I had expected her to be impressed by the devotion of these men. It was a labour of loyalty and even love, hauling up the heavy guns by means of great straps fastened to the rocks. But she didn't see it. She didn't see the point of it. What did they get out of it? she said. Except for ruptures. The comradeship, the pride of achievement, she didn't see it. Mahan expresses warm admiration, quoting the words of Horatio himself: *A work of the greatest difficulty which in my opinion would never have been accomplished by any other than British seamen.*

I quoted this too in the course of my dictation; it was important for the understanding of him, that pride in his men. But she was unmoved. One of the earliest of her interruptions. I was surprised at the time – I wouldn't be so surprised now. She didn't see the point. What was it *for*? I could hear her voice in the quiet room, that edge of impatience or slight annoyance in it that what she felt to be unreasonable always induced in her. *If it had been to help someone. You know, rescue someone. Even a cat. But just dragging guns up a cliff . . .*

This voice came to me from the walls, as voices often did. Not faces, not then. Mahan's reply came almost at once, jovial and easy. He didn't really want to argue with a lady. *To get men to do that, you need leadership qualities of the highest order, you would not expect them to be employed in rescuing a cat now, would you?*

A different voice, a different direction. *What did they get out of it?* Nasal, metallic – it was Badham. And the answer: *a pat on the back and a rupture.* But this was not Badham's voice, it had changed to Miss Lily's. The terrible suspicion came to me: were Miss Lily and Badham on the same side, were they in league? *We are talking about inspiration,* Mahan said, but no one paid him any attention. And that voice of Badham's was familiar, I recognized it now, it was the voice that sounded in my ears when I read aloud from Horatio's despatches.

This was frightening. I had to get up, do a bit of pacing. This time I chose *Trafalgar* by Alan Schom. Only one word in the title, no problem of choice. Unerring forefinger on the middle letter. Six paces to the silenced wall. These voices had broken my concentration, taken me away from Horatio and the morning when he lost his eye. It was getting on for seven.

Bastia was taken in May, thanks to Horatio and his faithful Agamemnons. Now there remained the third citadel, Calvi, difficult of access – there were no landing places nearer than four miles. Again guns had to be hauled up, this time by soldiers and sailors working together. Then, at daybreak on the 12th, the enemy opened a heavy fire. You were watching from a flat-topped rock that gave a view over the besieged fort when a shell burst on the sandbags on the ramparts, sending out a hail of stone splinters and sand, cutting and bruising you on the right side of the face.

At first you made light of it. In a letter to Fanny you said it was only a scratch. But it proved more serious. As I continued to pace back and forth, touching the 'A', spreading my palms against the wall, I pictured you alone in your cabin on the *Agamemnon*. It is a month after the surrender of Calvi and the expulsion of the French. You are bound for Leghorn to refit. You are still weak and tremulous from the malaria that returned to you in the fierce heat of that Corsican summer. You look in the mirror, clapping a hand first over the left eye, then the right. It is no longer possible for you to deceive yourself: the right eye is useless to you, always will be. The pupil is irregular, immobile, it has spread to cover almost all the iris, it knows the difference between darkness and light, nothing else.

I was moved yet again by this testing, childlike and lonely. I was passing the glass-fronted bookcase on my right, where I keep the books I particularly value, Nicolas's monumental edition of the letters and despatches, some of the earlier biographies. The light was reflected from the glass as I passed. On an impulse I broke off my pacing, advanced my face to the glass and placed a hand over my left eye. The eye that looked back at me was dazed and disabled by the shine of the glass but I saw it reflected: vague, cloudy, strangely shapeless and amorphous. It was not mine, and I recoiled from it with a fear that for some moments seemed to stop my heart.

I did not stay longer in my study that day. I remember that an immense weariness descended on me, my limbs felt heavy and it seemed hard for me even to hold my head up. I went to the big armchair in the sitting-room, got under my mother's rug and dozed away the rest of the morning.

This sort of daytime sleeping fit grew frequent as the days passed. I think it was a sort of subterfuge, a means of escape from Mahan/Badham, perhaps a way of bringing Miss Lily's return nearer. Ten weeks, she had said. That would take us to Monday, the 15th of September. I had decided to phone Avon Secretarial Services that day, to see if she was back.

In the midst of all this I did not neglect Horatio's calendar. I was ready well in advance to commemorate his second maiming, which took place three years later, early on the morning of the 25th of July. With three ships-of-the-line and a frigate he had been ranging from Lisbon to the coast of North Africa, hoping for a favour from the gods, a sight of the legendary Spanish treasure fleet, returning from South America. Now the rumour came that they had arrived, loaded with bullion, in the Canary Islands, Tenerife. What a prize!

Grigson was very good on the Tenerife engagement. I have never forgotten his lessons. The big map, glossy and smelling of hot glue, draped over the blackboard, Grigson stocky and nimble, a creature of fire with his reddish hair and the glinting pelt of his sports jacket, wielding a billiard cue, his own property, pointing out the routes, the distances. *Here is your Grade A in O-level history.* The pointer hovering, tracing, pausing and pouncing, keeping always to the rhythm of his voice and his movements before us. *Boys, we stood alone, the French had twice our population . . .*

Cadiz to Tenerife, a thousand miles. According to intelligence reports, Santa Cruz de Tenerife was ill defended. Reports also mentioned Spanish merchant ships in the harbour. A thousand miles, six days running before the wind, while the crews trained at the guns and the carpenters made scaling ladders for the assault. Then, faintly outlined against the sky to the south-west, the volcanic peaks of Tenerife, where Grigson's cue came to rest.

The intelligence reports were false, the fortifications were formidable. The sea approaches below the town were commanded by powerful batteries. Should they have attacked at all? *Boys, you must try to imagine the times they lived in and the men they were. In 1797 as in 1940 we stood alone. Any measure, any prospect of success, anything that could force the allies of France out of the war . . .* Grigson had a sense of the past, he should have talked to Miss Lily.

The plan depended entirely on surprise. Under cover of darkness a combined force of seamen and marines would put ashore in boats with muffled oars. Without warning they would attack the batteries on the heights to the north of the town. Grigson rolled up the map at this point and used coloured chalks on the blackboard. Red for the French batteries, blue for our ships, dotted white for the planned line of attack. Here is the bombship ready to open fire on the town; here are our three ships-of-

249

the-line anchored out of range. At dawn they will close in, ready to bombard the town. But that won't be necessary. With the guns taken by storm and the town threatened with destruction, the governor will capitulate, all bullion or treasure belonging to the Spanish will be handed over.

But it is not to be. Grigson shakes his head, the cue is grounded, the blue ships stay where they are. Strong offshore currents make it impossible for the frigates to land the men; and in their battle with the tides they are sighted by the enemy, the advantage of surprise is lost. The attack has failed. But when did you ever accept defeat? What did you say? *Thus foiled in my original plan, I considered it necessary for the honour of our King and country not to give over the attempt.*

Heat rose through Grigson's wiry, reddish hair, warming the air around him. The gestures of the hand not holding the cue were brief and strong, cutting or chopping motions. No one could long sustain his gaze. He approved of your words, we knew he approved by the tone in which he quoted them – I think it was the first time I ever heard your words spoken aloud. They came to me in Grigson's voice that July evening, while I waited. It was late, nearly midnight. I was waiting for one o'clock, the time of the wound.

The walls and ceiling of the study were shadowed. The only light came from the lamp on my desk. Your words, as spoken by Grigson, were in my mind. Then a surprising thing happened. After all these years of recalling the wound, remembering Grigson and his billiard cue and coloured chalks, it came to me that there had been one boy in that class at odds with the rest of us. Strange that I had not remembered him before. A picture of him came now into my mind, gradually, detail by detail. It was like peering at something under water that has been stirred, waiting for the tremors of the surface to subside. A sallow boy, large but not athletic. Heavy brows. Rather adenoidal. The nature of his questions came similarly slowly to my mind. A nasal voice. I think he wore rimless glasses. At that moment, when Grigson's theme was honour, this boy actually asked if it hadn't been wrong of Nelson to try again. This to Grigson, whose bristles of hair seemed to issue sparks, who perhaps misunderstood the question, not thinking any boy could be so lacking in *esprit de corps*. Well, certainly, it was wrong of him to lead this second attack in person, he was a rear-admiral and commander of the whole squadron, he was wrong to risk himself, but of course it was gallant too . . .

But no, that was not what this boy meant. I could not remember his name. What about the thousand officers and men Nelson took with him, only half of whom returned? This boy had been reading other texts than those furnished by Grigson. We were all against him, we shared our teacher's disdain for this insinuating outsider.

But he would not be silenced. The sea was rough, there were powerful batteries on the heights above the shore, the chances of success were almost nil. Is that what honour means? Was it the hope of Spanish gold that made you throw those lives away? *A kind of serial killer.* No, he didn't say that, the Badham boy didn't say that, Miss Lily said that. This boy had a limited existence. Why couldn't I remember his name? Why had I no memory of him in any other class, questioning any other teacher?

Wiped off the slate for all these years between. I tried not to think of him any more, but only of that doomed, gallant second attempt. Quarter to one now, fifteen minutes to go, you are already pulling for shore, you and the thousand others. Shortly before you have written a hasty letter to Sir John Jervis. *Tomorrow my head will probably be crowned with either laurel or cypress.*

Grigson approved of this too, but I was not in his class now, I was alone in my study, the class had gone, that boy had gone, who could tell where Grigson was? As the moment of the wound drew nearer I was quite alone. Laurel or cypress. You knew, you must have known, how expensive in lives it would be, how slight the chances of success. Even to get ashore under fire like that, let alone to storm the heights. A thousand men, all with a hope of life, and you wrote to Jervis as if there were only one.

What was it for? Miss Lily's favourite question. No use as a base, too far away, the Mediterranean was the vital zone. The point was the treasure. You were the commander of the squadron, you were entitled to one quarter. *No boys, personal greed did not enter into it, the objective was to cripple the Spanish by depriving them of the means to continue the war.* Yes, he was right, the times were desperate, the Spanish could not be brought to a battle, it was the only way. Think of the times they lived in, think of the men they were.

Three minutes to one. A heavy sea running. The boats are too crowded, many of them do not reach the shore, they capsize and the men in them are drowned. The Spaniards have seen us, the shore batteries open up while the boats are still hundreds of yards from land. However, you reach the harbour mole, you draw your sword, prepare to leap ashore. At that moment, as you raise your sword, your right arm is shattered by grapeshot. You make an attempt to pick up the sword with your left and to continue, but your strength fails and you fall. Bleeding heavily, you are laid in the bottom of the boat and they begin to row you back to the ships. But you will not allow them to return in an empty boat. Half fainting as you are, you will not let them proceed, you order as many men as possible to be gathered into the boat from the sea.

Thinking of this, I felt the familiar smart of tears. Tears always came to restore my feeling for him. That stoicism, that forbearance, that care for others. The same man, the author of the letter to Jervis . . .

The first ship they came up with was the *Seahorse*, commanded by your friend Fremantle, still out there in the night somewhere, taking part in that disastrous landing. But his wife Betsy is still aboard – she has been given special permission to accompany her husband. By now your arm is pumping blood in spite of the tourniquet, but you refuse to quit the boat. *I would rather suffer death than alarm Mrs Fremantle by her seeing me in this state when I can give her no tidings whatever of her husband.* You order them to go on, to find your own ship, the *Theseus*. At last they do so, but you will not be helped aboard. *Let me alone. I have yet my legs left and one arm. Tell the surgeon to make haste and get his instruments.*

You were magnificent. And to think that the later progeny of Badham have set this fortitude down to the effects of shock. No memory of that rotten apple in our class daring to say anything about it. Grigson would have come down on him heavily. *We stood alone against a powerful Continental aggressor. To the generations born since 1940 the situation is difficult to imagine.*

Long afterwards, in a Greenwich bookshop, perched on the top of a ladder to get at the dusty top shelf, I came upon a monograph: *Eyewitness Accounts of Nelson's Battles* by H. C. Grigson, MA (Leeds). It was the same man. I bought it and have it still. There is a brief biographical note at the back. Grigson was born in 1927. He was twelve when the war broke out, he would not have seen any fighting. That sense of crisis, of heroic isolation, he would have got it from others – parents, teachers . . .

The arm was cut off high up, near the shoulder. It was thrown overboard, on your orders. More terrible than the pain of the cut, or perhaps it was the expression itself of this pain, was the bitter coldness of the surgeon's blade. Always, afterwards, on any of your ships, you made sure that the surgeons warmed their blades before operating. It took them half an hour to sever the arm and bind the stump. Then – only then – they gave you opium to ease the dreadful pain.

I have on one wall of my study a framed facsimile, enlarged to double-size, of the first letter written with the left hand. This was two days after the loss of his arm. I got up now and went to look at it again, trying as I did so to avoid looking towards the glass-fronted bookcase which I was now rather nervous of. Wavering, very variable as to the size and the slant of the letters, all the same it is not bad for a first attempt when one considers that he was still sick and suffering and in a mood of deep discouragement. *I am become a burden to my friends and useless to my country.*

This on the eve of his great victory at Aboukir Bay, with the triumphs of Copenhagen and Trafalgar to follow! He rose from the ashes of defeat like the fabulous bird. So could I too, I resolved there and then. I would rise with him, above failure and discouragement, above my psychic mutilation. I would fight on. My battle would be Naples 1799 and I would win it for him. In the glow of this determination I took a new exercise book from my drawer, one of my specials, with strong covers and good, smooth paper. This would be my left-handed journal. I would not begin it yet, I would begin when he began, two days after the wound.

23

The July of mutilations and maimings gives way to glorious August, the Battle of the Nile on the first day of the month, in 1798. Of all his battles before Trafalgar this was the one I looked forward to most.

A night-battle, his only one. I was at my table in the ops-room by 5 p.m., laying the ships out, a bottle of my father's claret ready-opened at my elbow. I never drank before his battles, only after he had hoisted the order for close action.

Forty minutes to go. The long hoped-for, long sought-for engagement about to begin. Since April, Horatio has been scouring the Mediterranean in search of the French fleet. His squadron has been brought up to a strength of twelve 74-gun warships and three frigates. The situation is desperate. We have no base east of Gibraltar, the Mediterranean is a hostile sea. On land the French are everywhere dominant. We know they are about to leave Toulon with a fleet of transports and escorting warships commanded by Bonaparte in person. But we don't know where he is intending to strike. It could be anywhere in the region. An attack on Portugal from the east, through Spain? A break-through into the Atlantic and a descent on Lisbon that way? A landing in Ireland, now in open revolt against us?

It is our task to find out. A heavy responsibility on that great stretch of water, in those slow ships. In May we learn from a captured French corvette that the expedition is about to set sail. Fifteen enemy sail-of-the-line and twelve thousand troops are already embarked. The warships are under the command of Vice-Admiral François de Brueys, whose flagship is the gigantic *Orient*, 120 guns.

Still no one knows where they are going. They are sighted north of Corsica, steering south-east. An attack on the Two Sicilies? But that would be easier by land. Or Malta, which dominates the central Mediterranean? But thirty-five thousand men, which Bonaparte's strength is now believed to be, would be far more than needed for this. Some altogether more ambitious attempt it must be . . .

Late in July, from a Genovese brig hailed off Cape Passaro, we learn that the French have been in Malta, that the Knights Templar have surrendered to them, that they have filled the army's coffers with the treasures of the churches – and then left again, destination unknown.

In the solitude of the great cabin of our flagship, the *Vanguard*, with maps covering the table before us, we try to work it out, try to enter the mind of the enemy. Unlikely they have gone west, the prevailing winds of the season would make it difficult with transport ships. East then. Corfu? Constantinople, where the Ottoman Empire could be smashed at the heart? But Bonaparte's great enemy now is Britain, and the greatest threat to British interests lies farther east. We have detailed information about the French force now; in addition to troops and artillery it includes naturalists, astronomers, mathematicians. What would be the destination for specialists such as these? It could only be countries with ancient and esoteric civilizations. Egypt, the Red Sea ports. Then India, and a crippling blow to this most vital of our colonies. That must be it.

We set off for Alexandria. But what if we are wrong? What if the slippery crappos have doubled back behind us, taken Sicily? Then the failure would be complete. Not a gallant failure, as Tenerife was regarded, but a failure of judgement with disastrous consequences for the whole conduct of the war. Mistakes like that are never forgotten, never forgiven. If we are wrong our career is at an end. And we are handicapped, we are half blind in the metaphorical sense also, we have only 3 frigates, only three ships fast enough to scout ahead for information.

We are not wrong but for some terrible days it seems that we are. No sign of them at Alexandria when we get there; they are still on the way, we have outsailed them, but of course we do not know this at the time. Back to Sicily, no sign there either. Egypt again, but now there is no doubt: the French have been sighted from Greece, heading south-east for Egypt.

Four days later, at ten o'clock on the morning of the 1st of August, we sight once again the lighthouses and minarets of Alexandria. The harbour is crammed with empty transports, but there are no warships. Napoleon has landed. He is on his way to the destruction of the Mamelukes at the Battle of the Pyramids, and the conquest of Cairo.

Some minutes of terrible disappointment. Then we give the order to steer east along the coast, towards the delta of the Nile. At two in the afternoon, roughly three and a half hours ago, we see at last, with joy and relief, the masts and yards of the French fleet at anchor. On the halyards of the *Zealous*, second ship in the British line, the signal is hoisted: *Enemy in sight.*

You knew then that decisive action was a certainty. *Before this time tomorrow, I shall have gained a peerage or Westminster Abbey.* That is what you said. Why does it trouble me so now, after all these years? Is it because of her? Like the laurel and cypress remark before the attack on Tenerife. That was traditional, death or glory, the genuine heroic impulse. But this . . . All those men, all the blood and rending of the flesh that awaited only a few hours away. A peerage or a state funeral. If I were talking to Miss Lily I would not mention this remark of yours, she would call it monstrous. Still theatre, she would say, but a one-man show now, the others lining the decks to kick their legs, make up the chorus. Why I had begun to subject you to her opinion at all, that was the mystery. She was miles away in Derbyshire, why did I give her so much say? How could Avon Secretarial Services be expected to appreciate your heroic sense of destiny, the patriotic identification of Britain's interests with your own? Her face with that little frown on it, the slight flush that came to her cheeks when she was indignant about something.

The French ships are set out now, all 13 of them, anchored in their curving line. Their commander, Admiral de Brueys, whose last day of life this is, is an experienced seaman, a former royalist officer, reinstated by Napoleon. He has fought the British before, during the American war of independence. He has three 80-gun ships, the *Tonnant*, the *Franklin* and the *Guillaume Tell*, and one of 120-guns, his flagship, the *Orient*. For ships as big as this Alexandria Harbour is rather too narrow, he is afraid of jamming at the harbour mouth. So he has brought the ships eastward, here to Aboukir, and anchored them in a tight defensive line protected behind by the shoals and sandbanks of the bay.

I always used the top left-hand corner of my table for this battle, a triangular space taking up almost half of the total surface. The right-angle formed by the sides of the table represents the arms of the bay with the peninsula of Aboukir to the north and the Nile Delta to the south. The French line curves shallowly outwards towards the open sea, with the *Guerrier* in the van, the *Timoléon* in the rear and the mighty *Orient* in the exact centre. They are anchored, *but only by the bow*; they swing with the current, there are spaces between them. An error on the part of de Brueys, yes, but who could have supposed Horatio would try to pass through, risk the shallows inside the bay, notoriously treacherous? And at night, in darkness, without maps!

Other errors the French admiral has made, all springing from the assumption that his rear is secure. Believing that the attack must come from seaward, he has placed his strongest ships in the centre, his weakest and oldest in the van. And he has failed to ensure that his leading ship, the *Guerrier*, is anchored right up against the shoals, so as to prevent our ships from passing inside, between his line and the shore.

5.22 by my watch. There has been time to prepare for battle since that first sighting of the French, ample time – that leisurely preparation for mortal risk, as always I was troubled and excited by it as I set out the British ships in their rough grouping on the seaward side. Rarely can men have prepared to face death with more deliberation, more knowledge of it in every heart. The port lids are opened and the guns run out; hammocks are rolled up and packed in nets along the bulwarks as a shield against splinters and musket shot; the furled sails are wetted to reduce risk of fire; the damp sand is strewn on the gun-decks to prevent bare feet from slipping on blood. The gun-crews, stripped to the waist, stand by the lines of cannon, the surgeons wait in the cockpit, the marines in full uniform troop with their muskets to the upper deck watched by their lieutenants with drawn swords.

Our ships are fortunate in the wind; a brisk north-westerly fills their sails as they bear down from the north. As they approach they form line in obedience to your general signal, number 31: *Form line of battle ahead and astern of the admiral as most convenient.*

At a distance, from the open sea, the French line looks impregnable, set in a convex curve outward from the shoals, the sea behind seething white as it breaks against the sandbanks. The ten British 74s, hauled sharp to the wind, are already in the shallower water, sounding as they go, fifteen fathoms, thirteen, eleven, nine . . . One is out of action already, Troubridge in the *Culloden* has run aground. Here he is, in a frenzy of frustration, at the tip of the shoal stretching east from the bay. I try not to think further of Troubridge, thoughts of him distress me, renew that sickness of doubt, inappropriate on the eve of such a glorious victory. Troubridge was one of the two captains – Ball was the other – that you sent to Cardinal Ruffo, in Naples the following July, with your assurance that you would not oppose the embarkation of the rebels . . .

But now you are innocent still, you scan the French line with the eye of a commander set on immediate attack. Landwards, behind them, the sun is setting in the magnificent summer dustglow of the Levant. Their masts and yards are fiery, they ride on a molten sea. You see their weakness together with their beauty. You will throw your whole weight on their van and crush it before help can come. But the shoals are dangerously close. The *Zealous* is still in the lead, sounding as she goes, eight fathoms, seven . . .

The last moment for choice is approaching. You can stay outside, order your captains to anchor two by two opposite the enemy ships. This is what de Brueys expects. You can break through the gaps in the French line and attack from the inside. But how can you be sure there is enough water?

It is exactly 5.40 p.m. You give the signal for close action. I pour out my first glass. Now it comes, the moment of pure and perfect opportunity. Can we outflank the French by rounding his line and attacking from inside? From our flagship, here in the centre of the line, we shout across to Hood in the *Zealous*. Can he take his ship round the end of the enemy line? Hood shouts back that he will try. So to the *Zealous* falls the honour of being the first to round the point of the shoals. But I have been too hasty, it is still only six minutes to six, I must wait six more minutes before taking her round. I have been rather hasty with the wine too, in my excitement; the glass is almost empty and I am not due for another till 6.28, when the battle is joined.

These are the last moments of the day, before the swift descent of that southern darkness. I have turned off the overhead light, left on only the lamps at the ends of the table. This is the poised moment, everything is at risk, we are entering a strange bay at nightfall, without pilots, without reliable charts, moving in narrow waters among invisible reefs and shoals. The progress of the *Zealous* is slow because of her need to take continual soundings. She is overtaken now by Captain Foley in the *Goliath*. Foley has made a deduction and acted on it with a boldness worthy of his great commander. If the French have anchored their ships by the bow only, there must be water enough to allow for the swing. If there is water enough to allow for the swing, there must be water enough for another ship to pass inside.

Impeccable logic. The *Goliath* sweeps into the lead. Here she is. It is 6.28, time for another glass. The enemy have hoisted their colours and opened fire. Foley has crossed the bows of the *Guerrier*, raking her with a broadside as he does so, then passing on to anchor here, on the inner quarter of the *Conquerant*, the next French ship in line. Hood takes up his station opposite the *Guerrier*. Our ships follow round in order of sail, the *Orion*, the *Theseus*, the *Audacious*. As the fires of that sunset are quenched in the sea, the five leading British ships are all inside and at closest possible quarters, bringing a concentrated fire to bear on the enemy van, the more deadly as the French can make no adequate reply. Their guns on the shoreward side have not been cleared for action, they are cluttered with rope and tackle and mess furniture – another disastrous consequence of the French assumption that attack was bound to come from the open sea.

Our flagship, the *Vanguard*, is the sixth ship to come into action, the first to anchor on the seaward side. Here she is, abreast and within pistol shot of the *Spartiate*. Now she is hard-pressed, fired upon both by the *Spartiate* and the *Aquilon*, next ship in the French line. The *Minotaur*, Captain Louis, relieves us, ranging up to draw off the *Aquilon*'s fire.

7 p.m. Night has fallen in a thunder of guns. In a pall of smoke, lit only by gunfire, the five 74s of the French van, undermanned and only able to fire on the starboard side, are being beaten into helplessness by eight of ours settled like a swarm about them. My lamps cannot match the glimmer and flicker of the gunfire and the lurid flaring of the smoke, and my room is hushed – only the slight sounds of my miniature hulls scraping on the glass; but my table is beautiful, reflections glinting on the dark surface, changing with the movements of my hands and arms as I direct the ships.

The eighth and ninth in our line, coming into position opposite the enemy centre, sustain the heaviest damage. In the smoke-hung confusion the *Bellerophon* misses her chosen foe, the *Franklin*, first of the French 80s – at present being very gallantly attacked by one of our frigates, the 50-gun *Leander* – and fetches up abreast of the mighty *Orient*, a ship with double her armament. Within fifteen minutes her masts have been entirely shot away. She veers out of the line, completely disabled. I leave her here, over on the lee side of the bay. The *Majestic* also suffers heavy loss, her captain, Westcott, being fatally wounded in the throat by a musket-ball.

But we are gaining. Our ships are like a swarm – it is as if they are feasting on carcasses. No, not carcasses, bodies still twitching. Always the same tactic: pass along the line, gather on either side, concentrate the fire.

Now, with battle fully joined, comes the wound. You are standing on the quarter-deck with Berry by your side when a flying piece of scrapshot slashes your brow to the bone. A flap of flesh falls over your good eye and the blood flows thickly down, blinding you. Berry catches you as you fall. *I am killed*, he hears you say. *Remember me to my wife.*

I see you as you are carried down to the cockpit, I see the lamps down there, swaying with the roll of the ship and thud of the gun-carriages. There are seventy or so men already waiting there, in that shuddering heat, many of them gravely injured. You do not allow the surgeons to be told you are among them. Still blinded, your face a mask of blood, you wait your turn.

The surgeon probes the wound, pronounces the damage not serious – the visible damage, that is. You are in total darkness, you send for the chaplain and dictate messages for Lady Nelson and for Louis, the captain of the *Minotaur*, who had relieved your flagship from the dual fire of the enemy. *Your support prevented me from being obliged to haul out of the line.* This was before your wound had been dressed, while you lay waiting for the dressing. You could not see. That you should think of Fanny at such a time was natural enough. But a message of thanks to one of your captains . . .

Once again, as I thought of you lying there, that familiar prickle of tears came to my eyes. How could this behaviour of yours be named? It was something more than courage or endurance. It was *grace*, springing like a flower from the hard ground of duty.

Still blind, you hear cheering from above. The youthful Berry enters with what he announces as a 'pleasing intelligence', one of the great understatements of history this must be regarded, considering that he brings news of the most notable British victory at sea since the defeat of the Spanish Armada. The French fleet is shattered. The *Spartiate* has altogether ceased to fire, the *Aquilon* and the *Peuple Souverain* have struck their colours, the *Orient*, the *Tonnant* and the *Heureux*, though not yet captured, are no longer able to make effective reply to our shot.

News to bring you back to life. Time for my third glass. Your brow stitched and bandaged, you are settled in the bread-room in the hold, below the waterline, as far removed as possible from the din of battle. You send for your secretary to take down a despatch to Earl Spencer, the First Lord of the Admiralty. But the secretary is in a state of nervous collapse; at the sight of you, blinded by bandages and working the stump of your arm in a fury of impatience, he loses his nerve altogether and cannot write. There and then I dismiss him from my service. I push up the bandage, take the pen myself. *My Lord, Almighty God has blessed His Majesty's Arms in the late Battle . . .*

I am interrupted again by Berry, this time to report that the *Orient* is on fire. The surgeon has ordered me to stay quiet but with the usual disobedience I demand to be helped up on deck. The night is soft and warm, thickly hung with smoke. A reddish glow is creeping over the expanse of the bay. My head throbs and aches, it hurts me to focus my eye, but as the glow strengthens I can distinguish the colours of the ships, make out the situation of the battle, see the leaping flames on the poop of the French flagship. I tell Berry to do what he can to save as many as possible of the crew. At the same time I give orders that our shot should be concentrated on the blaze so as to hinder the enemy from bringing it under control. Many of the *Orient*'s guns are now disabled, but some on the lower deck are still firing, the French gun-crews serving them until the fire gets too close and they are driven off. I see the flames begin to race up her tarred rigging, flare blue along her newly painted sides. I know that the flames will be seeking paths downward, towards her powder magazine.

What I do not see – what no one in the British fleet sees – is the appalling fate of the French wounded, trapped below decks with their surgeons, all burned alive together. Or Admiral de Brueys, who had made all the wrong assumptions with both his legs shot away and tourniquets tied around the stumps, seated on a chair on his blazing deck, still facing his tormentors, still shouting orders to maintain fire, until another shot cuts him in two and puts him out of his misery.

A competent commander, not brilliant, not like you. The end he made has been a recurrent nightmare since I first read of it at the age of fifteen. Thoughts of it now wrenched me from the action. I was here, this was me in the basement, reaching for my glass. You were there on the deck of the *Vanguard*, pushing up your bandages for a sight of your beautiful, desolate victory.

The cannonade continues. Our ships aim their guns at the heart of the blaze. Swarms of sparks fly over the face of the water and in among the anchored ships. The British captains nearer the blaze cut their cables to get clear. At five minutes past ten, just at this moment, with a stunning detonation and a great flash of light, the *Orient*'s powder magazine explodes, a fiery wreckage is flung high into the night sky, hangs in its own light for some moments, then descends in a rain of masts, yards, red-hot ammunition, charred fragments of corpses, thudding on the decks of the neighbouring ships or falling back into the sea in a hiss of mingled smoke and steam.

This mighty bang is heard in Alexandria, fifteen miles away. After it, for several minutes, an utter silence lies over the bay. Then the guns start up again. The French van and centre have been destroyed, it is now the turn of their rear. By sunrise the full extent of our victory is apparent. Of the 13 French warships lying at anchor the day before 10 have been captured, one has been blown up and two have escaped. Aboukir Bay is a scene of utter desolation with listing, smoking ships and scorched bodies drifting in the shallows. As you truly said, *Victory is not a name strong enough for such a scene.* Once again we rule the waves, control of the Mediterranean is restored to us. Bonaparte is stranded on shore, the threat to India is removed, the French losses are six times ours. The remains of the *Orient* are in the depths of the bay, together with her butchered admiral and her treasure – the enormous sum of £600,000 in gold bars and diamonds wrested from the Swiss Republic and the Roman State to finance Bonaparte's Eastern expedition, along with the irreplaceable treasures of the Knights of St John.

A great action, demonstrating yet again the truth of Grigson's words to us so long ago and those of Bobby's teacher so recently. He would be with his mother now, in Derbyshire. I thought of the boy's face looking fixedly at me in the dim light of the *Victory's* gun-deck, a light similar to that here in my ops-room, where shadows lay on all sides beyond the arena of the table. *He says our sailors were the best in the world and we had better officers.* Quite right, my boy, quite right. It wasn't the ships, it was the men. They were better trained, more disciplined, they had superb morale. They cheered when they saw the *Orient* go up. What would Miss Lily say to that? She would go round it, she would find a question to which there was no answer. Something outside the records. Did a single one of them, officers or men, at the time or later, express pity for the crew of the *Orient?* Not as far as we know. The men cheered. The officers of course did not cheer but they did nothing to check the men.

I couldn't help it. All these years of celebrating the Battle of the Nile and now I had to listen to questions from Avon Secretarial Services, to try to understand the way this woman associated things together. She had soured his great victory with this talk about pity. Now, because of her, I was obliged to remember the way he talked about the battle himself, in Palermo, a few months later, as related by Captain Gordon, a Scot who was there as travelling tutor to the invalid Lord Montgomerie. I could not remember the words in detail, but Gordon's memoirs were up there in my study, on the shelf. It was only twenty to eleven, much too early to go to bed. I slept badly at night in any case and I was stimulated now by the battle and the wine. I decided to go up and check the reference.

I was moving towards the wall, towards the light switch. I think I had begun to reach towards it, actually extended my arm. I glanced aside — some sense had come to me that I was being watched, that my movements were being noted, registered. I looked to the right, where I sensed this interest lay, looked through the open door of the ops-room to the larger room beyond, my gallery of Nelsoniana so lovingly assembled over the years.

All the light there was came from the lamps at either end of my table. The farther of these cast a white pool, fringed by the pattern of the raffia lampshade, over the threshold of the door. The fringes seemed to shift, to eddy very slightly, as if prey to some remote disturbance. Beyond the door they drew together, made a narrow, wavering shaft into the next room, touched the straight outer side of the porcelain tankard commemorating Trafalgar, slid round the convex curve of the Copeland loving-cup with the hand-painted full-face portrait of him in one of its panels.

At the dim limits of this faint plank of light was the huge, papier mâché bust of him, roughly twice life-size, that stood in the centre of the floor. The face was turned directly towards me. Despite the dimness I was aware of the features, though I did not know whether I was seeing or remembering the yellowish complexion, the look of moisture given by the pulped and oiled paper, the heavy sweep of the cocked hat, the garish emblems painted on the breast. Whether seen or remembered, tonight he had a different, crueller face. That thick curl of the mouth . . . He looked like a god glutted with sacrifice. The eyes were not visible, they were shadowed by the hat as they always were in my dreams, but I knew that they would soon be levelled at me, that they would contain a deadly reproach. *You have let me down*, the

266

eyes would say, *you have failed to clear my name.* An angel's displeasure is horribly dangerous. I knew I had to get out before he showed his eyes.

I put the light on now and that helped. My heart thumped and my breath caught as I passed him. I felt a feverish heat in the glands at the sides of my neck. But I did not look. At the top of the stairs I remembered that I had left the lamps on in the ops-room, but I could not look behind me, let alone go back.

24

The lights in the basement burned for three days before I could bring myself to go and switch them off. And then I went almost at a run and didn't look at him, not at the bust, not at the portraits on the wall. If Miss Lily had been there I would have asked her to do it, on some pretext or other. She would not have been afraid.

I told myself I needed more time. But the time did not come. The basement stayed locked. Those few hours at the table, moving my ships about, celebrating our victory, drinking perdition to the damned French, before I felt him watching me, they were the last I could remember with any pleasure and they left me only bad dreams. Soundlessly the *Orient* went up again. Fiery fragments rained through my nights. A featureless figure in a cocked hat bobbed on the tide, then dived and sported like a dolphin among the spars and corpses, still with his hat on. De Breuys sat bolt upright in his chair among the flames, the stumps of his legs sticking out before him. His face was melting in the heat . . . I would wake to find my whole body rigidly braced, as if in expectation of some blow.

Habit is strong, however; it can hold you against terror, at least for a while; it can run parallel, a parallel track. In that time of my nightmares I made another trip to Seldon's in Sloane Street to buy a Staffordshire group depicting the moment of the fatal wound. No date on it but typical of the mid nineteenth century. Horatio has fallen, his lung pierced and his back broken. He is supported by Dr Scott, the chaplain, and Hardy, both very pink in the face to contrast with the stricken admiral's pallor. A curiosity, no value much, crudely made, with Horatio wearing an eyepatch, something he never did. But I had an open-fronted cabinet in the basement containing a small collection of such pieces and I thought I would add this one to it.

Strange to relate, while I was buying this piece and all the time I was bringing it home, my purpose remained clear: I would put it with the other things in the cabinet. I was sustained by the years of happy acquisition, by the prospect of that healing peace that used to descend on me when I was down there, moving about among my exhibits.

It was only when I got home and the piece was on my study-table that the first doubts came to me. However, I tried. I tried to pretend, to trick myself. I went with it in my hands to the basement stairs. I went halfway down, more than halfway. The door was there, deeply familiar, varnished brown, with the brass knob and the neat little slot of the lock waiting for my key. But already I was gulping and sweating. I began to feel that same hotness at the sides of my neck. Almost before I knew it I was back at the top of the stairs.

I never tried again. I remember sitting for a long time, back there in my study, looking closely at pale Horatio with his eyepatch, at his florid, tight-trousered helpers. He was not frightening here, he had no gaze. But down below there, in the basement . . . You, who rescued me from fear!

So it was that, in the days following the Battle of the Nile, I was obliged to face the fact that the basement was effectively out of bounds, that picture gallery, exhibition cabinets, ops-room were all closed to me. I was reduced to the bedroom, the armchair in the sitting-room with my mother's rug, the desk and walls of my study. Added to this was the fact that I could not get on with my book and could not believe Miss Lily would come back.

These were terrible days. I neglected to eat. I neglected to wash. I left a note for Mrs Watson asking her not to come any more and enclosing a cheque for a month's money. Without her ministrations the spiders thrived, the dust collected, the sink got clogged and little balls of fluff began to creep about in the passages.

There was one hope and it kept me moving through the hours. If I could solve the problem of Naples 1799, if I could show how wrong they were who accused you of treachery and falsehood, everything would fall into place again, everything would start functioning. You would look kindly at me, you and I would be together again as always before, the bright and the dark. Miss Lily would come back, we would work on the book, we would go for outings to the Maritime Museum at Greenwich and further afield to Burnham Thorpe, your birthplace, perhaps even, someday, abroad, Palermo for example, where you and Emma became lovers. I would not worry about being among so many foreigners, she would keep everything safe in her handbag.

I tried to write my thoughts in the left-handed journal. My writing had improved by now, it was much firmer. But no thoughts of my own ever came to me when I took up the pen in my left hand. The pages were covered by your words, not mine, snippets from the letters and despatches, written at different times and in different circumstances. They came to me without any searching, any effort of recollection. Vacant, pen in hand, I would let my eyes and my mind skim over them.

It was my good fortune to have under my command some of the most experienced officers in the English Navy, whose professional skill was seconded by the undaunted courage of British sailors . . . I have brought home a faithful and honourable heart . . . I shall return – if it please God – a victor; and it shall be my study to transmit an unsullied name . . .

An unsullied name – that was his wish, his dearest wish. Tears came into my eyes at the simplicity of it, at my failure so far to deliver it to him. I had been clinging, during these last few days, to the Fatal Misunderstanding Theory, which has been advanced by various of his biographers over the years. According to this, on that morning of the 26th of June both parties were labouring under a misapprehension: the rebels came out believing in the treaty, Horatio believed they had understood that the treaty no longer applied. Could this be possible? The trouble with it as a theory is that only the rebels' view of things had any circumstantial support. They had come out with their belongings packed and ready, books, linen, plate. They had embarked. Surely this meant they believed in the treaty. For what Horatio believed there is only the evidence of his own statements and these are sometimes confusing. His letter to Lord Spencer some fortnight later for example: *The rebels came out of their forts with this knowledge, without any honours, and the principal rebels were seized and conducted aboard the ships of the squadron.*

The knowledge they were surrendering unconditionally, you meant. But it looks from your words as if the seizure followed immediately on the surrender, whereas the rebels were allowed to embark before the ringleaders were seized. Haste? A careless oversight? How could one know? I was in chase of meanings and motives gone for ever, fishing in the past with nets always too coarse for the agile fish I was after, never getting more than the flash of a tail. It seemed like an ocean to me, and I went down into it with my crude equipment day after day. Ruffo and Hamilton, the subtle priest and the wily diplomat, could they have contrived, between them, to keep you in ignorance? But it must have struck you as odd. You saw the rebels come out. Through your telescope, from the deck of the *Vanguard*, you saw them come out through the sea-gates of their forts. You must have thought it was odd that people who knew they were going to be seized, put in irons and handed over to the tender mercies of Ferdinand and Maria Carolina would embark *with their luggage*. The real trouble with the Fatal Misunderstanding Theory was that it made you seem incredibly dense.

Such problems did not trouble Mahan of course. He did not see them as problems at all. His view of things was admirably clear. Ruffo was the trickster, he had taken advantage of the sailor's simplicity. A man such as Nelson, totally honourable and honest, does not suspect duplicity in others. He had promised not to hinder the embarkation and he did not do so; but he had never wavered in his refusal to accept the treaty. He would not stand by and see those miscreants go unpunished. They were traitors, friends to the cursed French, vapid theorizers, full of airy-fairy ideas, not an ounce of true grit among them.

Irish accent, faint but attractive. A bluff and likeable fellow Mahan. He flings his long legs out before him when he sits. Nothing mean or cramped about him. Laughter-lines in that weather-beaten face. A man whose conversation is frank and far-ranging, who exacts nothing from you. A man to repose in, have a drink with.

Badham comes into view, skulking behind, narrow-shouldered and dark-suited. A bitter smile of disbelief. *Nelson wasn't that stupid, nobody could be.* Those conflicting signals, all the confusion, it worked in his favour. Armistice and treaty, embarking and sailing, these are words we play with when vagueness suits us. He wanted them out of the forts, he wanted them hanged, let them think what they liked. Badham's glasses shine, he is wearing a wing collar, he raises one evil, black-gloved hand. I wait for Mahan to get up and give him a straight right to the jaw, but he seems not to have heard. If I could get round to the other side, get within range of that narrow skull . . . I found myself looking round the room for a weapon. It was at that moment of desperate impulse that the idea came, a kind of call. And it was associated from the first with the name of a man I had never met, but whose five-year-old notepaper I still had, a man named E. L. Sims, a resident of Naples.

It was appalling but it was undeniable. There was nothing more that I could do here. If I wanted to keep Horatio with me, I would have to go in person to that city. Naples must contain him still, must contain the truth of those June days. The rooms he ate in, slept in, the streets and buildings he knew, they were still there. Take a trip, Miss Lily had said – advice I had never intended to act on. Dread mounted within me. I was going to act on it now.

25

The salient facts about Sims were that he was an honorary member of the Nelson Society and that he had lived in Naples for a good many years and so must know the city well. He would be just the person to give me some tips, set me on the right track. That he was an honorary member was largely due to me, which I thought might give me some claim on him. Five years before I had seen an article of his in the *Historical Review* entitled 'Four Days in Naples', which dealt with Horatio's first brief visit to the city in the September of 1793, when he was thirty-four years old, a mere captain still and a faithful husband, and had both eyes and all his limbs and was in proud command of his spanking new ship, the *Agamemnon*.

I had been impressed by Sims's meticulous scholarship, the detailed way in which he charted Horatio's movements, the meetings with the Hamiltons and with the prime minister, Sir John Acton, the dinner at the Royal Palace, when he sat at the King's right hand, the breakfast aboard ship on the Sunday morning, when he was host to a distinguished company, including Lord Grandison and the Bishop of Winchester and family, the sudden request, shortly before 11 a.m., that his guests should quit the ship because a French man-of-war had been sighted off Sardinia and he intended to sail immediately to intercept her.

Nothing new in this, but by following the timing so closely and cross-cutting between events Sims had succeeded very cleverly in conveying the drama of Horatio's life at this time, the glitter of high society, the political manoeuvring, the looming death-struggle with France for supremacy at sea which was not to end until twelve years later at Trafalgar. Sims was a man with a sense of the clock, so much was clear, a man with a feeling for parallels. After several weeks of painful indecision I had written to him and he had replied with thanks, courteous though brief. Whereupon I had proposed to the committee that Sims should be invited to become an honorary overseas member. He had accepted the invitation, no more had been heard from him, but somewhere I still had the single sheet of his notepaper with at the head his address in Naples and – or so I hoped – the telephone number.

Of course, he might well have moved since that time. It was Friday afternoon on the 5th of September when I had the impulse to inflict grievous bodily harm on Badham. I knew that if I hesitated much or launched on any sort of debate with myself, I would never make the call. As if under the duress of a dream I opened drawers, fumbled among papers, finally found Sims's note. There was a telephone number at the head. Then it came to me that my passport might be out of date. I had not been out of the country since the trip to Tenerife with my father. After more minutes of search I found it: still seven months to run. I did not know the code for Italy – I had to look it up in the phone-book.

In the course of these harassing preliminaries the protection of dream wore off and my hands became unsteady. However, I did not dare to pause. A peevish, waspish sound to the ringing tone, foreign and far away. Could he be there, at the back of such a sound? Five years . . . Then a voice, without discernible accent but in some way familiar.

'Sims.'

The hiss of his identity seemed to hang in the air between us. There was an agitation in my throat but I contained it. I explained to him who I was.

'Yes,' he said, after a considerable pause, 'I remember that you wrote to me. Some years ago, yes. Where are you now? Are you in Italy?'

'No,' I said. 'No, I am here.'

There was what sounded like a thin clearing of the throat at the other end of the line. 'Here is always where we are,' the voice said.

'Here in London,' I said. 'I am planning to visit Italy, Naples in fact, and I wondered if we could . . . It would give me great pleasure if you could spare some time for me, I thought we might meet for a drink. Compare notes.'

'Notes?'

'As you know I greatly admired your article about Horatio's first visit to the city.'

There was again a pause, this time rather briefer. 'Horatio, yes,' Sims said. 'Well, it would have been very pleasant, Mr Cleasby, but I am leaving Naples soon and I'll be away until the end of the year, so I am afraid – '

I showed a promptness now I had not known I was capable of. 'When?' I said. 'When are you leaving?'

'At the end of next week.'

'I was planning to come more or less at once. You will still be there in the early part of the week?'

In a tone that I thought indicated resignation he said, 'Yes, in the early part of the week, certainly, I will still be here.'

And so it was all arranged. I would telephone Sims from my hotel on the evening of my arrival. We would meet and have a drink together.

Reaction set in immediately. I had some moments of giddiness moving away from the phone and then I experienced a sort of twitching behind the knees, distinctly alarming. It might have been an obscure symptom of hunger; nothing had passed my lips since the tea and digestive biscuits of the morning. Despite this weakness, I was pleased with myself. I had acted with decision, I had not allowed myself to be fobbed off. Something like Hotham's Action, when we nobbled the *Ça Ira*. I decided to celebrate by phoning the takeaway for a pizza.

There was a shadow over things, however, and it grew darker while I waited for the pizza to arrive. I would not be here for

Miss Lily's return. She was due back at the end of the following week – I had been ticking off the days. Now, after all this time of waiting, I would not see her before I left. It couldn't be helped, I knew that. Sims might hold the vital clue, perhaps even something he wasn't himself aware of. Armed with it, I would return, Miss Lily would commend my initiative, we would complete the book together, it would revolutionize Nelson studies . . . All the same, I felt heavy-hearted at the thought of missing her and when the pizza arrived I no longer wanted it. I had some red wine instead.

They were anxious days that followed. There were things I had not foreseen, not being an experienced traveller. It was short notice for early September, still the holiday season. I succeeded in getting a flight to Rome for the following Monday afternoon but there was no connecting flight to Naples available. I would have to go by train. I could have got the train ticket through the agency, but it didn't occur to me.

The whole thing bristled with difficulties. What should I pack, what should I wear for the journey? I had been shuffling around in old clothes for months, not changing very often. My shirts had been folded away too long, they had grubby marks along the folds; my trousers had horizontal crease marks made by the hangers. Before I could become a traveller, before I could present myself to Sims, I had to clean myself up, go to a barber, buy some socks.

I felt almost distraught, locking the front door, locking myself out, hoisting my case down to the waiting taxi. However, this state of nerves subsided, eclipsed by the different order of stress involved in finding my way about at Heathrow. On the whole I acquitted myself well there, I think. I lost some minutes waiting in the wrong queue, among people who were travelling Business Class; but I soon realized the mistake and moved on down to the right counter.

I got the train from Rome Airport to the central railway station without mishap, but I had a bad time at the station itself. I was confused by the crowd and the jostling movement, by the need to be constantly stepping out of the way. Untrustworthy-looking people in white caps with plastic peaks repeatedly asked me if I wanted a hotel. However, I found the ticket office, joined the queue. When I got up to the counter and met the dark, indifferent gaze of the clerk – eyes that had seen so many other eyes, so close, horrendous thought – at this last moment I asked for a single ticket, not a return, asked for it in English and with a sudden loud insistence, as if it might be denied me.

It wasn't, of course; the clerk's expression did not change by the slightest flicker. When I tried to ask about train times he shook his head, raised one hand in a gesture that seemed to take in the entire station. Information was to be sought out there, his job was selling tickets.

Clutching my little oblong of pinkish card, I walked away. I had a sense, exhilarating and alarming, that I was burning my boats behind me. This single ticket was a mark of my determination, my commitment. Without the truth I would not return. However, I had first to get to Naples. I still did not know the time of departure. The information office was full of people waiting and there was only one woman behind the counter to answer their questions. Here and there along the station concourse were large illuminated screens but these did not show times of arrivals and departures, as I was expecting, only a series of images fleeting and diverse, quite soundless: a woman undressing, drifting autumn leaves, oddly angled faces.

Anxiety fastened on me almost unawares. I found myself breathing open-mouthed as if I had been running. It was quarter past two. The heat of the day outside had flowed in, struck through the girders of the roof high above. I felt it pressing down on my head. I was still lugging my case. I thought of finding a left-luggage office, but what if I had to leave in a hurry? There was no friendly-looking buffet where one might have hoped to get tea and a jam doughnut in total anonymity, there was only a sort of glassed-in café, where waiters hovered about. You would have to sit down, catch the waiter's eye, struggle to make your wants known, worry about how much to tip. I could not meet the hazards of such a place until I knew the time of my departure and probably not even then.

I was not far from total anguish and immobility when I came upon a poster at the far end of the station, which had details of inter-city connections. There was a train to Naples at 2.46. A little star was printed after the time and I saw from the foot of the poster that this was a Eurostar train, distinguished with a note in both Italian and English, *Alta velocità, High speed*. There would almost certainly be an extra charge on a train like this. It was now 2.27 by my watch. A man in railway uniform was passing close to me. I stepped in front of him, swinging my case. 'Eurostar ticket?' I said to him loudly. He regarded me without much expression but not unkindly. I tried again. 'Eurostar ticket?'

He raised a forefinger as if testing the wind. '*Uno*,' he said. '*Binario uno.*'

Platform 1. We were then alongside Platform 22. Hastily back the full length of the station, humping my case. Sure enough, there it was, clearly marked, the Eurostar ticket counter. A strip of red digital lettering above stated that all seats had to be booked in advance. Five or six people were already queuing. It was 2.35. Minutes ticked away. I was sweating heavily, unable to prevent myself from gasping. I have always, from childhood, practised open-mouthed breathing as a relief from all manner of stress, and now it has become quite involuntary. I felt that people were looking at me but I did not return these glances. It had become immensely important, symbolical, not to miss this special, high-speed train. I understood now that the train itself was a part of the design, that I was being tested. A failure at this point could put my whole enterprise at risk.

At last my turn came. I paid the supplementary charge, received the white card that recorded my booking. Where did the train leave from? Platform 22, naturally. It was now exactly 2.43. I had three minutes to traverse the whole length of the station again.

In a panic of haste I set off. The blood throbbed at my temples, my vision was clouded, I heard my panting progress through the crowd. I made it with half a minute to spare. The brand-new train was there, towering above me, in all the gleam of imminent departure. I found my seat, collapsed into it, waited for the moment of drawing away.

We remained where we were, without explanation, for the next seventeen minutes, while my breathing returned slowly to normal, my heart quietened, the perspiration cooled on my body. I understood the whole thing now: there had been no need for haste, no need for fear, a period of error had been allowed for, *the train had been scheduled to wait.* This thought brought no ease of mind, merely increasing my sense of responsibility. It came to me now, in these moments of restored calm, came to me like a folding of wings, that it had not after all been fear of missing the train that had agitated me so but fear of what I was doing, of the mission itself, a fear no doubt quickened by the distress I had just been put through, but already there, already existing – I had brought it with me from Belsize Park. Miss Lily's face came into my mind, that flushed look of hers and her indignation when she met with something that seemed contrary to common sense. I was swept with a desolate sense of her absence and I seemed to hear her voice saying, 'But what does it mean, Charles, what does it *mean?*'

Her smile when she heard about the brandy. I hadn't minded it somehow. And Bobby's solemn stare . . . The progress of the train was smooth, almost silent. I felt weary but safe from harm for the moment, quite relaxed. The countryside south of Rome slipped by unheeded. I began to think again, in a wandering, sleepy kind of way, of that last voyage in the battered flagship, that long return to gratitude and grief. They took every care to keep you fresh, repeatedly draining the spirits off from below, topping them up from above. But the sentinel who was on guard beside your barrel got a bad fright one morning – he saw the lid lifting up and gave the alarm. Nothing supernatural in it; your body had absorbed most of the brandy and a pressure of gas had built up.

It was early in December when you arrived at Spithead, two weeks later when you made your way round to the Nore. When you were taken from the cask and inspected you were found to be in a perfect state of preservation. An autopsy revealed that your heart and liver and lungs were free of all trace of disease; all your vital parts were perfectly sound. You might have lived to a great age, the doctors said. But your remaining eye was going, in a few years you would have been completely blind.

They took you and put you in a plain coffin, one that had been waiting for you ever since 1798; made from the timbers of the *Orient*, the French flagship destroyed at Aboukir Bay. This was cased in lead and then enclosed in an outer coffin, encrusted with heraldic devices, your coat of arms, the stars of your orders, a crocodile representing the Battle of the Nile. In this you lay in state in the Painted Hall at Greenwich. Here the Prince of Wales came alone to pay his respects, that same Prince who had once caused you torments of jealousy. Next day the doors were thrown open to the people, who came in such enormous numbers that the governor of the Hospital panicked and called for extra troops. They were not needed, there was no disturbance, the people were docile with grief.

Three days later the grand river procession from Greenwich to London, the stately City barges with the black and gold of their cabins and the brocaded liveries of the oarsmen, your funeral barge towering above them with its huge canopy and its plumes of dyed ostrich feathers tossing in the wind off the river, the silent crowds lining the river banks. There was a moment which I had always felt to be significant, ever since first reading about it. I couldn't remember when – perhaps in the Grigson days. As your barge was brought alongside Whitehall Stairs the sky darkened and there was sudden violent squall of rain, lashing the bearers as they struggled to raise the coffin and place it on the waiting funeral car. This intervention of the sky was remembered and retold, those darkened moments when you quitted for ever the element that had seen your triumphs.

A vast procession had been assembled to escort the body to St Paul's; but there were too many soldiers, it was a river of red, the blue naval uniforms were almost overwhelmed. Just forty-eight men, seamen and marines from HMS *Victory*. The crowd roared its approval of them, they were cheered continuously as they marched past, proudly displaying the flags of their ship, two huge Union Jacks bearing the marks of the enemy shot and the St George's ensign, which they held up to view, ripped and shattered, amid the sobs and plaudits of the crowd. But silence fell at the passing of the funeral car. As it went by with its tall four-posted canopy and nodding plumes, bearing the gilded coffin high above the heads of the people, its progress was accompanied by a great rustling noise like the sound of waves on the seashore, as the thousands of male onlookers removed their hats.

The burial service was performed after the Office of Evensong. The coffin made its slow way up the aisle to the haunting music of William Croft's 'Burial Sentences': *I am the resurrection and the life saith the Lord.* But the piece most people remembered and spoke about came at the end of the service, just before the coffin was lowered to its final resting place in the crypt, the music composed by Handel for the funeral of Queen Caroline in 1737, with its ringing assertion: *But his name liveth evermore!*

Precisely at thirty-three and a half minutes past five the coffin was lowered into its grave and disappeared from public view. It was the Garter King at Arms – I tried to recall his name but could not – who proclaimed the style and the titles of the dead Lord: *Thus it hath pleased Almighty God to take out of this transitory life, unto his divine mercy, the Most Noble Lord Horatio Nelson, Viscount and Baron Nelson of the Nile, and of Burnham Thorpe, in the County of Norfolk, Knight of the Most Honourable Order of the Bath, Vice-Admiral of the White Squadron of the Fleet . . .*

I drifted into sleep before getting to the end of the list. I roused myself to produce my ticket when the inspector came, but for most of the journey I was comatose. I didn't take much notice of the surroundings until we were approaching Naples and I saw the tawny, crumpled summit of Vesuvius, familiar to me from a hundred illustrations. There were glimpses of the coast, a glitter of sea, a strip of bright sand, a vivid cluster of beach umbrellas, swallowed up almost at once by the ugly and haphazard jumble of buildings stretching up from the shore. On the other side, to my left, a constant, rippling line of mountains, bare, bluish in this afternoon light, rank on rank of them.

I took a taxi from the station to my hotel, the Santa Lucia, closing my eyes on the anarchic disorder of the traffic. This improved when we reached the wide seafront road where the hotel was. All the same, I was glad to climb out from the taxi into the flooding sea-light that came off the bay, glad to be able to understand the driver's English, work out the liras, give him a tip that seemed acceptable. Glad, in short, to have survived thus far. My visit was already assuming the characteristics it was to have all the way through, almost till the end: a surviving of encounters, a sense of having – only just – kept a step ahead. Horatio was in this city. I had to keep going till I found him. More than that: I had to keep on the look-out, keep my mind open for the truth when it came. I kept on, I was careful – almost till the end.

All the details of my arrival at the hotel were attended by this same sense of obstacles overcome: checking-in, ascending in the lift, following the porter down the quiet corridor, finally finding myself alone, still all in one piece, in my distinctly handsome room – they had given me one overlooking the bay.

Only now, in this first solitude achieved in Naples, about to reach for the phone, only now did I register the address of this hotel – such a famous name, it had not been necessary to mention the street. But I noticed it now on the brochure lying beside the phone: Via Partenope 46. Parthenopean Street. It was named after that short-lived republic whose fate had tormented me for months, named after those Neapolitan Jacobins whom Ruffo and his Calabrian irregulars defeated and drove into their forts, to whom the promise of safe-conduct was made and not kept, who came out in the end to cast themselves – you said – on the mercy of their notoriously unmerciful sovereigns. Did you believe it? Did you? It was that botched attempt at liberty, those heart-sickening deaths, that the street commemorated, not your loyal support of the Bourbon monarch . . . I felt a chill, something like premonition, as I took out my wallet, found the card on which I had written Sims's number, made the call.

'Ah, it's you,' he said without particular expression. 'So you have arrived.'

'Minutes ago,' I said. 'You see I lost no time in phoning.'

'No, you didn't.'

'I am very much looking forward to – '

'Did you have a good journey?'

The conventional politeness of this took me quite by surprise. The journey had nothing to do with it, I was on a mission. 'Yes,' I said. 'Quite uneventful.'

'Uneventful is always good,' Sims said. 'Especially on aeroplanes.'

'I was wondering if tomorrow we might meet . . .'

'During most of the day I am busy, unfortunately. There are so many things to see to before I go away. But late in the afternoon I would have some time, if that suits you. Or perhaps you would prefer the day after?'

'No,' I said, 'no, tomorrow would be fine.'

So it was arranged. Sims would come to the Santa Lucia at 5.30, we would have a drink together at the hotel bar. It was a great relief to me to have definitely fixed this appointment. Sims was a resident of this city, he would know Italian, he was a knowledgeable, scholarly fellow, he might put me on to something, new material, a line to follow up. I would have to be on the alert, it might be small, something Sims himself might not think was important. Something to establish your good name for ever and join mine to it. Entwined together, inseparable, vindicated and vindicator, the bright and the dark.

In the glow of hope these thoughts afforded me I went over to my window and looked across the bay. Your eyes saw this when you looked out from the balcony of your room in the Palazzo Sessa, residence of the Hamiltons, where you stayed. Not perhaps the immediate foreground lying just below me, the little harbour with its moored launches and yachts, the gently glimmering water warmed by the reflections of the boats to shades of ochre and pale orange. No, but you would have seen the more distant view, the open sea, the island of Capri with its ridged head and long jaw. Like some fabulous dragon. Perhaps you too made just that comparison in your mind, looking out from your room that September of your second visit, when you were falling in love with Emma Hamilton. Some warm evening like this one. Languid and feverish after your great victory at the Nile, still suffering from the strain of it and the shock of the wound. She moves quietly about in the room behind you, preparing something for your comfort. What you need most for your comfort is the enfolding of her lovely thighs, but this is five months away still, in Palermo, on a cold day of February. No heating to speak of, chilly marble everywhere in those Sicilian palaces, Miss Lily would not have liked it, she feels the cold. In the tent of the blankets a warm refuge, a mingling of breaths.

A white cruise liner was crossing the bay from right to left, in the direction of Sorrento. Immediately below me a policeman in a white helmet and pale blue uniform was directing the traffic. To the north, barely a hundred yards beyond the marina, was the Castel dell'Ovo, or Castle of the Egg, from which, under the eyes of the British fleet, some of the Jacobins, clutching the belongings they would never need again, were embarked on their transports. A massive, squat, square-topped building, windowless on the shore side. I could make out a poster on the façade, brightly coloured, with a figure on it that looked like Donald Duck but of course couldn't be. This castle was so close, only minutes away, I could leave it to the last.

It was after seven. Already there was some gathering of darkness in the air, strings of coloured bulbs on the café fronts and along the harbour railings had been lit while I watched. After the trials of the day I was tired. I would eat at the hotel, go early to bed. In this new place nightmare might give me some respite. I would be fresh next day, ready to search for him, ready to face Sims. I had high hopes of Sims.

26

I slept fitfully but better than usual. I had a strange dream, different from any I could remember. I was walking on smooth sand, gleaming wet, giving slightly to the weight. I was looking for something, stones of some kind that might be concealed in the sand, but I found nothing. The sand became more shining and softer, my feet made oily swirls in it, like oil spreading on a wet film. A white goat approached me, very shyly. I tried to encourage the goat to come nearer and it did so finally. I put my hand out to caress the goat but found that it had turned so that its rear was towards me. I felt my hand caught in a warm dry clamp. I thought at first it was the goat's prehensile anus but saw after a moment that he had a very long tail with a thick, fleshy bump at the end like a bullrush and this contained a kind of mouth, in which my hand was imprisoned. For some moments I tried to withdraw it, not violently but discreetly. I felt some disgust, some fear, but mainly a desire that no one should witness my humiliating predicament. No one did. Still politely tugging, I rose to wakefulness in the pale light of early morning. Slowly the sense of mystery and beauty and repugnance caused by this dream faded away, to be replaced by an uneasy question: why was there no reference to Palazzo Sessa in my guide-book, otherwise so packed with information? Why was it not marked on any of the maps?

Even later, setting forth, fortified by coffee and various pastries, the question still exercised me. I knew the way of course. I had traced it in imagination a hundred times, your triumphant coach-ride up from the waterfront, after the salutes of the guns, the swooning of Emma, the welcoming speech of King Ferdinand, sweating in his velvet suit.

Every detail of my walk that day has stayed with me. The glittering sweep of the bay, Vesuvius mild-looking in the early sunshine, the cindery tracks of its eruptions clearly visible, a group of policemen with gleaming revolver-holsters laughing and joking together at a street corner. Across the broad Via Marina, up to Largo di Castello, then steeply up again into the side of the Pizzofalcone hill. I was out of condition and had to take it slowly. The streets were narrow, paved with dark stone, the houses tall and close together. Full daylight had not arrived here yet, some residue of darkness still grained the air between the houses. There was a short alley ending in a cobbled yard with on one side a small church and on the other a vaulted passage opening on to the courtyard of the palazzo.

There it stood before me, Palazzo Sessa, official residence of the British Ambassador, rented by him from the Marchese di Sessa for £150 a year, a high rent for the time; before that home to monastic orders for something like seven centuries. Here Emma arrived on her twenty-first birthday, in the full flower of her beauty, cast off by Sir William's nephew, though not yet knowing it, soon to be the mistress, then the wife, of the elderly uncle. Here exhausted Horatio was brought after his great victory at the Nile, to be tended by Emma, to lie and watch her as she moved about the room, her full figure under the loose drapes. Here began their celebrated love.

I scanned the façade, every inch of it. I looked carefully at the arched entranceway. It was incredible: there was nothing whatever to record or commemorate the fact that the greatest hero in our national history had spent months of his life here at a time of crucial importance, when the fate of the city was hanging in the balance. Standing there on the dark cobbles of the courtyard, I looked up to the first floor, where your room was. A line of washing obscured the tall windows. Another went across from one side of the courtyard to the other. Somewhere inside the place a baby was crying with a blind, persistent woe, hardly pausing for breath. Across from me, at the foot of the stone steps that you must have mounted to reach your apartment, two women were standing together. They had been talking but fell silent when I appeared and looked closely at me. The place was a tenement, in multiple occupation. There was no way it could be entered, no way of finding that room of your fever and dawning desire, the room I had shared with you, as I had shared thoughts of Emma's body. With a sensation of bewilderment I raised my head to the clear blue of the day above me, clouds moving slowly in it, swifts wheeling high up. There was a sudden silence, or so it seemed, I thought I could hear the thin shrieks of the swifts, distant as they were, some message contained in them important for me to know. But it was the sound of mourning, it fell on my up-turned face, it touched my face like rain. His words printed on my mind, his courage that supplied my lack . . . The sky was blank, the birds were silent. I became aware again of the wailing baby, the glances of the women, the lines of washing. From somewhere behind me came music from a radio, thin notes, slightly distorted.

I turned away, went back through the vaulted passageway, past the church, back down towards the water. Everything I looked at seemed improbable, insubstantial. You saved their Bourbon majesties, you delivered Naples from the cursed French . . . Perhaps in the two forts where the Jacobins held out against you I might discover something that would save the day.

Castel Nuovo was the nearer, just across from the Royal Palace, on the seaward side. It took me not quite half an hour to walk there. Round, crenellated towers in dark stone, an incongruous triumphal arch in white marble, celebrating the taking of the city by Alfonso I of Aragon. I got my ticket from the small office adjoining the courtyard. Somewhere here, in a corner, royalist hostages were shot by the rebels, panicking as their time ran out. Perhaps over against the steps the killing was done, where now a group of schoolchildren clustered and chatted. Or against the wall, below the chapel – mass shootings generally seemed to take place up against something. Was this the deed of blood that determined you to deal harshly with the rebels, to regard them as beyond the pale, people to whom promises need not be kept? You see, I was still trying to find reasons. But the outrage was small, compared to what the royalist mob was doing in the streets of the city. No, you were against them from the start, you loathed their libertarian rhetoric, all that claptrap, that parroting of the bombastic, bloody French.

It was a question of getting up to the top of the castle, up to the ramparts, so I could look down over the sea-gates that the rebels came out of, see the view towards Sorrento as they must have seen it on that last day of their liberty, as they were embarked on the transports that became their floating prisons.

A flight of stone steps led upwards. I mounted quickly, a sort of excitement possessing me, a sense of possible revelation up there on the heights. I would see where the rebels came out along the mole, I would see them, by a stretch of imagination, as he would have seen them, waiting in his anchored flagship out in the bay, telescope to his eye, noting with approval that they were not being accorded honours of war. Perhaps, in this violation of the parallels, in this splicing of viewpoints, some essential clue might be vouchsafed me . . .

But on the broad stone landing of the second floor my way was barred by two attendants, who pressed with their palms at the air between us and uttered words I did not understand. I heard the slam of heavy doors closing. It seemed I was required to go down to the courtyard again. What had happened? It couldn't be closing time, it wasn't eleven yet. The attendants were shouting among themselves. A different sort of shouting came from the street outside, a heavy, reiterated chant. And from some invisible source, high above, other voices, thinned by distance.

The man behind the counter at the ticket office knew some English. Things were finally explained to me. A mass demonstration by the unemployed of Naples was going on outside, some of the demonstrators had infiltrated the fort, occupied the battlements, theirs were the voices I had heard shouting down. They were armed with clubs, the man said – he gestured with his hands to show the formidable nature of these. His face took on a look of painful sincerity. They were very bad people, he said, not genuine unemployed at all. There was fear of some violent assault on the picture gallery, the frescos in the chapel. Everything had to be locked and barred.

There didn't seem much point in hanging about waiting. It might take a long time to expel these intruders. I thought it likely that the riot police would have to be brought in. I made for the exit gates but found these barred too. Two attendants in hot blue suits, one on either side. Please open this gate. I made gestures of unbarring and opening. The attendants shook their heads, miming in their turn: more people with clubs just outside, waiting for a chance to break in. How long will this go on? Tapping my watch, raising my eyebrows. Shrugs all round, nobody knew. I was caught there, trapped between occupied battlements and barred gates.

It was hot, even in the shade of the courtyard wall. The remote harangues from the men on the battlements still came floating down. Straining my eyes against the glare, I made out two gesturing figures. One of them raised and waved what looked like a staff or short pole, thicker at one end than the other. Besiegers or besieged? Beyond them, the sky was glazed white, painful to look at. A moment of giddiness came to me and I felt in danger of falling. I stepped back, groped for the support of the wall, remembering as my vision cleared how Miss Lily had supported me the evening I had staggered, remembering the warmth of her hand under my arm.

There were other visitors, drifting around the courtyard or standing in the ticket office. A gaunt American couple, an Italian family, man and wife and two small fractious girls, a mixed group of young people, probably students. Hostages all, fellow victims of circumstance, we avoided one another's eyes. After something more than an hour the gate was unbarred, we were allowed to leave. There were no demonstrators in the street outside but a number of helmeted policemen waited there, standing in silent groups near the vans that had brought them.

It was quarter past twelve when I emerged. The sun swooped down as if it had been waiting in ambush just for me. Nothing looked the same. The street seemed wider than before, it was a river flowing with cars; looking across it was like straining to see a far shore. It was too far, there was too much glare. I felt the eyes of the police on me.

Lunchtime was approaching but I felt no smallest desire to eat. I set off walking, keeping the water on my right, stopping every now and again to consult my map. It took me nearly forty minutes to get within sight of the Carmine church. I had to cross the road, a hazardous business this, as there were side lanes as well as the main ones and no one took any notice of the traffic lights. I had to make a dash and only narrowly avoided being run over. This made my temples throb and I felt the beginning of a headache, a dull, persistent pain along the ridges of the brows. But it was cool and dim inside the church, all a harmony of variously coloured marbles. There was no one else there. I stood still for some moments absorbing the peace and silence of the place, the inlaid pilasters at their exact intervals, the stone heads of seraphim decorating the arches. Nothing much had changed since Ruffo's time, since that morning of the 27th of June 1799, when the cardinal had come here in state to celebrate a mass of thanksgiving for the fortunate outcome of the treaty negotiations.

He was happy that day – or so he gave it out. *Full of contentment that the English had not only recognized but themselves executed the treaty.* Sacchinelli again, the diligent secretary, writing after his employer's death. The words sounded now like an echo in the cavern of my mind, in this sumptuous, cavernous church. What was in the cardinal's mind as he intoned the 'Te Deum,' raised the Host that day? The rebels were already out of the forts, they had been jostled to their transports by Horatio's marines. How much did Ruffo know, how much did he suspect? Did he really think the Jacobins would be allowed to sail for France? Or was that mass a piece of ornate and solemn hypocrisy, designed to exculpate him, throw the odium of betrayal on the British?

The same questions. I was no nearer the answers here than I had been in my basement in Belsize Park. Standing there, with that dull band of pain along my brows, I felt the same sorrow, the same helplessness that I had so often felt at home in my study. Whatever one made of the documents, the truth of the past was beyond grasping, it lay in the looks exchanged, the tones used; and the eyes and voices had left no trace.

Out again, into the blinding sun. A walk of five minutes took me from the scene of thanksgiving, whether genuine or not, to the site of the indisputably genuine hangings which shortly followed. Piazza del Mercato, where the executions were carried out, where public executions had been carried out for many hundreds of years. A vast and desolate square between the dock area and the district of Forcella with a few nondescript stalls round the edges. Along the eastern side an open-air market for cheap leisure goods, plastic garden chairs, inflatable dinghies and ducks and paddling-pools, brightly coloured beach umbrellas, all set out on the cobbles. Some small boys listlessly kicking a ball around in a far corner. A Baroque church with a lead-coloured dome and eroded saints on the façade.

Somewhere here, in the middle . . . Whatever the rights and wrongs, the promises kept or broken, this is where it ended for the leaders of that short-lived republic. Day after day, through those summer months of 1799, they were brought here in batches to combine with hangman and pull-feet and make that triple-headed, dangling beast that had so haunted my imagination.

I squinted across the vast square. The flat light of afternoon lay over everything – there were no shadows. I found myself longing for the cool of night, for the dark, as they must have done as they were led out to die. The agony would be over, they would have found their own darkness. The troops withdrew at nightfall; their only purpose was to ensure that the executions were carried out. The corpses were stripped by the hangman and left hanging, sport of the populace. If they were not citizens of Naples no one would claim them, they would remain there. The *lazzaroni* would push and pull them this way and that. Cruelty, like other motions of the heart, needs time to warm up. With time they went from jeers to knives, slashing at the bodies, cutting off the ears, the nose, the testicles, hacking through the ribs. After that came the feast. The livers were roasted and eaten, here on the square, perhaps just where I was standing. It is related that a passer-by who refused to partake of this meal was killed on the spot.

You saw none of this, you saw none of the executions, you came nowhere near the contagion of the mob. You were . . . elsewhere. On board ship or in Sicily or dozing through the hot afternoons in the Palazzo Sessa. You heard it, you must have heard it, no one in Naples could escape it, that great roar of jubilation as the victim was launched into space.

The dome of the church opposite was clear in every detail. I had the impression of some quivering or disturbance in the air, like the single swing of an invisible pendulum. Then the square was blank again, drab, dusty, featureless, pressed down under the flat light. The garish beach goods, the occasional voices of the children, the squat little church . . . That great sum of terror and pain, I had somehow expected to find it reflected here; but there was only this bleakness and ugliness of the present.

Turning away, quitting the square, was attended by a curious sense of effort. No more than tiredness, I suppose, but I felt I could have stayed there a long time without moving, one of the derelict props of the place. It was twenty past two; Sims was coming to the hotel at five thirty; there would be time to see the other fort, Castel dell'Ovo, but I had omitted to find out whether it was open to visitors in the afternoon. Probably not, I thought. It was near the hotel in any case. I was exhausted, but the thought of resting or stopping to eat something did not come into my mind. I did not want to take a taxi, shrinking from the human encounter it would involve. Only Sims I wanted to see; I had hopes of Sims.

I was walking more slowly now; it took me more than an hour to get to the fort. I was relieved to find the gate open; but as I approached I was astonished to see that the figure on the poster over the entrance, which I had observed at a distance from my hotel room and which had so much resembled Donald Duck, was in fact Donald Duck, complete with jaunty sailor's cap and chortling beak and clumpy webbed feet. Above his head in bright red letters, *Il Mondo dei Paperi*. Ripples of light moved over the poster, cast up by the jiggling reflections of the harbour water. *Mondo* was world – the World of Donald Duck. After some moments of incredulity I understood: there was a Donald Duck exhibition taking place inside this venerable building.

It might be possible to bypass Donald, get a ticket for the fort only. I went through the vaulted tunnel of the entrance and spoke to the man inside the little glassed-in ticket office. I spoke carefully through the grid. Not Donald, please. But you couldn't have one without the other. I didn't like the man's eyes, they were small and black, I didn't like the way he stared through his glass wall, as if there were something wrong with me, something strange about wanting to give Donald a miss. It occurred to me now that I could ignore the exhibition altogether, go straight on past. I would walk past, make my way up to the sunlit bastions, inspect the cannon, still in their emplacements, look out from those heights over the water to where your ships lay at anchor.

But at the entrance to the exhibition I came upon two young people, a boy and a girl, they were wearing Donald Duck T-shirts, they had spotted the brightly coloured ticket in my hand, it too bearing Donald's image. They smiled in greeting, they held out catalogues, they thought I had come for him. I was too tired, too confused, the smiles and T-shirts were impossible to disappoint, I could not simply slink past, keeping my head down so as not to see their expressions change. I tried to smile, tried to assume the look of someone looking forward to a rare treat, and passed inside.

Once in there was no quick way out again. It was a one-way

system, arrows pointed from room to room. The exhibition was enormous, it occupied three floors, all of them strangely resonant with voices. Voices and echoes of voices, in the cavernous rooms; but no faces of people, none that I can remember, so terrible was the impact of the faces on the walls. All Donald's relatives were there, grotesquely blown up, staring down. Everywhere I looked I met their eyes, enormous, unshaded by lashes, horribly intent. The primary colours shrieked from the walls. The glands at the sides of my neck felt hot, I felt the run of sweat on my chest and back. Twice I tried to go back, to retrace my steps, but the way was barred by more young people in Donald Duck T-shirts. They smiled, they pointed at the arrows, I had to follow the arrows. The second floor was worse than the first, with the Scottish branch all represented and named in glaring capitals, Jack McDuck and Dirty Dingus and Sir Quackly, huge and terrifying in a top hat and spats. There was nowhere in the room to look, nowhere my eyes could take refuge from them. A moment came when I doubted my ability to walk across the room, expose myself to the barrage of those eyes, reach the stairs to the third and final floor, the only way out. I wanted to hide, to press back against the doorway. I was aware of my own noisy breathing. I made it to the slit of a window, peered out at a sudden, brilliant section of sea, the broken crest of Vesuvius, the mole of the fort along which the Jacobins made their way to be embarked. Here finally was the view I had wanted. Turning back, I encountered with an irrepressible leap of terror the enormous, baleful eyes of old Scrooge McDuck, the collective stare of a boatload of Jowly dog-pirates in black masks.

How long I stayed here, how I found the resolution to get out, I cannot clearly remember. In the end, keeping my eyes down, I forced myself to walk across to the foot of the stairs and mount upward. The third floor was better. There were no more mon-strously enlarged and malignant ducks, only a few of Donald's milder-eyed cousins, Molly Mallard, Cuthbert Coot, Luke Goose.

The last gallery was quite different from the others, devoted to copies of well-known paintings, faithful in every particular except that the human subjects had been replaced by Disney characters. I stayed here some time, waiting for my breathing to come back to normal, for that flush of panic to subside – fear with me was a fever, not a chill; the chill came now as the sweat cooled on my body. There was the Arnolfini Betrothal by Jan Van Eyck, with the Happy Hippos, Horace and Clarabella, as the engaged couple, and Caravaggio's celebrated Lute-Player, with Minnie Mouse plucking the strings.

As I stood before these travesties in the blankness of mind that followed upon fear, through my weariness, my headache, my strained sight, there came to me some dawning hope of revelation. These images imposed on images, this simpering Minnie, these toothy hippos, perhaps here, not outside on that sunlit sea, was the secret, the key I was looking for. This Vermeer, with a pinafored Snow White in the kitchen among hanging fowl and the utensils of an alien culture . . . If one could peel the layers away, find the truth below the image, before the original painter found it, before the first, deceiving brush-strokes. A memory came to me of the coloured stamps I had so loved as a small child, transfers, as they were called, about the size of a match-box top, backed by some thin, adhesive tissue. You peeled the tissue away, you pressed the stamp on a blank sheet and there, clearly printed, was the image. Angel fish, flamingos, a boat on a blue sea, a huntsman in a red coat. It would work on your skin too, particularly where the skin was pale and hairless, like the inside of the forearm. A transfer could only be used once but one could be superimposed on another and this was always a temptation and always regretted, resulting in botched shapes, blurred colours. Perhaps my earliest experience of sorrow, that remorse for the blighting of the pristine image, the knowledge it could never be recovered.

I was driven away by the arrival of a chattering group of children shepherded by an elderly lady, their teacher as I supposed.

Finally there was an escape route – stone stairs led down and away. Too late now to see more of the fort, I was due to meet Sims at half past five in the bar of my hotel. If I wanted to be there before him, there was time only to find my way out of this place, walk back past the little harbour, cross the broad road that ran along beside the bay.

I reached the air-conditioned haven of the bar with six minutes to spare. I felt sticky and dishevelled, but there was no time for a shower if I wanted to be in place first. The bar was long and darkly shining. Pale lights were already on behind the counter, though shaded sunlight still lay over the wicker chairs and glass-topped tables at the nearer end. Hobnobbing on the bar stools was quite out of the question, I knew my disabilities, I did not want to sit too close to Sims, I would not have been able to talk to him or meet his eyes. I went to the bar and asked for red wine. I took my glass over to the corner table farthest from the bar and sat with my back to the wall so as to observe the approaches. At this early hour I was alone there, among the tables. I drank some of the wine, which was good, full-bodied, dark ruby in colour – from Sardinia, the barman had said. Almost at once, with the first taste of it, my headache receded, my weariness disappeared, and I felt entirely alert.

He came at twenty-three minutes to six. I knew him at once, before he had reached the table, before he had broken into the smile, signal of uncertainty, apology in advance for possible mistake. I had never set eyes on him before, but I experienced a pang of delighted recognition. That large, loose-knit figure, the careless, slightly shambling gait, the light hair, tanned face, the lines round the eyes that came from scanning wide horizons – it was Mahan to the life.

As he drew near and I stood up to answer his smile, the impression grew stronger and stronger. He corresponded in every detail. So much so that when he held out his hand and said, 'Sims, Ernesto Sims,' I was momentarily at a loss for his meaning.

'Charles Cleasby,' I said. 'So kind of you to find the time for

297

me.' Somewhere between the beginning of this sentence and the end of it, the incongruity, the foreignness of his first name struck me. He seated himself opposite my chair, at the farthest remove, and I was pleased by this, it seemed like a mark of tact. I asked him what he wanted to drink – a waiter had materialized at his elbow. He asked for something called *carpano*, which I had never heard of but took to be a sort of aperitif. This again seemed slightly incongruous – I had set Mahan down as a whisky-and-soda man, whether on foreign verandas or by the hearth of home. I asked for another glass of the Sardinian wine. 'Good of you to give up your time,' I said, shyness causing me to repeat myself.

'Not at all. It is good to meet a fellow member of the Nelson Club.'

There was something in the tone of this that made me glance quickly at him. Nothing showed on his face. Did he know I was no longer a member? Why had I thought his eyes were blue? They were dark, almost black. But his long legs were thrust out before him, carelessly sprawled, just as they had been that day in my study. He was wearing a linen jacket, rather crumpled. A dark blue handkerchief fell in loose folds from his breast pocket.

'How are you liking Naples?' he said.

An odd question, I thought it. How could I tell him that Horatio's Naples and mine was a sticky trap, a smeared web? He lived in Naples. I could not risk giving him offence, he might withhold his help.

'Well,' I said, 'I'm not really here as a tourist, you know, I am here to try and pick up his traces.'

'Excuse me, whose traces are we talking about?'

'Why, his, you know. Nelson's. I have rather drawn a blank so far.'

I suspected nothing. In that first flush of confidence I began to tell him about my book, about the problem I had run into. 'I wondered whether you might be able to put me on to something,' I said.

I had spoken in a light tone, not wanting Mahan to think me

stumped but merely casting around. He had leaned forward in his chair. The red-brown stuff in his glass was hardly touched.

'A plaque?' he said. 'Did you expect to find a plaque commemorating Nelson on the wall of the Palazzo Sessa? One of those blue ones that they put on houses in London?'

This was not the tone I had expected; there was something harsh in it, something derisive, setting me on the defensive. 'Perhaps not a plaque,' I said, 'but something at least, something to mark his stay there.' *Ernesto.* And the eyes, dark, fathomless . . .

He looked down for a moment and his shoulders slumped in what seemed a long release of breath. 'My dear man,' he said, 'you have had a disappointing day, but you could walk round in this city every day for a year and you wouldn't see the slightest sign of Nelson anywhere, neither hide nor hair of him. Not a syllable. The Palazzo Sessa looks down over the Piazza dei Martiri. Did you look at the monument there?'

'No.'

'The martyrs in question are the Neapolitan Jacobins who went to the scaffold in the name of liberty in 1799, sent there through the good offices of Lord Nelson. This hotel is on a street named after the republic that Nelson helped to bring down.'

'Yes, I know that.'

'And do you know that if you went out of here and turned right you would come before long to the Via Caracciolo, a broad and beautiful avenue that runs along beside the sea towards Vomero? Or that if you went a little way up Via Santa Lucia, which is just behind us here, you would arrive at the little church of Santa Maria in Catena, which contains Caracciolo's tomb? That same Caracciolo, the Neapolitan admiral whom Nelson, on doubtful authority, had court-martialled for treason and condemned and hanged in the course of a few hours – he was already hanging there from the yardarm when Nelson sat down to dinner. It was Caracciolo's corpse that rode the waves, you remember? Yes of course, you will have read Parsons's account. The local fishermen recovered his body from the scrape in the sand where the English had left it without even protection from the dogs. Now he lies there in state, one of Italy's most honoured sons.'

He paused here and took a sip of the syrupy-looking liquid in his glass. He had been careful otherwise but ordering that drink had been a false move on his part. I knew now that he was not what he seemed. I knew I'd have to be very careful.

'You have come for the wrong hero,' he said. 'Caracciolo is the hero here. Heroes are always local.'

I saw the sudden, ironic twist of his lips as he said this. Thin lips. It was clear that heroes meant little to him, whether English or Italian. Mahan would never have said a thing like that. This was a person without ideals. A change had come over him while he spoke. He seemed narrower somehow in his chair, even his face seemed narrower and the hairline more receding. He was an impersonator, a dangerously clever one. But his disguise was slipping away.

'After all,' he said, 'they would not be likely to honour the memory of someone they consider responsible for the destruction of one of the most cultivated societies in Europe. Between the July of Ferdinand's return and the following March, 120 were put to death in Naples and the islands and 222 sentenced to life imprisonment. To say nothing of the hundreds given shorter sentences who died in Ferdinand's filthy jails. Very few of these were men of the populace, perhaps two or three. All the rest were nobles, officers, lawyers, doctors, professors and men of science and letters. In the exercise of his royal mercy Ferdinand strangled or decapitated or shut away the whole of the Neapolitan intellec-tual class. Do you appreciate the gravity of a loss like that? They cut off the head and left the trunk to the mob and the Church and the Bourbon tyranny. The whole south of Italy still feels the effect of that today.' He was shaking his head. 'And you come here to look for Nelson.'

'He was not responsible,' I said. 'How could he have known what would happen to them?'

These words of mine served only to give the person opposite me more power, I knew that. I was afraid of him but I could not prevent myself from inviting more harm, from putting my head on the block. It was why I had arranged the interview, I understood it now. I looked away from him, summoning resolution. There were more people at the bar and three men in business suits were sitting at one of the tables, but too far away to hear us. People were passing through the swing doors that gave on to the street outside, people entering and leaving. Rapid shapes of light were made by the swinging of these doors, flexing, spiralling shapes, gone as soon as glimpsed. This light had a reddish tinge – the awning outside the hotel was red, I suddenly remembered. The reception area lay beyond the doors, beyond the passing people and the play of light. It seemed strangely distant and the air looked thicker there, opaque and still, like cloudy water in a glass tank. It was suddenly quite clear to me that I had not come here to find Horatio at all: I had brought him here to be killed and myself with him. 'I intend to clear his name,' I said.

'Clear his name?' Even the voice seemed different now, thinner, more nasal. I nerved myself to meet the dark eyes. He was smiling, that same uncertain smile he had worn as he approached me, as if not sure of my identity. 'Have you read the Italian sources?'

'Those that have been translated.'

'But most of them haven't. I work at the National Library here in Naples, you know. It is one of the best in Italy – we like to think it is the best. I am in charge of the European history department. It contains the most extensive collection of local materials – chronicles, journals, eyewitness accounts – anywhere to be found. They don't leave you in any doubt as to what the rebels themselves believed. Even in early July, when they had been embarked for more than a week, they still believed they would be sailing for France. Gaetano Rodinò in his *Racconti Storici* tells us that Mario Pagano, who was subsequently executed, was still planning, as late as the fifth, to set up a fencing academy

301

when he got to Toulouse. Rodinò, as you will know, was a fellow prisoner of his on board one of the transports.'

'It is not a question of what they believed. Horatio acted in good faith, he needn't have had any knowledge of what they believed. How can he be held responsible for what went on in their minds?' It was my last attempt to fight back. I straightened myself, I looked the fellow in the face. 'There is no evidence,' I said. 'None whatever.' It is a terrible thing to face a cynic and put all your hope in a negative. 'Not a scrap,' I said, and I pressed my lips together to keep them from trembling.

I had looked away, but his voice came over to me, unhurried, unmistakably nasal now, slightly metallic: 'This is a case where the search for evidence complicates the issues and obscures the truth, as it has been doing now for two hundred years. You say there is no evidence, therefore we cannot know. That is false reasoning, Mr Cleasby. We should look first at what we already know, because it often precludes the need for evidence. If we know the painter's work, we don't need his signature on the painting, not necessarily, don't you agree?'

'We do if we have to prove it.'

'But we are talking about knowledge, not proof. What do we know about Horatio Nelson? A gifted naval commander certainly, but that does not help much. A hero, yes. Heroes never admit mistakes, let alone wrong-doing. Heroes need to succeed gloriously, it is obligatory, at least until the moment comes for them to die gloriously, and this was not his moment. We know he was inordinately vain, we know he could gobble up flattery by the cartload, we know he took in hatred of the French with his mother's milk, we know he was a lifelong devoted servant of monarchs, we know he was totally ignorant of Naples except for where it lay on his charts, we know he was besotted with Emma Hamilton, who was besotted with Queen Maria Carolina, who wasn't besotted with anyone but had a lively desire to save her kingdom from the French and avoid the fate of her sister, Marie Antoinette. She was just as set on winning as the admiral but a

302

lot more adaptable. Or perhaps I mean intelligent. My saviour, she said to him. Devoted Lady Hamilton said the same. The queen and the mistress. Do you not see what this comes to, the irresistible conclusion? Look at the picture. Do you really need a signature?'

I could not answer him. His loquacity amazed me; deliberate, unfaltering, with a constant edge of malice in it. Those wrinkles round his eyes that I had thought due to scanning far horizons came from squinting over books in his library. He was short-sighted, of course. He would have his glasses in a case in one of the pockets of his jacket. Rimless glasses.

'In order to satisfy his appetite for victory, in order not to disappoint those who hailed him as their saviour, in order to punish those who had dared to desire a republic on French lines . . . Do you not see? He could not fall short in any particular. In his way were a few hundred men and women who thought they were protected by a treaty, and an intractable warrior–priest named Ruffo, who had made the treaty with them and wanted to save his face. So a way was found, a form of words. The appearance of good faith was preserved. And lo and behold, the rebels come walking out into the arms of the British marines.'

So far I might have resisted; it was still, after all, in the realm of argument. But he had foreseen everything, even this vestige of resistance. He had planned everything in advance. He kept the killing stroke for the end.

'What does it matter, after all?' he said. 'Why should it matter?' That thin smile was on his face again. 'He was a man in a tight corner, wasn't he? We were at war with France, it was a struggle for survival, great issues were at stake. A spot of fraud, a few hundred expendable people, the statutory cover-up afterwards. Fairly standard for our times, isn't it? Or any other times, for that matter. Look at this century of ours, the things that have been done. Churchill made shadier deals and he is thought a great Englishman, whatever that means.'

'He was a politician.'

He leaned forward – he hadn't heard me. 'What was that?'

'Churchill wasn't a hero.'

'Oh, I see. It's because Nelson was a hero that they have been trying so long to keep the taint of falsehood from him. That's why he couldn't be allowed to do anything underhand. Well, heroes are useful, there is no denying that. Nelson was useful at the time and he has been useful ever since. The Royal Navy keep a silence for him on Trafalgar Day, don't they, and fly the flags at half-mast? Stirring stuff, especially now that most of the glory has departed.'

'He was a rebel too. He broke the line . . .'

My voice was again reduced to little more than a whisper. He gave no sign of having heard me. 'Don't you know it yet?' he said. 'Heroes are fabricated in the national dream factory. Heroes are not people.'

He was looking at me as he spoke but I could not meet his eyes. I looked down at his hands. One lay palm down on the table, the other was loosely curled round his almost empty glass. The nails were immaculate. The pads on the knuckles looked soft.

'You know,' he said, '*dulce et decorum*, sweet and fitting. Not to die for one's country exactly, not necessarily, but to dream of it and be proud. To deal with our fears by dreaming. There are no heroes out there, Mr Cleasby, there are only fears and dreams and the process of fabrication.'

He knew me, somehow he knew me. I was still looking at his hands.

'No heroes,' he said. 'Surely you know that?'

Soft, indoor hands. Quite hairless on the backs. *Of course.* The hair had been worn away by gloves, kid gloves, black . . . Why hadn't I seen it before? He was Badham.

I stood up quickly. 'Another drink?'

He made as if to rise from his seat. He didn't want me to get away. 'No,' I said, 'it's on me.'

'The waiter will come,' he said, but I didn't answer, I turned and walked over to the bar. There were more people there now, someone was asking for a drink, I had to wait and this was a good thing because it enabled me to gather myself together. Some sort of a plan had to be made. I had to prevent him from realizing that I knew his true identity.

I glanced towards him. He was sitting in the same position, with his back to the bar. Across the few yards that separated us I took in the details of his appearance, seen thus from behind: the slightly ridged line of his jacket collar, the strip of shirt above, a cream or pale yellow colour. The shirt seemed too tight, it creased the flesh of his neck into folds at the sides. Above this the hair on his nape grew in loose thin curls like delicate shavings of some pale wood. The bar had hushed around me, all sound had drained into this closeness of sight. But I must have shifted my position, moved a little closer to the counter of the bar. I met Badham's eyes! There was a narrow panel of mirror set in the angle of the wall behind my chair and he was watching my face in the glass. His own seemed to change now as he met my eyes, and I knew he had understood I was on to him.

There was no time to lose. There were no lifts on this side of the hotel, so I could not follow my first escape plan, which was to mount to the first floor and then come down by the stairs past the reception desk and out to the street. I would have to walk past him, there was nothing else for it. My heart was beating heavily and my throat had gone dry. He would assume I was going to the gents, or so I hoped. When I got opposite the swing doors I darted suddenly sideways, bumping into a porter with a luggage trolley and knocking my shin on one of the cases. And so I made it out into the street.

The sun was low over the sea now but still strong; I felt the heat of it as I stepped out from the shade of the awning. I must have crossed the road directly and gone down the steps, because I was suddenly there in the little marina where the white boats rested in their moorings, side by side. The boats didn't move but the surface of the water was shivering all over and this seemed strange, unaccountable, the masts and mooring ropes quite motionless, their reflections wriggling in the water like snakes, there was blood in among them too, a shuddering of red, as if the snakes were bleeding as they writhed. The cruelty that Badham had used against me came to my mind. A lump formed in my throat and my eyes filled with tears. The surface of the water glimmered and blurred, and it seemed to me that the ripples of blood were gaining, spreading, soon they would cover the whole surface of the harbour. I had to get away from this. I went back again, on to the pavement. The white rocks on the foreshore below me were dazzling in the sunlight. There was the gleaming sweep of the bay, the softly glowing crests of the promontories beyond. In this luminous moment the message came to me, like a pulse beat in the softness of the evening: *Villa Emma*. The little house that Hamilton built for her at Posillipo. Where we went to escape the foul city, where we walked hand in hand through the gardens above the sea. I would go there now, at once. She would be waiting. I would get a taxi or a bus.

I began to walk across the pavement. I was still almost directly opposite the hotel. I saw Badham come through the swing doors, pass under the awning and emerge on to the pavement. I saw him hesitate, look this way and that. I had the impression that he might be going to cross the road towards me. I went rapidly back down the steps. One of the boats had a black rubber guard tied to the bow and I saw this stretching and contracting in the water like a lung. I waited some minutes, then I went up again, holding myself in readiness for flight. There was no sign of him on the opposite pavement but this meant nothing in itself, he could easily have been hiding somewhere.

A man dressed in a dark suit and carrying a briefcase was approaching along the pavement. I moved into his path. 'Villa Emma,' I said. He raised his eyebrows and moved his head a little to one side. He had not understood, or so I thought at the time. 'Villa Emma, Posillipo,' I said. At this he smiled and made a sort of pointing gesture over his shoulder. There was a bus-stop not far behind him, twenty yards or so, and he seemed to be indicating this. I think he was about to say something more but then his expression changed completely, a cheeping sound had come from somewhere in the region of his heart. He thrust a hand inside his jacket and brought out the cheeping thing and spoke to it as if he wanted to soothe its alarm. At this moment a bus pulled in to the stop and one or two people began to descend from it. I was still afraid that Badham might be somewhere near. I ran the distance at an unsteady jog and clambered up.

The driver started up again as soon as I was on board. He did not look at me or ask for any money. I had to stand to begin with, the bus was full. It jerked and shuddered and swayed heavily on the corners. I found a rail near the door and clung to it. I could not see where we were going. It was very hot inside the bus; I could feel the sweat gathering on my scalp and in all the concave places of my body. Some of the people inside the bus struggled to a yellow box attached to the rail near the entrance. They thrust white slips at this and it made a ringing sound. I understood that they were stamping tickets which they must have had before boarding the bus.

People got on and off, and after a while I found a seat. We had left the sea and turned inland – I only noticed it now. The street ascended steeply, the sounds of the engine were guttural and grinding. It was now that the pair of them got on, a woman and a girl, the woman bulky and matronly with a red canvas shopping bag, the girl with a face from a nightmare bestiary, wedge-shaped, with a hideously elongated nose like the proboscis of an anteater.

I suspected nothing at first. All I felt was a sort of dread. The seats on this bus did not all face the same way, they were in two lanes separated by an aisle, and the four at the front faced towards the others. I was sitting in the most forward of these four. For the moment there was no one sitting opposite. What I was dreading came about. The two of them chose to sit side by side directly in front of me, face-on, the square-faced matron with the shopping bag on her knees and the monstrous girl with her staring green

307

eyes and flexible snout and chin receding to nothing. And both of them looked fixedly at me.

It was this fixity of regard that alerted me. I could feel their eyes on me all the time. Things began to fall into place. Badham emerging from the hotel, looking to right and left – that had been a signal. The man with the telephone, receiving instructions. The bus that drew up so opportunely, the driver who did not ask me to produce a ticket. And now these two, keeping me under observation.

They were cunning; every time I glanced at them they were looking somewhere else. The girl sat hunched forward. She was continually wrinkling the loose skin on her nose and opening her mouth in a snarling expression. She had on a white T-shirt with 'Louisiana Country Club' inscribed across the bosom. What did that mean? They could have been notified that I would be on this bus, but how could Badham have known I would get on it in the first place? Could he have watched me? I had not actually seen him walk away.

The girl was looking about her, still wrinkling her nose and snarling. She was looking at the other people on the bus. Suddenly I realized: it was an outing, she was enjoying herself, this was her best T-shirt. She was retarded, to say the least, and this woman was looking after her. Surreptitiously I scanned the woman's face. I was afraid but I had to do it. Broad cheeks, small deep-set eyes, an expression of placid resignation. Not the mother, a nurse of some kind, the girl's keeper . . . She had taken some trouble to change her appearance but I knew her now, I recognized her, I had last seen her leading away poor Penhas on the occasion of my father's funeral. Nothing to do with Badham. Her name was Mrs White. I felt a great rush of relief. I caught her eye and nodded slightly to show that I had understood and she blinked twice in reply.

We were on a level now, far above the sea, moving between large buildings with identical balconies. The roads were wider and there were pockets of greenery here and there, scattered groups of trees and clumps of brightly flowering bushes. There were not many people on the bus now, but a man was sitting opposite me on the other side of the aisle. I leaned forward and spoke to his averted face: 'Posillipo?' He turned and looked at me for some moments in silence. Then he shook his head and pointed in the direction the bus had come from. He called forward to the driver, who merely shrugged. Some minutes afterwards the bus stopped. '*Capolinea,*' the man said. He again pointed behind him, the way the bus had come. The bus driver got down from his seat and came towards us. '*Capolinea,*' he said.

Everyone was getting off, we had come to the end of the line. I understood now. They had wanted to keep me away from Villa Emma at all costs. Misled by the man with the telephone, I had boarded the bus on the wrong side of the road. Posillipo was in the other direction. The driver showed me his watch and made a little circle above it with his forefinger. One hour. I would have to wait an hour before I could get a bus back. The driver smiled, his moustache lifted. He made little chopping motions in the direction from which we had come. 'Posillipo.' He was in it too of course.

Everyone else was off the bus by now. I followed them. The driver got back into his seat and the bus drew away, gathered speed, disappeared in the distance. If this were the end of the line, where was he going? I thought I knew the answer to that. Mrs White and her charge had got off with the others. They were some way off, walking along together by the side of the road. I had no idea where I was or what I should do. It was ten minutes to seven. The sun was setting in silver cloud over a sea invisible from here. I was not proposing to stay where I was, in that empty place, alone and exposed, without cover of any kind. I was not such a fool as that. While I was still hesitating the signal came. Mrs White glanced slightly over her shoulder. I immediately began to follow, taking care to keep a distance between us.

The road curved away, I lost them from view. When I came

round the curve, there was no sign of them. But there was an unsurfaced road going off at right angles, with houses on one side and a stone wall on the other, bordering what looked like private grounds. After a while the road narrowed, the houses were less frequent. It was no more than a footpath. There was no sign of Mrs White or the girl. I had made a mistake somehow, I had misread the signal. I stopped at the edge of the road and stood still. Immediately, with this ceasing of movement, I became aware that I was being watched. I was in a trap. I could not simply go back the way I had come, it was too dangerous, it was what they expected. Then I saw that there was a gate in the wall on the other side, a little way farther along, a metal gate, painted green.

There was no padlock on the gate, just a simple bar. It opened quite easily. I was planning to make a detour, keeping within the shelter of the wall, until I could get back to the dirt road again at a point somewhere near where it joined the main road, find a hiding place where I could wait for the bus. But I was too much in fear of the open, I stayed in the shelter of the wall too long. When I finally hoisted myself over it and dropped down on the other side, bruising my elbows and jarring my legs in the process, there was no sign of the road. I was in what I took to be the grounds of some large house or perhaps hotel. A gravel path wound away through thick shrubbery. All I could do was follow this – I had lost all sense of direction now.

I came out on to an asphalt driveway and an empty car park with white lines marking the spaces. On the other side of this were some single-storey brick buildings that looked like offices and then a large white house with balconied windows. I crossed the car park, passed round the nearer of the brick buildings. Through a window I saw two men in long white coats talking together. They stared at me as I passed.

I began to walk more quickly. There was a pavement now, leading in the direction of the white house. A man appeared suddenly from a side-turning and walked towards me. He was passing a hand over his face, down and up again, with rapid repeated movements. As I drew opposite he stopped doing this but he kept his hand stretched over his nose and peeped at me over the top of it.

Someone called out, perhaps in greeting, someone hidden by an angle of the building. From an upper room I heard the sound of a woman's laughter, strangely sustained as if she were laughing also on the intakes of breath. A uniformed nurse came round a corner of the building with a very old man in a wheelchair. His face was tilted back and his eyes were closed, his sharp nose pointed up towards the sky. From the frame of his wheelchair there dangled a teddy-bear and a black monkey with glass eyes. The bear and the monkey jerked and danced – they were on strings of elastic. The old man's eyes were not closed, they were white slits, he was watching me. The nurse said some words I did not understand. She left the wheelchair and came round towards me.

I understood everything now. Mrs White and the girl were in it too, they had led me here. The men with white coats, the hand signals, the laughter . . . They had anticipated everything. There was no time to lose. I jumped over the low hedge that bordered the pavement, ran back across the car park and into the shrubbery. There was great power and freedom in this running at first. I ran in a wide circle, crashed through another low hedge, climbed a wooden fence and found myself behind the house on ground that led upwards through a straggle of bushes and bare earth and patches of burned-out grass.

That sense of freedom did not last. I was breathing hoarsely, open-mouthed, lungs straining as I climbed higher. A thin screen of trees, cluttered with ivy. I pushed through them and half scrambled, half fell down a bank on the other side into a deep-sided cutting, broad and flat enough at the bottom to walk along – it looked as if there might once have been a single rail track here. There were grassed-over mounds of stones at intervals along the way.

Down here the night had begun to take over, there was an advance of darkness between the banks. After a while I stopped and listened, but there was no sound of pursuit. When I judged the distance to be safe, I climbed up the bank on the farther side. I had to get up on hands and knees, and I was torn by bramble and thorny scrub. But when I reached the top of the bank I forgot my hurts. I was looking down over the distant lights of streets and houses and the vanishing gleams of traffic, looking beyond this to the glimmering radiance of the bay. The sun had gone, but the sea still held the last of the light in a luminous solution of silver.

This was what you climbed up to as a boy, climbing from the sheltered glebeland, from the riverside meadows where the parsonage lay, mounting the bridle path towards the high ground above the village, high above, between the shoulders of the downs, from where we could look down over sand and salt marsh, strands of gold and strips of shallow pool and at the verge, the real sea, the mass of it, seamed white or silvered over. Behind us great rafts of bright cloud and the soft gleam of the sun on wet sand ripples and mud flats and the glitter of dried pebbles and shingle up the beach. Curlews whistling above the marshes, the terns with their wild cries and plunging flight.

How often we had seen it together. But now I was alone and the light was fading, and I knew I had been brought here only for this, brought here alone to see the line of the sea as you saw it that evening in March when you were twelve years old, the evening before you left. It was the only point in all the countryside around from which to get a view of the sea. You came here in the fading light and looked at the sea, and you walked away to spend your life with the sea and when you did that you took my life with you.

What I would have done, how long I would have stayed there, I don't know. I thought everything was at an end. But then the miracle happened, the boy appeared. For some moments I could not believe it. Only a dark shape at first, surmounted by the pale

312

glimmer of the face. There below me, in the last of the light he came walking. Between the crest of the cutting where I crouched and the lights of the houses below, neither fast nor slow – it was a path well known to him. On his back a sort of bump, which I made out to be a small rucksack. Of course, his provisions would be there, his provisions for the journey. He was not going home to the parsonage, he was leaving, he was going away to spend his life with the sea, he was taking my life with him.

Down the slope again, through the thorns and scrub. I found a stone big enough, not too big. Panting now with the fear of being too late, I kept along the cutting out of hearing, out of sight. When I clawed myself up again he was still there below me, a diminutive figure, walking at the same pace, looking ahead of him. And now, when I had to get behind him, he started singing!

Incomprehensible words in a child's treble – your voice had not broken yet. A blunder of the first order, preventing you from hearing me as I drew closer behind you, my step uncertain in this difficult light. Perhaps at the last moment you heard or sensed something. But then it was too late, too late to turn on me the terror of your eyes. I struck downward at the small head, once, twice. The figure sank to its knees, half turning towards me, raising an arm. A sound came from it, not very loud, like sobbing but more liquid – as though there were some liquid in the throat. I struck again and he fell forward. I heard the crash of his fall.

Then I walked away, continuing the boy's path, keeping the lights below me. There was no need to hurry now. I had nothing to fear. I had done it, I had broken the line. Dark and bright angels meet at twilight, it is the only time. And when they meet they join. We can never lose each other now.